Not Our Crowd, Darling

Not Our Crowd, Darling

a novel

MICHAEL CRAFT

QUEST
·OVER·
PRESS

Book design and cover art direction: M.C. Johnson
Author's photo: Aaron Jay Young

Library of Congress Cataloging-in-Publication Data

Craft, Michael, 1950–
Not Our Crowd, Darling : a novel / Michael Craft
   ISBN: 979-8-218-67935-4 (hardcover)
   ISBN: 979-8-218-73734-4 (paperback)
   BISAC: FIC019000 Fiction / Literary
            FIC044000 Fiction / Women
            FIC050000 Fiction / Crime

First hardcover and paperback editions: November 2025

Questover Press
California • Since 2011

SOMETIMES, DARK SECRETS DON'T FADE WITH
THE YEARS. INSTEAD, THEY GROW DARKER.

Meghan Auric lives in self-imposed confinement atop a luxurious tower, the tallest building overlooking a small city on the Great Plains. Dark secrets and a long-ago betrayal put her there, while debilitating fears and guilt have *kept* her there. The upside: her much older husband's recent death has made her one of the wealthiest women in the state, and she intends to put those riches to a more noble use than he did.

Now, though, political developments in a special election begin to unravel what really happened some twenty-five years ago, offering her the chance to escape her gilded cage and to reap justice—as well as revenge. The downside: pursuing this truth would likely cause her to lose *everything*.

With a wry sense of humor that never fails her, Meghan searches for the courage to begin her journey from self-doubt and isolation. Getting there won't be easy, though, with obstacles along the way that threaten not only her lavish lifestyle—but possibly life itself.

"In this sparkling, suspense-tinged study of wealth and isolation, Craft introduces recently widowed Meghan Auric, who struggles with a terrible secret from her past. Craft wrings insight, pathos, and beauty from Meghan's rarefied milieu. He seizes the symbolic potential of her tower residence to heighten the suspense, evoke emotional resonance, and offer breathtaking views in crisp, lyrical prose."
— *BookLife Reviews* (EDITOR'S PICK)
from the indie review service of *Publishers Weekly*

"In Craft's novel, a middle-aged woman loses her wealthy, elderly husband and finds herself embroiled in a political crime caper. A slow-burning but ultimately uplifting novel of second chances, the tale deftly explores compelling themes of self-discovery, loss, and rebuilding self-respect."
— *Kirkus Reviews*

"I loved *Not Our Crowd, Darling*, in which some bad people actually get punished and journalism still makes a difference. Meghan Auric is a refreshing hero for our trying times, a moral intellectual trapped in a 'trophy wife' role who dares to confront past fears and speak the truth to power. She also makes amazing gelato."
— *M.G. Lord, author of 'Forever Barbie'*

"Wry humor, psychological revelations, and simmering mystery result in a novel that is embracing and engaging, spiced with just enough suspense to keep its outcome unpredictable."
— *Diane Donovan, Senior Reviewer, Midwest Book Review*

CONTENTS

Not Our Crowd, Darling

PART ONE : *The Building* 1
  Chapters 1 through 5

PART TWO : *Meghan's Dilemma* 83
  Chapters 6 through 16

PART THREE : *Scream Like a Girl* . . . 263
  Chapters 17 through 20

About the author 330
Acknowledgments 331
Author's note 332
About the type 334

PART ONE
The Building

CHAPTER
ONE

Death threats are no laughing matter, especially when they're backed by powerful interests. Perhaps I shouldn't have been so glib about the chain of events that was set in motion a few weeks ago, but the role of "damsel in distress" didn't suit me in the least. Better to shrug off one's woes with a dash of cynicism and a dollop of wit.

Our crowd, you see, didn't care much for high drama. Complacency and privilege were more our style. We didn't worry much about money or homelessness or lost glaciers.

On the morning when this began, however, I did feel a twinge of concern when a nurse poked her head around the door to the hospital chapel. Seeing me, she stepped inside. Her eyes were downcast as she approached with purpose and slid into the pew, sitting next to me. "Meghan Auric?" she asked. I nodded.

"Miss Auric"—she rested her fingers on my forearm—"I'm so sorry to inform you that your father has just passed away."

The hushed silence of the room, with its thick carpeting and upholstered benches, produced a ringing in my ears. It was accompanied by the claustrophobic feeling of being trapped in a miniature church, but there was no tang of incense, no flicker of candles. Up front was a table that might pass for an altar. On it was a dusty arrangement of artificial flowers, fluorescently backlit by a fake stained-glass window of plastic shards that formed a jagged design of milky, soothing pastels. Though I thought of the space as a chapel, it displayed no icons of any particular faith. Out in the hall, a sign on a brass stanchion had said: MEDITA-TION ROOM. QUIET, PLEASE.

For a long moment, I studied the nurse—more accurately, the nursette. I had recently turned fifty, and to my eyes, she looked impossibly young, too tiny to be entrusted with matters of life and death. When at last I spoke, I corrected her: "I'm *Mrs.* Auric. Eugene was my husband."

She gave me an odd look—as if she didn't quite believe me—then repeated, "I'm so sorry."

"An innocent mistake." The man's facetious words drifted from a few rows behind us, in the shadows. Startled, the nurse turned to look. The man sat languidly near the end of his pew, lolling with one arm stretched along its back. Suppressing a breathy laugh, he told her, "My stepmother is often mistaken as my father's daughter. Some people assume she's my sister—but she is most definitely *not.*"

Flustered, the nurse again said, "Sorry."

With a reassuring grin, I leaned close to her, saying, "That's just Gene; ignore him. Eugene *Junior* has an annoyingly flippant sense of humor—unlike his father, who had *no* sense of humor at all."

Laughing openly now, Gene got up, moved to our pew, and slid in next to the nurse, telling her, "Dad was eighty-five. That's a decent run for a lifetime of indulgence, so we can cut him some slack for being a grump at the end. Truth is, though, he was *always* a grumpy old man—at least since *I* came along."

I could vouch for Gene's assessment of his father as a perpetual churl, although my experience with Eugene Senior didn't begin until Eugene Junior was in his twenties. It should be noted that Gene was now forty-nine years old, nearly *my* age. Though I was technically his stepmother, we had never lived under the same roof. To Gene, I was just his dad's second wife.

The nursette ping-ponged her head from side to side, asking us, "Would you like to say farewell to your ... loved one?"

Gene asked, "He *is* actually dead, correct?"

She nodded. I bit my lower lip, avoiding eye contact.

Gene pressed on: "Did he leave any messages?"

"No, sir. He just slipped away. It was peaceful."

Gene leaned in front of her to look at me. "Well, Meg? Should we go up to his room?"

My mouth sagged. An obligatory, awkward scene at Eugene's death bed had zero appeal.

Gene could easily read my blank expression. "Or," he said, "maybe we should just go to lunch."

We were each absorbed in our own thoughts while walking toward his car—the sort of long black European sedan typically driven by someone in uniform, "the help." But Gene was an independent sort who took a measure of defiant pride in handling, on his own, the more mundane chores of everyday life. He jangled the keys in his pocket.

The contrast between the gloomy meditation room and the sunny parking lot could not have been more pronounced. It was a Thursday in mid-September as the chilly morning warmed toward noontide. A huge blue sky stretched over the Great Plains, the heartland, where the aptly named city of Fairview bustled and buzzed, an island of activity and arts and commerce that had risen from the endless fields of wheat.

Gene helped me into the car, then walked around to the driver's side, got in, and buckled up. Switching on the ignition, he turned to ask, "Did you really want to have lunch?"

I shook my head. "I just wanted to get out of there. Can you drop me at the building?"

He nodded. "Sure."

When he had pulled out of the parking lot and merged into traffic, I asked, "Does your mother know yet?"

He sighed. "Probably not." He tapped a button or two on the steering wheel, and a moment later, the sound of a ringing phone came through the car radio.

The call connected. "Junior?" said a woman's voice—the voice of Bibiana Auric, Eugene's first wife. "Any news?"

"Afraid so, Mom. Dad's gone. It was ... 'peaceful,' they said."

There was a long silence over the phone.

Gene continued, "Meghan was at the hospital with me. We're both in the car now."

I spoke up: "Hi, Bebe. Sorry for the bad news. Sorry for your loss."

We heard her heave a big, noisy sigh. It didn't sound like grief—more like relief at the end of an ordeal. She said, "Condolences to you, too, Meg. You were closer to him than I was—for a *long* time now."

"We knew it was coming, but it's still sad."

With a tone of resignation, she agreed, "End of an era." Then she chortled. "Have we run out of clichés yet?"

"Hope so," said Gene. "I'll be home in a while, Mom. Can I bring you anything?"

Bebe snorted. "Like what? Kleenex? Boo-hoo."

He laughed. "Okay, Mom. Later." And he rang off.

We sat without speaking as he turned the car at a downtown

intersection and cruised along the main boulevard, which was bordered on one side by a lush, green park with a pretty lagoon and a picnic area. It was a popular destination for office workers escaping their cubicles with their bagged lunches. On a perfect day like this, they'd be fighting for bench space.

These several acres of turf and trees served as something of a front yard for Fairview's tallest structure (by far) on the opposite side of the divided boulevard.

The thirty-floor Auric Tower, referred to by locals as simply "the building," had risen from the fertile landscape some forty years earlier as a visionary dream made real by an ambitious developer, Eugene Auric, at the moment when his self-made career had entered the maturity of unimagined success. That career's staying power, and the wealth spawned by it, had defined the modern history of Fairview, putting it "on the map," as they say, as the second-largest city—and without question the most prosperous—in an otherwise sparsely populated state.

During the early days of Eugene's career, business ventures had often taken him out of state, frequently to Chicago, and every time he went there, he stood on the Michigan Avenue bridge, gawking up at the Wrigley Building, enchanted by its fanciful architecture, its decorative detailing, and its shockingly pristine cladding of glazed white terra-cotta tiles. "Now, *that's* a building!" he told the architect he eventually retained. Eugene wanted something very much like the Chicago landmark to bear his own name, at home.

And now, there it was. Its lower floors weren't as sprawling as the Wrigley Building, but it was equally tall, with bigger windows, as well as playful design motifs baldly borrowed from the wedding-cake style of the original. The Fairview Chamber of Commerce always bragged that Auric Tower "dominates the community's skyline." But Eugene (dear old grumpy Eugene) always countered, "It doesn't 'dominate' the skyline—it *is* the goddamn skyline. Nothing else even comes close."

Gene slowed the car, asking me, "Which entrance?" The building, with its setbacks, occupied an entire city block, with the gleaming white tower rising from the middle. The front entrance, on Auric Boulevard, served the lower floors with its public spaces—shops, restaurants, and offices. The upper floors were occupied by residences, with their elevator lobby accessed by an entrance on one of the side streets. There was also a private entrance on the back street with a guard and no signage, which gave direct access to elevators to the top two floors, the penthouse. Nearby on the back street were overhead doors to the private garage and a loading dock with a freight elevator to the rooftop terrace and gardens.

I told Gene, "The north entrance is fine," meaning the residential lobby. "Ronda was going to leave some documents for me."

Gene turned at the corner and, halfway down the block, pulled over to the curb near the entrance. A car was parked in front of us. Under the canopy that jutted out from the building, the doorman was unloading packages. So Gene cut his engine, hopped out of the car, and came over to the curb to help me out.

I thanked him, then paused on the sidewalk. My head tilted back as my gaze scaled the walls of the building, which converged at a point in the sky. A single small cloud, a mere wisp of white, drifted through the deep green foliage of a tree poking up from the penthouse gardens.

"Unless I'm mistaken," said Gene, guessing my thoughts, "it's all yours."

After picking up the packet of documents at the service desk in the lobby, I waited to enter an elevator alone, then used my key card to commandeer express service to the twenty-ninth floor, where the doors slid open into the private foyer of the two-story penthouse.

No noise. No crowds. I was home.

Standing still in the quiet entry hall, I took a moment to close my eyes and breathe deeply. I felt the calming of my racing heart. I felt the panic, which had stuck in my throat, melt away. Feeling steadier on my feet, I walked from the hall and through the reception room, with my three-inch heels snapping on the teak parquet floor. Anyone, I suppose, might have been stressed by a morning that had marked the death of a spouse, the end of a twenty-five-year marriage.

But here's the thing: I felt this way every time I left, then returned to, the building.

The penthouse reception room, which lacked windows but had plenty of wall space, functioned as an art gallery, with few furnishings—just a center table with a fresh floral arrangement (changed every few days) and a tufted banquette for the restful appreciation of the paintings. The museum-worthy collection consisted entirely of works by twentieth-century American artists, in styles ranging from realism (Hopper, Wood, Wyeth) to abstraction (Diebenkorn, Morris, Pollock). I had already tagged most of these as eventual donations to the Fairview Institute of Arts, where I served as a longstanding member of its board of trustees.

The arrangement of roses, asters, and cut salvia, I noted, was beginning to droop.

Stepping from the gallery, past the library, and into the formal living room, I called, "Ashley? Are you here?"

Hearing no response from our young housekeeper—hearing,

in fact, nothing at all—I moved silently across the expanse of silk carpet and sat on a sofa near the far wall, where the view from a bank of windows skimmed past the treetops of the town, far below. At the edge of our city, the leafy green faded to the dusty yellow of vast, unbounded wheat fields, quilted here and there by razor-thin roads, all of it divided by the broad concrete ribbon of the interstate highway. Its multiple lanes shot out of town and seemed to curve with the earth, disappearing into the faraway horizon, where darkening fields gave way to the fuzzy towers and dank sprawl of the state capital, a city that its hope-filled founders had naively named Consensus.

My eyes drifted back to the sofa, where I had set aside the packet that was delivered by Ronda Trask, my late husband's personal, on-staff attorney and—some said—fixer. I zipped open the cardboard mailer and removed its thick stack of paperwork, a dreary assortment of stapled and paper-clipped documents, each littered with sticky-notes and a profusion of arrow-shaped demands for my signature. On top of the pile was a note on Ronda's stationery, scrawled in block letters: MEGHAN, SORRY FOR YOUR LOSS. MUCH TO SORT OUT. WILL DROP IN TOMORROW TO DISCUSS. TAKE CARE. —RT

Whatever it was, it could wait. I set the papers aside and leaned back into the cushions of the sofa. My eyelids felt heavy. As they closed, slowly, the expansive view from the windows blurred and dimmed.

And then, in the stillness, I heard a voice, faintly—a woman's voice, chatty and laughing, but distant. My eyes opened. I looked about. I knew the voice; it was Ashley Factor, our housekeeper. But where was she?

Sitting upright, I called out, "Ashley?"

As before, there was no response.

Outside the living room was a partial terrace, but I could see at a glance that there was no one out there. Which meant that she was probably on the larger terrace, upstairs.

I stood, crossed the room, and climbed the curved, floating staircase that led to the thirtieth floor. This area of the penthouse had a huge circular cutout between the floors, creating a glamorous two-story atrium with a multitiered art déco Lalique chandelier suspended through both levels. The setting had been photographed and published countless times—though the residence had never been identified in print or online because of Eugene's paranoia (perhaps justified) that the pictures might create jealousy.

He told me, "It could give bad ideas to the wrong people."

I scoffed. "And who, pray tell, are 'the wrong people'?"

He gave me a *knowing* look. "Not our crowd, darling."

I said nothing, but he knew that I had never considered "our crowd" to be "my crowd," except by marriage.

After stepping from the stairway into the upper level of the penthouse, I moved through an open area meant for entertaining—more of a party room than the living room downstairs. Passing the adjacent dining room and kitchen, I approached the glass doors that led out to the terrace, which surrounded most of the top floor. It was truly a roof garden out there, not just a perch with a view, but a spectacular open-air living space with comfortable furnishings that encouraged either quiet relaxation or lively conversation. The jaw-dropping forty-mile vistas were tempered—brought back to planet Earth—with potted trees, boxed hedges, and gracious beds of flowering plants. There was even a section of terrace behind the kitchen that was devoted to a working garden of vegetables and herbs.

From inside the glass doors, I saw Ashley standing a few yards away, under the ornamental tufts of a poodle-clipped cypress, talking to her phone, held at the end of a selfie stick. As I slid one of the doors open a few inches, she was saying, "... there's nothing but the finest for the lucky couple who come home to this bussin' mansion in the sky. You'd expect to find this in New York or Paris or maybe Dubai, but nope. All this wonderfulness is right here, smack in the middle of America's breadbasket. Don't believe me? Just look at all that *wheat*." And she slowly swung her arm, letting her camera capture the sweep of the far-flung fields below.

"Ashley," I said, stepping out to the terrace, "what do you think you're *doing*?"

"Oh! Hi, Meghan," she said, chipper as can be. When she had taken the housekeeping job two years earlier, she addressed me as "Mrs. Auric." Within a week, that had morphed into "Mrs. A." Two weeks later, she asked if she could call me "Meghan," and I was surprised that I instantly, eagerly, permitted it.

She reminded me of myself when I was younger. She was twenty-four when she came to work for us, two years out of college, smart, ambitious—and utterly ill-equipped to earn a living with a degree in theater. Oddly, she didn't think of housekeeping as "beneath her," and in fact, she liked not only the drop-dead surroundings of the job, but also the flexibility of the hours—she was here most days, most of the time, but not always, depending on our needs.

When Ashley was working here, she did so conscientiously. When she was not here, she kept creatively engaged as a blogger—more correctly, a "vlogger," I guess, pursuing an alternate calling as a "lifestyle influencer," whatever that is. She claimed to have thousands of followers and YouTube subscribers. This struck me as a specious basis for building any sort of meaningful career. (But then, to be honest, so did housekeeping. So there.)

Bottom line: I liked her. Plus, she was far more adept at anything digital than I was, and I had no children, so she was handy to have around.

At that moment, however, I needed to remind her, "No pictures in the house. No names. No addresses."

She crossed her heart. "Understood, Meghan. I was just shooting the view out here. No video in the house, ever. I promise."

Ashley was pretty and stylish, too—at least from the waist up. She had the makeup skills of a pro, complementing her flawless, creamy complexion. For her vlog, she wore a perky, spangly little top, with her blond hair done up in a playful frizz. Beneath the belt, however, "out of frame," she wore torn jeans and ratty sneakers.

After stuffing a few things into her backpack, she walked inside with me, and we made our way to the kitchen. It was not quite noon.

She said, "You're back earlier than I expected. Everything okay with Mr. A?"

The question took me by surprise—not only the gravity of it, but the fact that Eugene's demise had, at least temporarily, slipped my mind.

I must have looked dumbfounded, which Ashley decoded with ease. A tear slid down her cheek—theatrical training? "Oh, no," she said, setting her backpack on the floor. "Is Mr. A…*gone*?"

Though I have always been impatient with the various euphemisms pertaining to death, I nodded, telling her, "Yes, alas. Eugene has shuffled off this mortal coil."

She wrapped me in a big sloppy hug.

Earlier that morning, before leaving for the hospital, I had a sudden impulse to make gelato. Having spent so much time at home during the latter years of my marriage, I'd found both a practical and a creative outlet for unspent energies in, of all places, the kitchen, which became, in effect, my hobby shop. I harbored no fantasy of becoming a gourmet cook, but I was an adventurous and curious putterer. After installing the vegetable garden on the terrace, my tinkering took a more serious turn, followed by equipment upgrades in the kitchen itself.

On a lark, I had ordered a professional-grade Carpigiani gelato batch freezer, and the results of my experimentation with it were revelatory. Gelato was now "my thing." And early that Thursday morning, dreading the incumbent death watch at Eugene's intensive-care bedside, I abandoned my wake-up coffee and got busy with the Carpigiani.

As usual, I had a batch of previously cooked gelato base, essentially a custard, well chilled in the refrigerator. Now came the inspired, more intuitive part. Browsing in the fridge, I spotted a bottle of grenadine, that delectable red bar syrup used in concocting, among other things, the children's "mocktail" known as a Shirley Temple, which also involved ginger ale.

Having both of those ingredients on hand, as well as a jar of maraschino cherries to chop up (the ordinary sort, bright red—not the trendy, expensive dark ones), I soon had the Carpigiani humming. Twenty minutes later, I was transferring a gallon of my gorgeous pink glop into a deep stainless-steel tray, which I promptly slid into the freezer of the Sub-Zero. After an hour or so, before leaving for the hospital, I moved the tray to a separate compartment that was always held at a less frigid ten degrees, where the gelato would remain frozen, but more malleable.

I'd been dying to taste it after it was properly set. In fact, the gelato—not Eugene—had consumed my thoughts in the hospital's meditation room that morning.

Now, stepping out of Ashley's embrace, I asked, "Are you hungry?"

Wiping away a last tear, she nodded, smiled.

"Would it be too disgusting if we had gelato for lunch?"

She grinned. "Bring it on."

If I say so myself—and I do—it was fabulous. I scooped a second helping into both of our bowls, telling Ashley, "Grab your spoon. I want to show you something." And I led her out of the kitchen, across the party room, and into the main bedroom suite; beyond was its own private section of the roof garden. (The guest bedrooms, a home office, and workout room were on the lower level.)

The bedroom I'd shared with Eugene was easily the size of a suburban three-car garage—that's the bedroom *itself*, not including the dressing rooms, expansive closets, and two bathrooms. Though Eugene and I had shared the same sleeping space for the entirety of our marriage, we had not, routinely, shared the same bed.

We each had motorized king-size adjustable beds, which connected to a single *long* upholstered headboard. The room appeared to contain about an acre of mattress area—an exaggeration, to be sure, but the overall effect was ridiculous. Making things worse, the beds were situated on a platform in the center of the room, two steps up from the floor, which gave the whole setup an uncomfortably "royal" vibe. I hated it, but it must have been exactly what Eugene had wanted when he built the place, all thirty stories of Auric Tower, long before I came along.

Eugene was also a bit of a peacock, an obsessive clotheshorse. His closets dwarfed mine. During those many early business trips to Chicago, he'd sought out the city's finest custom tailors, and after countless fittings and ongoing purchases, he'd bought himself a recurring spot on the men's ten-best-dressed list. He wore *nothing* off the shelf—right down to his bespoke underwear. His dressing room was bigger than the bedroom itself, with his vast wardrobe catalogued and accessible with the touch of a button on a motorized conveyor rack.

"For *starters*," I told Ashley between swallows of gelato, "I want his bed *out* of here. Eventually, I'll rethink the whole space."

She nodded while eating. She didn't need to take notes. Serving not only as housekeeper, but also as house manager, responsible for coordinating outside help and services, Ashley would remember every detail.

"The clothes," I said. "They also need to go, but that'll take longer. I'll want to do some sorting and figure out how to give it away, donate it. I have no interest is *selling* it—but trashing it would be callous. Unthinkable."

She nodded. With a wrinkle of concern, she asked, "Will you be okay here? I mean tonight? Alone?"

I had to mull that for a moment, but only a moment. Setting aside my empty dish, I assured her, "I'll be fine. Over the years, and especially the last few weeks, I've spent many nights alone here—and truth is, I like it."

"Good. But if you change your mind, Meghan, just let me know. I'll be happy to camp out in one of the guest rooms for a while—if you want."

I smiled. "Thanks. But no." This conversation brought to mind that two of the guest rooms downstairs were originally designated as "servants' quarters" on the floor plans I later saw, which seemed logical enough, given the scale and grandeur of the penthouse. When I questioned Eugene about this, he explained that he was squeamish about live-in help, saying, "I just don't like the idea of people living under the same roof with us. This is *our* place, not theirs."

Similarly, in spite of his paranoia about the "wrong people" being jealous of his wealth, Eugene was squeamish about security technology within the penthouse itself. When the building was constructed decades earlier, it was outfitted with the usual precautions and cameras at the street level, the entrances, and lobbies, but the units within the building had no centralized security. In recent years, with the development of miniaturized cameras and Wi-Fi alarm systems, high-tech home security had grown much more common—but Eugene wanted none of it. "Who knows who'll be *watching* you, and *when?*" he asked with a toss of his arms.

"Ashley," I said, "another item for the list: get someone in here to propose some sort of discreet security setup."

"Now *that*," she said, "that's long overdue."

Leaving the bedroom, Ashley returned our dishes to the kitchen, and I went downstairs to the living room to retrieve the packet of documents I'd set on one of the sofas. Approaching it, I realized that I'd also left my phone there with the papers, so I sat down to check for messages.

All the emails were junk, but two texts caught my attention. The first was from Bebe, Eugene's first wife: LUNCH TOMORROW? SWAP WAR STORIES? HOW ABOUT THE BAR AT THE CLUB, HIGH NOON?

I replied: PERFECT. WE'RE ON.

The other message was from Faye Rubin, my therapist. Her

text had been sent about a half hour earlier: HEARD THE NEWS. (DOORMEN ARE WORSE GOSSIPS THAN HAIRDRESSERS.) IF YOU NEED TO SEE ME, MY TWO O'CLOCK JUST CANCELLED. WANT IT?

I would have no trouble getting there, as her office was in the building, which is why I'd sought her out some five years earlier. I replied: BRINGING GELATO.

An hour later, I left for my appointment. After changing elevators twice, I walked down a quiet hallway on the eleventh floor and approached the door labeled DR. FAYE RUBIN, PSYCHIATRIST. As I stepped into the waiting room, I was greeted by Marlene, the receptionist, who looked up from the check-in window with a somber expression, saying, "I'm so sorry for your loss, Mrs. Auric. Just have a seat, please. Dr. Faye will be with you shortly."

Sitting, I asked, "Do you have a refrigerator?"

She looked bewildered. "Sorry?"

I hoisted the little bag I'd packed. "I brought ice cream. If she'll be more than a few minutes, maybe you could—"

A door to the back office opened. "*Meghan*," said Faye, "great timing, lousy circumstances, come on in." Jewish, motherly, a bit saucy, Dr. Faye begged comparison with Dr. Ruth, but without the German accent. She was about ten years older than I was, around sixty—a seasoned professional at the peak of her practice, a working widow since long before we'd met.

After taking me back to her office and closing the door behind us, she stood quietly for a moment, studying me. "You're looking ... *great*," she said, more pleased than surprised.

I smirked. "Were you expecting me to wear black? A veil, maybe?" In fact, I was wearing a cashmere jacket and skirt—tweedy, muted green—the sort of autumnal hue that nicely offset my auburn hair (blond highlights), which I always wore in an un-fussy chin-length "boy bob."

Faye laughed softly while sitting behind her desk, gesturing for me to sit as well. "No, a veil is definitely *not* your style, Meghan. But let's face it—you must've had a rough morning."

With a wink, I set the bag on her desk. "Gelato helps."

This was not the first time I'd done this. Faye eagerly lifted the bag, opened it, and looked inside. Finding one covered Tupperware mug, one spoon, and one napkin, she asked with a wrinkled brow, "Nothing for you?"

"Trust me—I've had *more* than my share already."

She hesitated. "Hate to eat in front of you."

"*Eat*," I insisted. "Before it melts."

She tried a spoonful. "Oh. My. *Gawd*. It's like a kiddie cocktail!"

With a thumbs-up, I explained, "Grenadine."

Between bites, she told me, "Your best yet—bar none."

It really did please me to watch her enjoy it. She had helped me in so many ways over the years, and the pleasure of bringing her something I had made felt like a more heartfelt payback than hard cash—though she certainly wasn't shy about her fees.

"Yum," she murmured, placing the spoon in the mug and setting them aside. After tidying her lips with the napkin, she set that aside as well and opened a file folder—my folder—on the desk in front of her.

"Meghan Daley Auric," she said slowly, as if seeing me for my first visit. "What brings you here today?"

Wryly, I reminded her, "You texted me and pawned off a cancellation."

She shrugged. "I did, yes. Because your husband died this morning. I thought you might need to talk about it."

Dropping the banter, the *bons mots*, the bullshit, I quietly admitted, "I guess I do—or at least I *should* need to talk about it. Thank you for the nudge."

She paused as if searching for words—this was a first. And frankly, it alarmed me.

"Eugene...," she said at last. "Unless I'm mistaken, his death came as no surprise."

With a barely perceptible shake of my head, I said, "Of course not. He'd gone through a long period of declining health for a year or two, maybe three. He was simply getting old and not taking very good care of himself. One thing after another started going wrong. They'd patch him up, and he'd be better for a while, but then something else would come along. One of his surgeries led to a serious infection, which spread. He'd been in a hospital bed for the past month, getting worse. They called it 'multiple organ system failure.' And now—today—it's over."

Faye nodded. "And you're feeling an element of relief."

I nodded.

She asked, "Do you feel guilty about that?"

"Yes. And no. You can rationalize it either way."

"Yes, you can. And I commend you for your insight. Now, then: Relief is one thing. Guilt is another. But what about grief? Are you grieving?"

Long seconds slid by. "Honestly? I'm not sure if I'm grieving. Logically, if I'm not sure about it, I'm probably *not* grieving. I haven't cried, not yet. Am I horrible?"

Faye allowed herself a soft laugh. "Of course not. Tears aren't the only measure of past love and commitment." She seemed to hesitate before adding, "Did you love him?"

During our many prior sessions, I had often spoken of Eugene, but Faye had never asked me so bluntly about loving him.

"Eugene," I said, "was always good to me. He was thoughtful—and obviously had the means to be a generous provider. I have no doubt that he loved me deeply. In return, I was deeply grateful. I felt sincere affection for the man. But I don't know if that counts as 'loving' him."

Faye nodded. "Several times in the past, you've described yourself as a trophy wife. Let's talk about that."

"It's an accurate description," I told her with a shrug. "The marriage was his idea; I never pursued him. I simply wasn't interested. When he finally convinced me to say yes, I wasn't gold-digging—I was relenting."

"*That's* an intriguing perspective," said Faye, cracking a smile.

"We tell ourselves what we need to hear, right? I *needed* to believe that the 'transactional' roots of our marriage were nothing shameful—and I still believe that."

"And yet," Faye reminded me, "with the passing of years, you've become increasingly agoraphobic."

"Not to nitpick, but you diagnosed me as a *high-functioning* agoraphobe."

"I did. And I still stand by that diagnosis: You fear leaving home. Leaving the building causes you anxiety, especially if you're alone. This sometimes leads to panic attacks. You no longer travel, correct?"

"God, no. Haven't been on a plane in at least fifteen years. Not long after my last trip, I let my driver's license expire. Granted, things could be far worse. I don't *need* to leave the building to go to work, to run errands, or to haul kids around. I'm the first to acknowledge that I lead an uncommonly pampered life. Auric Tower may be a *gilded* cage—but it's my cage nonetheless, and that's what brought me to you."

She explained, "There can be many roots for your condition, but it often stems from some sort of psychological trauma. That could be something as simple as living with lies."

I asked, "By 'lies,' are you referring to the various justifications I've sold myself regarding my marriage?"

"Possibly, yes. With Eugene's death, there's a good chance that these issues could resolve themselves. I don't go along with the adage that 'time heals all,' but sometimes it can help."

I was skeptical. "At a deeper level, Eugene's death doesn't change a thing."

Faye sat back in her chair. "Expound on that, please."

I heaved a distasteful sigh. "I'll need to go back a bit—to my childhood."

She prepared to take notes.

"I grew up here in Fairview, an only child. My father died of a stroke when I was in high school. My mother, a teacher, was left with a modest house, no mortgage, and a decent income that allowed her to give me a comfortable upbringing. When the time came for college, I wanted to leave the state and broaden my horizons, so I managed to win a partial scholarship to Berkeley in California, where I earned a bachelor of arts in philosophy. Around the time I graduated, my mother was killed in a car accident here, and I inherited the house I grew up in. With no prospects for employment with a philosophy degree, I came home and took a clerical job at Fairview United Insurance."

Faye looked up from her notes. "That name is familiar—but not lately."

I nodded. "It changed hands a few years ago, bought out by one of the national agencies. But back then—this was twenty-six years ago—United was the biggest outfit in town, handling both property and health policies. My work was menial, but it was a paycheck; I was simply treading water. But I also met a guy who worked there, an agent, John White. Three or four years older than me, he was as bland as his name, but somehow, we hit it off. And before long, marriage was in the air—no firm date, no ring yet, but it was clear where things were going."

I hesitated before continuing: "Then something unexpected happened—something I regret. I haven't mentioned this before because it's a secret I've been forced to keep."

Faye asked, "Was it something illegal?"

I didn't answer.

"Even if it was," she said, "that was a *long* time ago. I'm no lawyer, but I think whatever happened is safely beyond any statute of limitations. Regardless, though, I would never report anything told to me in confidence by a patient. So if you're inclined, unburden yourself." She set down her pen and closed her notebook.

I gathered my thoughts, then told the story: "While John and I were working at United, he hatched a scheme, pitching it to me as foolproof. I was to falsify certain health-insurance records as a means of denying claims to policyholders, enriching the company through the reduced payouts to John's accounts. This would boost his career with United, which would in turn boost *our* future prospects after we married. At first, I refused. But I was twenty-four at the time, and he seemed more world-wise—and doggedly persuasive. When at last I gave in, I justified my complicity through immature thinking: I believed that I somehow 'deserved' compensation for a philosophy degree deemed worthless by the greed of the business world."

"Oy," said Faye, lifting a hand to her forehead.

"'Oy' is right. It took a while, but eventually the scheme was uncovered. And John? That prick disappeared—vanished—leaving me alone to face grave legal jeopardy."

"Were you ... *arrested*?"

I raised both palms. "Not so fast. Turns out, one of the agency's biggest clients, also an investor in the business, was the area's largest real-estate developer—none other than Eugene Auric, then fifty-nine. He had recently dumped his much younger wife, Bibiana, intending to find someone else, even younger. He'd had his eye on me and made a few advances that I laughed off. Then, when my legal peril became known to him, he swooped in to 'rescue' me."

Bug-eyed, Faye asked, "*How?*"

"His terms went something like this." I lowered my voice to a deeper register, paraphrasing Eugene's long-ago words: "I may not be the man of your dreams, Meghan, but marry me and I'll make your problems go away. We'll each be bound by our own dirty little secrets. Yours: you made some very bad decisions that affected people's health. Mine: I couldn't persuade you to be my wife based on my own merits, but only because I could help you out of an enormous jam. Being thirty-five years your senior, I will almost surely die first, and then, if our secrets are still intact, you will be heir to everything I have."

Faye said, "I'm stunned."

"So was I," I assured her. "Eugene even offered to put his terms in writing, in a prenup. Given my circumstances, I found the proposal attractive, but I doubted if Eugene could actually make my problems disappear. He surprised me, though, by turning to his lawyer, Ronda Trask, who handled the payoffs—and probably a few threats. Sure enough, this allowed me to clean out my desk at Fairview United, walk out of the office with an unblemished record, and begin planning the wedding that would be followed by a twenty-five-year marriage to a local tycoon."

Faye broke into a huge smile. "All's well that ends well, right?" Then, responding to my blank expression, she added, "Or am I missing something?"

I leaned forward in my chair, explaining quietly, "When the agency uncovered John White's scheme, its report detailed the results of the insurance records I altered."

Faye winced.

I told her, "People died."

CHAPTER
TWO

Living with lies was the root cause of my problems, according to Dr. Faye Rubin. She might have previously reasoned that my central lie, my "original sin," was agreeing to a loveless marriage of convenience. Or perhaps she suspected that I had, more venally, married for money. But no. My original sin was far worse, robbing policyholders of their lives. My subsequent sin was accepting Eugene's offer to get me off the hook. I wasn't proud of any of this; in fact, it haunted me every day. And this heavy guilt, this dirty secret—it clearly qualified as the elusive "psychological trauma" that Faye thought had triggered my stifling agoraphobia.

So my first night in the penthouse as a newly minted widow gave me plenty to mourn—not just the death of my husband, but also the complete loss of plausible denial of my wrongs, which had evaporated that afternoon when I verbalized those wrongs, sharing the secret with my therapist. I *needed* a good night's sleep, but the events of that day remained stubbornly active in my restless mind.

Gelato helped. So did booze. And finally, a Xanax.

Friday morning, I awoke earlier than usual, surprisingly refreshed. I was booked to meet Eugene's lawyer at ten, then lunch with Eugene's first wife, Bebe, at noon. This left me plenty of time for a vigorous session in our (now *my*) home gym, but not until after relaxing with coffee on the terrace, where I was reminded of my widowhood as soon as I picked up the rolled newspaper that rested on the tray next to a carafe of bold, steaming Arabica. I knew what to expect as I unfurled that day's issue of the *Consensus Times*, published an hour away in the state capital. News from Fairview was usually contained in its own section, but today a Fairview story had made its way up to page one. The headline said it all: EUGENE AURIC, DEVELOPER AND PHILANTHROPIST, DIES AT 85.

The bulk of the obituary had surely been written and kept in the can for some time, but a few quotes had been gathered since yesterday—tributes from Governor Swaine and a handful of business associates. *Nice job*, I thought. The tone was reverential. The praise, lavishly obsequious. The photos, heavily retouched. Eugene would have loved it.

I slowly tore the front page from the back page along the crease, careful not to damage even a word of it. It was a tribute that ought to be preserved in a plastic sleeve and tucked away in a leather-bound book of memories. Instead, I walked over to the ornate stone balustrade at the edge of the roof garden and held the sheet of newsprint high over my head, where the constant breeze tugged it from the pinch of my fingers. I watched as it drifted higher and higher in the updraft from the building, fluttering over the green of the town, then disappearing as a white speck somewhere above the sunny yellow of the wheat fields— far, far, away.

My workout in the gym took on a frightening intensity that morning. I usually spent an hour at it, but today's routine stretched to ninety minutes—cardio on the treadmill, followed by circuit training on various machines, and ending with free weights, which I forced up a notch. Was all this vigor meant to mask my underlying anxiety, or was I simply doing penance for gorging myself on yesterday's gelato? At least I'd had the good sense to send the remainder of it home with Ashley, who would not be working at the penthouse today.

Running late with my workout, I had to rush to get cleaned up and presentable for my meeting with Ronda Trask, Eugene's on-staff attorney and general factotum, who worked downstairs on the seventeenth floor, in the corporate headquarters of Auric Development & Holdings. I had rarely set foot in the company offices—that was Eugene's domain, dead or alive—so Ronda had suggested meeting on my own turf, in the penthouse.

Dingdong.

Checking my watch (precisely ten o'clock), I crossed through the reception room and opened the door to the entry hall, where Ronda had just emerged from the elevator. She carried not one briefcase, but two—one of them tan leather, the other oxblood.

She had recently turned sixty-five and had worked for Eugene for nearly thirty years. Now that he was gone, I wondered if her thoughts would turn to retirement—but I doubted it. Her work, it seemed, was her life. She never spoke of anything or anyone else, leading many to think she was a lesbian, not of the lipstick variety. Her brown hair, mostly gray now, was worn in a short, serviceable style, buzzed at the sides, and today she wore one of her no-fuss pantsuits (this one the color of wet cement) with black oxfords.

"Woo-hoo," she said, "look at *you*. Hope you didn't go to the trouble of dolling up for *me*."

"Actually," I admitted, "I'm meeting Bebe for lunch."

"My sympathies," she said dryly.

I grinned and offered a hug. "How are you doing? You've been with Eugene longer than *I* have—I'm really sorry for your loss."

"Aw, thanks, Meghan. I'll be fine. But we're here to talk about *you*." She flexed both arms, with both bulging briefcases still in hand. She wasn't very tall, but built like a fireplug—you would *not* want her following you in a dark alley.

"Here," I said, "let me help." I took the tan briefcase and led Ronda through the living room, past the library, and into Eugene's home office. He'd always referred to this room as his "den," which might have been a guy thing or maybe just old-fashioned, but either way, I didn't like the sound of it.

The room had bookcases and dark hardwood-paneled walls (walnut, I think) displaying several sports-themed oil paintings by LeRoy Neiman (not my cup of tea). There was a grouping of upholstered furniture, a game table with four side chairs, and of course a massive manly desk, which displayed a computer monitor and a variety of framed photos, including images of Eugene himself, his son, and his building, but nothing of his first wife ... or me. Behind the desk were French doors leading out to a small private terrace. Not big enough for furniture, it was sort of a glorified balcony.

I suggested to Ronda that we should sit at the game table, where we could sort through the material she'd brought. While she unbuckled one of the cases and began placing stacks of paper on the table, I asked, "How are things downstairs at headquarters? Who's running the show?"

She paused with her sorting and sat back in her chair. "Right now, by default, it seems *I* am. Eugene kept the top management highly compartmentalized. Guess he never thought much about a succession plan—or if he did, he never made it known."

I rolled my eyes. "Planning his successor would be admitting his own mortality—not his favorite topic."

Ronda snorted. "You got *that* right."

"There's a … board of trustees, isn't there?"

"Oh, sure. But that's just *advisory*. They don't do jack shit. They can't. Since day one, the company has been privately owned. And now"—Ronda beaded me with a stare—"you own it."

Though the words were jarring, I'd known for many years, at least in the abstract, that I would be Eugene's principal heir. "But," I told Ronda, stammering, "… but I have … I have no idea how to step into Eugene's job … or *anyone's* job."

She tossed her hands. "Piece of cake. You don't need to punch a clock. Just *delegate*."

"Oh." That sounded better. I could do that. "Can I delegate *you*?"

She gave a deferential bob of her head. "You can indeed."

So we covered a lot of ground that morning.

Aside from the day-to-day minutiae of running the Auric corporation, the most pressing item that Ronda needed to review with me was Eugene's estate plan, his living trust—a setup designed to avoid lengthy, public probate proceedings.

She herself had drawn up the trust for Eugene, and she assured me, "It abides by both the letter and the spirit of the prenuptial agreement that he had me draft for both of you twenty-six years ago, before you married." Having written the prenup, Ronda was of course privy to the secrets that had bound both Eugene and me.

"He was true to his word," said Ronda. "Because your agreed-upon confidences were never violated, the assets of his estate, with very few minor exceptions, now pass directly to you,

Meghan. He left token bequests to Bibiana, Eugene Junior, and a few charities, schools, and fraternal organizations."

I asked, "Bebe was well taken care of when they divorced, correct?"

With a firm nod, Ronda explained, "Eugene may have been a jerk for dumping her in order to seek out someone younger, but he was a total gentleman when it came to the settlement. He gave her a *substantial* portion of his assets at that time, no strings attached—along with a similar payout to Eugene Junior. They were both set up for life, and as far as I know, they've both been smart enough to invest and grow their fortune, rather than squander it. Bibiana must be fuckin' *grateful* for that divorce."

Fair enough, I thought.

"However," Ronda said, then paused.

Through a cautious grin, I asked, "Yes?"

A fleeting wave of concern passed over Ronda's face, then instantly disappeared. "Eugene recently added a codicil to the terms of his estate plan. But it's a *very* minor item."

"Exactly *how* minor?" I asked.

Ronda pulled a sheet of paper from a folder and cleared her throat before reading to me the single sentence of Eugene's codicil: "If, subsequent to my death, Meghan reveals that I played any role in exonerating her from crimes she committed while in the employ of Fairview United Insurance, her inheritance from me can be contested by my first wife, Bibiana, and my son, Eugene Junior."

I cocked my head, unsure of the implications of what I'd heard. The day before, I'd told the complete story of the prenup to Faye, my therapist, but I was sure it was safe with her. I asked Ronda, "Will Bebe and Junior be made aware of this codicil? Wouldn't that just tip them off to what Eugene wanted hidden?"

With an elaborate shrug, she said, "First of all, I didn't write this; Eugene did, verbatim. He didn't ask me to vet it or clean it up; he just signed it in the presence of our corporate notary and handed it over. I'm the executor of his trust, and in my judgment, it makes no sense to provide Bebe and Junior with a copy of the codicil—unless *you* go public with the prenup secrets. Which, *obviously*, you're not gonna do. Because you're a smart cookie."

I gave her a grateful nod.

She continued, "If you ask me, this codicil from the grave is simply intended as a don't-rock-the-boat clause."

"Is that a technical term? Or mumbo jumbo?"

She smirked.

As we continued discussing the various items on Ronda's list, she checked them off with eager slashes of a thick black Sharpie, declaring, "Done!" with each stroke.

"We're getting there," she assured me. "Now, then: Eugene's memorial. He left no instructions. What do you want? Big or small? Public or private? Religious or not?"

"Just ... *minimal*."

"Want me to handle it?"

"Please."

"Done!" Moving along, Ronda said, "The last year or so, he's been talking about having a portrait of himself painted, life-size, for the office lobby."

"Now, *why* doesn't this surprise me?"

"He set aside funds for this. Want me to handle it?"

"Actually ... no. Let me deal with that. I have a lot of contacts through the museum."

She nodded. "You're on their board, right?"

"Right. My college minor was art history, no more useful career-wise than a major in philosophy, but it added to my *bona fides* when I joined the board—not to mention, of course, that I was the wife of Eugene Auric. In any event, the museum job is volunteer work, and I love it. So I'll take care of the portrait project."

"Done! And one final item today: the press. We've been fielding quite a few calls downstairs from reporters who'd like to talk to you about Eugene and about your years together. I've spoken to all of them and told them not to count on anything, but I did make a list and agreed to pass along the requests to you." She removed a page from her folder and gave it to me.

The list included talking heads from all of the area's TV stations and one from CNN, but I wanted no part of that. Even though Marshall McLuhan once described television as a "cool" medium, I had no desire to occupy the hot seat in a broadcast interview, with my mumbles and squirms digitized for posterity. If, however, I couldn't avoid the media's probing curiosity, I would much prefer the edited thoughtfulness of print.

Ronda's list included newspaper journalists from Chicago to the east and Los Angeles to the west, with a smattering of others from the less populace regions between—and in fact I recognized several names from the *Consensus Times*, except one.

I asked Ronda, "Who's Chase Unger?"

She chuckled. "Cub reporter at the *Times*. New intern, I think—a kid out of college. They assigned him to the Fairview 'beat,' if there is such a thing, which must feel like Siberia. He was nervous on the phone."

"But I'm *sure* you put him at ease." I grinned.

"In *fact*, I tried to. He was polite and earnest, not pushy at all. He's not *from* here and didn't even seem familiar with the Auric name. Just a new hire following up on an assignment." Meaningfully, Ronda added, "He hasn't been around long enough to have an agenda."

"Unlike," I said, glancing over the list again, "most of these others."

"Do what you think best—or don't do anything at all. Sometimes, the less said, the better." She asked me for a few more signatures before gathering her papers and stuffing them into both briefcases.

Pushing back her chair at the game table, she asked, "Mind if I take a look at Eugene's computer?"

"Help yourself." I stepped over to the desk and switched on the computer, which had sat darkened and idle for the entire month of Eugene's hospital stay. It booted up just fine but needed his password. I hesitated.

"Ten to one," said Ronda, "it's the same dumb password he used for everything else—I *told* him how dangerous that is."

I thumped my forehead, then typed in: WRIGLEYWEST. (He'd always liked to brag that Auric Tower was "the Wrigley Building of the West.")

"We're in," said Ronda, eyeing the screen.

I moved aside so she could sit at the desk and get to work. Then I picked up the slim folder of papers she had left me. "If you need me," I said, "I'll be in the living room."

Holding the phone at arm's length, I gave myself a moment to reconsider. I weighed the upsides and downsides of calling a reporter—I didn't *need* to do this. But lots of journalists were trying to get through to me, and I reasoned that if I shut *everyone* out, they would collectively sense an untold story and go sniffing for it. On the other hand, if I openly approached a polite young reporter with no agenda and offered a coveted interview, he would very likely allow me to shape it as I saw fit. And because he worked for the *Consensus Times*, a perfectly respectable little paper with a sterling reputation, his story would go out on the wire services and be picked up wherever there was interest, forestalling any digging from the rest of the pack. This struck me as a sensible gamble.

I had already tapped in the number. Now I drew the phone near and punched the CALL button.

After a few rings, the line connected, and a young man's voice, which was not particularly deep or resonant, said, "Chase Unger, *Consensus Times*."

"Hello, Mr. Unger. This is Meghan Daley Auric, returning your call."

At first he said nothing, making me wonder if we'd been disconnected. But then he responded with a squeak, "*Really?*"

I laughed. "Well, *yes*. You did phone me, correct?"

"I did ... but I ... I didn't expect to hear back from you."

"Whyever not? But never mind, Mr. Unger. I understand you'd like to have a conversation about my late husband. I'd be happy to do that, but I think it would be *so* much better face-to-face, don't you?"

"Absolutely! We could meet over coffee—I'm buying. There's that big Starbucks not far from your building."

"That"—I envisioned the crowds, the milling, the lines—"*that* won't quite work for me. Perhaps you could come to my home, if you don't mind. How about tomorrow morning at, say, ten? Are you available on a Saturday?"

I could hear him swallow, sounding breathless. "*Sure.*"

"Wonderful. There's a private entrance on the back street. They'll be expecting you."

By the time Ronda Trask left the penthouse and returned to Auric headquarters on the seventeenth floor, I had a few minutes before needing to leave for my lunch date with Bebe at the Fairview Towne Club, which was also in the building. First, though, I decided to double-check my outfit. The club was very much "our crowd," and my husband had died only twenty-four hours earlier. My getup needed to blur the line between heartbroken grief and lighthearted acceptance.

I was wearing a nubby silk jacket and skirt of cinnamon brown, Valentino, with a beige blouse and a bright yellow chiffon kerchief knotted around my neck. Very autumnal and nicely coordinated—but the yellow seemed a tad cheery for my widowed circumstances, so I swapped it for another scarf, identical, but burgundy.

The penthouse elevator took me down to the residents' concourse, where I switched to another elevator, down to the street-level concourse with its main entrance from Auric Boulevard. As noon approached, the lobby was busy.

Bebe had been married to Eugene when he built Auric Tower, and she was also a founding member of the Fairview Towne Club, a private (and highly exclusive) women's club that had outgrown its original facilities near the edge of town. Because the hoopla surrounding construction of Auric Tower guaranteed that it would become *the* prestige address in the city, Bebe strong-armed the governing board of the club to approve moving it—then convinced her husband to reserve the second and third floors of his building for the club's new location. What's more, she finagled a grand (but private) staircase that rose directly from the main lobby to the second-floor entrance to the club. Tucked behind the staircase was a discreet elevator, accessible only by key card, for those inclined not to climb the stairs.

The two floors of the club included a bar, a dining room, a more casual café, meeting rooms of various sizes, a ballroom for larger events, a ladies' gym with steam room and sauna, a game room for cards and other genteel table games, plus offices and even a few sleeping rooms to accommodate speakers and celebrity guests. Membership was for women only, who needed to be sponsored by current members and submitted for committee review. Men were allowed in some of the facilities, but only as guests of members.

All were expected to abide by rules pertaining to—most notably—a detailed dress code for both ladies and gentlemen. Also covered were decorum, the restricted use of mobile phones (padded booths were provided for such use), and a general prohibition of photography on the premises, although it was permitted at special events where pictures might enhance the club's stature.

The dues for all this exclusivity were costly, but the initiation fee was nominal—exactly one dollar—unless the membership committee stamped your application NOT OUR CROWD, and then the initiation was quoted at an astronomical level that *no one* could pay, at least no one in Fairview.

As I approached the top of the staircase, the doorman admitted me, saying, "My deepest sympathies, Mrs. Auric. I hope you'll find comfort with your Towne Club family this afternoon."

I thanked him as I entered. (Much of the service staff, in fact most of it, was male. To the best of my knowledge, this was the result of no written policy, but I couldn't help wondering if the women in charge got a kick out of placing attentive, polished, well-mannered men in servile roles wearing custom-designed Armani uniforms of charcoal worsted gabardine.)

With nods and murmurs of thanks, I fielded condolences from everyone I passed while moving through the lobby of the club and into the barroom.

It was a traditional sort of bar space, with no windows, done up in red leather and dark wood, feeling more masculine than feminine—the only such room in the club. The bar itself had a dozen or more stool-height leather chairs. In the evening, it would be standing room only, but most of the seats were unoccupied that Friday at noon. To the side of the room, there was a short wall with three small semicircular booths. At each of them, the tufted leather seating could accommodate two people huddling at a tiny round table barely big enough for cocktails, though high enough for dining. Bebe always enjoyed the challenge of eating at these tables, finding that the cramped privacy had conspiratorial overtones that far outweighed any inconvenience. "Isn't this *fun*?" she once asked, leaning toward me over the table, practically nose to nose. "It reminds me of dining on a train—the Orient Express, no less—though I've never *done* it."

That Friday, none of these booths were occupied, but the middle one was reserved with a small brass placard engraved: MRS. AURIC. They had two such signs, since both Bebe and I were members, and she had chosen to keep her married name after the divorce.

When I entered the room, the bartender greeted me at once with a subdued smile and the requisite sympathies. He wore the same sleek outfit as the rest of the staff, but his jacket was a lively cardinal red. He asked, "May I get you something to drink while you're waiting for the other Mrs. Auric?"

As I paused to consider this (a good, stiff martini might do the trick), the club's general manager entered from the back of the room and snapped his fingers at the barkeep, telling him, "Two champagne cocktails for the Mrs. Aurics, please—on the house tab." Then he rushed over to where I stood and gently clasped my right hand with both of his. "On behalf of the Towne Club's entire membership and staff, Mrs. Auric, let me extend our *warmest* sympathies for your loss. We're *so* sorry." Despite his starchy, maudlin words, he didn't look any more saddened by the situation than I did.

"Thank you, Everett. How kind of you."

"Please," he said with a hand now touching the back of my shoulder, guiding me, "let me show you to your usual booth."

It was a tight fit, with my skirt squeaking against the shiny maroon leather. Just as I settled in, Bibiana Auric entered the room.

Now it was her turn for the royal treatment from Everett Burke. He had been with the Towne Club for more than twenty-five years, before my arrival, while Bebe was still married and living upstairs in the penthouse. A few weeks ago, he had mentioned that it was his birthday; he was now fifty-seven, which marked ten years since he'd lost his wife to breast cancer. There was an adult daughter somewhere who was busy with a career and a young family, so Everett was totally dedicated to the club. He had a suave sophistication that was a good fit for his position; just as important, he was *not* a gossip and was known for his discretion and propriety.

Among the club's "mature" membership (which is to say, *most* of us), he was judged a fairly hot commodity—and he looked *damn* good in that Armani uniform. His was augmented by a subtle ornamentation of the shoulders, a suggestion of epaulets, because he was our highest-ranking staff member. I couldn't blink away the image of a crush-worthy airline pilot.

As he helped Bebe into our booth (she, too, squeaked on the leather), Everett told her, "You have my deepest sympathies, Mrs. Auric."

She gave him a wry look, reminding him, "We weren't that close—*lately*. But thank you." Her outfit was consistent with her blunt words. While I had cautiously switched out a cheery yellow neckerchief for something more subdued, Bebe was looking festive enough for Mardi Gras. The colors of her ensemble were, in a word, riotous, though at least she'd had the good sense to avoid sequins (*never* at lunch, darling). She was now sixty-eight and, to be honest, looked older. My thoughts weren't meant to be judgmental; they were merely objective. If she felt that her attire lent a youthful air, she was wrong.

Everett told her, "Whatever you've been doing lately, Mrs. Auric, keep it up—you're looking *splendid* today."

She winked at me, croaking, "He can be *such* a bullshitter."

Indeed he could.

The bartender approached with the two champagne cocktails on a tray, which he passed to Everett, then disappeared. Everett placed the glasses on the table in front of us, saying, "With the club's compliments, ladies. *Santé.*"

We thanked him. As we sipped, he nonchalantly slid a captain's chair from a nearby table and placed it at the open front side of our table. Bebe and I frequently lunched at this booth, and more often than not, we would ask Everett to join us in conversation after we'd eaten. He now stepped back a pace and bobbed his head, telling us, "I'll check again with you later. Enjoy." Turning on his heel, he vanished.

Bebe paused to watch his retreat. Subconsciously, or maybe not, she licked her lips. Under my breath, I warned her, "Careful."

She heaved a showy sigh. "I know, I know: not our crowd, darling. Alas, he's 'the help.'"

After another sip of our cocktails, I sat back in the booth, smiling. "Thanks for suggesting this, Bebe. You seem to have adjusted very well to life without Eugene, so I could use a few pointers. I'm grateful for a bit of girl talk."

She snorted. "Girl talk for *you*, maybe. I'm old enough to be your mother."

"Nonsense." But in truth, Bebe would be a few years *older* than my mother, had she lived that long. This brought to mind another uncomfortable fact: Eugene had been nearly old enough to be Bebe's *father*. And he was *sixty* when I myself had married him, just a few years out of college. (No wonder I was in therapy.)

As if reading my mind, Bebe said, "People—*other* people—they never understand. But we did what we had to do."

I nodded. Although I fully understood how I myself had been compelled to marry Eugene (it almost felt like blackmail), I wondered aloud, "Did he twist your arm, Bebe? How?"

She laughed. "I twisted *his*. Let's face it—he was a prize worth pursuing. I mean, you and I, we both made out just fine, right?"

I couldn't argue with her thoroughly practical reasoning. Glancing about at our luxe surroundings, I reminded myself that the Towne Club occupied only a small slice of the entire *building* that I now owned. And the building, in turn, represented only a fraction of Eugene's vast holdings. "Yes, Bebe," I said, "we made out just fine."

We ordered lunch, and while picking at it, I asked, "How's Gene doing?"

"Junior? He's fine. Why do you ask?"

"Well, his *father* just died. At the hospital yesterday, he seemed totally unmoved, almost flippant. In truth, so did I, but I didn't have a *blood* relationship with Eugene."

Bebe said, "Junior's 'relationship' with his father ended when he moved away to college. By the time he graduated, Eugene and I had divorced. They hardly ever saw each other after that. I don't think they were very close to begin with, and *then* they had at least twenty-five years to grow further apart. I don't kid myself—I know that Junior, at forty-nine, is essentially a playboy, living at home with his mother. But it's his life, and the settlement gave him his own resources. I don't mind; in fact, I like having him around."

When our lunch was cleared, Everett stepped over to the table bearing two dessert plates. "Hope you ladies are in the mood for something wonderful—the chef's special *semifreddo alle mandorle*, frozen almond mousse with chocolate sauce and cookie crumbs."

Bebe and I glanced at each other. "We shouldn't," she said.

"But we will," I countered. "Thank you, Everett. Won't you join us?"

"Not for dessert, thank you, but perhaps coffee and conversation." He signaled a waiter to bring three espressos, then slid the chair out from the table and sat with us. He said to Bebe, "I hope everything has been to your liking, Mrs. Auric." Turning to me, he added, "And to yours as well, Mrs. Auric." He grinned.

This had become something of a ritual. Once we were all seated together, we switched to first names, but not until Bebe and I had invited Everett to do so. (For him to initiate it would be presumptuous.) So I gave Bebe a verbal nudge: "Okay, this time, *you* do the honors."

She beamed. Resting her fingertips on Everett's hand, she said, "Do feel welcome to call us Bebe and Meghan. We'd be *ever* so pleased."

"Why, *thank* you, Bebe—that would be delightful."

And instantly the three of us were gabbing away. All of us knew instinctively that gossip regarding members was taboo, as was the topic of politics, but a recent news story in that realm had transcended partisanship with developments that had captured broad public interest. I said, "I've been preoccupied for the last couple of days. Anything new regarding Vaughn?"

Three months earlier, Senator Grady Vaughn had returned from Washington and was staying at his wooded estate on the outskirts of Consensus. A fitness buff in his sixties, he routinely took a morning run along a winding trail on his property. But he did not return when expected one day, and a search team located his body a mile away from the house. The death was attributed to a heart attack.

Because he was only a year into his second six-year term, Governor Swaine called for a special off-year election to fill the remainder of Vaughn's term, while making an interim appointment of his own wife, Olympia Swaine, as a placeholder in Washington for the few months until November.

Six weeks ago, an open primary was held, narrowing the field of a dozen candidates down to two: Julian Wentworth, a member of the Consensus County board of supervisors, and Celia Flores Gamarra, the state labor commissioner.

"You mean," Bebe asked me, "you haven't heard about the medical examiner's inquiry?"

"No, I haven't. That's why I asked."

Everett leaned over the table and lowered his voice. "No formal report yet, but word is: Senator Vaughn's death is now deemed 'suspicious.'"

"Oh, *no*." All along, I'd sensed there was more to this than was first reported. "That's ... distressing, to say the least."

Bebe downed the last of the dessert from her plate. "Just politics as usual," she said, sounding far too cavalier.

"Turns out," I said, "I have plans to spend Sunday afternoon with friends, and I think Celia Gamarra will be there. Maybe she'll know something. She's a great gal, by the way."

Bebe gave me a look. "Not our crowd—if you catch my drift."

I caught her drift: Gamarra was Latina.

Everett said, "Whatever happened, it was certainly tragic. Senator Vaughn was *such* a gentleman—and a guest of the Towne Club at any number of events. In fact, he dined here with one of our members just *two nights* before he died."

With a hoot, Bebe said, "Hope the food didn't kill him."

Everett blanched.

I told him, "Bebe has a warped sense of humor. Pay no attention to her. And please do give my compliments to the chef. His *semifreddo* was perfection."

Bebe grinned. "It was to die for, one might say."

"Thank you," said Everett, ever the diplomat. "I'm so pleased you both enjoyed it. If you'll excuse me, please?" He rose from his chair, lifted our dessert plates from the table, and took them away.

Once again, Bebe watched his exit like a cat eyeing a tasty mouse. "Have I told you?" she asked me through a purr. "One enchanted evening, the stars aligned, and Everett Burke swept me off to an astral plane—if you catch my drift."

"Yes," I reminded her, "you've *often* told me about that singular experience. Lucky you."

I, however, was far better at keeping secrets than she was. So she'd never heard that I, too, had visited that astral plane. More than once.

CHAPTER
THREE

That Friday afternoon, as soon as I returned to the penthouse, I sat down and made notes regarding the *semifreddo alle mandorle* I'd had at lunch. One taste of it had me plotting to replicate the flavors in a gelato, and now I needed to make a list of ingredients while the sense memories of eating it still lingered. Preparing an experimental batch would be an enjoyable weekend project— the results of which I could take to the Sunday gathering that would include Celia Gamarra.

Once I had my grocery list in order, I turned to another project—finding the right artist to commission for a life-size portrait of my late husband. I had left a message with the museum director at Fairview Institute of Arts, asking if he had contact information for Dustin St. James, a local artist specializing in portraiture who'd been attracting interest and praise from cognoscenti on both coasts. Finding his phone number waiting for me in a text message from the museum, I called him.

After we'd spoken for a minute or so, I could tell he was skeptical—as if a cold call offering a plum commission must be a prank. But after I dropped the right names and ballparked the right figures, he asked eagerly, "When can we meet, Mrs. Auric?"

"Tomorrow," I suggested. "Saturday afternoon at Auric Tower. There's a private entrance on the back street. They'll be expecting you at two."

So Saturday shaped up to be a busy day—with the reporter Chase Unger visiting in the morning and the artist in the afternoon. Ashley would be there working most of the day as well, since she'd skipped Friday, and I was itching to see some progress with the various household matters that needed attention following Eugene's death.

A good place to start was his shamefully expansive wardrobe. Ashley had lined up a few charities that were eager to help rid me of this mountainous reminder of Eugene's vanity, but the sorting and packing could not be accomplished in mere hours—more likely days or even weeks—so these organizations had sent cartons and packing supplies up to us, which were now piled amid the disarray of the huge bedroom.

Thanks to Ashley's resourcefulness, a crew had already come in to remove Eugene's bed, leaving conspicuous carpet dimples and a gaping blank space next to my own bed on the step-up platform that morphed upward into our shared headboard. It looked like hell and would need to be addressed later, but for now, the extra space was useful as we began sorting and piling more than enough finely tailored suits to fill a haberdashery.

While working on this (I counted three dozen cummerbunds), I asked Ashley, "Have you looked into security systems yet?"

As if she hadn't heard me, she lifted a hanger from which dangled an odd pair of items. With an ugly grimace, she asked, "What on earth…?"

"Spats," I told her. "Keep them. A community theater might want them."

Tossing them into our "miscellaneous" pile, she said, "Fairview Security came up to have a look at the place, and they'll work up a proposal this weekend. I'll let you know when I get it. If you approve it, they can start installing on Monday."

I nodded. "Sounds good. If the proposal makes sense to you, and if you're confident the results will be unobtrusive and *discreet*, go ahead and approve it. The sooner, the better."

Ashley and I had gotten an early start that morning, and after another hour of fingering through Eugene's clothes, I'd had enough. It was now after nine o'clock. Not looking my best, I told Ashley, "I need to start putting myself together. A reporter is coming up at ten."

"Sure, Meghan. If I won't be in your way, is it okay if I keep working on this?" She thumped a filled carton on top of another near the door.

"Be my guest," I said, whisking off toward my dressing room.

Just before ten o'clock, refreshed and primped, I was sitting at the kitchen counter, phoning down to the grocery market in the residents' concourse on the eighteenth floor. My planned gelato would require some offbeat ingredients that I wanted to check on. The manager assured me that everything was on hand and offered to send them up right away.

"Let's wait," I said. "I'll be down later to do some browsing. You can send everything up after that."

"Of course, Mrs. Auric. Thank you for phoning."

Having a few minutes to spare, I did an internet search for Dustin St. James, the artist I would be meeting that afternoon. I was already familiar with much of his work, but I had no idea what he himself looked like. And—*well*, now—I was pleasantly surprised.

When the phone vibrated in my hand, I might have blushed, wondering if it was the electricity of attraction. But no. The guard at the private street entrance was phoning.

He said, "Mr. Chase Unger is here to see you, Mrs. Auric."

"Please send him up."

I went downstairs to the lower level of the penthouse, checked my hair in the mirror over the fireplace in the living room, then passed through the reception room and opened the door to the entry hall just as the elevator door slid open.

I'd known that Chase Unger was young (fresh out of college, maybe twenty-three, tops), but the kid in the thick glasses could have been in high school. He was at least four inches shorter than me, with a thick head of brownish blond hair, a cowlick, and (get this) freckles! He carried a thin leather satchel that reminded me of an old-timey student's book bag. A heavy navy-blue woolen shirt was worn open, like a jacket, over a checked button-down oxford shirt, and the outfit was completed with baggy, cuffed corduroys the color of chocolate milk. He was at once goofy-looking—and lovable.

My smile must have verged on laughter. Wide-eyed, he asked, distraught, "Is something wrong, Mrs. Auric?"

"Nothing at *all*," I assured him as he stepped out of the elevator. I moved forward, extending my hand. "A pleasure to meet you, Mr. Unger."

Awkwardly, he freed his right arm from the strap of his satchel and shook my hand, telling me, "My editor was *so* surprised when he found out I'd heard back from you."

I grinned, "And I'll bet he suggested a few questions for me."

"Plenty."

"Who knows?" I said brightly. "Maybe we'll get to those questions eventually, but I'd much rather hear what's on *your* mind, Mr. Unger."

"Um," he said bashfully, "most people just call me Chase."

"If that would make you more comfortable, I'd be happy to do that. And while we're at it, Chase, I'm Meghan."

He gave me a weak, dumbfounded smile—and I had a hunch he'd avoid addressing me at all.

I suggested, "Let me show you around first, and then we can settle down for a talk."

He followed quietly as I walked him through the public rooms of the lower floor. I did most of the talking; he said little more than "gosh" or "amazing" or "beautiful."

"And let's go upstairs. We can stop in the kitchen, and then sit down for a talk on the terrace."

Dutifully, he followed me up the swooping stairway in the central atrium. Eugene had built this space with one purpose in mind—to impress even the most jaded of visitors. As for sweet little unassuming Chase, he seemed so overwhelmed by this glitz that I feared it might trigger a bout of the vapors.

He was fine, though, when we stepped into the kitchen and I asked, "Would you like some gelato? I made it myself."

"Really? I didn't know you could *do* that—make gelato at home."

I waved a hand toward the Carpigiani. "One of those helps."

The batch I had setting in the freezer was fairly basic—pistachio—but to my mind, the timeless classic. I scooped a hefty serving into a glass bowl for him and a smaller serving for myself.

When he tried it: "My God, this is ... *wow*. Thank you."

Just then, Ashley walked in to fill her water bottle, needing a break from the project in the bedroom. "Oh, sorry to interrupt," she said. "Didn't know you were in here."

"Perfectly all right," I said. "Ashley, meet Chase. Chase, this is my helper, Ashley."

He set down his dish and stepped over to shake hands. As he did so, his face seemed to light up with a flash of recognition. "*Ashley?*" he said. "Ashley *Factor*, the blogger?"

"Vlogger," I said.

He told her, "I'm one of your subscribers. I'm a huge fan of your *Factor Moments* channel."

Ashley glowed, switching instantly to her video persona. "How *sweet* of you, Chase. You're a doll."

They were, I calculated, only three years apart, clearly of the same generation. With no subtlety whatever, I asked, "Is there someone special in your life, Chase?"

"No, I just moved here. Still settling in. Work, work, work."

Ashley told him, "Yeah, it takes some getting used to—life in Fairview. Lots of wheat, but it sorta grows on you."

Wistfully, I recalled, "I'm *from* here, and when I was in high school, it *did* seem like a lot of wheat. But my mother used to tell me, 'It's not *where* you live, but *how*.'" (If only my mom could see me now.) I asked Ashley, "You met Zack here, didn't you?"

She nodded. "Last year. At the time, I thought, *Maybe he's 'it.'* But ... I dunno."

I didn't know, either. When I'd first started hearing about him, I was happy for Ashley, but I cared about her, and my gut now told me that Zack was not, by any stretch, "it." He was a musician—a New Age marimbist, I believe—and the few times I'd met him, he seemed moody, entitled, and frustrated. He wore black all the time. He had baggage. And Ashley could do better.

Chase said, "Really nice meeting you, Ashley. But I shouldn't waste any more of Meghan's time." He turned to me. "I can't quite believe that you agreed to an interview. This could make a huge difference for me at the *Times*."

Rinsing our bowls in the sink, I told him, "Then we'd better get started."

Out on the terrace, Chase was again gobsmacked—the roof

garden, the views, the opulence of it all. It was too easy for me to forget that not many people actually lived like this. In fact, most people had never even set foot in such surroundings.

We seated ourselves across from each other in deeply cushioned chairs, shaded by a cheery pink-and-gray awning. Its scalloped edge wavered in the breeze. I could tell that the fledgling reporter was flustered while getting his notes organized, so I said, "Please, Chase, I want you to feel at home here. Just think of me as a friend, and let's enjoy this beautiful morning."

He took a deep breath and seemed more relaxed as he switched on his recorder and opened his notebook. "Thank you, Mrs. Auric—I mean, Meghan." Warmly, he added, "You're not at all what I expected."

Truly curious, I asked, "What were you expecting?"

"Well"—he struggled for words—"I mean, you're *really* rich, obviously, and I haven't had much exposure to 'your crowd,' so to speak. I thought you might be sort of... mean. Sorry."

"Nothing to apologize for. In fact, I know plenty of mean people in my crowd."

He laughed. "Can I quote you on that? Just *kidding*."

I laughed with him. "Don't you dare."

"So," he said, getting down to business, "you and your husband were together for twenty-five years. Two days ago, you lost him. How are you adjusting to life without him?"

"Well enough," I answered, perhaps too quickly. "As the years went by, we spent less and less time together—I mean, he was a *busy* man, and he loved what he did. I was never so insecure that I thought I needed to *compete* with his business. So I was here for him when he needed me, and I kept out of the way when he didn't. Recently, of course, he'd been very ill, so he hadn't been home for quite a while." For purposes of the interview, I thought

I'd better add, mawkishly, "I'm just so glad he's at peace now."

If Chase sensed I was being disingenuous, he didn't let on. Instead, he asked, "What can you tell me about Eugene Auric that might surprise people?"

"Most people have probably heard about his 'thing' for custom tailoring—he coveted that spot on the best-dressed list. But I'll bet they *didn't* know that he absolutely craved black licorice. Couldn't get enough of it."

Chase looked up from his notes. "Really?"

"Yes, really. Long ago, before I knew him, he started snacking on licorice to help him quit smoking. It must've worked—I never once saw him with a cigarette. So, in effect, he replaced the one craving with another. Since one of my hobbies is making gelato, I figured out how to replicate a licorice flavor, which is similar to fennel or anise—they come from different plants. Anise is sweeter, with a more powerful licorice flavor, so that's what I used, adding honey to the gelato. Eugene loved it. As far as I was concerned, it was *mezza mezza*."

"Cool," said Chase, writing quickly. "Nice detail. Now then, stock question: What was the happiest moment in your twenty-five years together?"

I flipped my hands. "Stock answer: When I realized how much I loved him."

Chase asked, "Care to elaborate on that?"

"No." How could I possibly say it? Certainly not for the record. Truth is, when I realized just how much I loved Eugene, it was the moment when I recognized that I didn't much love him at all.

"No problem," said Chase. "And the opposite side of that question, which you might not want to answer: What was the saddest moment of your marriage?"

I surprised Chase by answering without hesitation. "Our saddest moment was when I realized that we'd never have children. It just wasn't in the cards."

"Gosh, sorry. If you prefer, I won't print that—but it's very humanizing."

I shrugged. "It's not as if we ever *pretended* to have kids. Our marriage wasn't perfect, but it was a far cry from an Edward Albee melodrama. In the final analysis, we were a fairly conventional couple—we had our issues, and we dealt with them."

Chase said, "Turning to happier topics: What are you passionate about, Meghan Auric?"

Exhaling a thoughtful sigh, I told him, "Cooking. And gelato—you already know that. Gardening, too, which is a neat trick on the thirtieth floor—maybe you'll want pictures of my tomatoes. Recently, I've gotten interested in local politics. But going much further back, I'd have to say that my driving passion is art—as both a topic of study and a source of inspiration. I'm a modest collector myself, but I also devote time and energy to the Fairview Institute of Arts, which is so vital to the enrichment of this community."

"Nice," he said, underlining something in his notes.

The interview went on in this vein for another ten or fifteen minutes, then he said, "One final question, Meghan: How do you want people to remember Eugene Auric?"

"I hope he'll be remembered exactly as *he* intended to be remembered. He was many things, but first and foremost, he thought of himself as a builder, and *this building* is the monument he built for—and to—himself."

Chase nodded. "Fair enough. But the building, which is beautiful, is also impersonal. It's something he left behind, but it doesn't give much insight into the man *himself*. At a deeper level, how should our readers remember him?"

Then it clicked. "Earlier, we spoke of art. One of Eugene's last wishes was to have a significant portrait of himself painted for the lobby of Auric headquarters, here in the building. I've begun to explore those possibilities. I hope that this project, in the hands of a gifted artist, will leave a deeper, more meaningful insight into my husband's legacy. Sometimes, art speaks where words fail."

Chase stabbed his notes with a period. "And that's a *wrap*. Thank you, Meghan. This'll be great."

"My pleasure," I told him as we stood.

Stepping out from under the awning and into the direct sunlight of the terrace, we instinctively drew near to each other and wordlessly agreed that a hug was in order.

As we embraced, I said into his ear, "Any chance you'll let me check my quotes before you run them?"

He stepped back a pace, laughing. "My editor would have a *fit*. But sure. I'll show you the quotes before I send him the story."

I gave him a thumbs-up.

Removing a small camera from his satchel, he said, "Before I go, wanna show me your tomato plants?"

After lunch, I went down to do some shopping at the market in the residents' concourse. I could have phoned or texted my list to them, but actually walking through the aisles, pushing a cart, gave me a few minutes that felt like a semblance of normalcy, a safe and sanitized tether to reality, as if I was just an ordinary housewife out running errands. When I wheeled my cart to the waiting checker, though, he didn't ring everything up or give me a total or ask for identification. He simply set my cart aside, asking, "Shall I send this right up, Mrs. Auric?"

I glanced at my watch. "Could you deliver it later this afternoon—say, three thirty?"

"Of course, ma'am."

And four minutes later, I was back in the penthouse, ready for the arrival of the artist whom I hoped to commission for a portrait of my late husband.

At the stroke of two o'clock, the guard at the private entrance phoned me. "Mr. Dustin St. James is here for your meeting, Mrs. Auric."

I was standing inside the doorway to the reception room, facing the entry hall, when the elevator door slid open.

"Mrs. Auric, I presume?" he said with a wide, handsome smile.

"Mr. St. James," I said, stepping over to greet him. "It's an honor. Please—come in."

When we moved into the gallery space in the reception hall, he paused to admire the collection. As he studied the paintings, I studied him.

I already knew from my cursory sleuthing on the internet that he was thirty-five years old, with an undergrad degree from the School of the Art Institute of Chicago and a master's from Yale, where he had also taught. Five years ago, he'd returned from the East Coast to hometown Fairview in the plains of the heartland, where he claimed to draw inspiration from what he called "the vast nothingness." To accommodate his large-scale canvases, he'd snapped up a vacant warehouse on the edge of town and converted it into a studio and living space that was recently featured in *ArchitecAmerica*. He was now routinely referenced as "someone to watch" or "the 'it' boy" in the world of contemporary portraiture, drawing favorable comparison to such luminaries as Kehinde Wiley, Amy Sherald, and Jonathan Yeo.

And there he was, standing in my home. He didn't look like a wild-eyed bohemian or a starving artist. *Au contraire*, he looked thoroughly put-together and professional—no matted hair, no paint on his clothes or under his fingernails. A solid six feet tall, with piercing green eyes and an astounding mane of wavy black hair, he wore charcoal woolen slacks with a matching turtleneck and a black cashmere blazer. Fifteen years my junior, he was not unthinkably out of bounds, and I could easily entertain fantasies starring him in a dominant role. (But alas, I had read that he was gay.)

"Grant Wood? Edward Hopper?" he said, peering at the walls. "Pardon me for gawking, but I'm just slightly blown away, Meghan." Then he halted, backtracking: "Do you mind if I call you Meghan?"

"Why not?" I said with a giggle. (I never giggle.) "That's my name, Dustin."

He continued browsing. "And Andrew Wyeth? You seem to have an affection for regionalist realism."

"Yes," I told him, "and I have a special interest in so-called magic realism." Dustin himself was known for this style.

He gave me a curious look. "Then—who knows—it seems we might be a good match."

"I hope so. Let me show you into the living room. We can sit down and talk about the portrait I have in mind."

"Of course, eager to hear your ideas. And I brought along my iPad—my digital portfolio, so to speak."

The living room, being rather grand in scale, had many seating options, so I asked, "Where would you be most comfortable?"

"Uh, maybe over here?" And he led me to a small sofa—some

would call it a loveseat. This was the same sofa where I'd sat on Thursday morning after returning from the hospital. It had a direct view onto the lower penthouse terrace and the "vast nothingness" beyond. As we sat, he placed his iPad on the cocktail table a few inches from our knees.

In order to face each other while talking, we needed to pivot from the ends of the sofa, bringing my right knee within an angstrom of his left.

"First," he said, "please accept my condolences on the death of your husband."

"Thank you. It's ... a bit of an adjustment."

"I understand. My husband, Brad, died about a year ago."

"I'm *so* sorry." I placed my fingertips on Dustin's knee for a moment. "I hadn't heard."

"It was sudden, and he was far too young. I still think about him every day."

"I can appreciate what you're going through." But in truth, I couldn't. My recent thoughts about Eugene had been limited to the frustrations of cleaning out his damn closet.

With these preliminaries out of the way, Dustin and I reviewed the parameters of the portrait project I had in mind, much of which we'd covered on the phone when I first called him. Though the portrait of Eugene was to be life-size, standing, it would be impossible, of course, for Eugene to pose for it, so Dustin would need to work from existing photos of his subject. I assured him that I could supply seemingly countless images for reference.

"But," I added, "the 'literal' depiction of Eugene doesn't interest me as much as the overall treatment, the *interpretation* of the man, the vision you can bring to the portrait."

Dustin reached for his iPad. "This is so exciting, Meghan. I rarely encounter a commission that allows that sort of latitude. Let me show you some examples of earlier work."

We spent perhaps half an hour reviewing images of his portraits, leaving no doubt of his talents. But then I stopped him, explaining, "These are all gorgeous, Dustin, simply breathtaking. But I've already seen most of them—online, or in exhibits. I'm well aware of what you've done. What really excites me, though, is where you might go next."

Smiling, he set down the iPad and reached to take one of my hands into both of his. "I'd *really* like for you to visit my studio. You can see 'what's next' in several works I have in progress right now. More important, as we talk, I'll be able to sketch and to demonstrate my process to you in real time. I'd love to make you a part of the creative concept from the outset. I don't offer this lightly—most clients are a hindrance, a pain in the ass. But you're different, Meghan. This could be very special."

I felt a lump of panic rising in my throat. "Um ... that's incredibly tempting, Dustin, but ... it's difficult to explain ..."

He shushed me with a finger to my lips. "I've heard about that. I know it's a sensitive issue, so there's nothing you need to explain. I could pick you up at your door, at your convenience, and take you to my studio. The tour, the collaboration, can be as extensive or as minimal as you wish. And if, at *any* point, you're feeling anxious or uncomfortable, just say so—and I'll get you back here in five minutes flat."

My heart was pounding. My mouth was dry.

So I was surprised to hear myself tell him, "Tomorrow won't work. But maybe Monday afternoon?"

CHAPTER
FOUR

I had been invited to spend much of the following day, Sunday, at the home of two dear college friends, where we would enjoy an afternoon cookout. I didn't need to ask what I could bring—it was exactly the sort of occasion that called for gelato.

Saturday evening, I experimented with a small test batch, mimicking the flavors and ingredients of the Towne Club's *semifreddo alle mandorle*. After it had sufficiently firmed up in the freezer, I tasted a spoonful—very promising, but not quite there. So I saved the test batch for later, tweaked the recipe, and went to work on a larger batch for the cookout.

Late Sunday morning, when another tasting confirmed that my tweaks had succeeded, I packed about a gallon of the gelato in an insulated cooler. Then I took it down to the residents' street-level lobby and carried it out of the building. Idling at the curb was a sizable SUV, midnight blue, spiffed and sparkling in the slant of autumn sunshine.

"Thank you, Clarence," I said to the doorman as he helped me into the passenger seat and placed my cooler on the floor in back.

When the doors were closed, Theo Hudson leaned over from the driver's seat to greet me, and we kissed cheeks. After the obligatory sympathies, he said, "Lila can't wait to see you—it's been way too long."

As he pulled into traffic, leaving the building behind, I felt totally at ease. Theo and Lila were a Black couple I'd met while we were all at Berkeley. We had bonded at once, then shared an apartment for a year or so. A bit later, I was in their wedding. I should note that although Theo was a highly attractive man, it was clear from the outset that he and Lila were committed to each other, so I never, ever thought of him in any context other than deep friendship.

Because our history predated my association with Eugene, which then led to my agoraphobia, that condition seemed to have no effect on me when I was in the company of the Hudsons. Being with them always felt like returning to simpler times, when they knew me as Meghan Daley.

Theo and I now gabbed the way old friends do, speaking as if in code, in shorthand, with the missing details filled in by our shared history. After a few minutes, we were driving through the area of Fairview dominated by Lindencrest University, a small but prestigious private school where Theo was now a tenured faculty member.

Back in our Berkeley days, he had never even heard of Fairview, but because of our friendship, he and Lila had visited me several times after I'd returned home from college. They liked the place—and became familiar with Lindencrest. But they remained in California while Theo continued in grad school, achieving prominence as a scholar and author in the social sciences. A few years later, when a Lindencrest faculty position opened in Theo's field, he decided to go for it. And he won it easily.

"We finally finished that deck project on the back of the house," he told me. "So we thought today would be perfect for a cookout, before the cold weather sets in." With a laugh, he add-ed, "Nothing fancy, though. Sorry."

"It sounds like heaven," I assured him. Slumping back in my seat, I could have fallen asleep—as if knowing I would be in good hands, with good people.

The house was in a quiet, wooded neighborhood at the edge of a small lake near the school. Many of the residents were senior faculty members. The style of the Hudsons' home might be de-scribed as "modern rustic." It was L-shaped, with steep, opposing shed roofs that were clad with shake shingles and punctuated by black stove-pipe chimneys.

Theo steered the SUV along a narrow, curvy blacktop road, then turned onto the gravel driveway that led to the house. An-other car was parked there, a sporty coupe that I recognized as belonging to Adam Hudson, Theo and Lila's son.

When we got out of the SUV, I felt the cool breeze from the lake and heard the rustle of birds in the trees, but otherwise, all was quiet on that Sunday as morning nudged toward noon. It was hard to believe that my "gilded cage" atop Auric Tower was only three miles away—it felt more like a million. Theo grabbed the cooler from the rear seat and thumped the door closed.

Lila had heard us arrive and was waiting on the front deck of the house to greet me with a hug. Then she held me at arm's length, nodding. "Know what, Meg? I think we're both lookin' damn *fine*—for a couple old broads."

I laughed. "There's no contest, Lila. When it comes to the beauty department, you will *always* take the prize." It was true—she was still a knockout, and she was two years *older* than I was.

With a whisk of her hand, she batted away my compliment as if it were a pesky fly. "I understand you've been working with Theo on Celia's campaign."

I shrugged. "Stuffing a few envelopes."

Theo said, "More like: writing a few checks." He had been heavily involved with Celia Gamarra's local office for her Senate campaign, located on campus. He'd convinced me to join the cause by bringing Celia up to the penthouse to introduce us. Then he set me up with menial tasks I could perform from home.

I told Lila, "I do what I can."

She said, "Come on inside. Someone's been wanting to see you."

Inside the front door was a typical, contemporary "open concept" arrangement of living room, dining room, and kitchen areas, with a wall of sliding glass doors to the rear—which now led to the new deck. Outside, a younger man was fussing with the tank that fueled a gas grill.

Lila called to him, "Adam, honey—Aunt Meg is here."

He immediately dropped what he was doing and rushed in with Doogie, a sweet Shetland sheepdog that looked like a small, fluffy collie. After the requisite condolences, Adam broke into a beaming smile and hugged me. "It's been *forever* since I've seen you. You look *great*, Aunt Meg." (The "aunt," of course, was purely affectionate.)

I reminded him, "It has *not* been 'forever.' Forever was twenty-eight years ago, in California, when I first held you in my hands." I mimed holding something the size of a loaf of bread.

Adam's father turned to us from the refrigerator, where he was stowing the gelato in the freezer. "And look at him now—Adam's a full-fledged lawyer, working his way up in a top-notch firm."

Adam chuckled. "Well, top-notch here in Fairview, which is a *long* way from Manhattan."

Lila gave me a wink. "We're just glad he's still around. How long—who knows?"

Dingdong.

Doogie barked as Theo beelined from the fridge to the door. Opening it, he welcomed the candidate, Celia Flores Gamarra, who already knew all of us, and her husband, Nicolás Gamarra, whom I had not met. When we were introduced, he said, "Everyone just calls me Nick, Mrs. Auric."

"And around here," I said, "I'm known as Aunt Meg—though Meghan is fine, Nick."

Nick had brought wine, which Lila took from him, thanking him.

Theo told us, "Bar's open. What would everyone like to drink?" After we'd all responded, he and Adam stepped aside to perform bartending duties.

I went out to the back deck with Nick and Celia, enjoying the weather and admiring the view of the lake through a clearing in the trees.

Celia, I knew, was forty-four. She was well known in state politics as the labor commissioner, appointed by Governor Swaine. She had a thoroughly professional bearing and a no-nonsense campaign style, focused on facts, figures, and policy. Frankly, she often struck me as a bit uptight—part of the job, perhaps—but today she seemed more relaxed in the company of friends.

Her husband appeared to be about the same age, maybe a few years older, an affable, nice-looking Latino. Physically fit, he spoke with precision and no accent, projecting an image that struck me as conspicuously clean-cut.

I said, "I know quite a bit about Celia's background—these days, who doesn't? But what about you, Nick? May I ask what sort of work you do?"

He pulled his card from a pocket and handed it to me. "I'm a detective with the sheriff's department."

Consensus County sprawled from the capital city of Consensus all the way out to Fairview and well beyond. Because Fairview was more centrally located in the county, the sheriff's main headquarters was located here. Fairview also contracted with the county for local police services. Glancing at Nick's card, I said, "So you work for Sheriff Hewitt."

Under her breath, Celia said, "Don't get me started."

Nick laughed. "I try to stay neutral, but my wife and Stanley Hewitt don't see eye to eye on most things."

She countered, "We don't see eye to eye on *anything*. He's a far-right extremist with a badge and a gun."

"Maybe. Maybe not. But Stan's my boss, and I need to work with him—at least until the next election."

"He won't be up again for three years. A lot can go terribly *wrong* in three years."

Theo and Adam brought out our drinks, and Lila carried a stack of dishes over to the new picnic table, where the six of us would eat. For now, though, we settled in a loose circle of canvas director's chairs, sipping and chatting while something roasted under the hood of the grill, scenting the autumn air with a smoky tang. Doogie sat in our midst, but kept an eye on the grill.

Our conversation drifted from topic to topic, but frequently returned to Celia's Senate campaign—and her opponent, Julian Wentworth.

"What's he like?" I asked anyone.

My old friend Theo said, "He's polished. Slick."

Lila added, "Too slick, if you ask me. He's slimy."

Celia told us, "I don't like him, but he'll be tough to beat. As a county supervisor, he's already proven he's electable. I, on the other hand, was *appointed* as labor commissioner, so most voters don't know me yet."

Her husband, Nick, reminded her, "You got through the primary."

"True ..." She raised and drank from her glass of wine, as if saluting herself.

Nick said, "But enough of politics—for now." He glanced around our circle, and his gaze came to rest on the Hudsons' son. "Adam," said Nick, "we've never had a chance to talk. I know you're a lawyer, but the rest is a mystery."

Adam laughed. "I've never been called mysterious. So, what would you like to know?"

Nick shrugged. "What's important besides your job? Married with children? Still looking?"

I shared a grin with Adam's parents.

He said, "I'm gay, Nick. And yes, I'm still looking. I wouldn't call Fairview a backwater—not at all—but it's not a gay mecca, either."

Celia said, "Any man would be lucky to have you, Adam."

Nick nodded. "Keep looking. He's out there."

(I, of course, immediately thought of Dustin St. James—local gay widower.)

Theo had just answered his phone and now said to Celia, "It's Xolani. Wants to know if she can bring some papers over for your signature."

Wearily, Celia said, "Sure—if it won't be an intrusion."

"No problem at all." Then Theo spoke into his phone, giving directions to the house.

Celia told us, "Xolani Vahdat is my campaign manager. She's a treasure—but she cracks the whip."

We were finishing a delightful *alfresco* luncheon (supposedly "nothing fancy," indeed), so I went with Lila to the kitchen to plate up the gelato, when the doorbell rang.

"That'll be Xolani," said Theo, heading for the door, trailed by Doogie.

The woman who stepped in from the front deck was young, thirty tops, and of Middle Eastern descent. Slim and stylish, she wore slacks and a tunic with a silk Hermès head scarf—which was not a hijab, but I thought she might have worn it as a cultural nod to one.

"So sorry to trouble you on Sunday," she told Theo. Wagging a manila folder, she added, "This'll just take a minute."

He took her out to the rear deck as Lila and I followed with a few plates of gelato. Lila said to Xolani, "Join us for dessert, won't you? Mrs. Auric made it."

I piped in, "There's *plenty.*"

While Celia scrawled her signature on a raft of papers, Xolani sampled the gelato with moans of pleasure.

Theo asked her, "What's new on the campaign front?"

She dabbed her lips with a paper napkin. "Wentworth just announced that he's speaking at the Fairview Towne Club this week, on Wednesday."

"La-di-da!" said Celia with a hoot.

"Really?" I asked. "I'm a member and hadn't heard about it."

Xolani said, "Sounded like a last-minute deal."

I told Celia, "There's usually one speaker luncheon each week. Want me to see if there's a slot open the week after Wentworth? The club believes in equal time for politicians."

With a Cheshire grin, Celia turned to Theo.

Theo turned to Xolani.

Xolani dug out her card and passed it to me. "That would be

beyond fabulous, Mrs. Auric. Whenever you have a chance, let's coordinate calendars."

Long after Xolani left, the rest of us lingered, enjoying each other's company and appreciating the fine weather of a warm afternoon as it waned toward the cool of the evening. Planets began to wink in the twilight.

I nodded off in a butterfly chair, and when I woke, Celia and Nick Gamarra had gone. Theo told me, "They said not to wake you."

Lila asked, "Can I get you anything, Meg? Coffee? Decaf?"

"No, nothing at all," I said, feeling absolutely content—but a bit stumbly as I got up from the caress of the butterfly chair. My movement roused Doogie, who'd been snoozing at my feet.

Adam asked, "Can I drive you home, Aunt Meg? I was about to head out myself."

"Perfect."

With hugs and kisses, I said goodbye to Theo and Lila, telling them to keep the leftover gelato, but taking the cooler.

Then I zipped away with Adam in his sporty little coupe, with the cooler stowed in his trunk.

When we drove up to the building, the night doorman came out to meet us. Adam popped the trunk, then leaned over for a smooch, saying, "Good night, Aunt Meg. Sleep tight."

The doorman closed the trunk and helped pull me up and out of the car. As Adam drove away with a toot of his horn, the doorman saw me inside and handed me the cooler, asking, "Pleasant day, Mrs. Auric?"

"Yes, thank you. A *very* pleasant day."

A couple of minutes later, I stepped out of the elevator and

66

into the entry hall of the penthouse, where everything was lit for the evening, as programmed. Passing through the gallery, I made my way upstairs and took the empty cooler to the kitchen.

Entering, I noticed at once that someone had removed the test batch of gelato from the freezer and pigged out, leaving a spoon and what was left of the gelato, now melted, on the counter. This was ... *odd*, to say the least.

Stepping out to the main room, I called, "Ashley?" But I was certain she had not been there that day. Walking through all of the upstairs rooms, I saw nothing unusual at all.

So I went down to the lower level again, continuing my inspection, and everything seemed in order, just as I'd left it— until I opened the door to Eugene's den.

To call it a "shambles" would be an overstatement, a tad too melodramatic. But to say the room had been "ransacked" would be *le mot juste*.

Someone had made a thorough, zealous search of the room.

As I walked in and looked around, it was impossible to tell at a glance if anything had been taken from the drawers or the files that were left open. But it was obvious that Eugene's computer was missing—not the large monitor, which was still on his desk, but the CPU, the cube of electronics that was now gone from its cubby beneath the desktop.

The LeRoy Neiman paintings, alas, hadn't been touched.

CHAPTER
FIVE

Rather than phoning nine-one-one or the building's security office, I took from my pocket the card given to me that afternoon by Detective Nicolás Gamarra of the Consensus County sheriff's department. I knew that he and Celia lived in Fairview, and the card included his direct mobile number, which I called. When I apologized for phoning him at home, he assured me that I'd done the right thing.

Twenty minutes later, he arrived with two uniformed deputies. He himself was wearing the same street clothes he'd worn that afternoon—nice slacks and a pinstriped oxford shirt—to which he'd now added a tweedy sport coat. Under his jacket, I spotted the glint of gunmetal in a polished leather shoulder holster.

As I walked them from the elevator hall and through the gallery in the reception room, I paused. With a sweeping gesture toward the walls, I said, "If the intent was simple theft, they were stupid to miss *this*. These paintings are *far* more valuable than anything else on either floor of the penthouse."

Sounding dismayed, Nick asked, "There's no security system?"

With a shrug, I said, "Amazing, huh? Eugene didn't want to feel 'watched,' so there are no cameras on the premises—except in here, in the gallery. The paintings couldn't be insured without at least a 'passive' system in this room. There are no alarms, but there are, in fact, miniature cameras hidden in the millwork of the paneling near the four corners of the room. They're not actively monitored, but they continuously record at the security office for review—up to a week later." I concluded by giving Nick contact information for review of the video.

Noting this, he said, "Great, got it. But you *really* should consider tighter security for the whole penthouse."

I gave him a sheepish nod. "It's been on the to-do list. In fact, installation starts tomorrow."

Then I led them directly to Eugene's office. From the doorway, they saw the mess. I said, "The computer's processor was stolen. As to anything else—who knows?"

Nick made notes. One of the deputies took photos. The other one started dusting for fingerprints.

Nick wondered aloud, "How'd they get in?"

I said, "Assuming they didn't scale the exterior of the building, there are only three ways into the penthouse. First, obviously, there's the elevator you took from the ground lobby to my entry hall. But that's closely monitored, with sign-in required for guests, twenty-four-seven. Second, there's an emergency stairwell, accessed from a dead-bolted door in my entry hall, but that can only be opened one way—from inside the penthouse, not from the stairwell, where there's not even a knob on the door. Third, there's a freight elevator from a private loading dock on the rear side of the building, which goes directly up to the terrace surrounding the top floor of the penthouse. It's controlled only by keypad entry or by key card. I've never had occasion to use it myself, so you'll probably want to check it out."

Noting all of this, Nick nodded, then asked, "Can you walk me through the whole place?"

"Of course." And I gave him the complete tour. After checking the entry hall again, as well as the gallery and all the other rooms on the lower level, I led him up the curved staircase in the open atrium to the thirtieth floor.

At the top of the stairs, Nick halted, taking it all in. "I had no idea," he said. "This is just ... well, I'm speechless, Meghan."

Trying not to sound *too* jaded, I admitted, "It's a bit much. But it's home."

We made the rounds. And as we reached the main bedroom, I meant to apologize for the mess inside, but he was one step ahead of me and stopped in his tracks, warning me, "Stand back! The intruders might still—"

"No, Nick"—I laughed, interrupting him— "I've been sorting through Eugene's *obscenely* vast wardrobe, trying to get rid of it. Whoever broke in tonight, I just wish they'd absconded with a few armloads of his suits."

Nick cocked his head. "What was Eugene's size?"

"Not a clue. But trust me, he was *way* more portly than you." With a flick of my hand, I signaled for Nick to follow me, saying, "Now let me show you something *really* interesting."

Taking him into the kitchen, I pointed to the freezer tray of melted gelato on the counter—and the dirty spoon resting at the edge of the puddle. I said, "I know this sounds crazy, but I think the thief got into the freezer, helped himself to a snack, and deliberately left the evidence to be found—as if taunting us."

Nick snapped some pictures with his phone. "Wow. Intriguing. And I think you're right. I've seen this sort of cat-and-mouse stuff before." Putting his phone away, he asked, "You've touched nothing here, correct?"

"Correct. The only possible *other* explanation is that Ashley was here today, but I'm sure she wasn't. I'm talking about my housekeeper and helper, Ashley Factor. She'll be here tomorrow."

"Good. I'll want to get a set of exclusionary fingerprints from both of you, if that's all right." When I nodded, he said, "Now show me the terrace."

Crossing the kitchen, I pulled the door open that led to the vegetable garden.

He asked, "That wasn't locked?"

"We've never routinely locked any of the doors to the terrace. Up here, who'd get in?"

He reminded me, "That's what we're trying to figure out."

After exploring the terrace, Nick decided to come back during daylight to inspect the workings of the freight elevator. The two deputies had finished their job in Eugene's den—and had also processed the evidence in the kitchen—so Nick dismissed them, saying, "Reports on my desk by noon, please."

When they were gone, it was ten o'clock. Nick said, "I know it's getting late, but I want to talk to you about something."

"Of *course*," I said. We had seen the deputies out from the elevator lobby, so I led Nick back through the gallery and into the living room, where I suggested he sit in a comfortable armchair. Then I seated myself perpendicular to him at the end of an adjacent sofa.

"Meghan," he said, "I'm glad you phoned me directly regarding what happened here." There was something in his tone—he wasn't merely saying that he was happy to be of service to a friend. Confirming my hunch, he continued, "I don't know what's going on here, but I wonder if you're aware of a certain situation. For the last few years, your late husband's company has been hiring off-duty sheriff's deputies as security guards—at nights and on weekends—for the offices that are located on a lower floor of this building."

"Oh? I wasn't aware of that. Is that unusual?"

"No, not at all. In fact, it's a sensible kind of setup. But even so ..." He hesitated, then confided to me, "I'm going to slow-walk my report on your incident tonight, just till I have a better idea of what might be behind what happened."

I asked quietly, "Should I be ... *worried*?"

"It's probably nothing at all."

Monday morning, having not slept well, I got up early and downed two quick cups of coffee, debating whether or not I should cancel my afternoon visit to the studio of Dustin St. James. A third cup had made me cogent enough to decide that I should keep that appointment, as it would provide a needed diversion from the vexations of having my home invaded.

The invasion went well beyond Sunday's break-in. Monday now brought a crew of a half dozen techies and workmen to begin installing an updated security system. Monday also brought Ashley to honcho that project and to resume helping me dispose of my dead husband's clothes. Plus, Monday brought a sheriff's deputy to take fingerprint samples from both Ashley and me. (Ashley thought it would be cool to shoot video of that process for her vlog, a suggestion I promptly vetoed.) And Monday also brought Detective Nick Gamarra back to the penthouse with a couple of thuggish-looking characters to examine the workings of the freight elevator.

In passing, Nick told me, "Overnight, we reviewed yesterday's security footage from your gallery room, which revealed no one passing through from the lobby elevator while you were visiting the Hudsons' house. Meaning, we now know with certainty that the intruder got in from the terrace."

Aarghh.

Later that morning, I grabbed my phone when Dustin St.

James texted me, asking: STILL UP FOR TODAY'S MEETING? PICK YOU UP AT TWO?

Despite my frame of mind, I sent an upbeat reply: CAN'T WAIT!

Dustin, I thought, might enjoy some gelato. Being well-acquainted with his work and also having met him, I judged him to be a man of vigor and flash and dazzle. Plus, he was gay. The subtlety of pistachio or vanilla or even *semifreddo alle mandorle* might strike him as blah. But *pink* gelato? I had a hunch he'd be into it.

I still had all the ingredients I'd used for the Shirley Temple version I'd made four days earlier (the day Eugene died), so I made a fresh batch of it before lunch on Monday and was able to let it set in the freezer for a couple of hours before I needed to leave for my meeting.

When the doorman phoned to inform me, "Mr. St. James is here to pick you up," I already had the cooler packed. Determined to overcome my entrenched reluctance to leave the building—at least for this afternoon—I headed down in the elevator.

Dustin was waiting at the curb in a large vehicle, much huskier and boxier than a typical SUV, like something intended for a safari—with running boards, guardrails, and a crash bumper. Paradoxically, all this ruggedness was offset by the pristine detailing of its mirrorlike finish, painted a deepest crimson. The doorman helped me up and into it.

Dustin turned to me wearing a bright smile and dark sunglasses—looking every bit as alluring as two days before. He asked, "What's in the cooler?"

"Gelato." I set it atop the sprawling console that separated our two seats.

"How delightful," he said, then pulled away from the curb.

Five minutes later, we were cruising through a light-industrial area at the edge of downtown, where a section of warehouses had easy access to the interstate highway.

Conspicuous among a row of otherwise shabby, featureless buildings was the one I'd seen featured in *ArchitecAmerica*. Clean and minimalist, the outer walls contained expanses of plate glass, which looked as if they'd been squeegeed and polished that very morning. A wisp of raised, sleek stainless-steel lettering protruded from the smooth surface of the rust-colored front wall: DUSTIN ST. JAMES STUDIO.

After parking near the entry door (there were also a couple of truck-size garage doors at the far end of the building), Dustin hopped down from the vehicle and trotted around it to help me out. I had opted not to wear heels that afternoon, wary of gravel, but there was none. Every surface—exterior as well as interior—was painstakingly finished, with an eye toward function as well as aesthetics. Dustin seemingly hadn't worried much about the budget, and I could only conclude that this was the result of bountiful commissions.

Entering the building, I detected at once the distinct but unmistakable smells of linseed oil and turpentine—they were subtle, but they announced clearly that an artist, a painter, had been plying his talents here.

He gave me a quick tour. The studio and residential areas melded seamlessly, and as we passed through the kitchen—designed in an austere style that I would almost describe as "surgical"—he suggested, "Should we put the gelato in the fridge?"

"By all means," I said as I opened the cooler and handed him a clear Tupperware container of the pink concoction.

"Now, *that* looks fabulous," he said, popping it in the freezer.

"Can't wait to try it. And I know someone who would *love* it. Mind if I share some later?"

"Please do." But I had no idea who the *someone* was.

"Okay, down to business," he said, closing the freezer door. Then he led me back to the studio proper.

We stood in the midst of eight or nine portraits he was working on, ranging in size from a conventional head-and-shoulders format, perhaps thirty inches high, to a monumental family portrait (four adults, five kids, two dogs, and a baby) with life-size figures, measuring seven feet high by twelve feet wide. In these and all the others, the people were rendered in a highly realistic style—*hyper*-realistic, almost photographic. But in each work, the settings, clothing, and mood made unexpected departures from reality, giving the paintings a gloss of (for lack of a better word) magic. They were all in different stages of completion, which gave me a peek into Dustin's process of developing an adventurous new style, uniquely his.

With a cautious tone, he noted, "You haven't said much."

I grinned. "How could I? I'm blown away."

"Then ... you *like* what I've been doing?"

I nodded. "I'm so grateful you convinced me to come here."

"So let's sit down and brainstorm *your* project."

There were a few scattered chairs around the cavernous studio, but there was also a long worktable, with stools, and that's where he led me. As we approached, I could see that he had laid out numerous large sketches, and I immediately recognized Eugene's features in the figures Dustin had drawn. He explained, "I pulled some images of Eugene from online—very predictable stuff—and used them as references. But I'm sure I'll do better after you supply actual photos from life, not posed."

And then we *really* talked, excitedly sharing ideas while Dustin made new sketches—wadding up and trashing some of the old ones. I was so immersed in this process that I lost all track of time. It seemed like forever. But when I heard the front door open, then close, I checked my watch and discovered that barely an hour had passed.

"Hey, Dad, I'm home," called a girl's voice.

"We're in the studio, honey. Come and meet someone."

A moment later, a girl with Asian features and straight black hair—not quite a young woman yet, maybe ten years old—entered the studio. Wearing pink sneakers and carrying a backpack, she had apparently returned from school. She came over to the table and gave Dustin a hug.

"Honey," he said, "I want you to meet Mrs. Auric." Turning to me, he said, "And Meghan, I want you to meet my daughter, Nova Tanaka St. James." With a wink he added, "How's that for a mouthful?"

The girl approached me and offered to shake hands. "Just call me Nova, Mrs. Auric. I'm very pleased to meet you."

Shaking her hand, I said, "The pleasure is mine, dear. And please: call me Meghan."

Dustin told her, "Meghan brought us a treat. Care to try it?"

"Well, *yeah!*"

"Come on, then." And Dustin led the way to the kitchen.

Two minutes later, we were standing around the center island, eating from bowls. Dustin and Nova both wanted more, which I generously scooped out for them. He asked me, "Did you actually *make* this?"

"Guilty. Just a little hobby of mine."

"Well, it's *great*."

Nova said, "It's like a kiddie cocktail, but ice cream."

"That's exactly what I had in mind," I told her.

When we finished, Dustin asked her if she had homework. She nodded, so he suggested, "Why don't you scoot upstairs and get a jump on it? Meghan and I still have some things to talk about."

"Sure, Dad. And *thanks*, Meghan."

"You're very welcome, Nova. I'm glad you enjoyed it."

And off she went.

Dustin took our bowls to the sink and began rinsing them. Over his shoulder, he asked, "Surprised?"

"Totally." I laughed. "Nova didn't pop up in my Google search. She's an absolute doll."

"Her mother can take credit for that—Crystal Tanaka was a truly beautiful woman. We met at Yale while I was in grad school. She was a dancer."

I found myself on shaky ground, since Dustin was gay. Tentatively, I said, "It's none of my business, but I can't help being curious: Was Crystal a surrogate?"

"No, sorry for the confusion." He set down his towel and came over to me at the island. "Crystal was my wife—and Nova was conceived the old-fashioned way. But two years after Nova was born, Crystal died. It was sudden, and she was far too young. I still think about her every day."

"You poor *thing*," I said. "Then you came home to Fairview, started a new life with your husband, and lost *him*, too."

He tossed his hands with resignation. "What's that old expression—'unlucky in love'? First Crystal Tanaka. Then Brad Larsen."

We still had a few more details to discuss. I said I would take some time to sift through old photos of Eugene and have them delivered to Dustin. Then he asked about the timeline for the project, and I assured him there was no deadline: "I don't want you to feel pressured in the least. I want you to *enjoy* creating this."

When I asked about terms of payment, he said that the final figure would depend on the actual size of the finished work, but he quoted a dollar range that would not be exceeded. I found this agreeable and wanted to pay a deposit, "just to make the project 'official.'" He thanked me for offering this, then sent to my phone the address to use for electronic payment.

He said, "Regarding the finished size of the painting, you've told me that you want a life-size depiction of Eugene, standing. In that case, with an eye toward composition, I'd suggest a canvas that's eight feet tall. A pleasing proportion for the width would be about five feet. Are those measurements workable for the space where you plan to display the portrait?"

I nodded, but uncertainly. "It's been quite a while since I've been in the corporate offices, and I never paid much attention to the lobby, but I'll check it out and let you know. I *think* it has a high ceiling, so the eight-foot canvas should be fine."

Four o'clock was approaching when Dustin finally said, "What a productive afternoon. If there's nothing else, can I drive you home?"

"Let me just grab the cooler—you can *keep* what's left of the gelato."

"It won't last long," he assured me. Then, as I gathered my things, he called up the stairwell, "Nova?"

"Yeah, Dad?"

"I need to run out—taking Meghan home. Back in ten or fifteen."

Driving downtown, having dispensed with our business for the day, Dustin and I gabbed like old friends. I said, "Nova is *such* a sweetheart. Now that you're a single dad again, is the day-to-day parenting a challenge?"

"Nah, not with Nova. She's a great kid. The only 'problems' are occasional scheduling conflicts. Logistical stuff. Fortunately, my parents still live in town, both of them healthy and *fawning* grandparents, so they're always ready to help out."

I mused, "Built-in babysitters ..."

"Cheap, too." He laughed. After a pause, he asked, "I could tell that Nova really *clicked* with you, Meghan."

"I'm flattered. The admiration was mutual."

"Then, what would you think of—maybe—getting together for dinner some night? The three of us."

"Sure," I answered at once. "That would be lovely. Let me check my schedule." After scrolling my phone, I suggested, "Friday night?"

He thought for a moment. "That'll work. *Great.*"

"If you don't mind coming over, there are several good restaurants in the building. I'll figure it out and give you details later."

"Perfect."

Since "the building" was now on the next block, he asked, "Which entrance?"

"Ummm ... just drop me at the *front* entrance, on the boulevard. I'll go up to Auric headquarters and check the ceiling height of the lobby."

"How *very* efficient of you." Pulling up to the curb, he said, "So. Stay in touch."

"Sure thing." Since we were both strapped in with our seat belts, a friendly parting hug was impossible. Shaking hands would be too stuffy. So we both instinctively leaned over the console and kissed cheeks—a bit prim, but it did qualify as an inch forward on the intimacy scale. (Or had my imagination taken over?)

The passenger door opened. "Good afternoon, Mrs. Auric. Welcome back." The doorman took the cooler from me, helped me out of the vehicle, and shut the door behind me. I turned to give Dustin a wave of farewell, but his eyes were on traffic as he pulled away from the curb.

Auric headquarters occupied the entire seventeenth floor. An elevator from the main concourse took me up and opened into a small vestibule, separated by a glass wall and doors that opened into the front lobby and reception area of the offices. Some of the floors of the building had higher ceilings than others, and at a glance, I saw that this was one of them.

When I walked through the doors and into the lobby, two women looked up from their seats at the reception desk. The older one, recognizing me, stood. "Mrs. Auric! What a nice surprise. We haven't seen you in ... *such* a long time. Our heartfelt condolences on the passing of *Mr.* Auric."

"Thank you," I said. I had no idea of her name.

"What can we do for you, please?"

"Could you possibly get me a tape measure?"

"Well ... of *course*." She looked flustered. First, she whispered something to the other woman, who got on the phone. Then she picked up her own phone, punched a button, and had a terse, quiet conversation. Hanging up, she told me, "One tape measure, on the way."

Turning to examine the wall that would display Eugene's portrait, I could tell that it was at least twelve feet high, which would easily accommodate an eight-foot painting. There was currently a modern abstract painting hanging there—purely decorative, of little artistic merit—which appeared to be about eight feet high, and it was square. I noticed that the composition of the square shape against the wall looked good, and I thought I might mention to Dustin the possibility of a square canvas.

"Meghan!"

I turned to see Ronda Trask, my late husband's lawyer and fixer, rushing toward me from the inner offices. The two receptionists exchanged a discreet nod. Ronda seemed furtive and agitated, wearing a fake smile and a black suit that looked even more mannish than usual. She raised one sweaty palm to rake four stubby fingers through her butch-cut hair. With her other sweaty palm, she waved for me to follow her.

I was practically running as she chugged ahead of me, passing the quizzical glances of workers on both sides of the aisle. Arriving outside her office, she barked at her assistant—a fey young man with indigo hair—"*No* interruptions!"

She stepped aside for me to enter her office, then followed me in and banged the door closed.

"*What?*" I said.

"Sit," she said, trying to calm herself, "just sit."

As we settled in across from each other at her desk, I asked, "Can I assume you've heard about what happened in the penthouse yesterday?"

She waggled her hands manically and shook her head, as if my question was off-topic and trivial.

"Listen," she said, leaning forward with her elbows on the desk. "Remember John White?"

I jerked back in my chair as if she'd slapped me.

She asked, "Remember your supposed 'boyfriend'—the one

who screwed you at that dogshit insurance outfit—then disappeared?"

Trembling, I asked, "How could I ever *forget* John White?"

"Well, brace yourself, Meghan. That motherfucker is now known as Julian Wentworth—candidate for the United States Senate."

I nearly choked on the lump that rose in my throat.

PART TWO

Meghan's Dilemma

CHAPTER
SIX

Sitting there in Ronda Trask's office—with its unadorned walls, its sterile fluorescent lighting, its stacks of paper everywhere—I gripped the arms of the chair and closed my eyes, hoping the panic would subside. When my breathing became more normal, I blinked and looked at her, asking, "Are you certain about this? It sounds nuts."

With a steely nod, she assured me, "John White and Julian Wentworth are the same person."

"How long have you known this?"

"News to me—just heard about it today." But something in her tone made me doubt her.

I asked, "Who told you?"

She paused. Her eyes wandered. "Not at liberty to say."

"For Christ's sake, Ronda—don't play coy with *me*." I knew she had a reputation as an insider who also happened to be a bit shady. Technically, though, I was now her employer, so I deserved direct answers to my questions.

"Meghan," she said softly (a tone that struck me as unnatural to her), "I need to ask you to trust me: the fewer details you know, the better."

Frustrated, I asked, "Then why tell me *any* of it? Why drop this bomb on me about John White?"

She looked me straight in the eye. "Because I thought you

deserved to know it. I'm sure this news disturbs you—fuck, it disturbs *me*, too. But I decided to tell you about it because I'm guessing that, deep in your heart, you'd want to know the dirt on this asshole. Or would you rather be kept in the dark?"

"No," I admitted, "it's better to know the facts."

Ronda nodded. "Especially when you're not *supposed* to know those facts—right?"

I nodded.

"So now you know." She grinned. "And knowledge is power."

This knowledge, this secret, should have been apparent to me as soon as Julian Wentworth started making a name for himself— or so I reasoned. After all, I'd been intimate with John White for over a year, so I still had a clear mental image of what he looked like, back then. And now, as a politician aspiring for higher office, he wasn't shy about plastering the media with his mug—so why hadn't I recognized him? Because he had changed. A lot.

When we were a couple, John White was nice-looking enough, but a bit pudgy, which gave him a baby face, a softness. As an insurance agent, a number cruncher, his sense of style was (to put it charitably) pedestrian. In an era when shags were popular and Mohawks were still around, he wore a two-dollar crew cut.

But now, doing a quick search of images on the internet, I saw the complete transformation of the man who had become Julian Wentworth. At fifty-four, he'd aged, of course, and the years had given him an impressive maturity. He'd lost the paunch and was clearly no stranger to the gym. His face looked leaner and strongly defined. His sandy blond hair was handsomely styled, sporting flecks of silver, and the trim sideburns morphed into a fetchingly short, neat beard. The makeover extended to his clothes, mostly business attire in the photos, all of it impeccable, a far cry from the chinos and polos he had once worn. I had to laugh. Had he hooked up with one of Eugene's custom tailors?

If I squinted, I could see a trace of John in Julian, but I would never have spotted it without Ronda's tip-off. On Sunday, at the Hudsons' cookout, Theo had described Julian as "polished" and "slick," while Lila had countered that he was "slimy." Judging from the photos I was finding, they were both right.

Next morning, Tuesday, I was up and about before the workers would arrive to finish installing the new security system, so I could take my time lounging on the upper terrace with coffee and the latest edition of the *Consensus Times*, still folded and rolled in its plastic sleeve, next to the carafe. I let it sit there, untouched, while drinking my first cup of Jamaican Blue Mountain, a special treat. What made this morning different from most was that I'd been told by Chase Unger that his interview of me would run in today's edition.

As promised, he had earlier sent me the quotes that would be used in his piece, giving me an opportunity to tweak or even nix a few, but I found that he had faithfully rendered my words and had even, in a few instances, suggested alternate wording to capture what he perceived as my intended meaning. With a huge sigh of relief, I was able to give my *imprimatur* for everything.

However, I had not yet seen the story itself, its presentation, or photos, so it was with no small measure of trepidation that I now slid the newspaper from its wrapper.

Imagine my surprise when I found myself smiling up at me from page one. And—bless his little heart—Chase had actually snapped a decent photo. More than decent, in fact. It was perhaps the most pleasing picture of myself I'd seen in *years*, and it was fun. He'd posed me kneeling at (practically *in*) my bed of tomatoes with two freshly picked specimens, which I held pridefully with soiled fingers, near the lens. The tomatoes looked *gorgeous*, I looked nearly as good, and everything was backdropped by the distant treetops of Fairview and the wheat fields of Consensus County, basking under the sapphire dome of a huge autumn sky.

The photo stretched the width of the page, with the story's headline appearing in the sky:

Meghan Daley Auric
is not afraid to get her hands dirty

The tone of the story was light and breezy, not at all maudlin—considering that it had been prompted by the recent loss of my husband. Chase skillfully humanized the situation and managed to depict me as someone more nuanced than just a grieving wealthy widow.

This called for another cup of Blue Mountain, which I sipped and enjoyed while reading through the story a second time.

"*Hey* there, Tomato Lady," said Ashley as she arrived for work, popping out from the kitchen. "Something tells me *you'll* be the talk of the town today."

"What nonsense," I said with a laugh—a tad too modestly. "I doubt if anyone will even *notice* it."

But they did. My phone began to *ping* with the arrival of chatty texts, and there were so many calls, I stopped answering them, letting the congratulatory messages pile up in voicemail.

When two techies arrived to complete their work on the alarm system, Ashley brought them out to the terrace, and they, too, offered cheery greetings to the Tomato Lady. I played along—but wondered how soon I would grow weary of this cleverness.

While they worked, Ashley spent an hour or so in the bedroom, packing up a few more cartons of Eugene's clothes. Then, when installation of the security system was complete, she and I both joined the technicians for a demonstration of the system's features and use. I was pleased that the cameras had been concealed so artfully (even out on the terrace, you couldn't spot the tiny lenses peeping from the overhangs until they were pointed out), but I was horrified when one of the installers deliberately tripped the alarm to show us how it worked.

The screech was so deafeningly *LOUD* that it triggered the onset of a panic attack, and I was certain that I would be dealing with more false alarms than actual intrusions. They turned it off. With hands on hips, I told them, "*That* is totally unacceptable."

They looked at each other. Shrugged. One of them assured me, "It's the best in the business."

I replied, "The whole point of this is to provide peace of mind, but every time I activate the system, I'll be a nervous wreck. I can't live that way."

The other guy told me, "No reason you can't leave the alarm feature off. Just use it as a 'passive' system, like you already have for the paintings."

"Perfect. Could you kindly disable that hideous ... *klaxon*?"

"You got it, Mrs. Auric." And it took him less than a minute to reprogram the system's defaults. "There," he said, "done."

My weekly appointment with Dr. Faye Rubin was scheduled for that afternoon at one o'clock. Although the day of our weekly meetings was flexible, they were always at one. Because she worked in the building and was never booked during the noon hour, that gave us the option to meet in the penthouse, rather than in her office. We could begin a bit early, perhaps over lunch, and still finish a fifty-minute session in time for her to go downstairs for her two-o'clock.

That Tuesday, Ashley had planned to work only in the morning (she had arranged to record a vlog episode with the city's top hairdresser that afternoon), so I phoned downstairs and let them know that Dr. Rubin was welcome to come up to the penthouse at twelve thirty.

I prepared a light "lady lunch" consisting of bruschetta, iced mango tea, and of course gelato, made with the last of that season's fresh strawberries.

At twelve thirty, as Faye stepped out of the elevator in my entry hall, I raised a palm in a gesture of warning: "If you call me the Tomato Lady, we're through."

She gave me a bewildered look. "I guess you *do* need help."

With a laugh, I told her about the story in the paper.

"Didn't see it."

"Well, I happen to have a copy."

So she read it on the terrace while we picked at lunch. "I think you handled that very well," she told me. "Great picture, too."

"Thank you."

"Don't mention it, Tomato Lady."

When we finished the gelato, Faye helped me take everything inside to the sink, then we both settled again on the terrace, sitting under the awning where Chase Unger had interviewed me on Saturday. I put on my sunglasses. Faye opened the folder she'd brought, organized her notes, and clicked a ballpoint pen.

"Now, then," she said. "We last met on Thursday, after Eugene died. In the five days since then, how have things been going for you?"

"Mixed reviews. Some good, some bad."

She nodded. "I'm in the same boat. We all are. Life is always a mixed bag. Start with the good part—tell me what happened."

"I left the building. *Twice.* Earlier, the hospital visits, those don't count—that was just fulfilling a duty. But I had an outing on Sunday, then another on Monday, and I *chose* to make both of those excursions."

Faye arched her brows. "That *is* good. Any regrets?"

"Surprisingly, none. I've told you about the Hudsons before—Theo and Lila."

Faye's pen was active, scribbling notes. "College friends. Berkeley. Black."

"Yes. They invited me to a Sunday-afternoon cookout at their place. Their adult son was there, a lawyer—he's called me Aunt Meg since he was old enough to talk. When I'm with them, it always feels so 'right,' as if I'm with family. So comfortable. No stress. I fell asleep in a chair near their picnic table."

"All those years with Eugene," said Faye. "Did those times feel comfortable and 'right'?"

I took a few moments to ponder, to recall. "Rarely," I said. Pondering further, I revised my answer: "No, never. I never felt 'at home' with Eugene, not the way I do with the Hudsons."

"Then ... you must have had a wonderful afternoon."

I nodded, smiled. "Celia Gamarra was there, too—you know, the Senate candidate. Theo is heavily involved in her campaign, and he's drawn *me* into it, as well. Hope she wins. *Boy*, do I hope she wins."

"I understand," said Faye—though of course she didn't *completely* understand my position, not yet.

I asked, "Curious about my *other* escape from the building?"

She flipped a page. "Fire away."

"One of Eugene's last requests was to have a portrait of himself painted, to be hung in the lobby of corporate headquarters. He wanted it life-size, standing."

Faye couldn't suppress a soft laugh. "I don't suppose *he* ever underwent psychoanalysis."

"Are you kidding? *He'd* just end up lecturing the shrink."

"So ... how did this get you out of the building?"

"I approached a talented young painter, Dustin St. James, who's best known for his portraits."

"Oh, *sure*," said Faye. "I'm familiar with his work. Also his background—he relocated from the East Coast and has his studio here."

"Correct. He's *from* Fairview, originally, and his parents are still here. So I met with him at the penthouse on Saturday, and we both had a good vibe about the project—so *much* so, he convinced me to visit his studio. I was there yesterday afternoon, and he's agreed to the commission." I paused before adding, "I really like him."

Faye looked up from her notes. "Expound on that."

"He's a top-notch portraitist, incredibly talented. He values my input on the project and respects me not only as a paying patron, but as someone firmly grounded in the arts. And on top of all that ... he's hotter than hell."

"Ahaaa ..."

"Yes, ahaaa. In parting yesterday, we kissed cheeks in the car, which doesn't mean a thing, or does it? And he's fifteen years younger. And he happens to be gay, and had a husband, who died too young. And before that, he was married to a woman, who died too young. And with the woman, he had a daughter, who's about ten and lives with him, and she's precocious and delightful—*all* of which doesn't mean a thing, or does it?"

Faye set down her pen. "This may sound like an understatement, Meghan—but there's a *lot* to unpack there." Her lips sputtered.

I joined her in laughter.

A small plane had appeared earlier as a mere speck in the sky, coming from the west, possibly from Consensus. It drew closer now, looking larger and better defined, painted school-bus yellow. I could barely hear the engines as it passed over the building, heading east.

As our laughter waned and the plane vanished, I said to Faye, "Dustin's daughter. Her name is Nova, and she had a similar effect on me as the Hudsons' son, named Adam, who's twenty-eight and gay."

Faye's brow pinched. "It sounds as if Nova and Adam are nothing alike. But they had a similar effect on you?"

"They did. I thoroughly enjoyed being with each of them—which served as a bittersweet reminder that I never had kids of my own."

"Do you regret that?"

"Mildly, yes. Early on, Eugene and I *tried*—but not with much persistence. He was past sixty and already had an adult son, so he was indifferent to starting over. He gave it a shot or two for *my* sake, figuring I had the motherhood instinct, and I guess I did. But regardless of the dynamics of who-wanted-what, I never conceived. We didn't explore the possible medical reasons—which would have ended up 'blaming' one of us for the failure."

"So," said Faye, "the intimacy tapered off early in the marriage."

I nodded. "It was gradual, but we knew where things were headed. From the start, I hadn't found him physically attractive."

"But he obviously found *you* highly attractive."

"I guess so—he pressured me to marry him. But he was getting older and developing some health issues, so let's just say that the sex drive, for both of us, 'petered out.' Honestly, it didn't seem to bother him. He still had his trophy wife, which is all he wanted in the first place."

Faye reminded me, "But after a few years, your agoraphobia set in and took hold. Didn't that limit his opportunities to use you as an armpiece and show you off?"

"If it did, he never groused about it. I think he liked the idea that I was tucked safely away in the tower for his private appreciation—as if I were the crown jewel in a collection of pilfered art. And keep in mind, Faye: I was, and still am, just fine with socializing *inside* the building. His office was here, as were many corporate events. The club and other restaurants allowed us to entertain here frequently. When he *really* wanted to make an impression, we had parties in the penthouse—and I was always there for him, a wife and hostess who did him proud."

Faye was making careful notes of all this. While she focused on her writing, I grew silent—and thoughtful. When she set aside her pen, I said to her, "I've been curious about something."

"And what might that be?"

"I recently turned fifty. Is motherhood still possible—or even advisable?"

She took off her glasses, sat back, and studied me for a moment. "You've never mentioned if you've reached menopause."

"Still having periods. No hot flashes."

"Then you're probably not there yet, but the average age for menopause to begin is fifty-one, so you're getting close. At the onset, natural pregnancy is sometimes still possible. Sometimes, even after menopause, IVF can be successful, but miscarriages and other complications are common. There's a lot that can go wrong, and personally, I wouldn't recommend it. But I can refer you to an obstetrician if you're really *serious* about this—"

"No," I interrupted, "I am *not* serious about it. Just curious about options."

"Alternately," she said, "there's always adoption or fostering." As an afterthought, she added with a grin, "Or stepchildren—if you connect with a guy with kids of his own."

I returned the grin and tapped the brakes: "Not so fast, Faye."

She flipped to another page of her notes. "Okay," she said. "You told me earlier that, since our last meeting, you've had some good developments and some bad developments. Your two excursions from the building were good, and your portrait project with the artist seems promising. Changing gears now, what went wrong?"

With a snort, I repeated, "What went wrong? For starters, how about a home invasion?"

She stiffened. "You *must* be joking."

"I am not." I then recounted to her what I'd found after returning home from the Hudsons' cookout on Sunday evening—Eugene's ransacked den and the bizarre, messy remnants of a gelato snack in the kitchen. I also explained, "That very afternoon at the cookout, I met Celia Gamarra's husband, Nick, who's a detective with the sheriff's department. So I called him that night, and he came over to investigate. He later confided to me—rather *ominously*, I thought—that he intends to slow-walk his report."

"*Why?*"

"Because some of the deputies in his department work as off-duty security guards—nights and weekends—downstairs in Auric headquarters."

"So what?"

"I'm not sure. But Nick seems to think they could have some connection to what happened up here in Eugene's den."

"Oy."

I continued, "And that's merely 'bad incident' number one. Ready for number two?"

"I dunno ...," she said warily.

"You're already aware of my long-ago, devastating experience with John White at United Insurance. And I've told you about spending Sunday afternoon with Celia Gamarra, the candidate, at the Hudsons' home. As you've probably heard, her opponent in the election is Julian Wentworth. Know anything about him?"

Faye shrugged. "He's a fascist—scary as hell, but not uncommon these days."

"Mm-hmm. Well, get *this*, Faye: late yesterday, I learned from Eugene's attorney that John White, who supposedly 'vanished' many years ago, is now none other than Julian Wentworth."

Faye looked stunned, confused, and skeptical. But then she brightened, telling me, "If this is true—if Wentworth was involved in an illegal scheme that *killed* people—what a scandal! That filthy *paskudnik* wouldn't stand a chance of being elected."

"But," I said, "that scheme involved *me*, too, so I can't even consider bringing it to light."

Faye nodded gravely. "I understand: The shame. The legal jeopardy."

"Not only *that*, but the same lawyer also informed me of a recent codicil that Eugene added to his estate plan: if I reveal *any* of what happened at United, I could lose ... everything."

Through a squint, Faye asked, "By 'everything,' do you mean the penthouse, the building, the company, its holdings, its assets ...?"

I confirmed, "The works. So here's the pisser: Wentworth deserves no role whatever in government, and at a purely personal level, I would love to blow the whistle as revenge for his betrayal. But if his wrongdoings are revealed—by me or by *anyone*—I will be royally screwed."

After thinking this over, Faye agreed, "Yep, that's a pisser."

I noticed that she had taken no notes while I shared this new background, but I felt the need to emphasize: "Please understand that I'm confiding all of this to you under strictest doctor-patient privilege ... or whatever."

She mimed zipping her lips, a playful gesture that was surely intended to put my mind at ease. Still, I fretted. I wanted to trust her. I *had* to trust her—because my words had put my fate in her hands.

That night, before retiring, I went to the new control panel in the bedroom and activated the security system. It beeped to the pulsing of a tiny yellow light while the readout counted down from ten. It then went silent as the yellow light turned red. The readout informed me: SYSTEM ARMED.

I puttered about needlessly for a few minutes, hoping to reassure myself that the audible alarm had in fact been disabled.

Then I finally went to bed ... turned out the last of the lights ... shut my eyes. But they wouldn't stay closed as I stared at the ceiling through the darkness, terrified that if I did fall asleep, I'd be haunted by nightmares of that ghastly shrieking siren.

My night, though initially restless, was undisturbed—no intruders, no false alarms, no ugly dreams. When at last I drifted off, I slept soundly. In fact, I did not wake up until much later than usual, when Ashley arrived at eight thirty on Wednesday morning. She bounded into my bedroom, intent on resuming the task of sorting and packing Eugene's clothes, only to discover the twisted lump of my body under the sheets, squirming.

"Yikes!" she squealed as I freed myself from the bedding, blinking at the daylight. She said, "I'm so *sorry*, Meghan. I assumed you were out on the terrace having coffee."

Lifting a palm to my forehead, I croaked, "You were wrong about that. But it's not a bad idea." After clearing my throat, I asked, "Could you be a lamb and get the coffee going? It's all set up—just push the button."

Wrapped in a robe and settled on the terrace with my first cup of coffee, I had no expectation of finding a photo of myself on the front page of the *Consensus Times*, as had happened the day before. But when I pulled the newspaper from its sleeve and let it unfurl in my lap, I found, instead, a large page-one photo of Julian Wentworth staring up at me.

So much for easing into my day. I was suddenly on high alert, heart racing, as I skimmed the article, which concerned the candidate's planned luncheon appearance that day at the Fairview Towne Club. Just the thought that he and I would be in the same high-rise building was enough to gag me—all the worse, we would be in the same *room* together.

I didn't notice the byline until I had finished reading the story and set down the paper. Since Chase Unger had been assigned to cover the Fairview beat, he had now made it to the front page two days running. The story seemed to be a basic rehash of a campaign press release regarding the event, accompanied by a file photo of the candidate. Since Chase's story contained no direct quotes from Wentworth, I assumed the cub reporter had not been granted access to him.

Picking up my phone, I found Chase's number and sent him a text: WILL YOU BE AT TODAY'S LUNCHEON?

A moment later, his reply: AFRAID NOT. PRIVATE EVENT. NO PRESS.

Drumming my fingers, I grinned. Then I typed: I HAVE AN EXTRA SEAT AT MY TABLE. WANT IT?

He sent back a yellow-faced emoji depicting googly-eyed astonishment. Chase wrote: YOU BET! THANK YOU, MEGHAN!

I sent him a thumbs-up, then wrote that he should wear a coat and tie, meeting me in the club lobby at eleven thirty.

Setting aside my phone, I lifted the newspaper again, gingerly, taking care not to even *touch* Wentworth's photo—but I studied it. The caption identified him as speaking to supporters at one of his rural campaign offices yesterday, so this was the most recent picture I had seen of him. He was standing in the midst of a small crowd, with his face no bigger than a thumbprint, but I could discern with my own eyes that, yes, he was indeed the man who had betrayed me long ago. He now looked so confident, so brazen, so pleased with himself. While I hated to admit it, the years had been *very* good to him; he looked youthful and toned. Although he was dressed in a business suit, it was tan and smartly tailored—nothing stuffy about it—and I could not blink away the image of an athlete preparing for the race of his life.

Behind him, partially obscured by his square-shouldered manliness, stood a woman, pretty enough in a cheesy sort of way, with straight blond hair down to her ass. Was she old enough to drink? The caption described her as Wentworth's "recent companion," Ivy Quick.

Although I was dreading the thought of sharing the same space with Wentworth—and breathing the same air—I was also, suddenly, feeling rather smug. He could *not* afford to have me recognize him (although, of course, I was already on to him). What's more, I was secreting a reporter into an event where Wentworth believed he could speak candidly to a well-heeled crowd that he surely considered "his base." There were needles to be threaded here. The game was on.

At eleven thirty, from the building's ground-level main concourse, I ascended the grand staircase to the Towne Club's second-floor entrance, scanning the crowd for Chase Unger. The atrium rang with the excited chatter of those arriving for the event. The attendees were mostly club members—older women, some with male guests—and judging by the piercing, nervous laughter that echoed in the cavernous space, many of the gals were just a little too eager to meet the hunky middle-aged guest speaker in the flesh.

When I got to the top of the stairs, there was a backup at

the door to the club lobby, where the staff was checking names against a guest list. I saw Chase standing off to the side, looking fidgety, checking his watch, having apparently been denied entry at the door. I hailed him with a yoo-hoo and a wave of my hand. He instantly brightened and slinked through the crowd to my side.

"You're looking *nice*," I told him, linking arms with him as we made our way forward. He wore a navy blazer, white shirt, and striped silk tie with the same corduroys that he'd had on when we last met. Paired with his boyish stature and looks, the outfit might have been mistaken for a school uniform.

"I have *one* necktie," he told me. "Glad you like it."

I laughed. "Eugene had, literally, hundreds and hundreds—and he never looked better than you do."

Chase shot me a grin. "I think you're exaggerating. But thank you."

I really *liked* this kid. The day before, during my therapy session with Faye Rubin, I'd told her how my mothering instincts had been piqued by two young people—Adam Hudson and Nova Tanaka St. John—both of whom I'd interacted with in the context of their parents. It now occurred to me that I knew nothing of Chase Unger's background, except that his gig at the *Times* was his first job out of college. I said, "May I ask your age, Chase? I'm guessing … twenty-three?"

"You're *good*."

"And your mother …?" (I guessed she was about my age.)

"She's in Iowa, with Dad, where I grew up." Chase added, "She just turned fifty."

On a roll, I asked, "And what does she do—besides bragging about *you*?"

"She's a librarian."

How sweet, I thought.

Stepping up to the door, I told the man with the list, "Mr. Unger is my guest."

"Of course, Mrs. Auric." He swung the door wide for us.

A few steps into the lobby, I leaned to tell Chase, "Well, you're in, kid. Got your camera? Recorder? Notes?"

He discreetly patted his pockets, nodding. As he had not brought his satchel that day, the oversize pockets of his baggy corduroys came in handy.

A waiter stepped over to us with a tray. "Champagne? Mimosa? Iced tea?"

I took a mimosa; Chase asked for iced tea. I told him, "Have a *drink*—I don't mind."

Under his breath, he reminded me, "I'm *working*."

As the doors to the ballroom had not yet been opened, the lobby was getting crowded and loud, with people trying to mingle and socialize before being seated.

Eugene's first wife, Bibiana, spotted me. Waving, she beelined toward me with Eugene Junior in tow. She couldn't *wait* to tell me, "Lovely article, *Tomato Lady*."

Laughing it off, I said, "Thank you, Bebe. Please meet my young friend, Chase Unger." I did not mention that he was the reporter who'd written the article, nor did he mention it while exchanging pleasantries with Bebe or Gene, who introduced himself.

"My *dear*," Bebe said breathlessly, leaning close to me, "did you *see* the piece in this morning's paper about Mr. Wentworth? He seems to be *just* what this state needs in Washington. He's one of our crowd."

Parroting Bebe's tone, I leaned near, speaking from the side of my mouth: "*Not* our crowd, darling—he's a fascist."

Bebe looked stricken. Chase struggled not to laugh. But Gene laughed heartily, saying, "You *tell* her, Meg: Wentworth is no better than Vaughn was. Even *worse*, if you ask me."

Chase, being new to the area, asked Gene, "By 'Vaughn,' you're referring to the senator who died, correct?"

Gene nodded. "Right. The *revered* old Grady Vaughn was in the pocket of every PAC and special-interest group that came calling. And they *all* came calling because *this* state, with such a sparse population, makes it real cheap to buy a senator. Grady Vaughn happily sold his office to anyone with a cause—*if* they had the bankroll to back it up."

Bebe said, "Now, Junior, don't be such a cynic."

"I'm not a cynic, Mom—just a realist. Vaughn absolutely *wallowed* in graft, and I'm damn glad he's gone."

Bebe heaved a disgruntled sigh. "That's enough. I need a drink—a *real* drink, if you don't mind. Junior, please see me to the bar."

"Of course, mummy dearest." Gene gave us an imaginary tip of the hat, took his leave, and walked Bibiana out of the lobby.

Someone tapped my shoulder.

When I turned, Everett, the club manager, was standing behind me, grinning. "Mrs. Auric," he said, "such a pleasure to see you again today—or would you prefer to be called the Tomato Lady?"

"I would *not*, thank you."

"Sorry." He laughed. Then he turned to Chase, extending his hand. "Welcome to the Towne Club, sir. Any friend of Mrs. Auric is an honored guest here."

NOT OUR CROWD, DARLING

They shook hands and introduced themselves, but Chase did not mention that he was a reporter.

Returning his attention to me, Everett said, "Before we start seating people for lunch, I thought you might like to meet our guest speaker."

Gulp. (Hadn't planned on that.) "But," I said, "he must be so ... *busy* ... preparing his speech or whatever."

"Not at *all*," said Everett. He's gabbing with a few top donors in the library, and when I mentioned you were here, he asked if he might offer condolences on the loss of your husband."

Chase's reporter's instincts had clearly been roused—the look in his eye urged me to go for it.

"Well then," I said, resigned to something unsavory, "I suppose I should see him."

"Excellent." With a deferential bob of his head, Everett led us out of the lobby, down a hallway, and then stopped at the library door, which was closed.

He gave it a brisk double-rap, then turned the knob and opened the door, leading us in.

Perhaps a dozen people were standing about, talking pleasantly. Although we were in a women's club, everyone in the room was a man except for me and a younger woman, whom I recognized as Ivy Quick. When I'd seen her photo in that morning's paper, I'd judged her with a degree of snark, thinking she was merely "cheesy" and too young. But now, seeing and hearing her in person, I realized that my restrained reaction to her had been too charitable.

How shall I put this? It should truly offend my feminist sensibilities to describe Ivy as a bimbo—but God almighty, that's what she was.

She really wasn't worth the focus I was squandering on her, but that, of course, was simply a delay tactic—because standing only six feet away from her was the candidate himself, Julian Wentworth.

He was talking with a fat man who had the bearing of a Monopoly banker, but Wentworth's glance kept drifting in my direction. Old moneybags then pumped the candidate's hand and ambled over to Ivy with a hungry, calculating look. She pulled out her phone to take a selfie with him.

As if on cue, Everett stepped me forward to Wentworth, who, smiling, closed the distance between us. Everett recited our names to each other, then bowed out. Chase Unger moved closer, slightly behind me, but I offered no introductions, as I thought Wentworth might recognize Chase's name from the *Times* byline.

Mouthing sympathies for the loss of my husband, Wentworth extended his hand. There was no graceful way to avoid shaking it, so I did—but I really hated touching him, as if handling a reptile, a snake.

"On a happier note," he said, "it was such a pleasure to read the story about your gardening." With a quiet laugh, he added, "But I won't stoop to calling you the Tomato Lady—which seems entirely too condescending for a woman of your obvious intelligence and charm, *Mrs. Auric.*"

His emphasis of my married name sounded oddly deliberate, as if telling me with a wink: *I know who you are.*

I parried: "You're laying it on a bit thick, *Supervisor Wentworth.*"

He chortled. "Yes, perhaps I was. This formality is unnecessary, don't you think? Just call me Julian."

I didn't bite. "Just call me Mrs. Auric."

He grinned. "*Touché*, Mrs. Auric. It's a name to be proud of."

Even if he had *not* known me—and betrayed me—twenty-odd years earlier, he would still be aware that I was Eugene Auric's widow. He'd already said that he'd seen the prior day's newspaper story. What's more, as a county supervisor, he was broadly involved in local government, and my husband was the county's leading businessman. Surely, their paths had crossed often, and anyone who knew Eugene also knew that I was his wife.

So I didn't know quite what to make of this interplay regarding my last name. I didn't think he was dumb enough to expect me to say, *You might remember me better as Meghan Daley*. Instead, I simply asked, "Did you know my husband?"

"Of course. We had dealings from time to time. I came to think of him—quite humbly—as a friend. In fact, just a week before he was hospitalized for the last time, he made a major donation to my campaign committee. I hope, Mrs. Auric, that today's luncheon remarks might convince you that I'm also worthy of *your* support to represent you in the United States Senate." He smiled benignly.

I said, "I know nothing about your stand on the issues. Do you have a published platform?"

"Not ... *exactly*. I much prefer the direct approach of communicating with voters personally."

"*All* of them? That's quite a trick, isn't it?"

"Tiring, I admit—but that's why I'm here today."

Chase Unger stepped up from behind me. Standing at my side, he said, "Mr. Wentworth, I'm new to the area and still getting up to speed on this election. I understand you're a current member of Consensus County's board of supervisors. But going back, how did you get your start in local government?"

Wentworth gave Chase a haughty look, telling him, "That background is *very* extensive—too deep to get into right now. You'll find a detailed CV on my website, wentworthforsenate.com."

"Thank you," said Chase. "I'll take a look at that."

"So will I," I said through a bland smile.

"Wonderful," said Wentworth. "And at the top of the homepage, you can't miss the CONTRIBUTE button."

Gag me.

Chimes sounded throughout the club, indicating that the ballroom was now open for seating.

While Chase and I were returning from the library to the lobby, I said to him quietly, "A word of advice: Tread carefully when questioning Wentworth about the past. You might get more out of him if you don't put him on the defensive."

"I noticed that. But why would he get defensive about his past?" With a laugh, Chase added, "Is he *hiding* something?"

My turn to laugh. "We *all* have secrets. Don't we?"

Looking a bit crestfallen, Chase told me, "I dunno—I don't *think* I have any secrets."

"Stick with me, kiddo. You'll learn a few."

If he was put off by that, he didn't let on. In fact, he seemed to brighten at the prospect of lessons at the knee of the master.

In the ballroom, round tables were set for nearly two hundred people, with eight or ten seated at each. The club was long aware, however, that I was uncomfortable being forced to socialize at large tables, so at events such as these, I was always provided with one of the two smaller tables that had been set for four, placed symmetrically near the front, where they did not appear to be anything special—merely filling out space to complete the layout of the room. (Membership, as they say, has privileges.) All tables were set with white linen, Limoges china, and fresh flowers.

There was an oblong head table, with the speaker and other dignitaries seated facing the crowd, and behind them was a small elevated stage with a podium flanked by video screens.

I led Chase to "my" table, front and left, where the other two seats were always reserved for the other Mrs. Auric, Bibiana, who was apparently still in the bar with Junior. I chose my chair, and after Chase had seated me, I asked him to sit at my left. (Bebe, if she was still coherent and vertical, would sit, as usual, at my right.)

The crowd was filling in fast as the service staff, all in Armani, poured water and iced tea, then delivered salads and baskets of bread—the luncheon would need to move along briskly to accommodate the program, which would begin as soon as dessert and coffee were on the tables.

Eugene Junior propped up Bebe as he lurched with her through the crowd and delivered her to our table. When he got her seated and placed a fresh martini in front of her, he told me, "That oughta keep her quiet."

"Don't count on it," she croaked.

While Bebe and I fell into conversation, Eugene Junior and Chase Unger got better acquainted on their side of the table, sharing a laugh or two while forking their salads.

The party at the head table seemed to just pick at their lunch, finding it unseemly to be on display while chowing down. A few of them left the table to make their rounds with the guests, oiling and schmoozing their way through the room. One of the dignitaries—and I use the term loosely—was Sheriff Stanley Hewitt, who now sauntered toward our table, as it was the nearest to where he'd been sitting.

"Oh, Christ," I told Bebe, "here comes that nitwit sheriff."

She countered, "I think he's rather *nice*, in a butch sort of way."

Hewitt approached me first, offering condolences, for which I thanked him. Then I introduced him to Chase, with whom he shook hands too heartily, before moving around to Junior and Bebe, who knew him well.

Prior sheriffs had always worn business attire, a professional look that befitted the administrator of a sizable public department. Hewitt, however, was a different breed. Even at dressy occasions, he chose to be "the man in uniform," wearing khaki head to toe with heavy black leather boots, which matched his wide leather belt and his always conspicuous holster, cradling a huge, ugly six-shooter. All that leather actually creaked as he made his way around the table. I was surprised he hadn't added a bullet-studded bandolier to cover his indecorous potbelly. He projected the image of one bad hombre—truly a piece of work—looking inanely aggressive in such refined surroundings.

Next to approach our table was a man I didn't recognize. Nor did he know us. Stepping between Bebe and me, he asked, "Mrs. Auric?"

When we both answered—"Yes?"—he was confused but not the least bit shaken. In fact, his manner was smooth and personable as we explained our connection.

With that bit of awkwardness dispatched, he said, "Then allow me to extend sympathies to *both* of you on your recent loss of Eugene. My name is Kyle Pollard, Julian Wentworth's campaign manager. He asked me to pop over and introduce myself."

Both Bebe and I shook hands with him. While he and Bebe

chatted, I couldn't help but compare Kyle to Xolani Vahdat, campaign manager for Wentworth's opponent, Celia Gamarra. Kyle and Xolani struck me as about the same age, maybe thirty— young, polished, presumably intelligent, definitely climbing. But the cultural contrast could not have been more stark. Kyle would make a perfect poster boy for a button-down Ivy League MBA program; Xolani was a definitive woman of the world.

Kyle was now crouching by the table, at eye level with Bebe, telling her, "Then you *know* what's at stake, Mrs. Auric. It'll take a man like Julian Wentworth in Washington to help put things back together—the way they *should* have been all along, in-formed by traditional *values*." He grinned.

Bebe burbled, infatuated by him.

But he scared the shit out of me.

When at last the cedar-planked salmon had been cleared, a cakey charlotte of mixed berries was served as dessert. Coffee was poured.

Everett Burke had appeared at the podium and now clinked a glass, drawing everyone's attention. For the benefit of outside guests, he introduced himself as the club manager, then intro-duced everyone sitting at the head table. Finally, he told us, "Please extend a warm welcome to Kyle Pollard, who serves as the campaign manager for today's guest speaker. Kyle?"

As Everett bowed out, he pulled his phone from a pocket and snapped a few pictures, signaling that it was permissible to do so at this event, despite the usual club rules.

Pollard stepped up to the podium, greeted by a typically sub-dued Towne Club round of applause.

"Thank you, everyone," he said, surveying the room. "I think most of you already know Julian Wentworth, but it's my duty and pleasure today to share a few details of his upbringing—details that he himself is far too modest to mention."

Oh, brother. I rolled my eyes.

"I'll bet you didn't know," Pollard continued, "that Julian grew up in a military household, moving with his parents from base to base during his formative years. I'll bet you didn't know that his father was on a tour of duty in Vietnam and died there during the chaos of the fall of Saigon, when Julian had barely entered grade school. I'll bet you didn't know that before Julian entered high school, his sainted mother died in an aviation training exercise, leaving this proud son of patriots to fend for himself in the world—and fend he did—eventually earning a full scholarship to study political philosophy at Oxford." With a chuckle, Pollard added, "That's Oxford, *England.*"

The room responded with smattered applause.

Pollard rambled on: "I'll bet you didn't know..."

No, I *didn't* know any of this. In fact, I knew that the man now posing as Julian Wentworth had no such background. I leaned over to Chase Unger and whispered into his ear, "Are you recording this?"

He nodded, tapping his phone on the table.

"Try to verify some of it—because it *all* sounds phony to me."

Chase removed a small notebook from his pocket and jotted something to himself.

Pollard told a few more iffy tales about Wentworth's accomplishments. And then: "Without further ado, ladies and gentlemen, please welcome—your friend and mine—our next United States Senator, *Julian Wentworth.*"

The crowd gave the candidate a slightly more enthusiastic

round of applause than they had bestowed on his flack, but it was clear that this esteemed assemblage wasn't yet sold on him—they wanted to hear what he had to say first.

"Thank you. Thank you." He raised his arms and patted his hands downward, as if asking his audience to be seated—but there had been no standing ovation. A few of the guests snapped pictures of the moment from their tables. From the corner of my eye, I saw Chase retrieve his camera from the pocket of his corduroys and place it near his notes on the table.

When silence reigned, and it was cringeworthy, Wentworth began, speaking softly, "My friends, we're a nation in deep trouble, divided and angry, in urgent need of the soothing balm of unity. Impossible, you may think. But the answer—the solution we *need*—is right there, right in front of us, exactly where it's always been. The founding, *traditional* principles of this great American experiment—one nation, under God, the Christian God—"

Oops. I wasn't the only one to wince.

But he kept at it, and when he *finally* finished—whipping himself into a frenzied appeal for votes and money and "faith in our sacred mission"—a few people clapped, but it wasn't sufficient to mask the clearing of throats and the creaking of chairs.

He stood there, smiling benignly, although he'd surely expected more enthusiasm. "Well, then," he said, clearing *his* throat, "I'd be happy to take a few questions."

Hands shot up.

"Yes, ma'am?" he said, pointing to someone in the middle of the room.

She asked about abortion, contraception, and a woman's right to make decisions about her own body.

He said he supported equal rights for everyone, but would ultimately leave all such matters for the states to decide, in keeping with the intentions of the Founding Fathers. Then he quickly moved to another question, acknowledging "the gentleman in back."

An old guy, a member's husband pushing ninety, asked, "Why don't you tell us something about your 'recent companion'—I think that's what the paper called her. She's quite the looker."

Awkward though the question was, Wentworth seemed relieved to escape a thicket of more pressing issues. "Ivy?" he said. "Care to join me up here?"

In a flash, she was up from the table and posing next to him onstage—all smiles and knees and teeth and hair—prompting quite a few photos from the crowd. Referring to Wentworth as her "main squeeze," she joined him in the expected song and dance: how they met, what their favorite pig-out foods were, what they were reading for pleasure, what hobbies they dabbled in, and on and on.

When Ivy sat down (eliciting applause far more enthusiastic than Wentworth had received, at least from the men), the Q&A continued, with an even mix of trivial and serious queries. But after ten or fifteen minutes, the room's energy was spent.

"Anything else?" asked Wentworth. It was evident from his tone that he hoped to wrap it up. "Last call," he said playfully, eagerly.

And that would have been the end of it. Except, that was the moment when Eugene Junior, sitting across from me at our table, raised his hand.

"Ah!" said Wentworth. "Down in front: Yes, sir?"

I hadn't been paying much attention to Junior, but it was now apparent that when he'd accompanied Bebe to the bar, he'd joined her in a martini—or two. Unlike the other guests who'd asked questions, he chose to stand, and he had a bit of difficulty doing so, needing to steady himself with a hand on the edge of the table. What's more, the prior questioners had not identified themselves to Wentworth.

"My name is Eugene Auric, Junior," he said through a slight but discernible slur. "But you, Mr. County Supervisor, *you* are most welcome to address me as Gene. Or just Junior."

A wave of snickering passed through the room as Wentworth, clearly amused, said, "Thank you, Gene. And please, call me Julian."

"Okay, Julian, so here's the deal. You and I have never met, but I'm pretty sure you knew my father."

"He was an amazing man," said Wentworth, "and my condolences on your recent loss."

"Right. Sure. Thank you. So…when my parents divorced a *long* time ago, both my mother and I were set up very nicely—set up for *life*—so you might say that things have been pretty easy for us."

Sitting next to me, Bebe had grown tense, shuddering with humiliation. Gripping the table, she leaned in her son's direction and whispered (loudly enough for much of the room to hear it), "Do sit down, Junior, and *shut up*."

He dismissed her comment with a flick of one hand, telling Wentworth, "My own *mother* likes to gripe that I'm just a 'playboy'—her word. And God's truth, maybe I am. But you know what, Mr. Supervisor? Being 'just' a privileged gadabout happens to have a few advantages—beyond martinis before lunch. You see, it also gives me the freedom to focus, to really *focus*, on a few serious, vital interests. And in recent years, I've come to realize that no issue is more pressing than climate change and its effect on the environment. I mean, we're facing total *disaster*, right?"

"Well"—Wentworth hemmed—"there are studies supporting both sides of that argument."

"Bullshit. We're in a mess of our own making, with only one possible way out. And that's why I have this *passion*: mandating the development and implementation of all forms of clean, renewable energy."

A few scattered guests clapped with enthusiasm, but most sat stiff and silent. Wentworth tried to lighten the moment, joshing, "Sounds like *you're* running for something, Gene."

Gene replied calmly, "No, I'm not. But you *are*. And if you're elected, you'll have a big say in how we move forward with this crisis. Will you help? Or will you sell your vote to the bad guys?"

Gently, seriously, as if instructing a child, Wentworth said, "Now, Gene: I share your concern for these issues. Sure, there may be differing opinions. But *seriously*? There are no 'bad guys'— not when it comes to something this important."

"*Hah!*" Gene took a step forward from the table, laughing with incredulity. "No bad guys? What about the guy they just buried, the guy you wanna replace? When I voiced these concerns, *frequently*, to Grady Vaughn, his reply was always the same: 'We're looking at it. We're studying it. Blah, blah, blah.' But what did he actually *do* about it? He was pushing for legislation that would allow the strip mining of noxious compounds right here in our home state—bad enough, right? But he *also* supported new attempts to route a crude-oil pipeline from Canada directly through our wheat fields. This was *nuts*. This was *evil*. And frankly—"

I closed my eyes, hoping Gene wasn't going to repeat what he'd said earlier in the lobby. But he did:

"—and frankly, I'm damn glad he's gone."

The gasp was universal. But it was short and quick. Then silence—till someone belched (the planked salmon had been a tad spicy), providing a bit of comic relief.

"Well now," Wentworth said blithely, "I seem to have lost track of the question."

Timid laughter drifted through the room as Junior staggered back to his seat, flumped into it, and crossed his arms. His chin dropped to his chest.

Wentworth said, "One more question?" With a wink, he added, "Let's make it a really *tough* one this time."

Again the timid laughter, but there were no raised hands.

And then, next to me, Chase Unger's hand shot up.

Wentworth glanced in our direction but pretended he didn't see Chase's hand. "Anyone?" he asked, peering toward the back of the room.

Chase then waved and waggled his hand but wasn't acknowledged. Earlier, in the library, Wentworth had turned defensive when Chase asked him something about his past, and it seemed he was still wary.

So I raised *my* hand. Would Wentworth dare to ignore me?

Seeing me, he was suddenly flustered—pinched brow, squint of the eyes—but he recovered in a flash. "Ah, Mrs. Auric," he said. "What can I do for you?"

I graciously suggested, "You could let me cede my time to my young friend, Chase Unger."

"Of course," he replied with a thin, tight smile. "What's your question, Mr. Unger?"

Chase, like Gene before him, rose to face the podium. "The earlier question, sir, was asking about your stand on the late Senator Vaughn's environmental policies. But my own question is about Grady Vaughn himself."

A wave of relief seemed to relax the candidate's features—at least the kid wasn't trying to dig into Wentworth's own past.

Chase continued: "As you're probably aware, there have been recent developments at the county medical examiner's office. They're now taking another look at the cause of Senator Vaughn's death."

This was not news—it had been a topic of public speculation for nearly a week, and the room now buzzed with the whispering of compared notes. Everyone, it seemed, was on top of this, and everyone had a different theory as to what had *really* happened.

With a dopey shrug, Wentworth said to Chase, "It was a heart attack, wasn't it?"

Before Chase could respond, ditzy Ivy Quick turned to look up from the head table to tell her main squeeze at the podium, "*No*, sweetie. They're saying Vaughn's death was *suspicious*. I'll bet he was *poisoned* or something."

Dismayed, Wentworth said, "But that's ... impossible."

Chase told him, "No, Mr. Wentworth. The medical examiner is now convinced that the apparent heart attack did not arise from natural causes."

"What *was* it, then?"

Chase replied, "They don't know, sir. Still working on it. I was hoping *you* might be able to update us regarding progress of the investigation."

Wentworth gripped the podium with both hands and hung his head for a moment, as if in prayer. The room was hushed.

When he raised his head again, he looked to the ceiling, as if peering into the heavens, telling us, "Grady Vaughn was one of the finest men I've ever known. He was a statesman, a patriot, and a man of deep faith—I looked up to him as a model of integrity, and I still take inspiration from his life and his work. Losing him was a dreadful blow. But now, learning there might have been foul play, it's just ... incomprehensible." Wentworth hung his head again.

Pollard, the campaign manager, stepped up to the stage, gently coaxed the candidate away from the podium, helped him down to the ballroom floor, and led him out through a side door.

Chase, like many others, snapped pictures.

It was all a bit much.

During the confused lull that followed, I leaned to tell Chase, "I don't believe for a minute that Wentworth hadn't heard about the medical examiner's suspicions."

Chase nodded, adding something to his notes.

People began to rise from their chairs, but the club manager rushed up to the podium, clinking a glass. "One announcement before we adjourn, please." When the chatter subsided, he said, "Next week, our speaker's luncheon will be held a day earlier than usual, on Tuesday, so that we can present, in a timelier manner, an appearance by Mr. Wentworth's opponent in the senatorial race, Celia Flores Gamarra. You'll receive a registration email later this afternoon. Thank you."

The chatter resumed and swelled, with everyone now on their feet, herding slowly toward the doors. I leaned to tell Bebe from the side of my mouth, "I hope Gene didn't drive today."

"No"—she heaved a languid sigh—"my driver brought us."

Her son took her arm and walked her to the nearest exit.

While Chase gathered his things and stuffed his pockets, the manager, Everett, stepped over to us from the main table, where he'd finished thanking Wentworth's party for attending. He said to me, "If you're in no hurry to leave, Mrs. Auric, I wonder if I could discuss something with you."

In turn, I asked Chase, "Can you find your way out?"

"Of course, Meghan. Thanks so much for this. I'll be in touch." And he took off.

The room was clearing out, but quite a few guests remained, standing in clumps, catching up. I asked Everett, "What can I do for you?"

"Perhaps..." He hesitated. "Let's talk in the library."

I nodded. Then we walked out to the hallway that led back to the room where Wentworth had earlier met with donors.

Now, as we walked in, the room was empty, tidy, and freshly cleaned. Everett closed the door as I seated myself on a long leather Chesterfield sofa facing the dark fireplace. Stepping over to me, he asked, "Do you mind if I sit with you, Mrs. Auric?"

"Not at all, Mr. Burke. Please make yourself comfortable."

"Thank you, Mrs. Auric."

As he sat, a mere foot away from me on the cushion, I said, "You're welcome to call me Meghan, you know."

"Why, *thank* you — that would be delightful." Then he clammed up and glanced about, looking nervous, which was most unusual for him.

"Everett?" I said. "What's on your mind?"

"I'm afraid this is somewhat delicate, Meghan." Looking handsome as ever in his uniform with its mock epaulets, he slid an inch or two closer to me on the tufted leather cushion. Clearing his throat, he said, "I would never wish to offend you by saying anything inappropriate, but there's a subject I'd like to broach that calls for candor. May I speak plainly?"

With raised brows, I assured him, "I wish you *would*."

He took a deep breath first. "In the past, Meghan, we have occasionally—and discreetly—'enjoyed each other's company.' While it may be crass of me to mention your husband's passing, this obviously 'frees you up,' if you'll pardon the expression."

With an elaborate, queenly gesture, I intoned, "You are pardoned." Then I grinned. "Yes, Everett, we've certainly had fun. More important, we've helped each other through some difficult times. I can say without hesitation that we're dear, close friends"—I winked—"with benefits."

He extended his cupped hands, inviting me to place mine in his. When I did, he said, "So I can't help wondering if...perhaps ...we might consider spending more time together...if we might explore the possibilities. I suggest this, of course, with no expectations, but simply to let you know that I would be open to it."

Leaning forward, I lightly kissed his cheek. Sitting back again, I smiled. "I won't say no. But it's *much* too early for me to say yes."

"Of course. I understand."

"Could you give me some time to think about this?"

He tapped my chin. "That's all I ask."

Theo and Lila Hudson came to the penthouse that evening at eight. I had invited them over for cocktails and dessert—just a casual get-together of old friends, minus the midweek rigmarole of fussing with a sit-down dinner.

A trailing sliver of the sun sparkled on the horizon as we carried our drinks out from the kitchen to the roof garden. The sky was a dusky blue—with an arc of gold where it met the curve of the earth. It would be dark soon, and a rush of chilled air rustled the wheat fields as it spread like a wave of nightfall, advancing from the edge of the world.

"Brrr...," said Lila, hugging herself as we got settled on the terrace, sitting around a stone cocktail table in armchairs with plump, striped cushions.

I offered, "Would you like to go back inside?"

"You kiddin', honey? I'll be just fine with that million-dollar view."

"And I brought your sweater," said Theo, handing it to her.

As she slipped it on, I reached to turn a gas valve that lit a fire in a small sandpit that indented the center of the table.

"Now, *that*," said Lila, "... that is just about perfect."

After we skoaled, then sipped our drinks, Theo said, "Bring us up to date, Meg. How did it go at the luncheon today? Was Wentworth a hit with the upper-crust ladies of Fairview?"

I paused, attempting a poker face, knowing that Theo's question was not mere chitchat—he was ardently committed to his friend Celia Gamarra's defeat of Wentworth. My delay in responding gave Theo a worried look. Squirming in his chair, he said. "Celia's in trouble, huh?"

I broke into a smile. "Maybe not. Granted, the Towne Club's membership skews a bit older, a bit patrician—"

Laughing, Theo interrupted, "A *bit*? The club's roster is the very definition of 'white Anglo-Saxon Protestant.'"

Wryly, I reminded him, "I was raised Catholic."

Lila reminded *me*, "But it didn't stick, Meg, and when you married Eugene, you became an *honorary* WASP."

I nodded. "Yeah, guess I did."

"No matter," she said. "We still love you."

"Likewise. But that's not the point. The *point* is this: despite the club's perceived pedigree, Julian Wentworth's luncheon appearance was *not* his finest hour."

Theo broke into a grin. "He bombed?"

"Pretty close. At least his 'recent companion,' Ivy Quick, lent a bit of spark to his presentation. Some of the older gentlemen in attendance seemed to think she was, and I quote, 'quite the looker,'"

"Ugh," said Lila, "that *snip*."

Shifting the topic back to Wentworth himself, I gave Lila and Theo a complete rundown of what had happened, concluding with the candidate's sappy tribute to the late Senator Vaughn— and his own supposed ignorance of the suspicious circumstances of Vaughn's death. "If you ask me," I said, "Wentworth was putting on an act, playing for sympathy from the crowd to compensate for a lackluster event."

Weighing this, looking pleased, Theo said, "And next week, it's Celia Gamarra's turn."

"Right," I said, "and the date's been set—it's next Tuesday. Can you be there?"

"I'm not teaching that day," said Theo. "Celia is checking to see if there's room at the head table."

"Skip that—too stuffy—I'd like for both you and Lila to come as *my* guests, at *my* table."

They looked at each other, nodded. Theo said, "Sure, Meg. Thanks."

Our conversation tapered off for a few minutes as we gawked at the sky's transformation from blue to black. A planet appeared, stunningly bright (probably Venus), then another (maybe Mars or Jupiter). The spectacle seemed to demand our silence.

But I wanted to say more. I was *very* tempted to tell Theo and Lila that Julian Wentworth was once known as John White, the man I'd planned a future with at United Insurance. The Hudsons had known John as well as me at that time, and they were mystified when my relationship with him ended abruptly, followed by my unlikely marriage to Eugene. "No," I had replied to one of their more pointed queries back then, "I am *not* pregnant with Eugene's child."

The Hudsons were—then and now—my best friends, and it tore me apart that I could not confide to them what had happened all those years ago. Nor could I tell them how those past events had a bearing on the current senatorial race. Celia Gamarra's campaign could surely put this information to good use, and my desire for her to win was as strong as Theo's, but I had not yet been able to sort out the potential blowback of revealing the complete backstory—the secrets that had clouded most of my adult life.

Setting my drink on the cocktail table, near the flames, I asked them nonchalantly, "Have you heard what happened while I was at your house on Sunday?"

They glanced at each other and shrugged. Theo turned to me. "No. What happened?"

"The penthouse"—I tossed my arms and emitted an exasperated sigh—"was broken into."

"Huh?" They took turns saying, "That's crazy." "Were you in danger?" "Who did it?"

But I responded with a question of my own: "Has Celia Gamarra *not* mentioned this? Her husband, Nick, is the detective on the case."

"No," Theo assured me. "And knowing Celia, I'm sure she *would* have mentioned it. Nick must not have told her."

I said, "He seemed intent on keeping everything low-profile. I guess I'm grateful—wouldn't like to have it in the news."

"But *why*?" said Theo. "Simple burglary?"

Lila asked, "What was the break-in *about*?"

And once again, I needed to keep them in the dark. "Listen," I said, "I'm dealing with quite a lot right now. I'm sorry to come across as so tight-lipped and mysterious, but please bear with me."

Lila nodded. "How can we help, Meg?"

And just then, I thought of their son, the lawyer who knew me as Aunt Meg. I said, "Could you let Adam know that I need a bit of help untangling some thorny legal matters? I need a lawyer." Though I didn't say it, I thought it: *I need a lawyer who isn't Ronda Trask.*

Theo said, "We'll talk to him tonight, Meg."

CHAPTER
EIGHT

On Thursday morning, I realized that a full week had passed since Eugene died. I had told Ronda Trask to take care of his "arrangements," which I wanted to keep minimal. She took me at my word. Eugene had since been cremated, with plans vaguely announced for a "celebration of life" to be held sometime next spring, supposedly Eugene's favorite season (a fanciful detail that was news to me). When Ronda offered me the urn, I asked her, "Just hang on to it, would you?" At least I could put *that* circus out of mind while dealing with all the other crap—the estate plan, the codicil, the reappearance of John White, and the frightening political ambitions of his transformed alter ego, Julian Wentworth.

That Thursday, Ashley arrived early to resume the project of sorting and disposing of Eugene's finery. I worked with her on it for about an hour, going through every pocket, as Eugene had an annoying habit of losing things that he'd failed to retrieve from his own clothes—fountain pens, dental floss, a solid-gold tooth-pick in a leather pouch, a heavy fraternal ring mounted with a sizable diamond (at least two carats). Some of his custom-made suits had small flapped pockets *inside* the jacket pockets, intended for keys, change, a hidden credit card, or an emergency stash of hundred-dollar bills. We discovered samples of all such items, including a condom still in its foil wrapper, stamped with an expiration date ten years past.

I trashed the condom, pocketed the ring, and split the hundreds with Ashley, telling her, "A parting thank-you from Mr. A." Then I asked her to continue sorting by herself, as I needed to put in some time at the gym—just one floor beneath the bedroom.

An hour later, I returned to the bedroom, sweaty and still panting. Ashley was wrestling with a large wardrobe carton, about the size of a washing machine, nudging it to the far side of the room, as I asked her, "What was the name of that self-defense instructor? Gus?"

She stopped and caught her breath, thinking for a moment. "Gustaf Magnuström."

From time to time, I had brought in various practitioners to supplement my at-home workouts—yoga, Pilates, aerobics—and when I mentioned this a year or two ago to Faye Rubin, she suggested self-defense lessons, which might help to quell my fear of leaving the building, particularly when I was alone. Ashley nosed around for recommendations, then called in Gustaf for a trial session, to see if we would click.

Ashley now reminded me, "After six lessons, Gustaf said there was nothing more he could teach you—he gave you a gold star."

"There was no gold star."

"It was a figure of *speech*, Meghan. He said you were one of the best students he'd ever trained."

With a snort of laughter, I noted, "I *still* can't leave the building alone, so maybe I need a refresher." Although that was a logical-sounding reason for bringing Gustaf back, I knew there was more to it: the man who now called himself Julian Wentworth had really worried me, and I feared the great unknown of what might lie ahead. Any form of self-defense now seemed like a good idea—but I didn't trust myself with a gun.

"Okay," said Ashley, "I'll track down Gustaf and get you set up with him." Then, with a grunt, she pushed the wardrobe carton the last couple of feet to the wall.

I wasn't finally cleaned up and put together for the day until nearly noon. On days when Ashley came to work early, I often prepared a simple lunch for the two of us, and that Thursday it would be a chilled pasta salad with cubed chicken, which I'd worked up the night before.

Passing through the bedroom on my way to the kitchen, I told Ashley, "We can sit down for lunch in ten or fifteen minutes— whenever you're ready for a break from this."

"I'll be ready in *ten*," she assured me. The piles of Eugene's clothes were getting bigger, not smaller, and it seemed we'd barely made a dent in the inventory from the motorized rack in his dressing room.

"Oh, Meghan?" she said as I turned to leave.

I turned to face her. "Yes?"

"Is it okay if Zack comes up for a few minutes? He has something for me to sign—for that Mexico trip we're planning in January."

I nodded. "Good time to head south." But I was a fine one to advise this—having not left the state in *how* many winters? I added, "Zack can stay for lunch if he wants." But I hoped he wouldn't—not being a big fan of "the boyfriend."

"Nah," she said, as if reading my mind. (Or was my disdain

for him written plainly on my face?) She continued: "He never keeps a tight schedule. No telling when he'll get here."

"Ah." His tendency to run late was consistent with my impression of him. So Ashley and I enjoyed lunch together, uninterrupted.

Sometime before one, as she was loading the dishwasher, she answered her phone, then told me, "He's on his way up."

Two minutes later, when Ashley admitted him from the elevator hall, I had positioned myself in the living room, lounging on a daybed near the windows, pretending to read a thick novel. I heard them chatting as they passed through the gallery, shoes clacking on the parquet floor. "Oh," said Zack when they entered the living room, "howdy, Mrs. Auric. Long time, no see."

I set the book aside. "Hello, Zack. Welcome. I hear you're taking Ashley off to Mexico this winter."

He had already handed a folder to Ashley, who now seated herself at a game table to sign a few documents.

"Actually," Zack explained, "it's Ashley who's taking *me* to Mexico. I'm still a struggling musician."

Right, I thought. *And Ashley's still a struggling housekeeper.*

As if reading my mind again, Ashley told me, "The trip will give me scads of great material for *Factor Moments*," referring to her lifestyle vlog.

Yeah. Well. Maybe.

Zack loped over to the table and watched over her shoulder, checking that she didn't miss any of the dotted lines. As usual, he wore all black, with his dark hair pulled back tightly into a slim, foot-long ponytail. He was perhaps ten years older than Ashley, around thirty-five, which was, I noted, the same age as another artist I knew, a painter, Dustin St. James.

It would be harsh of me to belittle Zack for not having achieved the level of artistic acclaim in his own field that Dustin enjoyed in his—success in the arts is always subject to the vagaries of timing, luck, trends, and connections, not to mention talent. Even so, I couldn't imagine that Dustin, if he had been less favored by fortune, would now fleece a younger lover (of either sex) for a pricey week of sun and fun. Zack, to my mind, was simply a taker, a user. For Ashley's sake, at the very least, I hoped he was bussin' in the sack.

I heard him say, "... that guy who's running for election."

With piqued curiosity, I sat up on the daybed.

Ashley turned in her chair. "In the park? Across the street?"

"Yeah," said Zack. "Some sorta rally."

I stood.

Ashley said to me, "Julian Wentworth—weren't you at lunch with him yesterday?"

"Indeed I was. And I don't think much of him—at *all*."

Zack shrugged. "Well, *they* do, Mrs. Auric. That guy's on *fire*."

I bristled. "How dare he!" I almost added, *In my own front yard!* But that would have been presumptuous, even for an Auric.

Ashley stood, handed Zack the folder of signed papers, and rushed over to me, wide-eyed. "Let's go down there—check it out—I'll get some video."

And I suddenly faced a stark black-and-white dilemma: I was absolutely itching to get down there and find out what was happening... *but*... I hated to leave the building, and I hated crowds, especially strangers.

Ashley was in mind-reading mode again: "I'll go with you. We can hold hands if you want. And Zack will be with us, too."

He said, "Sure, Mrs. Auric. Might be a blast."

Ashley added, "If you panic, we can come right back."
Dare I do it?
"Just ... give me a moment." I needed to pop a pill first.

We took the elevator down to the residents' concourse, then another down to the public concourse on the ground floor, where the arched main entrance led out to Auric Boulevard—with the park directly across the divided street. Spotting me, the doorman used his fob to control the crosswalk signals, stopping traffic in both directions. Flanked by both Ashley and Zack, holding hands with both of them, I darted forward, leaving the building behind as we plunged toward the greenery—and the imagined mayhem—beyond.

Stepping up to the opposite curb, I heard the rev of engines as traffic resumed on the wide boulevard behind us. People mingled ahead of us, some of them strolling into the park, but it was no throng, no mob. Some of them carried shopping bags or lunch sacks—which seemed to surprise me. Had I been expecting pitchforks and torches?

I let go of Ashley's and Zach's hands, feeling foolish for having clung to them. "I should be all right now," I told them.

Ashley paused on the sidewalk and looked into my eyes. "I'm here for you, Meghan. Whatever you want, just say the word."

"What I *want*," I said, glancing between the tall stone obelisks that framed the entryway to the park, "is to see what Wentworth is up to."

"Follow me," said Zack. "The rally was over by the pond."

We entered the park, where people lingered at picnic tables before heading back to their offices. A few WENTWORTH FOR SENATE signs were stuck haphazardly in the ground, with arrows pointing toward the lagoon. The distant sounds of patriotic music and raspy chants from bullhorns echoed across the water, muffled by the trees.

Walking toward the rally, which seemed to be winding down, we passed clumps of people who were leaving. Some of them wore WENTWORTH buttons. One of them wore a silly stovepipe hat, wrapped with a campaign poster: I'M WITH WENTWORTH. A frumpy lady was telling her companion, "I *love* that guy—he's one of *us*." Trailing a few feet behind them, an older man in work clothes told a younger man in uniform, "If he's good enough for Ivy, he's good enough for me." The soldier nodded, laughing. "Can't argue with that. There's hope for all of us." In the next wave of those leaving, a couple of young women gabbed with excitement. One said, "At least he's not some old fart." The other, nearly giddy, replied, "Fuck—he's hot!"

This was ... *interesting*, to say the least.

The day before, I had expected Wentworth to dazzle his audience at the Towne Club luncheon, where he was among the affluent and well-educated—a crowd of movers and shakers, by anyone's definition. Those were the people who would most naturally be receptive to his pro-business, anti-regulation stance, clearly stated on his website and during all of his interviews. But the reaction to him at the luncheon had been tepid at best.

The people leaving his rally today, however, struck me as less fortunate on the socio-economic curve—and plenty defensive about it. I sensed that their support was rooted in an anger that, somehow, Wentworth had overcome. They didn't care a whit about the wonky intricacies of financial theory because they had no dog in that fight. Clearly, though, they had liked what they heard from him—because he had told them something they *wanted* to hear. And I had a hunch what it was.

Nearing the perimeter of the rally itself, I saw that my hunch was correct. A banner: IN GOD WE TRUST. Another: ONE NATION, UNDER GOD. Posters: CHRIST IS THE ANSWER. More posters: CHOOSE LIFE, ABORTION IS MURDER. Yet another: CONTRACEPTION KILLS.

The candidate was at the podium, wrapping things up. "So have another hot dog, and don't forget to vote in November. I give you my solemn word: If you elect me, I will be there for you in Washington. I will turn *your* vision of this society into *our* vision, a unified America where laws find their authority in the rule of God. Keep the faith, my friends. And God bless America!"

A full load of vomit hurled from my throat and splattered on my shoes as a scratchy recording by Kate Smith blared from an over-amped circle of loudspeakers.

Ashley didn't notice my distress—at first—because she was busy shooting videos of the scene. But when I grabbed her arm for support, she was instantly back in the moment. She stuffed her phone away and found a fistful of Kleenex in her bag, then began helping me clean up.

Zack checked his watch and said, "Sorry, ladies. Gotta run. *Later!*" And he abandoned us.

From the corner of my eye—a snotty eye still clouded by my upchuck—I saw a man rushing toward me. As he approached, my vision cleared, and I recognized him as Kyle Pollard, Wentworth's campaign manager. "Jesus *Christ* ...," I muttered.

"Mrs. *Auric*," he said, alarmed by my unsightly appearance. "We're delighted to see you again, but ... are you *okay*?"

Grabbing another Kleenex from Ashley, I dabbed my lips before telling him with a feeble laugh, "Must've been the hot dogs."

"Well, that's just *terrible*. I'm *so* sorry. We'll have a word with the purveyor, of course."

"Of course." I picked a fleck of something from my teeth.

"Can I get you anything? A bottle of water?"

Ashley told him, "No need," as she produced a bottle from her bag and handed it to me.

I thanked her and downed a few swallows, clearing my throat of the bile. Pollard was still standing there, watching me. His concern surely stemmed not from my mortifying accident, but from fear that the rally had failed to produce its intended effect on a potential major donor. I asked him curtly, "Is there anything else?"

"Uh, no, ma'am. I hope your day improves. And again"—he backed away—"I'm sorry."

When he was out of earshot, I turned to Ashley. "I thought he'd *never* leave."

"What a turd," she said, "if you'll pardon my French."

"*Quelle merde*," I quipped.

Ashley finished tidying me up. She licked a finger and dabbed something from my cheek. "Let's get you home," she said, "and see if we can't clean up those shoes."

They were a pair a suede Ferragamos, comfortably chic—but beyond redemption.

"Yes," I agreed, "let's get me home." And I took her hand as we retreated from the rally, heading back toward Auric Boulevard.

While waiting for traffic to stop at the crosswalk, she asked me softly, "See?"

"What?"

"That was nice, right? You should get out more often."

I eyed her for a moment. And we burst into laughter.

Getting off the elevator in the penthouse entry hall, I slipped out of my shoes, which Ashley whisked away to the laundry room, where she would attempt a rescue with brushes and solvents. (Good luck with *that*.)

While I padded through the reception room, barely noticing the paintings displayed there, the phone in my pocket buzzed, so I paused to pull it out and check the readout: GAMARRA CAMPAIGN. Intrigued, I sat on the long upholstered bench in the middle of the gallery, then answered the call. "Hello?"

"Hello, Mrs. Auric. So sorry to bother you. This is Xolani Vahdat, at Celia Gamarra's campaign headquarters in Consensus."

I said, "Yes, of course, Xolani—no bother at all. What can I do for you?"

"Well, *first*," she said, "a huge thank-you for getting Celia booked for a speaker's luncheon at the Towne Club next week. I doubt if we'd have gotten in without you. I'm just calling to confirm that you've offered to host Theo and Lila Hudson at your table, correct?"

"Absolutely correct—I'm happy to help." My eye drifted to the Edward Hopper painting centered between the others facing me. It depicted a scene in a bucolic landscape that could have been Fairview, where a figure, a woman, seemed caught in a dark and aching loneliness.

Xolani said, "That's perfect, Mrs. Auric. It's so thoughtful of you to take care of the Hudsons—plus, it relieves the squeeze at the head table, which is still in flux."

I repeated, "Happy to help. You'll be there on Tuesday?"

"Of *course*," she said with a playful tone of understatement. "A campaign manager's duties never end."

"I saw your counterpart at yesterday's event, then again at a rally in the park, just a few minutes ago."

With a low laugh, Xolani told me, "Watch out for Kyle Pollard—he's a sinister sorta guy."

Sinister, I thought. That was the word for the dark loneliness of the Hopper painting. The woman wasn't sinister, but the setting itself was.

Xolani continued, "Unfortunately, we didn't hear about Wentworth's rally till the last minute, so we couldn't get anyone over there for a bit of reconnaissance."

I asked, "Are you aware that his campaign is pandering to Christian nationalists?"

"Sure. He can't win *solely* by promising giveaways to the billionaire class. He also needs a critical mass of zealous foot soldiers—who vote."

I mused, "Onward, Christian soldiers..."

"*Right.*" Xolani laughed. "But I doubt if he actually believes the stuff he feeds them."

'No," I assured her, "he doesn't." I could vividly recall that the John White of twenty-odd years ago was no crusader—he was a profound cynic regarding *all* religions.

Xolani said, "Fortunately, *our* candidate doesn't play those games. Celia focuses squarely on the issues of good government that can make life better for *everyone*—with *no* culture wars."

"Amen." My tone was deliberately flippant. Just then, I noticed Ashley in the living room, passing by the far end of the gallery, holding my shoes at arm's length. I called her name.

When she popped into the gallery, I signaled for her to wait as I said into the phone, "I might be able to get you some video from today's rally. Interested?"

"And how," said Xolani.

So I put a hand over the phone while explaining the situation to Ashley, who agreed to share her raw footage. Then I handed the phone to her, so she and Xolani could arrange the video transfer. When they had worked out the details, Ashley returned my phone and left with my shoes—which now looked even worse than when they were splattered with vomit.

I asked Xolani over the phone, "All set?"

"All set. And thanks. When Celia decided to get into this race, she did it to set things *right*. Oh, sure—beloved old Grady Vaughn had the reputation of a saint, 'the people's senator'—but make no mistake. He was as venal and grubbing as the worst of them. And his environmental policies were not just shameless, but *brazenly* shameless. He sold out the people of this state, and he threatened the very *existence* of future generations. Off the record, Mrs. Auric: whatever it is that happened to Grady Vaughn, I'm glad he's gone."

Her words lingered in my ear long after our call ended. Xolani, like my late husband's son, Gene Auric, had applauded the suspicious death of a sitting member of the United States Senate.

That same afternoon, around three o'clock, Theo and Lila's son, Adam Hudson, came up to the penthouse for a private conversation. The night before, I had told his parents that I was interested in retaining him for legal services, and he was quick to follow through.

Ashley was just leaving for the day when Adam arrived, and they exchanged pleasantries at the elevator as the door slid closed on Ashley.

Alone with Adam in the entry hall, I said, "Thanks for coming on such short notice."

He hugged me. "Of *course*, Aunt Meg. But what's *wrong*? My folks sounded worried."

"Frankly," I admitted, "so am I." And I led him into the living room. Since he was visiting in a professional capacity, I suggested that we sit at a table near the windows, facing each other as if from opposite sides of a desk.

When we were seated, he set his briefcase on the floor and folded his hands on the table. With a warm smile, he said, "Talk to me, Aunt Meg."

I heaved a breathy sigh and cleared my thoughts. "You were too young to remember when this happened—twenty-six years ago—you'd have been about two. I was working at Fairview United Insurance, and there was some trouble."

Adam nodded. "Mom and Dad have mentioned there was some 'weirdness' back then, but they've always said they didn't know the whole story. According to them, you were practically engaged to some guy who worked there, but then the relationship suddenly fell apart, and you married Eugene. My folks were stunned."

"I don't blame them. I was pretty much stunned myself."

Tentatively, he asked, "Care to enlighten me?"

I weighed my words. "This is highly sensitive—I mean, obviously—that's why I wanted to talk to you."

He grinned. "I won't 'tattle,' even to Mom and Dad. If you want to retain me, that establishes an attorney-client privilege."

"On TV," I recalled, "the lawyer always makes it official by asking for whatever change the client has in his pocket."

He laughed. "Okay, Aunt Meg, if it helps assure you that we have a bond of confidentiality, go ahead and pay me from your pocket."

I never carried change. And my wallet wasn't on me. But I went through the motions of checking my pockets. "Oh!" I said. "Here we go." And I pulled out the heavy fraternal ring—with the big diamond—that I'd found in Eugene's clothes that morning. Dropping it into Adam's palm, I said, "That ought to cover today's session."

Hefting it in his hand, he laughed. "Do ya *think*?" Squinting closely at it, unable to make sense of the elaborate tooling and symbols, he asked, "Exactly what is this?"

I shrugged. "Some club Eugene belonged to."

Adam frowned. "Probably racist."

"Probably. Maybe. I don't know—he was always truly fond of your family—but the people he hung out with, who knows? So sell it."

He pocketed the ring. "Payment accepted. And you are now— *presto*—my client. Speak your mind."

So I told Adam ... everything: The long-ago insurance scam. John White's disappearance. Eugene's offer to "fix" the situation if I married him. The terms of his trust. His codicil from the grave. His dodgy attorney, Ronda Trask, who had arranged it all. The recent break-in at the penthouse, which might have involved off-duty sheriff's deputies. The resurfacing of John White as Julian Wentworth. And the consequences I might suffer for exposing everything, which I *really* wanted to do, but feared that I could not.

Adam took copious notes, occasionally interjecting questions or making comments of perplexed disbelief.

Concluding my recitation, I summarized, "It's complicated."

"That doesn't *begin* to describe your situation, Aunt Meg. It breaks my heart that you're going through this, but thank you for trusting me to help you sort this out. If it makes you feel any better—I'm on it."

Leaning back in my chair, I did feel better. "But there's one more point," I told Adam, "and I think it's crucial to determining how everything else plays out."

"Okay. You have my undivided attention."

I explained, "Wentworth surely knows who I am. But he doesn't know that *I* know who he *was*."

Adam nodded slowly, "Meaning, he thinks the entire deception has succeeded. He thinks you're still in the dark."

"Right. And if he feels safe, then I can feel safe. But if he ever feels threatened by me, then all bets are off."

"Phew."

We reviewed his notes again and determined a course of action: Adam would research the relevant laws and, if appropriate, get private investigators involved with the case. I gave him copies of Eugene's bulky trust documents and the one-page codicil. Then we rose from the table, hugged, and left the living room, walking through the gallery to the elevator.

Before pushing the DOWN button, I said, "There's something else I've been wanting to tell you about." I smiled.

"Not another legal problem, I hope."

"Not at all. You see, Adam, I've recently made the acquaintance of a local painter, a portrait artist named Dustin St. James. By any chance, do you know him?"

Adam scrunched his face in thought. "Sorry, no. *Should* I?"

"Well, he happens to be gay, and I—"

Adam laughed. "We don't *all* know each other, you realize."

"I suppose not, but I couldn't help thinking that you might *like* Dustin. His husband died about a year ago, so I know he's available. Thirty-five, I think. *Very* good-looking."

Adam seemed interested. He asked, "Is he into Black guys?"

I thought of Dustin's Asian wife, Crystal Tanaka, and his mixed-race daughter, Nova, as well as his late husband, Brad Larsen, a name with a vanilla ring to it. I told Adam, "I think Dustin takes a fairly... *versatile* approach to life."

"Cool."

"Shall I send you his contact info?"

Adam asked, "If I reach out to him, can I use your name?"

"Of *course*." I sent Adam a message from my phone.

When his phone buzzed, he glanced down at it, then looked up, grinning. "Aren't you just the foxy little cupid?"

By attempting to set up Adam with Dustin, I was not inviting competition to horn in on my own possibilities with Dustin. Rather, I was abandoning those fantasies, which I had come to recognize as not only foolish, but degradingly desperate. By inserting Adam into the equation, I was neatly (and rather nobly, I thought) removing myself from these uncertain dynamics—and in the process, I was restoring my sense of dignity.

So. There. One less thing to stew about.

My timing of this cleansing was good. Because, not an hour later, I was faced with an altogether different wrinkle. The guard at the ground-level private entrance phoned to tell me that Chase Unger was here, asking if he might come up for a few minutes. "He says it's important."

"Certainly," I said. "Please send him up."

I had been fussing with a new batch of gelato in the kitchen, so I went down to the lower level of the penthouse to wait for Chase in the entrance hall.

When the elevator door opened, the young reporter said, "I'm sorry for intruding, Meghan, but I thought you'd want to hear this directly."

"That's just fine, Chase. Thanks for coming over." I led him through the living room and over toward the stairway. "Gelato? I'm playing around with *dulce de leche*."

"Sure!"

Up the stairs we went—and into the kitchen, where I scooped the gelato, still quite soft, into bowls. Sitting on stools at the counter, we both tried a taste. Chase signaled two thumbs-up.

I asked, "So: What's your news?"

"I did some deep fact-checking on Wentworth's background details—all that bragging on him that his campaign manager did at the Towne Club luncheon."

With a snort of a laugh, I recalled, "Both parents, military heroes—orphaned before high school—scholarship to Oxford. Talk about claptrap."

Chase gave me an odd, steady look. "It *all* checked out."

Literally, I dropped my spoon. "Impossible," I said. "I know for a *fact* that that man's parents were alive and well *after* he finished school—at a community college just north of Consensus. Oxford my *ass*." I laughed at the thought of it, the *absurdity* of it.

Chase told me, "I made an online request for expedited verification from the university's Degree Conferrals Office, and just before I came over here, I got an automated response by email." He showed it to me.

When I read it, my jaw sagged, my pulse raced.

"Wentworth," I said, "seems to have friends in *very* high places."

CHAPTER
NINE

Perhaps I should have understood from the outset that if some-one was attempting to install a manufactured candidate in a high federal office—someone with a totally fake identity—the people behind it would make damn sure that the candidate's invented background would pass the routine sniff-testing of journalists and other fact-checkers. While I had no direct knowledge of how this might be done, it surely *could* be done, as evidenced by the work of witness-protection programs and espionage agencies. With the right connections—and enough money—just about anyone could be reborn as an orphan of military heroes or a graduate of Oxford.

I told Chase Unger, "Be careful with this," but I couldn't tell him why. I told him, "Whatever's going on here, it's bigger than we think," but I couldn't make him privy to the background that I actually knew.

Friday morning, during my regular workout at home, I was net-tled by my inability to confide in Chase. Granted, he was a *kid*, fresh out of college, working for the local rag. If he were to beat the galactic odds and find a Pulitzer in his future, it was still *way* down the road of his career. With the current dire state of newspapers, though, I had to wonder if his career would be dead-ended before he even had a chance to make a go of it.

He was eager and dedicated. At a gut level, I knew that I could trust him. But I didn't know if I could trust *myself* with the consequences of exposing Julian Wentworth. It would make a hell of a story for Chase—indeed, the stuff of Pulitzers—but it would also upend my life. So I needed to tread with care.

When I finished my workout, I went upstairs to my bedroom, where Ashley was dutifully—doggedly—engaged in the never-ending quest to rid the penthouse of Eugene's vast wardrobe. "Christ," I said as I entered the room, "it smells like mothballs in here."

"I noticed. Yuck. Maybe we're reaching the lower limits of Mr. A's stuff."

"Don't count on it. I'll pitch in after I get myself cleaned up. Finding any hidden treasure today?"

"Nothing of interest. It's there on your bed."

I went over to inspect the fruits of Ashley's scavenging: a few stubby pencils from Eugene's golf club, a dusty unwrapped cough drop, scraps of paper with illegible scribblings (MICROBLEXS? ANTIJYEZCUFF? SHITSTORK?), and two wrapped condoms, both dried to a crisp, one yellow, one pink. Huh?

While walking off to my dressing room, I turned and asked, "Were you able to reach Gus Hoozit?"

"Gustaf Magnuström. Yes. He said he was 'tickled' that you want him back. He'll be here Monday at nine."

"Good." A moment later: "Uh ..."

She turned to look at me. "Yes?"

"Uh, maybe later, after lunch, you could help me ... pick out a dress?"

Her eyes widened with astonishment.

I explained, "Dinner with a friend. He's a bit younger."

My dinner date with Dustin was *not* a "date." When he first suggested it, while driving me home from his studio on Monday, the idea seemed spontaneous and friendly, by no means a nudge to take "us" to the next level. What's more, the get-together was also meant as an opportunity for me to get better acquainted with his daughter, Nova, because our earlier brief encounter had been so pleasant. Meaning, this would not be a cozy dinner for two, and the third party would be a child.

I admit, when we made these plans, I had found his suggestion tantalizing, wondering if (just *maybe*) he was exploring "possibilities" that were not yet clearly defined. By instantly, eagerly agreeing to these plans, I could hardly deny that I myself was curious about where—if anywhere—the evening might lead. Meanwhile, however, I had dismissed that notion as both unlikely and unseemly, deciding to make an offering of Dustin to Adam Hudson. So tonight was to be merely a chaste and chummy night out.

I had made arrangements for dinner at a restaurant in the building, reserving a table for three at Tableau Magenta, which was always excellent—and I thought that Nova would find it less stuffy than the Towne Club. We were booked for seven o'clock ("dinner at eight" struck me as unreasonable for a child), and I told Dustin that if Nova would enjoy seeing the penthouse first, they could come up at six thirty.

That afternoon I was more nervous than usual when guests were expected. Eugene and I had entertained so many bigwigs from the worlds of business and politics, I had lost count, and those blowout occasions always involved extensive food preparation and full bar service. Tonight there would be none of that—just a simple walk-through tour for one man and his child, maybe a quick drink—but the knots in my stomach seemed more fitting for a royal visit. (What did *that* tell me?)

Regarding what to wear, Ashley urged me to keep it simple: "You're telling me you're not hot for this guy, but I'm not so sure. Either way, don't tart it up. You'll just scare him off—and what would the *kid* think?"

I reminded her, "I *never* 'tart it up.'"

"Of course not," she conceded, "but you know what I mean: less is more."

Sound advice. I chose a classically tailored silk jacket and skirt of chocolate brown with matching silk kitten pumps. To brighten it up, I added a magenta silk scarf (to coordinate with the color scheme of the restaurant), and just a *bit* of gold bling.

At precisely six thirty, the doorman phoned me. "Mr. and *Miss* St. James are here, ma'am."

And at six thirty-two, I greeted them at the elevator in my entry hall.

"Good evening, Mrs. Auric," said Nova, stepping forward and offering me a shake of her right hand. Bringing her left hand around from behind her back, she extended a small bouquet of white rose buds and baby's breath.

"*Thank* you, Nova. How very sweet of you. And remember—I'm just 'Meghan.'"

Dustin stepped up to me with a casual kiss on the cheek. "Hi, Meghan. Thanks for having us up. Nova's been eager to see the place—and you."

I took her hand. "Let's have a little tour then, shall we?" We began in the gallery.

Dustin explained to his daughter a few technical points relating to some of the paintings. She listened, nodding, and seemed genuinely interested in his mini-lecture.

While they studied the art, I studied them.

No surprise: Dustin looked great, as usual. But tonight he'd taken it up a notch, looking more formal in a dark worsted suit, the color of steely graphite, with a silvery silk pocket square. Instead of a shirt, he wore a fine-knit mock turtleneck, a shade or two lighter than the suit. His handsome shoes were blucher-style black oxfords.

Nova wore a slim-tailored mannish suit of black tuxedo cloth, a natural choice with her straight jet-black hair. Under the jacket was a black silk blouse with a Nehru collar and plump silk buttons. Her shoes: black patent-leather flats. At ten years old, with maturing facial features but not yet busty, she projected an exotic look of androgyny—and a supremely self-confident sense of personal style. I could imagine her as an adult, stepping up to the podium to conduct an orchestra, pausing to acknowledge thunderous applause before turning to a hundred musicians and raising her baton.

She turned to me. "You could start your own museum, Meghan."

"Not a bad idea. Now, let's get these flowers in water."

So I led them up to the kitchen and found a small vase. Dustin arranged the flowers while I took Nova outside to see the terrace.

Looking over the balustrade, she said, "It's like a map of the town—with trees." Her hair fluttered in the building's updraft. "Where's Dad's studio?"

"Over ... *there*," I said, crouching next to her, pointing.

She looked at me quizzically. "It's so *small*."

"All a matter of perspective, Nova."

"Oh."

Ten or fifteen minutes later, after we had walked through the entire penthouse and returned to the gallery on the lower level,

Nova said, "Your house is really beautiful, Meghan."

"Thank you, sweetie. Happy to share it with you." I checked my watch. "Perfect timing. Shall we head downstairs for dinner?"

Nova gave an eager nod.

Stepping over to the elevator, Dustin said, "I'll drive"—and he pushed the DOWN button.

Several of the building's better restaurants, including Tableau Magenta, were on the sixteenth floor. We got out of the elevator, and I led the way.

"Good *evening*, Mrs. Auric," said the host, whose name I couldn't remember. "It's an honor to have you back. This way, please."

He showed us to one of the prime tables surrounding a round reflecting pool at the center of the dining room. Above the pool was a dome of equal diameter in the ceiling, from which hung a stunning Baccarat chandelier—with magenta crystals. Despite the restaurant's name, the tables themselves were not magenta (they had traditional white linen napery), but the sturdy cut-glass water goblets were magenta, and the tidy flower arrangements on each table contained a mixture of red, pink, and white blossoms. The staff wore hot-pink boutonnières, but that's as far as the color theme went, and it was a perfect knockout. (Had the theme been taken much further, the room would have looked like a bordello.)

We were showered with attention, as a child on the scene was something of an anomaly. Nova had a Shirley Temple, lending another vibrant touch of magenta to our table. For Dustin and me, I ordered—what else?—a bottle of rosé Dom Pérignon. "It goes with *everything*," I noted, as if the splurge could be justified by its practicality.

Although Nova's mother, Crystal, was of Asian descent—with both parents born in Japan, I learned—Nova herself had never been there. And since Crystal had died when Nova was two years old, the girl never assimilated her mother's culture. Her eating habits were similar to those of most American girls of her age, squeamish about meat, but willing to try anything. Fish was no problem, and she *loved* shrimp.

So we all began with salads, and for her main course, Nova ordered a shrimp cocktail—described as featuring colossal prawns. Dustin and I had no qualms about beef, choosing chateaubriand for two, to be carved at the table.

After the salads, during a lull between courses, Nova said to us, "Excuse me. I need to find the restroom."

I set my napkin aside. "Come with me, dear. I'll show you where it is."

Dustin got up and helped me with my chair, giving me a wink as I rose from the table. With my handbag tucked under one arm, I led Nova out of the dining room and down a hallway.

When we reached the restroom, she paused outside the door. With an impish grin, she told me, "I really didn't need to 'go,' at least not *that* bad."

I returned the grin. "What's up, kiddo?"

Lowering her voice, she said, "I think Dad really likes you."

"I like *him*, too. He's so talented. And I'm thrilled that he wants to paint my late husband's picture."

She gave me a goofy look, as if I were dense. "Not *that*. I mean, he really *likes* you."

I played along. "Ohhh ... he likes me as a *friend*?"

She laughed. "*Something* like that. Know what I mean?"

"Maybe." I knew, of course, what Nova meant. But I also thought she was probably mistaken. It would be easy for a girl of her age to nurture fantasies of her single father finding love. And besides, I told myself, Dustin was gay—regardless of whatever circumstances or predilections had led to Nova's birth. To my mind, a more realistic fantasy for Nova might focus on Adam Hudson joining the family, although Dustin hadn't met him yet.

Nonetheless, Nova knew her father much better than I did, and even at ten, she might have voiced instincts that I would be foolish to dismiss. "As long as we're here," I said, "I should freshen up."

I held the door to the restroom open as Nova stepped inside. I followed. While she scooted into one of the stalls, I opened my bag at the vanity and glanced in the mirror. A touch of powder wouldn't hurt.

As we arrived back at the table, Dustin rose to seat me, asking, aside, "Girl talk?"

I assured him, "More like woman-to-woman."

It seemed that the serving staff had also been awaiting our return. The moment we three were seated, they appeared at our table, presenting the colossal prawns, carving the chateaubriand, grinding pepper, refilling glasses, and then—*poof*—they vanished.

"*Bon appétit*," I told my two charming companions.

Dustin raised his champagne glass. "To you, Meghan. Nova and I are delighted to spend the evening with you."

"Cheers," said Nova, raising her kiddie cocktail. She was on her third, and when she smiled at me, her teeth were pink.

The meal was splendid, and after the initial oohs-and-aahs, we settled into easy, pleasant conversation.

Setting his fork at the edge of his plate, Dustin told me, "I had a thought about your husband's portrait. Do you mind talking shop?"

"Not at *all*. What's your idea?"

He turned in his chair to face me more directly. "Well, first of all, I *love* your suggestion to use a square canvas, rather than the conventional vertical for a standing figure. Eight-by-eight feet will give the work such a *monumental* feel. The square does, however, present a certain compositional challenge: the figure alone seems lost in all that space. So—bear with me here—what if we do a whimsical nod to tradition and create an *equestrian* portrait of Eugene standing with a horse?"

My eyes bugged. "Eugene never got within a mile of a horse."

Dustin slumped. "No go, huh?"

"*Au contraire*—it's perfect. It's so bizarre. And wonderful."

He touched my hand. "Know what I love about you, Meghan? You're so open-minded, so adventurous. *This* will be fabulous. I already have a few sketches—can't wait to show you."

"Can't wait to see them."

With a chuckle, he sat back in his chair. "What a difference—working with the right client. You know, I did a portrait for Governor Swaine. He was a pleasure to deal with, a good guy, and I was proud of the results."

"You should be. Swaine's portrait was one of the reasons I sought you out."

Dustin gave me a humble bow of his head. "Thank you. But on the other hand, working with Senator Vaughn was a total *disaster*."

"Oh? I didn't know that you'd painted him."

"I *didn't*. That's the whole point. At first, I agreed to the commission, but as soon as we got into the conceptual stage—talk about 'creative differences'! I guess he was in his sixties, but he had the attitude of a fossil in his nineties, totally stuck in the past, so I returned the deposit. During our final discussion, we practically came to blows. I've never 'fired' a client before, but believe me, it felt great. And now, quite frankly—"

I cringed, hoping he wouldn't say it. But he did:

"—frankly, I'm glad he's gone."

I wagged my head. "Sorry to hear this. Grady Vaughn was a guest in our home a number of times, and he was always more than gracious to both Eugene and me. But I've come to understand that *many* people had issues with him."

Our table chat lightened as we segued from the main course to dessert. The restaurant's specialty was listed on the menu as MAGENTA VELVET CAKE, which I'd had many times and now recommended to my two guests, adding, "Try it with ice cream." Servings were brought for all three of us.

Tasting it, Nova squealed with delight. Dustin groaned—sounding a tad orgasmic, which brought visions to mind that were not quickly blinked away.

We lingered awhile with coffee (Nova switched from Shirley Temples to milk), enjoying each other's company and the afterglow of a leisurely top-notch meal.

Dustin checked his watch. So did I: nine fifteen. He said to me, "It's not *that* late. If you'd like to get out of the building for some fresh air, maybe you could come over to the studio, and I could—"

Wryly, I suggested, "You could show me your etchings?"

He laughed. "Sorry, didn't mean it that way. But I *could* show you the equestrian sketches."

I mulled this for a moment. I noticed Nova facing me from across the table, giving me a discreet but eager nod.

"Sure," I told Dustin. "Thanks for suggesting it." Then I signaled a waiter, who came to the table.

"Yes, Mrs. Auric?"

"Check, please."

The waiter grinned, explaining, "Mr. St. James already took care of it, while you and the young lady stepped away earlier. Enjoy your evening, ma'am." He retreated.

I turned to Dustin, chagrined. "That's ... not fair. You're my *guests*."

He gently shook his head. "You're my *client*."

"But I never would've ordered the Dom Pérignon if—"

"Stop that. I'll write it off."

I sulked. "I should've taken you to the Towne Club—your money's no good there."

He shrugged. "Maybe next time."

The doorman had Dustin's huge safari-style cruiser brought up from the underground garage, and it was now parked, idling, at the curb in front of the building's main entrance. Dustin helped his daughter into the back area while the doorman helped me up to the front passenger seat, then thumped the door closed. Dustin got in behind the wheel, and away we went.

Nova was gabbing with me about a dance class she was taking twice a week after school. With my head turned to see her as we spoke, I paid no attention to where Dustin was driving.

Perhaps five minutes later, he slowed the vehicle and stopped at the curb in a neighborhood I didn't recognize; his warehouse loft was nowhere to be seen. At the nearest house, a porch light was on. When he gave a quick toot of the horn, a woman opened the door and waved.

Dustin got out and helped Nova retrieve an overnight bag

from behind the back seat. Then he crouched on the parkway to hug her, saying, "Give Gramma a kiss for me."

Nova skipped along the sidewalk and up to the porch. When she was indoors and the light went out, Dustin drove us away.

After three or four minutes, we were in the warehouse district, pulling into his parking court. He cut the engine. I turned to him in the near darkness, noting, "It seems you've ditched our ten-year-old chaperone."

He smiled. "Is that a problem? Should I take you back?"

I hesitated ... briefly. "Weren't you going to show me those sketches?"

He left the vehicle, came around to my side, and helped me down. Then he walked me over to the entrance to his studio.

After unlocking the door and opening it, he stepped aside so I could enter the vast, dimly lit space. He followed me in and closed the door.

There were no sketches.

Or maybe there were—but I never saw them.

CHAPTER
TEN

Saturday morning, I had the penthouse to myself. Ashley wouldn't be coming in at all that weekend, but I did get a text from her while I was doing some warm-up stretches for my workout. She asked: HOW WAS THE DATE? Immediately after that, she sent a big yellow winky-face with a vulgar pink tongue hanging out.

I replied: NOT MUCH TO REPORT. SEE YOU MONDAY.

There was, of course, plenty to report, at least from a gossipy perspective, but I wasn't sure how much I'd tell her, if anything at all.

A particular detail from my overnight adventure with Dustin stood out among the others. It wasn't our coy game of mutual consent...or the moment I first saw his naked body...or his gentle lovemaking. What struck me most was an offhand comment, his unexpected compliment, when he called me "buff." The way he said it, he was entirely approving—and I found it empowering. It certainly kicked the energy level up a notch.

Now, in my home gym, I was running on the treadmill, about a half hour into it, when my phone buzzed with an incoming email. It was from Dustin: FORGOT TO SHOW YOU THE SKETCHES.

Slowing down to a walking pace, I scrolled through the six images. Then I typed: LOVE THESE! NUMBER 4 WOULD BE

PERFECT, BUT MAYBE TURN THE HORSE AROUND?

A minute later, Dustin asked: WITH EUGENE RESTING HIS ARM ON THE HORSE'S ASS?

I replied with a thumbs-up emoji.

The following morning, I was *still* basking in some residual afterglow from the unforeseen developments of Friday night. So the day that was now dawning seemed inordinately serene as I settled on the kitchen terrace with my coffee, a bowl of mixed berries with a soft gob of lemon gelato, and the thick Sunday edition of the *Consensus Times*, still rolled and wrapped in its plastic sleeve.

I assumed the paper would include some coverage of the special election, and when I unfurled it, the front page confirmed my hunch, with a variety of stories about aspects of the two campaigns. There was nothing flashy, though—no sensational headlines, no burning controversy—and my first impression was that the coverage seemed dry and wonky, needing more photos and fewer columns of the gray, unbroken text.

But one of those columns, below the fold, caught my eye because it was under Chase Unger's byline. The smallish headline, presumably written by some bleary-eyed editor, had no flair whatever: WENTWORTH SENDS MIXED MESSAGES.

Had I not known the reporter, I'd have probably skipped the story. But I did know the reporter, and his opening paragraphs grabbed me at once:

> Appearing at campaign events in Fairview last week, U.S. Senate candidate Julian Wentworth presented two strikingly different versions of himself to two strikingly different audiences.

On Wednesday, speaking to the elite membership and guests of the Fairview Towne Club, Wentworth toed the party line on such issues as taxes, regulation, and climate, assuring his audience that, if elected, he would be a staunch friend of business, with a closing nod to traditional values.

On Thursday, however, while appearing at a public lunchtime rally in Auric Park, his campaign took on the character of an evangelistic revival meeting, replete with hot dogs and a Kate Smith recording of "God Bless America." The crowd carried banners decrying not only abortion, but also contraception. Wentworth, in turn, promised that, if elected, he would work toward legislating Bible-based laws for the nation.

Chase's story did not end on page one, but continued inside on page five. When I turned to it, I saw that the story was longer than I had presumed, filling the entire page and including several photos. One of the pictures, taken by Chase from his table at the Towne Club, showed Wentworth at the podium, head bowed, during his soppy tribute to the late Senator Grady Vaughn, whose seat he hoped to fill.

The other photos were scenes from the rally in the park: the crowd with their signs, looking more like a zeal-stricken mob; a close-up of a fervent woman in prayer, kneeling in the dirt; and Wentworth at the podium with his hands raised in a feverish, priestly gesture. The rally photos were arranged on the page with a group caption and a shared credit line: *Screenshots of video by Ashley Factor, courtesy of Celia Gamarra for Senate Campaign.*

The story itself wound its way around the pictures and down

the page. I found myself skimming until I reached the closing paragraphs:

> Julian Wentworth is a charismatic figure with an extraordinary backstory that is likely to impress voters of any stripe. And he has been known to the public in recent years through his able service on the county's board of supervisors. But he is not without his critics.
>
> A credible source has told the *Times* that dubious claims have been made by Wentworth's campaign regarding his background. Specifically, the source said, "I know for a fact that (Wentworth's) parents were alive and well after he finished school—at a community college just north of Consensus." This contradicts the candidate's official bio, which states that he was orphaned before high school and later attended Oxford University.
>
> The *Times* has been unable to reconcile various disputed facts and has reached out to the campaign for clarification or comment. No response was received prior to deadline.

Lounging on my chaise, I chortled while setting aside the newspaper. Now, *that* would surely cause a few headaches for Wentworth and his crew. Gloating over these developments, I poured another cup of coffee from the carafe and ate a spoonful of berries, now dripping with the tangy, melted gelato. Delightful. Savoring another mouthful of berries, I wiggled my toes in the warmth of the morning sun.

When I had suggested to Xolani Vahdat, campaign manager for Celia Gamarra, that she might be able to make use of Ashley's video from the Wentworth rally, I was pleased that she wanted the footage, but I had no idea of what she might do with it. That she simply offered it to the *Times*, I thought, was brilliant. The pictures spoke for themselves, and their publication served my purpose—without my direct involvement.

Thoughts of the Gamarra campaign led to thoughts of Celia's husband, Nick, the detective investigating the prior weekend's break-in at the penthouse. He'd said he planned to slow-walk the report of his findings, but I couldn't help wondering if I'd missed something.

I must have been sending brain waves—because Nick phoned me around noon that day, asking if I had time to see him. "There are a couple of updates we should discuss."

I asked him to come over around two o'clock.

At one minute past two, when he stepped out of the elevator and into my entrance hall, I said, "Good to see you, Nick. I've been wondering where things stand."

He nodded. "It was a busy week, but I'm *starting* to make sense of what happened. It's a long story."

"Then let's sit down." I led him through the gallery and into the small library off the living room. I rarely went in there, as the room's general appearance reminded me of Eugene's den— bookcases, hardwood-paneled walls, leather furniture—but no LeRoy Neiman paintings. I had hung, instead, a pleasant landscape by a minor French impressionist who'd never made it into the "legacy" crowd. His vision and technique fell short of masterful, but his warm palette in the depiction of a wheat field reminded me of views from the penthouse during late afternoon.

Before we were seated, I asked Nick, "Can I get you anything? Water?"

"No, Meghan, I'm fine."

I motioned for him to sit on the loveseat beneath the painting. I sat in one of two club chairs that faced him. Windows on either side of the painting revealed a similar landscape beyond the outdoor terrace. Since the library had no direct access to the roof garden, I had planted its terrace with a patch of leaf lettuce, providing a vivid burst of green.

Nick wore a sport coat, as he had during prior visits, but I noticed that he'd brought nothing with him today—briefcase, files, evidence kit, whatever. He crossed his arms and breathed a quiet laugh. "What are you looking at?"

"Sorry," I said. "It seems you're always dealing with paperwork—notes—but today, nothing."

With a smile, he said, "Most observant of you, Meghan. Today's visit is unofficial. Off the record. Get it?"

"Got it." I mimed locking my mouth and tossing the key.

"You can *speak* of these matters," he assured me, "but for now, only to me."

I nodded. "Then this sounds fairly... sensitive."

"Very. And I'm not telling you these things because I like sharing secrets. The point is, I think you might be able to help."

"I hope I can," I said. My instincts told me that Nick was one of the "good guys" in law enforcement—not in it for the ego or for the badge of authority, and serving no agenda other than equal justice for all. How could I *not* comply with his request for help? The problem, of course, was my knowledge of particular past events that I simply couldn't share with him, not without risking ... everything.

"So," said Nick, "let's talk about the break-in. Your exclusionary fingerprints—and those of your helper, Miss Factor—were everywhere we'd expect them to be, but they were nowhere that would suggest involvement in this crime." He grinned. "So you're off the hook. It wasn't an inside job."

"Glad to hear it," I said wryly.

"As for the mess of ice cream left in the kitchen, that tells us nothing—except that the intruder is deliberately, brazenly screwing with us. And finally, the freight elevator. By process of elimination, we know with near certainty that it was used to gain access to the penthouse. But there were no fingerprints or other evidence of who did it. Normally, the elevator would've been *lousy* with prints, but it was wiped *clean*—a clear indication of foul play."

I tossed my hands. "So we've got nothin'?"

"No, we *do* have an increasingly uncomfortable possibility."

I had a hunch where he was headed with this.

He explained, "There is absolutely no evidence of what individual, or individuals, were actually responsible for the break-in. They left no trail at all, and that isn't easy—meaning, whoever was behind this was a pro. Could it have been someone from inside law enforcement? You bet. They'd have exactly the sort of training to pull it off."

I took a deep breath, then reminded Nick, "You told me before that Auric headquarters employs off-duty sheriff's deputies for security at nights and on weekends. If they're clever enough, that would probably give them access to passcodes and such that would facilitate the penthouse break-in. Right?"

"Correct. But what was the motive? It seems that the only thing *taken* from the penthouse was part of a computer—while some of your artwork is worth *millions* and was ignored. So the intrusion had nothing to do with the robbery of valuable goods. Instead, they were obviously *searching* for something, which they believed was in your husband's home office, and to me, that suggests that the object of their search was ... *information* of some kind."

I nodded slowly. "Eugene was a notoriously private man, but his mistrust of others sprang from a single obsession—protecting his business, his brand. And in that realm, let's face it, he was pretty damn good."

"None better," Nick agreed. "Just look at what he's built."

"But," I said, "how does any of that even *conceivably* involve the sheriff's department?"

Nick pondered this for a moment. "Not a clue."

I asked him, "In the course of your investigation, have you talked to Ronda Trask?"

He rolled his eyes. "The lawyer?"

"I know, I know—she takes some getting used to. But she was probably Eugene's most blindly loyal staffer. He used to joke that she was his 'fixer.'"

"Everyone," Nick assured me, "has always referred to her as Eugene's fixer. In fact, I didn't even know she was a *lawyer* till I talked to her last week."

"Can you tell me what you talked about?"

"Sure. I asked her about the security setup with our off-duty deputies. I wanted information like names, schedules, pay—and what they actually *do* at Auric headquarters while none of the usual staff is around."

"Wouldn't those details be on file at the sheriff's department?"

"Probably. But I didn't want to be the one digging into it. I didn't want the word to get around that I was asking questions."

I found his reply sobering. "You mean, there might be consequences? Ramifications?"

He shrugged. "Depends what is—or isn't—going on."

"So, was Ronda helpful?"

"She was. Gave me all the specific info I requested—except, she had no knowledge of what the hired guards actually *do* there. Maybe they eat doughnuts all night. Or maybe they rifle the files."

I said, "I'm *sure* the offices have security cameras."

"They do. But the cameras are monitored—guess where—at the sheriff's department."

As Dr. Faye Rubin might put it: *Oy.*

I sensed that my meeting with Nick was wrapping up, but then he said, "There's another matter with developments you might want to know about."

With a cynical lilt, I told him, "I can hardly wait."

He said, "This isn't public knowledge yet, but it soon will be. The county coroner and the medical examiner have completed their forensic review of Senator Vaughn's supposed 'heart attack.' The exhumed body was reexamined for agents that cause or mimic cardiac arrest—and the testing revealed the presence of hydrogen cyanide. Scrupulous physical examination then revealed an injection point that had previously gone unnoticed—between the toes of the left foot."

Stunned, I sat back in my chair, asking, "This happened while Vaughn was out for a jog in the woods?"

"Yes. The most likely theory is that an assailant encountered him during his run and temporarily overcame him by some means—possibly chloroform or ether—leaving no signs of a struggle. He then removed one of Vaughn's shoes, injected him, replaced the shoe, and left him to die."

I mumbled, "Senator Vaughn was ... *murdered.*"

"Yes."

"Do you think—and I know this sounds crazy—do you think

there could be a connection between Vaughn's murder and the current election?"

"There's no evidence of that, but we haven't looked into it yet. In any event, I know that Celia—*my wife*—had zero involvement in what happened to Vaughn."

"Of course she didn't. But Julian Wentworth strikes me as capable of anything."

Nick asked, "Why would you say that?"

"Did you read that article in this morning's *Times*—the dispute about his background?"

"I did. It was intriguing, to say the least. But it left me wondering who this 'credible source' might be. When I asked Celia about it, she said she thought the source might be *you*."

I faked an airy laugh. "Where would she get *that* idea? But please let her know: I'll do whatever I can to make sure Wentworth isn't elected."

Nick sat forward with his elbows on his knees and looked me in the eye. "Meghan," he said, "whatever's going on here, these guys play rough. They play for keeps. So watch your step."

That evening, while fussing in the kitchen, I was interrupted by the buzz of my phone, but I didn't recognize the number of the incoming call.

Connecting, I mumbled, "Hello?" When I wasn't sure of the caller, I tended to lower my voice a bit, as if "disguising" it— the aural equivalent of fake glasses and a rubber nose. I must've sounded ridiculous.

He said, "May I speak to Meghan Auric, please?"

I countered, "May I ask who's calling?"

"Kyle Pollard, with Julian Wentworth's Senate campaign."

Hmmm. "Hello, Mr. Pollard. This is Mrs. Auric."

He asked, "Is this a good time to talk?"

"That depends on why you're calling. What can I do for you—write a check, maybe?"

"While that would be lovely, Mrs. Auric, I just wanted to ask how you're doing. At Julian's rally on Thursday, you seemed a bit—shall we say—*distressed*. Everything better now?"

"Much," I said. "But the Ferragamos are hopeless."

"The who? I don't think I know them."

"No"—I laughed—"apparently you don't. But the point is: It wasn't the hot dogs that made me ill. It was Julian's messaging. Did you see this morning's story in the *Consensus Times*?"

"Of course. And it left us wondering about a few things. The pictures, for instance. Did you feed those to the Gamarra campaign?"

"Why would you think that?"

"Because the photos were credited to Ashley Factor. We did a background check and learned that she's employed by you. She also has a video blog, which we checked, and she looks exactly like the woman who was with you in the park. Naturally, this leads us to wonder: Who's side are you *on*, Mrs. Auric?"

"Not that it's *any* of your business"—I was fuming now—"but I wouldn't vote for Julian Wentworth if my *life* depended on it."

"That's a *very* provocative statement. Equally provocative was the quote in the story—from a 'credible source'—questioning Julian's impeccable career and education. He seems to think the unnamed source was *you*. Wherever would you come up with such outlandish ideas? With the stakes so high, you could be facing a monumental libel suit, Mrs. Auric."

Before I was able to lash out at this snot-nosed dweeb, I heard him cover the phone while talking to someone in the room with him. He came back on the line, telling me, "I have someone standing here who wants to speak to you."

After the phone was handed over, I heard a new voice—Wentworth's—telling Pollard, "Now get out. This is private." I heard the sound of footsteps and a door being closed.

Then Wentworth said through the phone and into my ear, "What the *fuck* are you up to, Meghan?"

So I said it: "I know who you are, John White. And I know what you did."

"You don't know *shit*. You were a crazy bitch back *then*; you're even worse *now*. And if you start spreading your fucked-up fantasies, you'll lose far more than I will—because I know what *you* did all those years ago. Trust me: you have *no* idea how much is riding on this election. So back off. Your life depends on it." *Click.*

I shouted to the disconnected line, "Go to hell, fucker!"

Then I set down the phone. My scowl morphed into a grin. Before I'd answered the call, and feeling wary of the unknown number, I'd set the conversation to record as a voice memo.

Just in case.

Although I had the recording, there wasn't much I could do with it—the consequences would be at *least* as harmful to me as they would be to Wentworth. But after the phone call that evening, my emotions were dominated by anger more than fear.

The cat-and-mouse phase was over. Wentworth and I were on the same page. He now knew that I had figured out his past identity at United Insurance. He also knew that I had figured out that his Senate candidacy was not one man's altruistic mission to advance the art of statecraft. Rather, I suspected that he was merely a figurehead, a puppet, a slickly packaged stand-in for unnamed backers who were seeking to advance their financial interests by duping low-information voters with irrational bromides about their gods and their grievances.

In short, Wentworth was just another for-sale politician. We both knew this.

But what he did *not* know, at this point, was that I knew that Senator Grady Vaughn had been murdered. I knew the "how," but not the "why." And this left me wondering what, if anything, Wentworth himself knew of these developments.

By the next morning, Monday, my focus began to shift. After a full night of stewing, I was still angry—*very* angry—but now the fear was setting in. Wentworth's campaign manager had threatened a "monumental" defamation suit. Wentworth himself had threatened my financial security, my freedom, and in none too subtle words, my life.

Grateful that I'd had the foresight to retain Adam Hudson's legal representation four days earlier, and equally grateful that I'd confided in him the full background of my dilemma, I now set aside my morning coffee and picked up my phone, scrolling for Adam's number. It was too early for a call, so I left him a text: PLEASE PHONE WHEN CONVENIENT. NEW DEVELOPMENTS. MUST DISCUSS.

An hour or so later, he replied: TIED UP IN COURT ALL DAY. SHALL I COME OVER AT 4:30?

I sent emojis of a thumbs-up and a big red heart.

When Ashley arrived that morning and came into the bedroom, I turned to ask her, "How do I look?"

With a nod of approval, she said, "Ferocious."

I was barefoot and wearing a karate gi—jacket and pants—the heavy canvas kind with a student's neutral-colored cloth belt. Gustaf Magnuström would arrive soon for my self-defense lesson, and although we would not be practicing karate, he had recommended the uniform for its sturdiness and its freedom of movement. During our initial sessions some two years earlier, I had come to appreciate the gi for its comfort and classic styling. Since then, I'd acquired a modest collection of lighter-weight gis in cotton or silk, using them as loungewear at home and, more recently, pajamas at night. But today I was wearing the real thing, meant for action.

Standing in front of a mirror, I practiced a few of the moves Gus had previously taught me, while Ashley went into Eugene's dressing room and returned with a double armload of his custom-made suits, which she dropped in a pile on the floor.

Hands on hips, she said, "Aren't you forgetting something?"

I paused, gazed at myself in the mirror, and repeated a kick.

"Not *that*," she said. "I want the dirt on the date."

I echoed her stance, hands on hips. "It was *not* a 'date.'"

She gave me a "get real" stare. "Did you sleep with him?"

Sounding a bit uppity, I reminded her, "That is *none* of your business, Ashley."

She smirked, mumbling, "Yep—I knew it."

I slumped. Then laughed. Sitting on the edge of the bed, I patted the mattress, and Ashley sat next to me. Through a grin, I insisted, "It wasn't planned. It just happened."

"Nice. Was he good?"

I nodded—but said nothing.

"Will you see him again?"

"Of *course*. Dustin is working on a portrait of Eugene, so we'll have *many* meetings."

"Sweet setup."

"It's not a 'setup.' It's business." Reconsidering, I added, "Well, it's art *and* business, but it's not as if we're having an *affair*. I mean, he's gay."

She asked, "But he performed just fine, right? Times have changed, Meghan. Things aren't so black-and-white as they used to be. Sounds to me like Dustin's sex drive is rather…*flexible*."

I shrugged. "Lucky me, then."

Gustaf Magnuström had an *enormous* olive-drab duffel slung over his back as Ashley brought him into my home gym, where I'd been setting out exercise mats and doing some stretches, anticipating his arrival. When Ashley left us, I said, "Welcome back, Gus. You look a bit like Santa with your bag."

He did have a white beard, but it was short and trim. And unlike Santa, Gus was lean and ripped. He clearly had some Viking in him—tall and blue-eyed. "*Ja*," he said, "a bag full of goodies for Meggy."

But the contents of the bag were actually for *him*. I helped him unpack it, as it was stuffed tight with protective gear that reminded me of a hockey goalie's uniform, but on steroids. The whole point of these lessons was for me to attack him—mercilessly—as if defending myself from an assailant.

He reminded me, "If you feel threatened, and running isn't an option, don't hesitate to fight back, even if the bad guy is bigger than you—because you're quicker, and you're smarter. And don't be ashamed to 'fight like a girl.' It can be very effective. Bite him—but *mean* it. Bite hard and hang on. Bite off an ear, if you can get to it. If he forces his penis near your mouth, you know *exactly* what to do. Take off the tip—and make *him* scream like a girl. Trust me, he'll back off damn quick."

"I'm not sure if I could do that."

"Of *course* you could. You could also scratch. Dig deep. Put those pretty nails to *use*. And don't forget about eye gouging. I'm not talking about Three Stooges horseplay—do it to save your life. You need to aim *beyond* the eyeballs. Aim for the brain, even if you break a finger or two doing it."

"Jesus, Gus."

With a soft smile, he said, "Hopefully, it won't come to that, Meggy. But if it ever does, just remember that you have powerful weapons of last resort. In any event, we won't be practicing *those* techniques today."

"Thank God."

"*Ja*, thank God." He laughed. "Fortunately, we have my sure-fire Magnuström Method."

Wryly, I asked, "Did you ever get around to filing that with the trademark office?"

"*Nej*, but it's on the to-do list." While Gus strapped on his protective gear, he continued his lecture: "There are many ways—many possible moves—to fight off a bad guy, but if you're standing face-to-face, up close, your best option for turning the tables and dominating the situation is ... what, Meggy?"

I dutifully responded, "The Magnuström Method."

"*Ja*. And what does that involve?"

"Knee to the balls, foot to the ankle." It was like a mantra. I'd said it—he'd said it—hundreds of times.

He nodded. "Very good. Granted, a kick with your foot, with a hard shoe, might do more damage to his groin, but it's also more likely to throw you off balance and land you flat on the ground—where you do *not* want to be. So: Use your knee. Stabilize yourself by holding on to him with both hands, then lift one foot behind you, and shove your knee directly into the target. *Give it all you've got.* At this point, he's off guard, but you don't wait for part B. In a single, fluid motion, raise your kicking leg to the side to gain momentum, then drive your foot into the side of his ankle. *Give it all you've got.* Let go of him, and he *will* fall to the ground—pissed, but temporarily helpless. Then you run." Gus paused before adding, "Or, if you'd prefer, stick around and beat the crap out of him. Better to run, though."

I nodded. "Got it: knee to the balls, foot to the ankle."

"Okay." Gus, now fully padded and protected, rose up in all his bad-guy manliness and approached me aggressively.

When he drew near, I grabbed his sleeves and summoned everything I had: knee to the balls, foot to the ankle.

And he landed on the mat with a stunning *thud*. The dumbbells clattered in a nearby rack.

When he caught his breath, I reached for his hand and helped him up. "Again," he said.

Again the dumbbells clattered.

After another round of this, he said, "Okay now: shoes."

I had been barefoot in my gi, but since there was no way of predicting what my state of dress would be when a potential assailant might pounce, I always practiced these moves first without shoes, then in sneakers, then in heels.

The Magnuström Method worked its magic regardless of what I was wearing, including the third time I downed Gus while wearing four-inch stilettos.

"Zowie," he said, writhing on the mat, panting. Looking up, he told me, "That was a good one, Meggy. Gold star."

My weekly session with Dr. Faye Rubin was scheduled for that afternoon at one. We weren't able to meet for lunch first, so I went down to her office on the eleventh floor.

When I entered her waiting room a few minutes early, I got a strong whiff of something like Parmesan cheese, with overtones of oregano. Marlene wasn't behind the reception window, so I assumed she was back in the break room, where she'd probably microwaved leftover pizza or lasagna for lunch. It smelled quite good, turning my thoughts to Italian food and, of course, gelato. I hadn't attempted spumoni lately...

"Oh! Mrs. Auric—I didn't hear you come in," said Marlene, appearing behind her window. Could I possibly get your signature on a couple of updated forms?"

"Certainly." When I stepped to the window, Marlene leaned over her desk to give me the paperwork and explain what was needed. At close range, her breath had the overpowering smell of industrial-strength mint, with lingering notes of the masked garlic—nudging the gelato fantasy far from my mind.

"Thank you," she said. "Dr. Faye will be right with you."

I had no sooner sat down again when Faye popped out from the inner sanctum and welcomed me to come back with her.

When we were situated in her office, she jogged a few files on her desk, plucked one out, and set the others aside. Tipping her glasses low on her nose, she said, "Meghan Daley Auric...," and opened my notes. "We last met six days ago, on Tuesday. How was your week?"

"Eventful."

"Expound on that, please."

"Well," I said with a touch of pride, "I left the building two times, as I did the week before."

"Good." She smiled. "Tell me about those adventures."

"My first outing was on Thursday, but I need to back up a bit. Last time we met, I told you that I'd learned that John White— the man who betrayed me long ago at United Insurance—had resurfaced as Julian Wentworth, the Senate candidate. I actually encountered him at a Towne Club luncheon on Wednesday."

"*That* must've been tense."

"It was. He now looks *entirely* different than before, and I didn't let on that I knew his secret, of course. So, when we were introduced, I was cordial—although I didn't go so far as to pretend I supported his politics. Interestingly, his speech sorta bombed that afternoon. But the next day, Thursday, it was a different matter when he held a rally in the park across from the building."

Faye nodded. "I saw the story in yesterday's paper. Were you there?"

I nodded. "That was outing number one. Granted, I didn't go far—just across the street—but with the crowds and the milling, it took a *lot* of resolve on my part. Then I threw up."

Faye gave me a wink. "Proud of you, Meghan."

"Thank you. Now, since you've read the story, you're aware that Wentworth was pandering to the religious right, and the crowd ate it up."

Faye shuddered. "Hideous."

"And you're also aware that there's some controversy over Wentworth's background—his education and such."

She studied me for a moment. "Yes. The 'credible source.' Was that you, Meghan?"

Bug-eyed, I asked, "*Why* does everyone figure that out? Wentworth's opponent, Celia Gamarra, saw through it. Then, last night, Wentworth himself called to tell me that *he* saw through it. And get this—he threatened my life."

Faye sat back, astonished. "Surely, you've reported this to the police."

I shook my head. "Not yet." Then I thought of something. "Can you get away for an extended lunch tomorrow?"

"Possibly. Why?"

"The Towne Club is hosting Celia Gamarra as a speaker—equal time, since Wentworth spoke last week—and I have a table, so I hope you can join us. But the point is: Celia's husband, Nick, is sure to be there, and he's the sheriff's detective who's been investigating my penthouse break-in. I don't know how much I can actually *tell* him about my history with Wentworth, but I should at least lay some groundwork and make him aware of the threat."

"Yes," agreed Faye, "you definitely *should*. And yes, I'd be delighted to attend."

"Wonderful." I made a note on my phone to update my table logistics with the club.

During this pause, Faye used her desk phone to ask Marlene to juggle Tuesday's appointments, allowing her to get away for a long lunch.

When she hung up, she said to me, "You told me you'd had an 'eventful' week—but a death threat really pushes the limit. What did Wentworth say to you?"

"He told me to back off—because my life depends on it."

"How did you react?"

"Oddly, I found the threat anticlimactic, as if I'd known it was coming—because I was *already* infuriated about something he said earlier. When I told him that I knew he was John White and that I knew what he'd done, he said, 'You don't know *shit*. You were a crazy bitch back *then*; you're even worse *now*.' He also referred to my 'fucked-up fantasies.'"

"Unfortunately," said Faye, "this is *not* too surprising. When you called him out on his misdoings, you gained the upper hand. So he not only belittled you; he attempted to make you doubt your own memories of what had happened. It's a common—but desperate—technique."

"Gaslighting," I said.

"Precisely." She grinned. "But it sounds as if it didn't work. It sounds as if his pomposity only steeled your resolve."

I noted, "You do have a way with words, Faye. No wonder I gladly pay you so much."

"Thank you. But seriously—regarding the threat—if you haven't filed a police report, how *are* you dealing with this?"

"I had a self-defense lesson this morning. I have an appointment with my lawyer this afternoon. And last week, a new security system was installed in the penthouse."

Faye scribbled in her notes. "Very good. Proactive and appropriate. Now, then: you said you had two excursions from the building last week. What was the second one?" Looking up from her notes, she added, "And I hope it wasn't as menacing."

Glibly, I told her, "At least I didn't throw up."

She laughed. "That's a good sign. What happened?"

"Last time we met, I told you about Dustin St. James, the artist, correct?"

She checked her notes. "Yes. You've commissioned him to do a portrait of Eugene. He has a precocious young daughter. And, to use your own words, he's 'hotter than hell.'"

I affirmed, "That would be Dustin. His daughter, Nova, had really clicked with me when we first met, so Dustin suggested getting together, the three of us, for dinner. I invited them here Friday evening, and we ate in the building—at Tableau Magenta."

Faye's brows arched. "Nice. How was it?"

"Superb, as always. Except, he pre-arranged to pop for the check, which mortified me—but it was also sort of, I dunno, *heartwarming*."

"Why were you mortified, Meghan? Are you simply uncomfortable accepting gifts? Or did it make you feel you weren't in control?"

I pondered this awhile. "Now, *that's* a good question. Generally, I have no problem accepting gifts. And I haven't had much experience being 'in control'—not during my time with Eugene, certainly. But yes, I think I did need to feel in control of the situation on Friday night."

"Why?"

"Because I didn't know where the evening might lead. Because I didn't even know where I *wanted* it to lead. But I wanted to retain the option of backing out, and to do that, I had to be in control. So the possibility of *not* paying the check—that never even crossed my mind."

With a soft smile, Faye asked, "And then what happened? Where did the evening lead?"

I grinned. "It led straight back to his studio—after dropping off Nova with her grandparents."

Faye sat back in her chair, tenting her fingers beneath her chin. "We psychotherapists have a highly technical term for this sort of situation: Did you do the dirty deed?"

"Indeed we did."

"Did you feel pressured?"

"Not in the least. When we arrived at his place, he asked if I wanted him to drive me home. But I declined his offer, asking, 'Weren't you going to show me your sketches?'"

Faye sounded skeptical: "Did you *see* any sketches?"

"Not till the next morning."

"Hmm." Leaning over her desk now, taking notes, she asked, "So then. Your overall experience that night—on a scale of one to ten—how was it?"

"Nine, easily. Ten, possibly. It was up there."

"Oy. But you said he's gay, didn't you?"

I waggled both hands. "That's what I *thought*, but I guess he's versatile or 'bi' or 'fluid' or maybe pansexual ... or *whatever*." Then I paused. "Uh-oh."

"Yes...?"

I counted back on my fingers. "Four days ago, on Thursday, I met with Adam Hudson. I told you about him—he's the son of my two best friends from college, Theo and Lila Hudson, and he's always called me Aunt Meg, and he's a lawyer now."

Faye recalled, "And he's gay."

"Yes. And he's coming over later this afternoon because I've hired him to help me sort out the legal ramifications of my past association with that asshole who now calls himself Julian Wentworth. In particular, I need to get a better idea of what could happen if I blow the whistle."

"You're considering that?"

"Of *course*. The last time I saw you, Faye, I simply wanted to get *back* at Wentworth—for what he did to me as John White. I wanted revenge. But now? I have a pretty clear picture of what Wentworth is up to politically and socially, so I'm just *itching* to bring him down—for the common good. But if I try to do that, regardless of whether my motive is noble or not, there will be serious consequences for *me*. And that's why I've retained Adam Hudson."

Faye nodded. "Okay. But I'm confused: while you were talking about Dustin St. James and his sexual inclinations, you stopped yourself and said, 'uh-oh.'"

I groaned. "Last week, I was convinced that Dustin was gay and decided that my fantasies about him were off-base and would only cause me grief. So, when I met with Adam on Thursday, I tried my hand at a bit of matchmaking. I gave him Dustin's contact info, thinking the two of them might make a cute couple—also thinking that Adam might make a darling 'second daddy' for little Nova. But now? Look at it this way: I tried to set up my best friends' son with another man I've since had sex with."

Faye echoed my earlier assessment: "Uh-oh."

Objectively, there was nothing "wrong" with all of this. I was not actually Adam Hudson's aunt, nor were we any sort of blood relatives. And even if we *were* related (which we were not), we faced no legal, ethical, or (to my mind) moral proscription against enjoying the "company" of the same man. Still, I could not deny the ick factor.

At four thirty, when Adam got off the elevator in the penthouse entry hall, he set down his briefcase and pulled me into a big, sloppy hug. "I've been worried all day about your text—and so sorry I couldn't get here sooner." He kissed my cheek.

This gentle intimacy, while perfectly innocent and conveying only affection, did nothing to assuage my squeamish thoughts of setting him up for a tumble with Dustin St. James. I assured Adam, "You have *nothing* to apologize for. I can't expect you to drop everything the instant I call. But I'm happy you're here now."

He stepped back, holding me at arm's length and looking into my eyes. "What happened, Aunt Meg?" He seemed even more fraught than I was.

I suggested, "We'd better sit down." Then I led him into the living room, where we sat at the game table—resuming the same seats we'd occupied during our first meeting, the week before.

Since he'd come directly from a day in court, his bulging briefcase was stuffed to capacity, with its strap barely latched. Before setting it under the table, he retrieved a file and legal pad. Then he leaned forward on his elbows, asking again, "What happened?"

Warily, I said, "Now, don't freak out, but Julian Wentworth phoned me last night, and—"

"Was he calling about the story in the *Times*?"

"Yes. And—well, I recorded the call. Want to hear it?"

"Of course."

I set my phone on the table, explaining, "The first voice on the line is Wentworth's campaign manager. Then Wentworth himself takes over. Listen."

I played the entirety of the conversation, which ended with Wentworth saying, "So back off. Your life depends on it." *Click.*

Adam was gobsmacked. After rattling his head to clear his thoughts, he said, "First, smart move to record the call, Aunt Meg. This alone could end his campaign. But more important— he threatened your *life*. Have you reported this?"

"No, not yet. And you already know the reason why I haven't done so: he and I are equally dependent on each other remaining silent. I'll be at an event tomorrow where I intend to talk to De-tective Gamarra, Celia's husband—not sure how much I can ac-tually *tell* Nick, but he needs to know we've had 'developments.'"

"He sure does," said Adam. "You're referring to tomorrow's luncheon at the Towne Club, correct?"

"Right. Your parents will be there, at my table—but please don't mention this to them."

"Whatever you say, Aunt Meg." When he finished writing a note, he said, "It might be a good idea if I had a copy of that recording, in case anything ... happens."

I nodded, "That's an excellent idea—but I'm not sure how to share it with you."

"May I have your phone for a moment?"

I handed it over.

He did some tapping and typing, then waited briefly—till his own phone buzzed. "Got it," he said, returning my phone.

Intrigued by this bit of wizardry, I asked, "Can you show me how you did that?"

"Of course." He ran me through the process—simple enough— then asked, "Do you feel you're in any immediate danger?"

"Honestly, no. I think the threat was a scare tactic and a warn-ing. I doubt if anyone is lurking out there, gunning for me."

"I hope you're right. But needless to say, from this point forward, the byword needs to be 'caution.'"

"Understood." I told him about the self-defense lessons and the new security system, also reminding him, "And now I've got *you* working on my behalf. So I feel well prepared for ... come what may."

He nodded, smiled. Opening his folder, he told me, "Following up from last week's meeting, I have a few things to report. First of all, I've been studying Eugene's estate plan and the revocable trust—which became *ir*-revocable upon his death. Nothing peculiar about it. As stated, you are indeed named as his trustee and principal heir. Granted, the provisions regarding secrecy of the insurance fraud are, shall we say, *strange* for a document of this sort, but you had not violated those provisions at the time Eugene died, so you 'passed the test,' as it were. And his assets have passed to you."

"But then," I reminded him, "there's that new codicil."

He dug it out. "Weird, isn't it? A single sentence: 'If, subsequent to my death, Meghan reveals that I played any role in exonerating her from crimes she committed while in the employ of Fairview United Insurance, her inheritance from me can be contested by my first wife, Bibiana, and my son, Eugene Junior.'"

I said, "I'm not even sure what that *means*—that my inheritance 'can be contested.'"

"Right," said Adam. "*Anyone* is free to contest the terms of *any* will or trust. Their challenge may have no merit, but they don't need 'permission' to try it, as implied by the codicil." He waggled the sheet of paper. "Frankly, I have no idea what the mechanism would be for enforcing this."

"The mechanism," I said, "would be Ronda Trask, who drew

everything up—except for the codicil, which was Eugene's doing. As the executor, she seemed a bit stumped by it herself, but she called me 'a smart cookie' and simply advised me to keep my skirts clean, so to speak."

Adam thumbed the edge of his folder. "From what I hear, Trask is the sort of person you cross at considerable peril."

"Yep. So ignoring the codicil would be ... perilous."

Through a squint of concern, Adam asked, "Big picture—Ronda Trask—do you trust her?"

"Largely, yes, but not completely. If I did, I wouldn't have hired *you*, right?" Speaking more to myself than to him, I added, "There's a fine line between caution and paranoia—and I seem to have lost sight of it."

"Okay," said Adam, moving on, "aside from the codicil, I found nothing peculiar about the estate plan. But I did some research on a different matter, and the results were, in my opinion, *beyond* peculiar."

Intrigued, I asked, "Regarding what?"

"The insurance scam. From what you've told me, that whole 'episode' at United was the catalyst for everything that's happened to you since. Consider: John White's betrayal. Eugene's ironhanded marriage proposal. Your struggle with agoraphobia. The codicil from the grave. And now, Julian Wentworth making death threats. *All* of this goes back to the insurance scam."

"Christ," I said, wagging my head, "if only I'd been a little more *mature* back then. If only I'd refused to get involved with the scheme—things would be entirely different right now. Talk about a fork in the road. Talk about dumb decisions and unforeseen consequences."

"True enough," said Adam, wise beyond his years, "but the course of your life has also had its rewards."

I glanced at my surroundings. "Yes, perhaps." Then I shrugged. "I hesitate to ask, but what was so peculiar about your research of the insurance scheme?"

"I found ... *nothing*. I figured that a scam like that, involving the loss of policyholders' lives, would surely leave at least *bread-crumbs* of a trail—committee reports, lawsuits, class-action payouts, news stories, or even just rumors. But I couldn't find a thing. Granted, that was pushing thirty years ago, but the internet was up and running by then, and I wouldn't think it *possible* for all traces of the scheme to be scrubbed from cyberspace. It's as if it never happened."

"It *happened*," I assured him. "Eugene said he'd get everything fixed. Ronda Trask was his fixer. Apparently she earned her keep."

This reminded me of the baffling disappearance of John White and his reappearance as Julian Wentworth. The makeover, the transformation, the degree from Oxford, all of it defied logic and probability. But nothing, it seemed, was ultimately impossible—not if you had the money, the connections, and a deeply devious mindset.

"One more thing to report on," said Adam, grinning.

"What?" I couldn't imagine ...

"I owe you a huge thank-you, Aunt Meg, for putting me in touch with Dustin St. James."

I gasped, but disguised it as a mild cough. Recovering, I asked blithely, "Oh?"

"I was spending some extra time in the office on Saturday, and then things got quiet that afternoon, so I decided to try giving him a call."

Saturday, I thought. *The day after my night at Dustin's studio.*

"So," I said, "I assume you reached him ..."

"Yeah. He sounded nice enough. I told him I'd read the

profile of him in *ArchitecAmerica*, which in fact I'd dug up. I apologized for reaching out but wondered if—*maybe*—he'd like to meet for coffee or something."

Fussing with the hair at my temple, I asked, "Did you, uh, mention *me*?"

Adam paused. "*Sorry*, Aunt Meg. I know you said I could use your name for an introduction, but while I was on the phone with him, I felt it might sound sorta lame—like I was being *set up* or something. So I kept you out of it. Hope you don't mind."

"Not at *all*."

"As it turned out, he was interested. So we met for a coffee date on Sunday morning—yesterday—that big Starbucks down the block from here."

"Nice. How'd it go?"

"Fine. Great. I was a little nervous, wondering how he'd react when he saw that I'm Black, but *no* problem—I could tell he sorta dug it. We talked for a half hour or so. Then he needed to pick up his daughter somewhere. No follow-up plans, but we agreed to stay in touch."

"And...? Any more phone calls?"

"Not yet. Thing is, I wasn't quite sure what to make of him. While we talked, I picked up a strange kind of vibe—maybe I'm just not used to the 'artist thing.'"

I nodded. "They see the world differently. Some people, non-artists, can find it difficult to connect with that."

"Yeah, maybe that's it. Still, I liked the guy and thought I wouldn't mind seeing him again. So I went back to the office on Sunday afternoon, preparing for court today, but I took a break and did a little more research on Dustin, just to see what would pop up on LexisNexis—an information database that lots of law firms use."

NOT OUR CROWD, DARLING

With a laugh, I said, "No convictions, I hope."

"No, of course not. Nothing like *that*."

Something in Adam's tone made me ask, "But ...?"

Adam seemed to weigh his words. "You mentioned to me that Dustin had a husband who died a year or so ago. Did you know that, earlier, he had a wife in Connecticut, while he was teaching at Yale?"

"Yes, Dustin told me all of that. His wife's name was Crystal. Their daughter is ten now. Her name is Nova."

Adam nodded. "And the wife died."

I recalled, "Dustin told me he was 'unlucky in love.'"

"That might be true," said Adam, "but he was *quite* lucky to have jumbo insurance policies on both spouses, who each died within two years of marrying him."

I felt my brow pinch. "Was any of this deemed suspicious?"

"The second insurance company thought so. And on the face of it, the circumstances are *obviously* suspicious. But the investigation went nowhere—they've got nothing on him."

"Hmm. Nonetheless, that's rather perplexing ..."

"It is," agreed Adam. "I firmly believe in the presumption of innocence, and I'm willing to give Dustin the benefit of the doubt. But just the same, I've kinda cooled on the idea of getting involved with him. Any thoughts, Aunt Meg?"

"I think you should follow your heart, Adam."

On the one hand, I'd dodged a bullet: I no longer needed to fret that my "nephew" would be bedding Dustin. On the other hand, what in God's name had I gotten *myself* into?

CHAPTER
TWELVE

Ashley asked me, "Any word from da Vinci yet?"

I turned to her with an admonishing look. "His name was *not* 'da Vinci.' As any art historian will tell you, he is correctly referred to as 'Leonardo.'"

Because Leonardo had painted the *Mona Lisa*, Ashley knew that he was, among other things, a famed portrait artist. And because he was probably the *only* portrait artist known to Ashley, she had borrowed his name (or what she *thought* was his name) as an alias for Dustin St. James, whom I had commissioned to paint a portrait of my late husband. Get it? While this bit of whimsy struck me as too cute by half—and I made a showy point of bristling whenever she said it—I also found it rather endearing.

We were at work again in my bedroom on Tuesday morning, the day after I'd learned how Dustin had seemingly profited from the death of not just one spouse, but two. Ashley persisted: "Any word from him yet?"

"No." I plucked another stale condom from one of Eugene's pockets and trashed it.

"Well?" she said. "Just *call* him." With a teasing tone, she reminded me, "It's not considered unladylike anymore."

"I *know* that." My inflection sounded testier than I'd meant. I exhaled a long, noisy breath, calming myself. "Look, Ashley, it's sweet of you to take an interest in what I'm doing—or not doing—with Dustin, but he's *not* at the top of my mind. I have a lot going on at the moment."

While she was well aware of my self-defense lessons, she knew nothing of the death threat. She stepped over a pile of clothes on the floor and touched my arm. "I'm really sorry, Meghan. I know how busy you are with the Senate campaign. Work before pleasure, huh?"

"Something like that."

Resolutely, she told me through a smile, "Well, I hope your gal wins."

"Thank you. So I assume you're *voting* for Celia?"

She looked befuddled. "I've never voted."

"*Ashley*, you're twenty-*six*. Don't you want to have a *say* in your future? How you vote is none of my business, but don't let other folks make decisions *for* you." Grinning, I added, "I'm imparting this advice from the perspective of my advanced years and hard-earned wisdom."

She laughed. "Advanced years! You're looking pretty buff to *me*, Grammaw."

She wasn't the first to describe me as "buff"—and my mind reeled with sense memories of the last time I'd heard it.

Later that morning, while putting myself together for the Towne Club luncheon, my phone buzzed with an arriving text. It was from Dustin: GOT A MINUTE TO TALK? PLEASE CALL WHEN CONVENIENT.

My first inclination, I confess, was to pounce on it. It had been four days since I'd seen him on Friday, and it was three days since we'd emailed each other the following morning, concerning his sketches. I did not, however, want to appear too eager and fawning. After all, the basis of our relationship was business—the commission of the painting—and I was the customer, so I would reply at my leisure.

That said, our relationship now had an added dimension, beyond business, and I didn't want to give the impression that I was playing hard-to-get. (God forbid—even if I had an inkling that he might be sizing me up as target number three.) So I decided to reply within an hour, before heading down to the club.

Forty-five minutes later, when I finished puttering in my dressing room, I walked through the bedroom, telling Ashley, "I'll be leaving in a few minutes. Help yourself to lunch when you want."

"Thanks, Meghan. Have a nice time." She'd found another pair of spats, which she dropped in the pile being saved for the community theater.

I descended the stairs to the lower level of the penthouse and entered the library, where I had conversed with Detective Gamarra on Sunday afternoon. The room had a fresh appeal to me since I'd noticed the vibrant effect of the beds of lettuce beyond the windows. Feeling clandestine, I closed the door, took out my phone, and sat on the loveseat beneath the impressionist painting of wheat fields. Then I typed a response to Dustin's text: IF IT'S A GOOD TIME TO TALK, I HAVE A FEW MINUTES.

Within ten seconds, my phone buzzed. Connecting the call, I answered, "Hello, Dustin?"

"Madame Auric?" he said playfully. I pictured him lolling in his studio, taking a break from some project—phone in one hand, the other flourishing an artist's brush like a long cigarette holder. I envisioned that glorious mane of wavy black hair. Frumpy old Leonardo, indeed!

"All's well?" he asked.

"Busy. Lucky to still be in one piece." My small talk may have sounded banal, but he wasn't aware of the weighty truth behind it.

He said, "The reason I called—other than missing the sound of your voice—I wanted to give you a progress report on Eugene's portrait. Still very much at the sketching stage, just working through a few ideas. One of which, I keep coming back to. But it's a little offbeat, and you might not care for it."

I reminded him, "The horse idea—now, that was *plenty* offbeat, and I loved it."

"So hear me out. The horse was a compositional consideration—also a bit tongue-in-cheek. But now, working with the sketches, I've realized that the horse also works *thematically*, as well as compositionally, with the scale of the eight-by-eight canvas. Visually, it's so *monumental*."

That word kept coming up. I couldn't help thinking of campaign manager Kyle Pollard's threat of a "monumental" defamation suit.

"Anyway," Dustin was saying, "the more I studied Eugene's photos, the more I visualized him in—*wait for it*—Napoleonic garb." He paused. "Reactions?"

Pondering this, I thought aloud, "Not cartoonish. More like magical realism. Heroic—but with a dark side."

"Wow. You've read my mind, Meghan."

"Then I think, *yes*—you should develop that idea. I'd love to see what you do with it."

"Wonderful. I'll get busy and let you know when I have something." With a soft laugh, he added, "Nova keeps asking if you and I have talked."

I thought, *So does my housekeeper.* But I told Dustin, "Well, you can now report to Nova that we have indeed talked. Give her a kiss for me?"

"Absolutely—and she'll love that you asked me to do it. She's fond of you, Meghan. Maybe another get-together sometime?"

"Sure. Why not?"

Awkwardly, he said, "And, uh, *this* time, I won't palm her off to the grandparents."

I laughed—but found little joy in this detail.

He added, "Unless, of course, you'd prefer otherwise. It's your decision."

"I'll need to give that some thought." (It wouldn't take *much* thought. My druthers were a total no-brainer.)

So. I was satisfied, at least temporarily, that Dustin harbored no fiendish schemes—other than to stuff my paunchy dead husband into a Napoleon costume. This I *had* to see.

I found myself laughing about it as I got off the elevator on the ground floor of the building and made my way across the main concourse, heading toward the grand staircase that rose to the Towne Club entrance on the second floor.

To avoid any check-in confusion, I had asked my luncheon guests to meet me at the foot of the stairs. And there they were: reporter Chase Unger, my friends Theo and Lila Hudson, and psychiatrist Faye Rubin. They had apparently figured out that they were all waiting for *me* and had subsequently introduced themselves, as they were now facing each other, chatting amiably.

Lila was first to spot me. "Meg, honey! We *love* your friends. We should have another cookout—both Chase and Faye are most *definitely* invited."

Theo said, "Great idea, sweets, but maybe after the election. Things are getting hectic."

Lila gave him a look. "It'll be *cold* in November."

He raised his hands in playful surrender. "Okay, okay, I give in—whenever."

Taking Chase's arm, I said to the others, "I assume you've met my young reporter friend from the *Consensus Times*. Chase Unger wrote the 'tomato lady' story—as well as that scorcher on Saturday about Wentworth's rally in the park."

Faye said, "Truly *splendid* work, Chase. I'll be watching for your byline."

As they sang his praises, Chase leaned close, saying, "Thank you, Meghan."

I suggested to everyone, "Shall we?" And we climbed the stairs together, joining the throng at the club entrance.

Once inside, we were approached by waiters in the lobby, bearing trays of iced tea, lemonade, and mimosas.

We made our choices, gabbed, and mingled a bit, but the five of us didn't wander far from each other. I kept an eye out for Bebe, who had not met my guests but would be at our table, needing introductions. I didn't see her, though—and hoped she wasn't in the bar, pounding martinis before noon. Then I spotted Everett, the handsome manager with epaulets, wending toward us through the crowd, and I assumed he would step me aside to follow up regarding our previous conversation—about exploring the possibility of more freely enjoying each other's company. While I was reluctant to advance that topic (not there and then), I was a bit dismayed when the shoulder he tapped was not mine, but Theo's.

"Mr. Hudson," he said, "I wonder if I might bother you for a moment."

"Yes?"

"I'm the Towne Club manager, Everett Burke, and today's speaker, Mrs. Gamarra, asked if you could join her briefly in the library."

I found it telling that although they had not previously met,

Everett had made a beeline through the throng when he approached Theo and addressed him with confidence. Clearly, Theo had been described to Everett as Black—and Theo happened to be the only Black man in the very crowded room. Such was life in the rarefied surroundings of Fairview Towne Club.

Theo told the rest of us. "Duty calls—strategy session, I guess. I'll catch up with you." And he left, with Everett leading the way.

Then I *did* feel a tap on my shoulder.

I turned. "Ah. Hello, Gene—and Bebe, too. I was wondering when you'd appear."

Eugene Junior told me, "We got waylaid in the bar." His hands were empty, but Bebe carried a martini.

She made an effort not to spill it—but it sloshed over the rim and wetted her wrinkled fingers as she said to me, "So here we go: Act two. Curtain going up."

"Beg pardon?" I asked. "Act two?"

"Wentworth was *last* week," she explained, "and that dreadful Gamarra creature is *this* week."

"If that's how you feel about her, Bebe, I'm surprised you're here today."

"Wouldn't miss it for the world," she assured me. "I'm so *terribly* open-minded."

"*Oh*," I said, minding my manners. "Introductions are in order. Bebe Auric and Gene, you already know Chase Unger, from last week, but I'd like you to meet two dear friends of mine. First, this is Lila Hudson, whose husband, Theo, is also joining us, but right now he's backstage, so to speak, with Celia Gamarra. He's involved with her campaign." I turned to Bebe, adding with a jolly laugh, "So *behave* yourself."

Ignoring me, Bebe moved her martini to her left hand and

extended her right hand (wet with gin) to Lila, exchanging a lady-jiggle. "A pleasure," Bebe said, then looked away.

"Also," I said, "I'd like you to meet Dr. Faye Rubin, who truly keeps me sane—she's a psychiatrist."

Bebe cocked her head, studying Faye. "Dr. *Rubin*, is it?" When Faye nodded with a smile, Bebe took a sip with her left hand, then extended her right, repeating the jiggle. "A pleasure."

Faye turned to Lila, standing next to her, and they resumed an earlier conversation.

Bebe, eyeing them, leaned into me, spilling a bit of gin on my sleeve. Under her breath, she asked, "Whatever *were* you thinking? Not our crowd, darling—if you catch my drift."

I caught her drift: Lila was Black, and Faye was Jewish.

I must have looked appalled by her comment because Eugene Junior tugged me aside, telling me, "You ain't seen nothin' yet. Wait till you get a load of who Mumsy invited to our table."

This ... did not sound good.

Our table had grown. It still occupied its prime position, front and left, but instead of the previous tidy four-top, the circle of white linen was now considerably wider and set for eight. (I had four guests. I myself brought our party up to five. Bebe and Gene made seven. And the eighth setting, still unaccounted for, was Bebe's mystery guest.)

Bebe and I, the two Mrs. Aurics, assumed our usual seats, which provided the best angle for viewing the head table and the onstage podium. I put Chase at my other side, as before, giving him a clear shot for pictures. Faye sat next to him, and Lila sat next to Faye—convenient for girl talk. The next open chair was saved for Theo, who had not yet reappeared.

Bebe reserved the seat next to her for her mystery guest. Which meant that her son, Eugene Junior, ended up at the one remaining chair, between the two saved seats, facing me across the table, but with his back to the stage.

When we had settled in, two servers circled the table in their impeccable gray uniforms, unfurling napkins, pouring water, and placing at each setting the first course, a chilled autumn bisque of yellow tomatoes and puréed parsnips, garnished with squash blossoms.

As at last week's luncheon, there were perhaps two hundred people seated in the ballroom, and the crowd's muted conversation crescendoed a bit as Celia Gamarra and her party entered from a side door without fanfare and seated themselves at the head table in front of the stage. Theo came in with them but would not be sitting with them, so the manager directed him over to our table, where he took the unoccupied seat between his wife and Eugene Junior.

"Welcome back," I told him. He and Junior had quickly introduced themselves, so I now said, "Bebe, I'd like you to meet Theo Hudson, Lila's husband. And Theo, this is Bebe Auric, who was Eugene's first wife."

Theo instantly rose from his chair and came over to shake Bebe's hand, telling her, "An honor, Mrs. Auric—I've heard so many nice things about you."

"A pleasure," she said dryly, then tried a spoonful of the soup, wrinkling her nose. (Though beautifully presented, the bisque must have been an experiment of the chef—which would surely not be repeated.)

As Theo returned to his chair, I asked him, "Is Celia psyched up for her presentation? We can't wait to hear what she has to say."

Bebe snorted. I elbowed her.

"Sure," said Theo, "Celia's always well prepared. But there was a bit of confusion behind the scenes. Sheriff Hewitt showed up—unexpected—so there was some last-minute juggling of plans, to get him seated at the head table."

I grimaced. He was easy to spot up there, forever the man in uniform—to my eye, the thorn among the roses. I asked, "What's *he* doing here?"

"He's our *sheriff*," said Bebe with high umbrage. "He's welcome anywhere, anytime."

I snorted. "Whatever you say, Bebe. Sure, he was here last week—with Wentworth—they're in *bed* together, so to speak. But trust me: Tin Badge Hewitt isn't here to support Celia."

With a smug smile, Bebe suggested, "You might do well to make note of that, Meg. The sheriff knows what's best for our county." She nudged her soup aside and centered the martini glass in front of her.

Amiably, Theo said, "Reasonable people may differ, but it's always wise to hear each other out, Mrs. Auric." He was speaking to Mrs. Auric the *elder*, I noted. But she wouldn't even deign to look at Theo. He added, "And if you compare the two candidates' positions, you'll find that Celia is *far* more friendly to women's issues."

Gene, sitting next to him, said with a pleasant laugh, "*Touché*, Mr. Hudson." And he raised his iced tea to clink Theo's glass. (I was relieved to see that Gene had not been day-drinking with his mother this time.)

Through a snarl, Bebe told him, "Zip it, Junior."

A voice from behind said, "Excuse me, Mrs. Auric?"

We both turned. "Kyle!" said Bebe. "You made it."

It was none other than Kyle Pollard, Julian Wentworth's campaign manager. At the previous week's luncheon, he had fawned over Bebe, who, in turn, had practically drooled on him while he hunkered at her chair, exuding his Ivy League polish and blathering about Wentworth's traditional values. He'd clearly made an impression on her, as he was now her special guest. He'd also made quite the impression on *me*, just two days earlier, when this snot-nosed dweeb phoned to threaten me with a libel suit.

Bebe patted the empty chair next to her, saying to Kyle, "I saved you a seat." After he sat, she leaned to tell him, "Skip the soup—it's crap."

My guests and I stared at him, agog. I was amazed that Bebe had found it appropriate to invite him. Junior simply sat back in his chair, crossing his arms and chuckling while watching our reaction to his mother's stunt.

And it *was* a stunt—this was a brazen and deliberate attempt to provoke a bit of discord and draw attention to herself. Having seized the limelight, she hogged the moment and snapped open her purse. "Oh!" she said to Kyle. "I thought you might put this to good use." She flourished a check before handing it to him.

Kyle glanced at it, then his eyes bugged. "Mrs. *Auric*—you're amazing. On behalf of Julian's campaign, I thank you."

Theo and Lila looked at each other, concerned.

Watching this interplay, Gene pulled a checkbook from the inside pocket of his sport coat, clicked a pen, filled in an amount, signed the check, ripped it out, and handed it to Theo, telling him, "I don't know how to fill in the payee, but I'm sure you can take care of it."

Theo looked at it, laughing. "I can indeed. Thank you, Eugene."

Following Junior's lead, I opened my purse and wrote a check. So did Faye Rubin. After we passed the checks down to Theo, he tucked all three of them into his jacket, looking *very* pleased.

When the main course was served—a chicken-and-cheese thing—the head table merely picked at it, as was customary, while a few of the dignitaries got up from their seats to roam the dining room and glad-hand the guests.

As had happened the prior week, Sheriff Hewitt sauntered over to circulate at our table first. He spent a long minute or two crouching between Bebe and Kyle—smiling and laughing and chawing—then his various items of black leather creaked as he stood again. He made his way slowly around the table, chatting up Junior and each of my guests, in constant campaign mode for his own office, even though he could not be challenged again for another three years.

Finally, when he arrived at my chair, I turned to hear what he had to say. But he said nothing. Instead, he studied me with a soft smile and a fatherly gaze. Then he raised a hand, giving me a few slow wags of his index finger, as if I'd been naughty, as if warning me. And two fingers below that, he wore a heavy fraternal-style ring with a sizable diamond, indistinguishable from another ring I'd seen a few days earlier. His grin was so cocky, I was tempted to stand and give him a taste of the Magnuström Method. (But of course I didn't.) Then he winked and walked away.

Bebe had seen none of this, sitting with her back to me while engrossed with Kyle Pollard. She was saying, "And there's plenty more where *that* came from."

This left me feeling...not exactly angry, but troubled. I leaned into their conversation, telling Bebe softly, "If you're talking about money, we *both* know where it came from. Everything we've got—it came from Eugene."

She shrugged. "Of course it did. He was always 'the provider.' He loved that role."

I nodded. "Yes, he did. But you seem intent on giving away a fair chunk of it to a politician you barely know. Would Eugene do that?"

Considering this briefly, she said, "I'm sure he would."

"*Why?* I mean, that doesn't sound like Eugene at all."

Bebe turned her back to Kyle and sat facing me directly. "The late Senator Grady Vaughn. Eugene *liked* him."

"So? A *lot* of people liked him. And others didn't."

She explained, "Eugene gave Grady Vaughn his *start* in politics. It was over thirty years ago, when Vaughn was young and promising. Eugene got him appointed to a *commission* or something, not sure."

If that had in fact happened, it was long ago, while Bebe was living in the penthouse, before I was even a twinkle in Eugene's eye. I told her, "I never knew that. Interesting. But that has nothing to do with *this* election."

"Of course it does. Senator Vaughn was an *institution*, a great man, and Julian Wentworth is now his—whatchamacallit—his intellectual heir."

I must've looked stunned. "*Why* would you think that?"

Bebe flipped her hands. "Just looking at him, just hearing him—it's obvious, isn't it? He's one of *us*."

"I don't buy into that at all. It sounds so ... *tribal*."

She looked bewildered. "Anything wrong with that?"

"Bebe, if you actually need to ask that question, I am *not* the person to answer it."

She had already demonstrated to me that she was beyond reasoning when it came to matters of class and identity, which she clung to as if for dear life. She had also convinced me that she was gullible enough to write any check, in any amount, to validate her membership in "our crowd." To feed that need, she would probably not hesitate to contest my inheritance. And that frightening prospect now seemed very real—*if* she was prodded by Eugene's codicil from the grave.

While mulling this, I noted that both Celia Gamarra and her husband, Nick, were still seated at the head table, but others had joined the sheriff in circulating through the ballroom. Celia's campaign manager, Xolani Vahdat, was now heading toward our table. She spotted me at once and quickened her pace. In her slim slacks, silky tunic, and vibrant head scarf, she was like an exotic flower—a breath of fresh air—in the staid, leaden surroundings of "the club."

"Meghan!" she said, stepping next to my chair. "Thank you *so* much for making this happen today." She leaned over my shoulder to kiss my cheek. And that's when she glimpsed Kyle Pollard—her counterpart in the competing Senate campaign. She stiffened.

Bebe also stiffened. Watching Xolani, she was clearly put off by the young woman's otherness. (Though Bebe's reaction was insufferable, I took pleasure in her discomfort.)

Xolani saw none of this—she was focused on Kyle. She asked him directly, "May I ask what *you're* doing here, Mr. Pollard?"

Bebe answered for him: "He is my *guest*, whoever you are!"

"Bebe," I said, "this is Xolani Vahdat, campaign manager for *today's* speaker. And frankly, I understand her dismay at finding 'the competition' at a private event."

Xolani tossed her hands. "Competition? More like an interloper."

Bebe repeated, "He's my *guest*."

Kyle jumped in, asking me, "As long as we're on the topic of interlopers, *why*, pray tell, did you sneak in that reporter last week? The Wentworth campaign made it perfectly clear that his appearance was a 'no press' event."

I leaned close to Chase, slinging an arm around his shoulders while telling Kyle, "I am a member of a private club and was under no obligation to honor your wishes while you were on my turf. Mr. Unger is a friend, and he was my guest at that event, as he is at today's—which, by the way, will be open to the press at the conclusion of lunch, so that the people will hear what *our* candidate actually has to say. We have nothing to hide. It seems that yours *does*."

Junior offered me a quiet "Bravo, Meg."

But Kyle was pissed. "My candidate has *nothing* to hide—despite your unfounded innuendo."

"Then why were you so upset by the reporting of last Thursday's rally with that bunch of religious nutjobs? It seems you're running a *stealth* campaign."

With restrained patience, Kyle explained, "Julian talks to his constituents on their own terms. He's a man of the people."

I laughed. "He's a chameleon. A two-face. He stands for anything that might help him grub an extra vote."

Kyle brought it down a notch, shaking his head. "I have no idea what your 'issue' is, Mrs. Auric, but you clearly don't know the same Julian Wentworth that I do. And I'm serving *proudly* in his quest for higher office."

I had provoked Kyle for one purpose—to find out how deeply he understood his candidate's background—and now I had the answer. Because of his evident confusion regarding the source of my animosity toward "Oxford grad" Julian Wentworth, I concluded that Kyle was unaware that his candidate was not who he seemed. Kyle knew *nothing* of the man once named John White—or his buried past.

When lunch was cleared and while coffee was being served, one of the ballroom's side doors opened, admitting a small corps of reporters, a half dozen or so, including a cameraman from a TV station in Consensus, who set up his gear front and center. The others sat in a row of folding chairs that had been aligned near one end of the head table.

Everett Burke approached the podium, clanged a glass, and introduced Xolani.

After she was greeted by polite applause, she ran through the usual round of thank-yous. Then, with a change of tone, she said, "Now, let me tell you about a woman I've come to know very well in recent weeks. She's a woman I think of as a close and trusted friend. And she happens to be running for a seat in the United States Senate."

We heard that Celia was the only child of hardworking immigrant parents, born here in humble circumstances. Inheriting that work ethic, she excelled in school throughout her formative years, then attended the state's leading university on a full scholarship, graduating with highest honors. Twenty years later, her appointment as labor commissioner by Governor Swaine capped a distinguished career of public service, during which she earned a glowing reputation for her commitment to, and focus on, whatever task was at hand. We also heard about her husband Nick's exemplary career in law enforcement, as well as the couple's tireless dedication to volunteer work for a long list of organizations devoted to bettering the quality of life in their community and throughout the state.

"Ladies and gentlemen," said Xolani, "please welcome Celia Flores Gamarra."

I was surprised by the enthusiasm of the applause—not raucous, not thundering, but it signaled an eagerness to hear her out.

"Thank you," she said, "for such warm greetings. I suspect that most of you don't know me very well. My work in government has always been behind the scenes, where I've considered it my mission, my duty, to make our tax-supported institutions work better for *every* citizen of our great state. Along the way, I have never sought publicity or glory or wealth, finding the satisfaction of well-practiced statecraft to be reward enough. But now, voters in the recent senatorial primary have seen fit to put me forward as a candidate for higher office—*much* higher—and I'm here today to ask for your consideration ..."

As Celia continued, she projected humility in her accomplishments, but also self-assurance in her proposed solutions to the many vexing problems of the day. The attentive crowd listened in silence, until she ended with a simple "Thank you."

And *boom*—an instantaneous standing ovation. Not *everyone* stood, of course. The elderly and infirm weren't up to it. The apolitical, who'd simply come for lunch, didn't care. And certain partisan diehards remained glued to their seats. (Bebe and Kyle sat there looking at each other, rolling their eyes and doing the "bored clap" thing.) But most of us were on our feet.

Celia seemed almost embarrassed by this response, shushing the crowd and motioning for everyone to sit down. When things got quiet enough for her to be heard, she said, "I don't want to intrude too much on your afternoon, so if you have any questions, let's get right to them."

Hands shot up, but none so vigorously as Eugene Junior's, waving to be seen.

Celia pointed to him. "The gentleman in front, please. Yes, sir?"

Gene stood. "What about the proposed pipeline?"

She didn't hesitate: "I oppose it, and if elected, I would vote to block it."

"Thank you!" He sat down and pulled out his checkbook to write another contribution.

Sitting next to me, Chase Unger waved for Celia's attention and flashed her a wide smile.

She smiled back. "Yes, young man?"

He stood. "Thank you, ma'am. Chase Unger, *Consensus Times*. On Thursday, your opponent told supporters that, as a senator, he would work toward, quote: 'a unified America where laws find their authority in the rule of God.' Your thoughts on that, Mrs. Gamarra?"

She sighed. "I respect everyone's right to believe any religion they choose—or none at all—but the First Amendment clearly prohibits the sort of nonsense suggested by my opponent. Next question?"

In the end, Celia's presentation was an unmitigated success. Nine days earlier, she had lamented about the prospects of her low-profile campaign, fearing that Wentworth would be tough to beat. But based on the Towne Club's reaction, her chances appeared to be improving.

My guests and I mingled with many others who stayed to chat with her while the rest of the crowd was leaving. Nick Gamarra spotted me and came over to thank me for getting Celia a slot on the club's luncheon schedule. "This could change everything," he told me.

"Hope so." Then I turned from the others to ask Nick, "Can you stay a few minutes to discuss something?"

"Of course. What's up?"

"Follow me." And I led him out of the ballroom, through the lobby, and into the quiet, dimly lit bar. On a Tuesday, pushing two o'clock, it was deserted; there wasn't even a bartender on duty. I asked Nick to join me in one of the tiny round booths. The tufted leather cushion of the high-backed seat nearly surrounded us, providing the sort of space conducive to gossip—or secrets.

I said, "First, Nick, how did it go with your unexpected tablemate today—Sheriff Hewitt?"

"That *was* a surprise. But nothing tense—I've worked with Stan for years, so we get along, no matter what. But he *did* ask if I had any updates on the break-in at your penthouse. It's been over a week, and I haven't filed a report yet. I told him, 'Nothing but dead ends, but we're still working on it.' He bought that, told me to keep him posted, no biggie. He gave no indication of knowing that I suspect there were deputies involved in the break-in."

I shrugged. "Well, *that's* good—I guess."

He asked, "Any news from your end?"

I hesitated. "Yes... there's been a development you should know about. But you'll want more details than I can give you."

The glint of his shoulder holster peeked out from beneath his suit coat as he leaned toward me. "Then tell me what you *can*."

I lowered my head, as if ashamed, which was ridiculous. "My life has been threatened."

Appropriately alarmed, he asked, "Who *did* this?"

I blew a long, slow whistle. "I can't even tell you that, Nick. I'm sorry. It would open *several* cans of worms."

"Then how can I possibly help? Do you need protection?"

"No, I don't think so—at least not yet. But I do want you to know that I have an audio recording of a phone call, and it pretty much clarifies everything. Unfortunately, I am *highly* motivated not to share it. At some point, who knows? So I've opened a text message and attached a link to the recording, which I can send to you on a moment's notice, if needed. I want you to know that this *could* happen."

He sat back. "I want to help. But you're not letting me."

I lowered my head again, and this time I was indeed ashamed—for putting him in an impossible position.

As I was leaving the barroom with Nick, Everett Burke noticed me from the lobby and approached. "Could I have a minute of your time, Mrs. Auric?"

I turned to Nick, saying, "Keep in touch. I will, too."

When he was gone, I suggested to Everett, "In here?" Then I led him back into the barroom and sat at the same little booth. The seat was still warm.

Everett joined me, saying, "Mrs. Auric—"

I interrupted: "Meghan is fine."

"*Thank* you, Meghan. As you might have guessed, I'm curious if you've had any thoughts about our last conversation."

"I've been a little busy, Everett"—now, *that* was an understatement—"but yes, I've been considering your suggestion. And for the time being, please understand, I'm not inclined to resume our previous intimacy."

"Ah"—he looked crestfallen—"but I do understand."

"However, you also suggested that we might simply spend more time together. So I'm wondering if you'd care to get away for a while tomorrow afternoon."

He perked up. "That could be arranged. Easily."

I told him, "One of my favorite places *anywhere* is the Fairview Institute of Arts. I'm a member of their board, and I've donated a few works, and it's just a lovely setting for a bit of quiet time. Interested?"

"Of *course*, Meghan. Shall I drive us there?"

"No. I'd prefer to meet you. Shall we say, perhaps, the main lobby at two?"

With a warm smile, he told me, "It's a date."

CHAPTER
THIRTEEN

My morning workouts had taken on an intensity and urgency of late. Again on Wednesday, I felt driven to push myself toward unknown goals. How could I set goals with so much uncertainty swirling about me? So I kept pushing forward, fearful that whatever I did, it wouldn't be enough. Tomorrow, Gustaf Magnuström would return for another lesson, and I hoped he could instill in me a better sense of direction. For now, though, I was on my own.

I had been on the treadmill for forty-five minutes, at a pace that felt like a sprint, so I was grateful to be interrupted by the buzz of my phone. The readout for the incoming call said: FAIR-VIEW GENERAL HOSPITAL.

Dialing down the treadmill to a strolling pace, I picked up the call. "Yes? This is Meghan Auric."

"Mrs. Auric," said the voice, which sounded too young, like the nursette in the chapel on the day Eugene died, "this is Emily at Fairview General. How have you been feeling?"

I held the phone at arm's length, giving it a quizzical look, as if it had posed a question in Swahili. Returning it to my ear, I asked, "*What...?*"

More loudly, Emily repeated, "How have you been feeling, Mrs. Auric? Tomorrow will be two weeks since the loss of your loved one." She must have still suspected that Eugene was my father, not my husband.

"I'm *fine*, I guess. Why do you ask?"

"Well, we do offer grief-support services that might—"

Interrupting, I assured her, "That won't be necessary."

"Oh, okay, perfect." She sounded as if she was checking off items on a list. "Also, no one has stopped by to pick up your loved one's personal belongings. If they haven't been claimed in two weeks, we usually donate them to our resale shop."

"Great," I said, "why don't you just do that?" I had no desire to retrieve the clothes that Eugene had been wearing when he was admitted to the hospital for the last time. I still hadn't processed everything *else* he'd left behind.

"Um ... it seems your loved one was wearing a heavy gold watch. It says 'Patek Philippe' on it." She mangled the pronunciation, but I got the idea. She continued, "They thought you might want that back. Also, we have his wallet—with cash, credit cards, other items."

I stopped the treadmill. "You're right, Emily. I probably *should* get that back." Dreading an outing to the hospital, I added, "I suppose I'll need to sign for it."

"*Someone* will. You could designate someone and let us know in advance. Or"—she paused, checking that list again—"I see you live at Auric Tower. We could bundle everything up and drop it off. But we'll still need a signature."

With a tone of mock formality, I said, "Then I authorize you to drop it off with any of our doormen. They are all *completely* trustworthy, and they'll be happy to sign for me."

"*Perfect*," she said. (I'd have sworn that I heard the stab of a period on her clipboard.) She concluded, "You can expect to have everything in a day or two."

"Well done, Emily. Many thanks."

Concluding my workout, I went up to my bedroom. Ashley had arrived for the day and was busy again, sorting through the detritus of Eugene's obsession with custom-tailored finery. Walking through the room, I told her, "Brace yourself. More on the way—from the hospital."

"Piece of cake. That can't be much."

"I *love* your can-do attitude. I've been dealing with plenty of crap lately, and it has me in knots. All I do is wonder: *What's next?*"

Ashley dropped a brass-buttoned double-breasted vest onto a pile of at least twenty others she'd collected. "You're *much* stronger than you think, Meghan. I've watched you—especially these past two weeks—and trust me, you're holding up just fine. *I'd* be a basket case, dealing with everything you're going through."

"I don't believe that, but it's sweet of you. How about we take a little break this afternoon?"

She reminded me, "My time is your time."

"Here's the deal: I'm meeting someone at the museum this afternoon for some ... relaxed conversation. I'd like for you to drive me. While I'm there, you can spend the time enjoying the place on your own. There's plenty to see. Have you been there?"

"It's been *ages*—I was a kid—a school field trip, I think. I remember liking it, but it's kinda dressy, right?" She spread her arms, displaying her housework attire. Although she generally presented herself with a keen sense of personal style, today's grubbies were not intended for hobnobbing with the culture crowd.

I shrugged. "We're about the same size. My dressing room is open to you—wear whatever you'd like."

"Really?"

"Of course, 'really.'"

She looked better than I ever had, wearing a simple ensemble raided from my closet: silk blouse, a waist-length bolero jacket of sapphire-blue velvet, and slim designer jeans, all of it paired with Italian loafers and a bit of silver bling—interesting, I noted, that she had avoided the more predictable choice of my gold jewelry. With fresh eyes, she had managed to combine my things in such a way that the overall effect was surprisingly youthful. (Or maybe *not* so surprising—as she was young enough to be my daughter.)

Taking one of Eugene's cars, a long white high-powered German coupe with blood-red leather seats, we looked like a couple of classy gals out for a leisurely spin around town. As we neared the Fairview Institute of Arts, Ashley glanced over from the driver's seat, asking, "Important meeting this afternoon?"

"Not... really."

She laughed. "That sounded rather evasive, Meghan. None of my business—but what's up?"

There was no point in keeping secrets, since I was bound to fill her in eventually, so I said, "Don't read too much into this, but there's a man who works at the Towne Club—the manager, in fact—and we've previously enjoyed the occasional *liaison*."

"*Well* now," she lilted, "don't *you* get around?"

"While I admit to *nothing*, whatever may have happened in the past won't happen today, obviously—not in a public museum. It's just that Everett and I haven't been able to 'talk' lately, as friends. We see each other often at the club, but he has a keen sense of propriety in his position there, so we've set aside some time on neutral ground."

Ashley grinned. "Sounds romantic. Is he dreamy?"

"For his age, yes."

"How old *is* he?"

"A few years older than I am. Fifty-seven, I think."

"Oh." Ashley sounded deflated. "So he's no Dustin St. James, then."

"No." (Not by a long shot.)

Parking was no problem on that Wednesday afternoon, and when we entered the building, it was evident that the admissions volunteer had been trained to recognize me at once: "*Welcome,* Mrs. Auric. What an unexpected pleasure to see you today." He disengaged the turnstile, allowing both Ashley and me to pass freely. "Enjoy your visit. And I'll let Mr. Yorba know you're here." He was referring to the museum director.

In the sprawling main lobby, a sprinkling of patrons wandered about, gazing at several large-scale sculptures. Others paused to read signage at the entryways to three temporary exhibits.

MODERNISTAS: MIDCENTURY MEXICAN MURALISTS
·
WORKS ON PAPER: LIVING INTAGLIO MASTERS
·
LIGHT + SPACE: FRACTAL ART IN CHAOS THEORY

"Fractals!" said Ashley. "I'm in!"

I had *no* idea what she was talking about.

She asked, "Okay if I shoot some video? I'd love to post about this."

Others were taking pictures. I told Ashley, "I think it's fine— but no selfie sticks or flash."

"No problem. Just text me when you want to leave, and I'll find you. Have fun." She wiggled her fingers goodbye, then headed off, in search of fractals.

On the opposite side of the lobby, other entryways led off to galleries featuring the permanent collections. Visitors came and went, crisscrossing the polished terrazzo floor, but the vibe was unhurried and respectful—almost reverent—as one might expect in a church. This had always been one of the rare public spaces that did *not* trigger my agoraphobia. This temple to the arts was my safe space.

I spotted Everett Burke coming through the turnstile, checking his watch. I checked mine: two on the nose. He was smartly dressed, as I would expect. Since he had come from the club, his trousers were probably those from his gray uniform, but he had switched the jacket for a sport coat of his own, in a bold nubby tweed of black and white. He'd also ditched the understated black necktie of the uniform, replacing it with a bolder one of solid Hermès orange—he had a good eye and a fearless sense of style.

He brightened as he saw me and rushed over to meet me. "I hope you weren't waiting long," he said as we kissed cheeks.

"Nope. Just got here. Thanks for taking time out of your day for me."

"The pleasure," he assured me, "is entirely mine."

"Have you been here recently?"

"A few social events. But I haven't spent much time in the galleries. Perhaps you could be my guide."

With a sly come-hither of my index finger, I led him from the lobby. The route to our destination first passed through a gallery of Americana. As we entered it, we faced, on the opposite wall, an antique quilt, hung in a frame and protected by glass—in which I noticed a reflection of us as we approached. The head-to-toe image was faint and ghosted, not clear and mirrorlike, but I could recognize my face as well as Everett's. And I was surprised, indeed astonished, to see that we looked like a *couple*—

not merely a man and woman who happened to be walking side by side, but a perfectly credible, matched-and-mated *couple*.

I wasn't the only one to notice it. "Hey," said Everett, "we look pretty good together, don't we?"

"Hmm?" I asked, as if I didn't understand what he was talking about, as if I hadn't seen us in the glass. And before he could explain, I directed, "This way," sidestepping the quilt and heading toward another gallery.

We passed through the landscape collection, the abstractionists, the surrealists, and then arrived in the portrait gallery. I told him, "Portraiture has been on my mind lately." Apparently, at that moment, no one else shared my obsession, as we were alone in the sizable, oblong room. There wasn't even a guard (though cameras peeped from every corner of the ceiling). I suggested, "Shall we sit?"

There was a long cushioned bench running lengthwise through the center of the room, a configuration similar to that of the gallery room at home in the penthouse, although this equivalent space in the museum seemed larger by tenfold. I sat near the middle, facing portraits by Flemish masters: Peter Paul Rubens, Michiel Sweerts, Jan van Eyck, Rogier van der Weyden, and on and on.

I said quietly, "They're magical, aren't they?"

Looking at me, not the paintings, Everett said, "They've never had that affect on me before—not until someone special pointed them out."

"Today, of course, it's all just point-and-shoot"—I thought of Ashley, her phone, and her fractals—"but there's something so *human* about brushes, canvas, and paint. Even now, centuries later, you can still *smell* it. The varnish, the warmth, the love."

Everett took my hand and kissed the tips of my fingers.

I turned to him, smiling, thinking of Dustin St. James.

We moved to another gallery, this one devoted to still lifes, an ageless genre that provided a sweeping survey of world art, the span of its cultures, their stylistic periods—ancient and modern. We slowly browsed the entire room. Again, we were alone. And once more, we sat on a bench.

Everett said, "Meghan? Where do you want to be in, say, five years?"

I gave him an odd look. "*Geographically?*"

"No." He explained, "Where ... in life?"

"Everett," I said, shaking my head, "right now, I'm having trouble looking ahead five *days*. Five years from now—I can't even grasp the *concept* of that."

"Let me be a little more specific. Five years from now, do you see yourself together with someone? Or alone?"

I had to chuckle. "You make it sound so stark, being alone. Until two weeks ago, I'd been married for twenty-five years. It wasn't *awful*, but I wasn't particularly happy, either. For now, I'm in no rush to 'settle down'—with *anyone*."

"Of *course* you're in no rush." He grinned. "That's why I asked about the five-year plan."

Returning his grin, I said, "All options are very much on the table."

That seemed to assuage him. (Once again, however, I was thinking of Dustin.)

I suggested, "Care for some fresh air?"

He laughed while making a gesture that encompassed all the paintings in the room. "What's the matter? I thought you *craved* the smell of it—all that varnish, warmth, and love."

Ignoring that, I asked, "Have you seen the gardens?"

He shook his head. "I didn't know there *were* any."

"Actually, there's only one, and it's not very big, but it's extraordinary."

Outdoors, at the juncture of two wings of the building, a small courtyard, perhaps thirty feet square, was protected from the winds but open to direct sun. An anonymous donor (no, not yours truly) had come up with the idea of using the space for an installation of shimmering organic-looking objects by a renowned glass artist from the Pacific Northwest. Set against two expansive walls of dazzling white marble, dozens and dozens of plantlike glass forms, predominantly red, rose from a bed of shiny, crushed black granite, creating a fantasy garden of foliage, spikes, and sprouts, some of which stood eight feet tall.

Across the courtyard, wispy trees provided a shady area where limestone plinths served as benches for the restful appreciation of this jaw-dropping spectacle of sunlight and glass.

Everett couldn't help wondering aloud, "Who keeps it so *clean*?"

I shrugged. "Volunteers? Very *careful* volunteers."

That afternoon in late September, the angle of the warm sunlight added a golden glow to the entire scene, while a breeze carried the cool hint of early autumn.

Sitting next to me, Everett took my hand again. Last time, he kissed my fingertips. Now what? He looked into my eyes, saying, "Thank you."

Skeptically, I asked, "For what?"

"Everything. A perfect afternoon. Your company."

His typical politeness and geniality had begun to feel more like persistent fawning, so I was relieved when we were interrupted.

"Meghan?" called a man's voice from behind.

When we turned, Petro Yorba, the museum director, came out from the building and approached us at a trot. We stood.

"I got a message from the desk that you were here," he said, "but I was tied up in a meeting with the board's auditors."

"Can't walk out on *them*," I said wryly.

He laughed. "Well. They're gone. They're happy. And I *couldn't* be more delighted that you're here." He smiled so broadly, it must have hurt. (But he knew where his bread was buttered.)

Turning to Everett, he extended his hand and introduced himself.

Everett reciprocated, saying, "An honor to meet you, Petro. I keep hearing that you've brought a whole new spirit of life to the organization."

"Too kind of you. But thank you so much."

"Well, it's *true*," I insisted. "Under the previous regime, we'd never even *heard* of fractals." I laughed airily.

Petro seemed unsure of what to make of that.

In his early forties, he was an up-and-coming figure in the museum world, recruited from the West Coast, where he'd worked miracles at a struggling regional museum that boasted plenty of old money, but was held back by too many old ideas. His arrival in Fairview had predictably nudged some deadwood from the board, which I had felt was long overdue. So he thought of me as one of his core group of allies—and he skillfully displayed the sort of long-range vision that *deserved* my support. Most important, he was driven by a goal of making the museum more accessible and meaningful to a younger generation of art lovers.

I asked him, "Everything okay with the audit?"

"Yes, thank God. They're satisfied that we're living within our means—but I've never felt that we should be content standing still. We need to have the leeway to recognize that next 'big idea.' There's always one out there, waiting, just beyond the horizon."

Obligingly, Everett asked him, "So … what's the next big idea?"

Petro grinned. But rather than answering Everett, he turned to tell me, "I've been waiting for the opportunity to talk to you about this."

"Uh-oh. Sounds expensive." I laughed—but wasn't joking.

Petro said, "This'll take a bit of explaining."

"I'm in no rush." Then I asked Everett, "Do you need to get back to the club?"

Checking his watch, he nodded. "I probably should—there's usually a midafternoon crisis or two before dinner service. Do you mind if I abandon you?"

"Heavens, *no*." I tried not to sound eager.

"Well, then, I guess I *will* run along. But this has been lovely, Meghan." He hugged me. Turning to Petro, he said, "Keep up the great work—and good luck with that big idea."

Petro and I said our farewells to Everett, then watched as he disappeared into the building.

With a smirk, I told Petro, "Cut to the chase. What's up?"

He hesitated. "You took me by surprise today—a very *pleasant* surprise, but I haven't prepared a formal presentation."

"In other words," I said, "you haven't polished your pitch."

"Exactly. So I'll need to wing it. Shall I open some champagne?"

"Are you that *sure* you'll be celebrating?"

"Not at all. But I need a drink."

"Oh, my," I said. "This *does* sound expensive."

Petro led me indoors, and we went upstairs to the founders'

lounge, a private room for use by major donors during large events. He used the keypad to open the locked door, then closed it behind us after we entered.

The lounge was furnished with club chairs surrounding round cocktail tables. I took a seat at the grouping nearest a wall of windows, which looked out to the courtyard, with a view of the glass garden below.

Petro stepped behind the bar, grabbed two chilled champagne flutes, and appropriated a bottle from a locked cooler—good stuff, French. Then he brought them over to our table and sat with me. He popped the bottle, filled the glasses, handed one to me, and raised his own. With a wink, he said, "*Santé.*"

After tasting it—"How divine"—I set down the glass and said, "Talk to me, Petro."

He took a deep breath. "Meghan," he said, "I've come to appreciate that your understanding of art—and your *passion* for it—is second to none in this city, possibly the whole state."

I grinned. "Not very subtle, but flattery *could* get you everywhere."

He continued: "The Fairview Institute of Arts has long been this city's most significant cultural asset. It's well funded and well attended, a true treasure in our midst. The Institute has various facilities and functions, but primarily, we're known for our museum—with its collections, galleries, and exhibitions."

I nodded. "I have a hunch you're about to say, 'But...'"

He nodded. "But ... if you think about it, our museum, like almost any art museum, serves a function that's essentially *passive*. We collect and exhibit the art—the public comes in to see it—then they go home. We hope they've been pleased and enriched by the experience, but that's the end of it. Sure, we hope they'll come back for more, and many do, but that merely repeats the cycle. We put up art; they look at it. Period."

"So," I said, "are you contemplating a museum experience that's more ... interactive?"

"That's a good guess, Meghan, and it has merit, but that's not what I'm driving at. I'm thinking bigger. I'm thinking about education. In fact, I'm thinking about a school—an actual, brick-and-mortar, primary and secondary *school*. Something along the lines of: The School at Fairview Institute of Arts."

"Would its purpose be to train artists?"

"Of course, but not exclusively. Its main purpose would be to provide a first-class general education, heavily endowed to admit a broad swath of students, including those from underserved communities and disadvantaged environments. Their education would be *anchored* in the arts, with the existing museum serving as a resource or lab. Many of the students, but not all, would be here to build a foundation for actively pursuing a life's *work* in the arts. All artists need nurturing—not only in mastering the skills of a particular medium, but also in history, theory, and creative thinking. Our school's purpose would be to provide *all* of that."

I asked, "By 'arts,' do you mean visual arts?"

"At first, yes, but I'd love to pursue other phases. To start, we'd focus on the traditional 'fine arts.' If that progresses well, we could add 'applied arts,' such as design. And finally, we could venture into phase three, the performing arts."

I blew a low whistle. "Those are *very* ambitious plans, Petro."

He grinned. "In the immortal words of Daniel Burnham: 'Make no little plans. They have no magic to stir men's blood.'"

"Where do you even begin?"

He flipped his hands. "Land, obviously. And believe it or not, that problem is already solved. There are two square blocks behind the museum that have fallen out of use. The city wants them redeveloped and would sign them over to us for practically nothing. Which leaves a much bigger nut, yet to be cracked."

I rattled off, "Buildings, staffing, endowments..."

"Yep," said Petro, "that's pretty much the scope of it. None of this would happen overnight, of course. It would be an ongoing project for at least five years, maybe ten—the point being, it would *not* require complete funding up front."

I reached for the bottle, topped up his glass, then mine. I asked, "Start to finish, how much are you looking for—total?"

He cleared his throat. "Because so many aspects of the project are still being defined, I have only *estimates* of the budget, but if you're looking for a ballpark..." He paused. Then he spoke the number.

I winced. (But I could probably swing it. And I loved everything I'd heard.)

Petro said, "A commitment of that magnitude would fall into the category of a *legacy* donation. It would certainly entitle you to naming rights. Our working name for the project—The School at Fairview Institute of Arts—is admittedly a bit prosaic and descriptive. Alternately, you might prefer something along the lines of Auric School of Arts, or Meghan Auric School, or Meghan Daley Auric School."

"Or," I mused, "Meghan Daley School."

Petro traced an index finger around the rim of his champagne flute. "That would be *totally* your decision."

I told him I'd think about it.

He chuckled. "I didn't expect to get a check *today*."

"Seriously," I said, "this is well worth exploring, and I'm grateful that you came to me first."

He offered, "Shall I open another bottle?"

Laughing, I stood. "Don't you dare."

He stood. "I should tidy up behind the bar, but may I see you down to the lobby first?"

"Thank you, no. I need to catch up with my assistant."

He offered a hug, then a kiss on the cheek, thanking me profusely before walking me to the door and holding it open.

Leaving the founders' lounge, I told him, "I'll be back in touch soon."

When the door closed between us, I ambled over to the interior balcony, which overlooked the atrium of the main lobby. Standing at the railing, I took out my phone and checked messages—nothing urgent. As it was now past three thirty, I assumed that Ashley would be ready to leave, so I sent her a text: CARE TO HEAD BACK? MEET IN THE LOBBY?

Watching the phone, I noted that the message had been delivered but not yet seen. My eye wandered across the atrium to the building's main entrance, where two women brought five young children through the turnstiles and led them into the vast space of the lobby below.

I guessed that the women were both mothers and had planned to pick up their kids after school, then drive them downtown for a bit of culture. They were all nicely dressed, and the kids had apparently been coached about expected behavior—no squealing, no running, and above all else, *no touching*. They had probably been told that the museum was a special, wonderful place. Maybe they were told to behave as they would in church. Whatever the moms had told them, it did the trick. Silently, the wee ones toddled up to an enormous bronze Botero sculpture of a pudgy reclining woman, and their eyes stretched wide, filled with amazement. They had entered an unknown world where fantasy was reality, where nothing was impossible. They were hooked. They giggled. And they pointed. But they didn't touch.

My smile widened as I considered an ironic twist that had marked my own excursion to the museum that day. While Everett Burke and I were touring the galleries, he asked if I had a five-year plan, wondering how I envisioned myself after that amount of time: attached or single? Responding truthfully, I told him that I was unable to plan the next five *days*, let alone years. Within the hour, however, Petro Yorba had all but sold me on a different sort of five-year plan—building a school—a project that could take far longer.

My gaze drifted while I mused about this, and again I noticed the turnstiles at the entrance. A familiar lanky figure in black passed through, then walked quickly to the middle of the lobby, where he stopped, hands on hips. Zack's foot-long ponytail switched as he looked around, as if searching for someone. *I wonder who ...*

Then Ashley emerged from one of the galleries (the one featuring intaglios, not fractals). Walking with purpose, she took her time, and her face bore a hardened expression, which I'd never seen before. Zack rushed in her direction, meeting her behind the lolling Botero woman's rump, where they were hidden from the children's view. They were, however, squarely within my line of sight.

They spoke quietly and quickly. Zack's manner was so furtive, I hoped this wasn't a drug delivery, but then I saw him simply counting out some cash that Ashley gave him—receiving nothing in return. He looked up from the money in his hands and said something to her. She raised her voice slightly, but enough for me to hear her say, "It's all I've *got*."

They exchanged a few more lines of tense but inaudible conversation, which ended when she leaned into his face, telling him, "Good-*bye*, Zack!"

They stared each other down for a moment. Then he stuffed the cash in his pocket and headed for the exit at a trot. She just stood there, stiff and angry. Her shoulders heaved as she breathed deeply, needing oxygen.

I immediately phoned her.

She looked at the readout, then took the call, answering brightly, "Yes, Meghan. Ready?"

I asked, "Are you all *right*, Ashley?"

The concerned tone of my voice must have clued her that I'd seen what happened. She looked about, asking, "Where *are* you?"

I waved from the balcony. "Up here." When she spotted me, I added, "What was *he* doing here?"

She waved me down. "I'll tell you in the car."

The children were making their way around the sculpture now, agape at their discovery of its gargantuan butt crack.

Pulling out of the parking lot, Ashley gunned it. But she'd said nothing.

I reminded her, "I'm listening..."

She exhaled loudly—and took some pressure off the gas. When we'd slowed to the legal limit, she said, "That, uh ... that didn't go so well."

"What did he want?"

She flumped her hands on the wheel, stating the obvious: "Money."

"Does this happen a lot?"

"All the time. And I've *asked* him, I've *told* him, not to bother me when I'm working. But there's always an excuse, an emergency. It's always *urgent* that I help him out, like it was today. He owed *somebody* for *something*, and he had to have it—*right* now."

I asked, "Why put up with that? Every time you give in, you're just enabling him."

Wagging her head, she said softly, "I know. I know. But no more. It's over. He's history. I told him to get lost." She paused, then sputtered with laughter. "Actually, I told him to go fuck himself."

"Good girl!"

Awkwardly, she extended her left palm over her driving hand, begging a high five. (Not my style, but I complied, figuring she'd earned it.)

"Know what?" she said, laughing again, but this time it was a laugh of disgust. "Just *yesterday*, I finally got that Mexico trip paid off."

"I hope it's refundable."

"Nope. The package was a pretty good deal, but the catch is: advance payment, nonrefundable."

"Well," I said, trying to sound upbeat, "the trip is *months* away. Maybe you can find a friend to go along and pitch in."

She shrugged. "I'll go alone if I have to, but not with Zack. He's...*weird*."

I was tempted to ask, *So you finally noticed?* But I kept that comment to myself.

B ack at the penthouse, I told Ashley that she could knock off for the day. When she headed for my dressing room to change back into her own clothes, I said, "Why don't you keep the bo-lero? It's *so* cute on you—and I haven't worn it in years."

She turned back, stunned. "But it's ... *couture*."

"It is. And it's yours."

She protested no further.

About five minutes later, she left—wearing it.

With little to do that evening and not feeling especially hun-gry, I decided to have a simple dinner sent up from the club, ask-ing for delivery at seven. While waiting for it, I could try another gelato experiment.

Spumoni had been on my mind for a couple of days, and I had gathered the ingredients for the three flavors—pistachio, cherry, and chocolate. The recipe was more complicated than most be-cause each flavor had to be prepared in separate batches, which would later be combined—loosely marbleized when not quite frozen.

While I was getting everything organized on the kitchen is-land, my phone buzzed with an incoming text: CAN YOU TALK? IF SO, CALL. It was from Dustin St. James.

The gelato could wait. I rang him at once.

He picked up. "Meghan! That was *quick*."

"Well, I ... *happened* to be available."

"Do you *happen* to be available tomorrow night?"

A bit too coyly, I replied, "Depends what you have in mind—but I have nothing on the calendar."

"Here's the thing: I've been working on sketches, and I can't *wait* to show you something. But I don't want to send you a pic-ture; you should see it for real. We could have dinner here and make an evening of it. I'll cook, if you trust me, and of course Nova will be here, too."

"Sounds wonderful, Dustin. Let's do it. Can I bring gelato?"

"I was hoping you'd ask. Can I pick you up?"

"I was hoping *you'd* ask. What time?"

"Is six okay? It's a school night for you-know-who."

"Perfect."

He lowered his voice. "And because it's a school night, I really can't ditch our chaperone this time. She needs to wake up in her own bed and start the next day on schedule."

"Got it. I absolutely understand."

How could I *not* understand? In fact, I found it endearing that Dustin needed to look out for his daughter's best interests. Besides, I told myself, plenty of other meetings—and *opportunities*—would surely lie ahead.

CHAPTER
FOURTEEN

Thursday marked the last day of September—exactly two weeks since Eugene's demise. This morning, I had a follow-up lesson booked with Gustaf Magnuström, but he needed to meet with me earlier than usual, so I didn't even bother with coffee or the *Consensus Times* before getting into my gi and arranging the exercise mats in the penthouse gym.

Ashley hadn't arrived by the time the doorman phoned to say that Gus was on his way up, so I met him myself at the elevator in the entry hall. While walking him through the living room on our way to the gym, I paused to ask, "Where's your bag of tricks?" I was referring to the oversize duffel that he normally brought, stuffed with his protective gear.

"I left it in my van," he said.

"Won't you need it? I'm getting pretty good at the Magnus-tröm Method."

"And that's the whole point, Meggy. You're more than 'pretty good.' You've mastered it—and there *is* such a thing as being overprepared. God forbid that you'll ever need to use these techniques, but if and when you do, you want to call up something that feels second-nature, not something that's been practiced and practiced and practiced..."

"You make it sound sorta Zen," I said while leading him into the gym.

"*Ja*, it is, I guess."

"Okay... but if we're not going to practice the Method, what are we going to do?"

"That's up to you, Meggy. You paid for an hour. How would you like to use it?"

"Well, as a matter of fact, I've been feeling at loose ends with my normal fitness training—it seems that no matter how much I do, it's never enough. It's exhausting, physically and mentally. It feels counterproductive."

He nodded. "*Ja*, Meggy. We need to talk." And he seated himself on an exercise bench.

I dragged a second bench over and sat on it, facing him. "I need to set some realistic goals, but I have no idea what the goals *should* be. I mean, training is all about numbers, right? How many pounds ... how many reps ... how many miles. But whenever I decide on a number, then work toward it, it starts to get easy, making me feel that I'm *cheating* or something. So I keep pushing myself harder and harder, but that doesn't feel right, either."

He shook his head. "Keep *that* up, Meggy, and you'll kill yourself. You're not competing for a gold medal—you're doing this for your health and stamina and *peace of mind*."

I sighed, slumping where I sat. "'Peace of mind'—that sounds so good. But lately, I've felt nothing but anxiety."

He placed his hands on his knees and leaned toward me a few inches. "Okay. You need to set some goals, but let's forget about numbers completely."

Skeptically, I asked, "What's a goal without numbers?"

"Everything, maybe. Tie your goals to your passions."

"Translate, please."

"What floats your boat? What jazzes you?"

I lolled my head back, closed my eyes, and thought about it.

"My garden ... gelato ... art ... and lately, I've been getting obsessed about decency in politics."

Gus chortled. "Good luck with that last one."

Opening my eyes, I admitted, "Yeah, it's grim."

"So let's look at your other passions. You mentioned your garden and gelato. I'd call those more of a hobby than a passion—unless you're planning to open a restaurant."

"God, *no.*"

"So let's talk about art."

I brightened. "Art history was my minor at Berkeley. I'm a reasonably serious collector. I've been on the board of trustees at the Institute of Arts for many years. And *now,* they're thinking of starting a school—I'd like to be involved with that."

Gus arched his brows. "Why?"

With a shrug, I rattled off, "Education is important ... the arts are important, at least to me ... and I'm now in a position to really *help,* by putting Eugene's money to use in ways that he'd *never* consider."

Gus eyed me with a quizzical look, waiting. "You're talking about a *school,* Meggy, and why it's important to you. What about ... children?"

I clapped a hand over my mouth with such force, I nearly lost my balance on the bench. "Of *course,*" I said, lifting the hand to my forehead. "Of course—the *kids.* That goes without saying, doesn't it?"

He smiled. "Talk it through ..."

Standing, I thought aloud while pacing: "I don't *mind* that I have no children. That 'empty craving' you sometimes hear about, that's not me. But I *have* thought—if circumstances were different—I might be a pretty good mother. At least I'd *try.* I'd give it my all. And I do seem to have an instant rapport with young people. Surely, that's a promising step in the right direction."

I thought of Ashley. And my "nephew" Adam. And cub reporter Chase. More recently, ten-year-old Nova St. James. And just yesterday, those five wondering tykes, mesmerized by the Botero sculpture.

"Gus," I said, "you're a genius."

He crossed his arms, breaking into a satisfied smile.

He had helped me find a hidden passion, and in doing so, he had helped me set a goal.

After Gus left, it was time for me to start my day properly with my usual morning routine, postponed by the early session in the gym, which had proved more emotionally strenuous than physically taxing—but thoroughly enlightening.

Ashley had arrived, then shared a quick cup of coffee with me in the kitchen before retreating to the bedroom for another deep dive into Eugene's sartorial excesses.

I poured a second cup for myself, then took it and the morning paper out to the terrace. The sky, I would have sworn, looked different. September—now creaking through its final hours toward the cusp of October—had tilted Mother Earth in such a way that the sky was suddenly, observably crisper, drier, bluer, with the delicacy of glass. A small bird (we didn't see many on the thirtieth floor) flitted in the branches of a topiary fig tree; its dainty chirp could barely be heard, floating on the gentle breeze.

Settling into a chair under the striped awning, which offered no shade from the low slant of the sun, I set down my coffee and slid the rolled newspaper out of its sleeve. Like so many smaller-market dailies, it no longer made any pretense of delivering "timely" news. Now that it was actually printed God-knows-where, the earlier deadlines meant that most stories were two days old by the time readers saw them in print. So I was eager to see what kind of coverage the *Times* had given Tuesday's luncheon with Celia Gamarra—better late than never.

The story was indeed on page one, and it carried, as expected, Chase Unger's byline. Its headline: SENATE CANDIDATE GAMARRA WINS OVER HIGHBROW CROWD. There were two photos, one a close-up of the candidate speaking at the podium, the other showing a wide angle of the dining room as the guests stood to applaud.

Chase's opening paragraphs made the point that although the Towne Club's membership was often characterized as "elite," Celia's audience proved to be warmly receptive to her "no-nonsense theory of governance." Further into the article, her prepared remarks were quoted at length, including this pertinent excerpt:

> "I suspect that most of you don't know me very well. My work in government has always been behind the scenes, where I've considered it my mission, my duty, to make our tax-supported institutions work better for *every* citizen of our great state.
>
> "Along the way, I have never sought publicity or glory or wealth, finding the satisfaction of well-practiced statecraft to be reward enough.
>
> "But now, voters in the recent senatorial primary have seen fit to put me forward as a candidate for higher office—*much* higher—and I'm here today to ask for your consideration."

As on Tuesday at the event, when I'd first heard those words, I was struck this morning by Celia's humility in conveying her accomplishments as well as her goals. She considered it her calling, her *job*, to serve the people, expecting nothing in return—other than the awareness that she had done her job well.

I set down the paper, feeling embarrassed. More accurately, I felt ashamed.

There I was, perched on the rooftop terrace of my penthouse, sipping coffee and claiming exhaustion from the earlier heart-to-heart with my trainer—in my at-home gym—while *other* people were actually out there in the world, *working*, struggling to pay bills, worried about leaving things in better shape for their children and for the next generation at large.

I pulled the phone from the inside pocket of my gi and placed a call.

"Good morning," said the polished voice of a receptionist. "Fairview Institute of Arts, director's office. How may I help you?"

"Is Mr. Yorba in yet, please? This is Meghan Auric."

"He *just* came in, Mrs. Auric. Let me connect you."

Moments later, Petro said, "Meghan! Have you had your coffee yet?"

Laughing, I explained, "I got an earlier start than usual today. Two cups already—but still need a third."

"Well, it's a delight to hear your voice—at *any* hour. And at the risk of sounding like a broken record, let me *thank* you once more for your enthusiasm yesterday—regarding the school."

"And that's why I'm calling, Petro. Something's been troubling me. I've been having some second thoughts."

Dead silence on the line. Then: "Um, would you like for me to ... come over and see you? I could pull together some specific details of the proposal, and we could try to find a way forward ... if that's, uh, possible."

Though I had not intended to make him squirm, I couldn't help but enjoy the groveling. With a chuckle, I said, "My apologies, Petro. I might have misrepresented my 'second thoughts.' My enthusiasm for the project has only *grown* since yesterday."

"Oh … *really*?" The relief in his voice was palpable.

"Yes, really. My second thoughts, you see, pertain to the naming of the school."

"Oh! *That* presents no problem whatever. As I mentioned yesterday, you would hold the naming rights—the decision is totally yours."

"Even if I wanted to call it, say … Meghan's Artsy-Fartsy Academy?"

Through a nervous laugh, he explained, "Obviously, the board would need to retain a *modicum* of veto privilege."

"Obviously," I agreed. "But here's my concern. Incorporating my name or Eugene's or even simply 'Auric' in the school's name, for all posterity—that now strikes me as pompous and bigheaded. I think this wonderful venture should be named exactly as your first instincts suggested: The School at Fairview Institute of Arts."

Petro was predictably relieved to hear my suggestion, but also astonished by it. "Most people can't *wait* to see their name on a building."

"Yeah, I've noticed that. I live in Auric Tower."

Returning to the kitchen, I set the *Times* on the counter and refilled my empty mug with that third cup of coffee. My bare feet kissed the tile floor as I moved the newspaper over to the center island and spread it open. After leafing through it (it was shockingly thin that day, with half of it devoted to sports), I returned to page one and skimmed through Chase's story again. Nodding, I confirmed my earlier impression that he was a surprisingly mature and insightful journalist, for a kid of twenty-three.

I mean, what was *I* doing at that age? I was stuck in a dead-end job at United Insurance, where I would soon be lured into a fraud scheme, falsifying health records—an unsavory episode that would then lead me into a forced marriage. At *least*, however, I now had some hope of partial atonement for my long-ago bad judgment. How? By funding a noble, selfless cause, a school without my name on it. As for the victims of the insurance scheme, perhaps I could find a way to make direct compensation to their families, thanks to a staggering inheritance—*if* I could hang on to it.

And the surest way to hang on to it was pretty simple—"don't rock the boat"—according to Ronda Trask, the attorney who still served as executor of Eugene's trust. What's more, she was confident that I would follow that advice because she judged me to be "a smart cookie."

Nonetheless, while standing there in the kitchen on that sunny Thursday morning, this smart cookie picked up her phone and sent a text to Chase Unger: ARE YOU FREE TO STOP BY LATER TODAY? MAYBE AFTER LUNCH? SOMETHING TO DISCUSS.

A minute later, he replied: SURE. TWO O'CLOCK?

I sent him a thumbs-up.

Naturally, I was riddled with doubts as soon as I set down the phone. Other than unleashing a shitstorm, what did I actually hope to accomplish by confiding secrets to a reporter?

For starters, I was sitting on a good story that any reporter would drool over, and if anyone was to get the scoop about Julian Wentworth's background, I wanted it to be Chase. If he broke this news, it would be his career-defining moment. What's more, the things I knew about Wentworth could probably doom his Senate campaign—a highly desirable outcome that had an equally desirable flip side, electing Celia Gamarra.

But there were dangers in pursuing any of this with a reporter as my mouthpiece. I had been threatened with a libel suit, not to mention the *death* threat—plus, I could be wiped out financially if Bebe Auric ever got it into her booze-addled head that she might bankroll a fascist to victory by contesting my inheritance.

So I had a *lot* to sort out before spilling the whole story to Chase—*if* I decided to go through with it. I thought about it in the shower, while I was finally putting myself together for the day. I thought about it during lunch, while Ashley prattled snide recollections of Zack, now *persona non grata*. And I was still thinking about it at two o'clock, as I walked from the living room and through the gallery to meet Chase at the elevator.

"Hi, Meghan," he said as he arrived. "I was so surprised to get your text this morning."

I stepped forward for a friendly hug. "Frankly," I said, "I'm still sorta surprised that I sent it."

"Oh? If this isn't a good time, I could—"

"Nonsense. Thanks so much for coming. Shall we?" And I led him back to the living room.

Ashley was passing through, carrying a carton of Eugene's clothes down from the bedroom. She occasionally stacked these boxes in the elevator hall, where one charity or another would later pick them up.

Chase said brightly, "Hi, Ashley! Need help with that?"

She blew her bangs—"Yeah, guess I do"—and set the box on the floor.

He said to me, "'Scuse me, please," then trotted over to Ashley. She said, "There's a hand slot on both sides. One each?"

"Perfect." And the two of them hauled the carton away.

As they returned, Chase was saying, "*Loved* the video you gave to the Gamarra campaign—from the Wentworth rally."

"That was really Meghan's doing."

"But it was *your* video—audio, too. There were no reporters on the scene, cuz they didn't *know* about it. Your recording made my Sunday story *possible*. Without it, we had nothing. Huge thanks. Nice job." He smiled.

She smiled. "Thank *you*, Chase. That's so sweet."

I caught her eye, twitched my brows, gave her a visual nudge.

She smirked. Turning to Chase, she said, "Catch ya later," then headed upstairs again.

Strolling Chase toward the library, I hooked an arm through his, telling him, "You'd never know it, but she's going through a rough patch."

"Oh, *no*. Why?"

"Man trouble, naturally. He was a louse. Between you and me—glad she dumped him."

"She *did*?"

"Mm-hmm ..."

The cozy library, in which I'd seldom set foot, was my new favorite setting for a *tête-à-tête*. Funny, I thought, how the beds of leaf lettuce out on the terrace had changed my perception of the room. Before, the space had struck me as a stuffy, wood-paneled *box*. Now it was truly a room with a view—including the lovely irony of a lush and living green garden on the twenty-ninth floor.

When I shut the library door, Chase settled on the loveseat beneath the painting of wheat fields. I sat in one of the club chairs that faced him.

He pulled out a reporter's spiral steno pad and then placed, on the table between us, a recorder. When he reached to switch it on, he asked, "Whatever's on your mind, Meghan, is this for the record?"

I hesitated. "Actually, no. Not yet, anyway."

"No problem." He removed the gadget from the table and closed his notebook.

I explained, "What I would like to do is simply share some background that *might* be useful for a later story. I can't tell you *everything* today, and I apologize for that, but I'm in the middle of a situation that's extremely complicated—and possibly dangerous."

His brow wrinkled. "Should I be worried, Meghan—about *you*? That's the main thing. Let me help. Screw the story."

I couldn't hide my gentle gasp, overcome by his affection and concern. "Chase," I said, "you should *not* be worried, not that way. I'll be just fine." Wishful thinking, but my words seemed to satisfy Chase, who leaned back, appearing more relaxed.

"So," he said, "I'm guessing this has something to do with the election."

I nodded.

He said, "More specifically, I'll bet it's about Wentworth."

Again I nodded.

He recalled, "Before, you told me that parts of Wentworth's bio weren't true."

"*None* of it's true."

Chase reminded me, "But his campaign stands by every word of it. And the Oxford degree checks out."

"I know, I know—it *supposedly* checks out—but that only confirms the depth of his deception. Clearly, some *very* powerful people are behind this scheme."

Chase looked skeptical. "So...there *is* a scheme? Are you saying that there's more to this than just a slippery politician who's padding his résumé?"

"*Yes*. I hesitate to invoke the word 'conspiracy,' but I'm certain: that's what's going on."

"How do you know this?"

I didn't like telling him, "That's the part I can't share with you. But trust me, it's explosive."

"I *trust* you, Meghan, and I believe you. But this 'explosive' knowledge you have—could you at least give me a *hint*?"

I thought carefully. "Wentworth is not the man he seems."

Pondering this, Chase asked, "You mean: he lies? Or: he has no scruples, no morals? Or: he pretends to be whatever candidate that different voters may want?"

"All of that is true enough"—I shook my head—"but that's *not* what I meant. So I repeat: Wentworth is not the man he seems."

Chase gave this some more thought. Then he grinned. "You mean: he's literally a *different person* altogether? You mean: 'Julian Wentworth' is an invented identity?"

Clearing my face of any expression whatever, I sat staring at Chase, unblinking. His eyes widened. I reminded him, "You never heard that from me."

"And...when *might* I hear that from you? If what you've implied is true, people need to know about it, and fast."

I told him, "I have no way of knowing, yet, if I'll ever go public with any of this. For *your* sake, Chase, I hope I will; it's a fabulous story. But for *my* sake, I hope I won't have to."

He asked, "If you do go public, do you have any proof?"

"In fact, I do—a recording of a phone conversation."

"Now, *that* could be interesting. Any chance I can hear it?"

"Tell you what," I said. "Detective Gamarra also knows that the recording exists, and I've set up a link in a text that I'm prepared to send him—if and when I decide to move forward. I'll add you as another recipient of that text. If I ever press SEND, you'll get the scoop at the same moment when law enforcement gets the evidence."

"Sounds good."

I mused, "It would be the final nail in Wentworth's coffin. Unfortunately, it could also ruin *me*."

Wryly, Chase noted, "Tomato Lady speaks in riddles."

I laughed. "Try *that* for a headline."

When we emerged from the library, Ashley was passing through the living room, having come from the direction of the elevator. She was carrying a standard cardboard Bankers Box, considerably smaller than the carton that she disposed of earlier.

She explained to me, "This is what the hospital sent over— Mr. A's belongings. One of the doormen just brought it up."

"Ah," I said. "I'll go through it upstairs."

She nodded and walked over to the stairway, but then turned back to us, asking Chase, "Have you ever been to Mexico?"

That piqued my interest.

Chase told her, "Once, spring break, in college."

"Did you like it?"

"Well, *yeah*. The hot weather felt great—in March. And I got to work on my Spanish."

She said, "The heat feels even *better* in the dead of winter, and I've got a week booked in Los Cabos for January. The package is for two—if you're interested."

His knees seemed to go weak. I thought he might faint, but he pulled himself together, burbling, "*Sure*, I'm interested ... but I'm *not* sure if I can get vacation time so soon ... just started at the *Times*. Want me to look into it?"

"Yeah." She smiled. "*Do* that. And I'll shoot you some info about the trip. Can Meghan give me your contact—?"

"Of *course*," I piped in.

After Chase left (in something of a daze, I should add), I went upstairs and into the bedroom with Ashley. She set the file-size box on the bed. The top had been sealed all around with heavy, clear packing tape. Also stuck to the lid was a sign-off sheet from the hospital, with signatures of everyone who had handled the package.

Ashley popped into my dressing room and came back with a sharp pair of scissors, handing it to me. I used one of the blades to zip open the tape, then removed the lid. Most of the box was filled with the last clothes worn by Eugene, but near the top was a packing list and a heavy manila envelope containing smaller items.

Opening the envelope, I found the Patek Philippe wristwatch, Eugene's wedding ring (a plain gold band), an oversize nail clipper (also gold), and his wallet. He had never been one to stuff a wallet—he carried only the essential IDs, two credit cards, and always a dozen crisp hundred-dollar bills. I counted out the cash, splitting it with Ashley, who raised her eyes to the ceiling and said, "Thank you, Mr. A." With a sputter of a laugh she turned to me. "And thank *you*, Meghan."

Setting all of that aside, I reached into the box to remove the stack of clothing—and my phone buzzed with an incoming call.

Stepping away from the bed, I checked the readout, mumbling, "Wonder what *she* wants."

Connecting the call, I said cheerily, "*Hello*, Bebe. What a nice surprise."

"Well, I just wanted to catch *up*," she said in an odd tone. Since it was now midafternoon, I assumed she'd been tippling for a while. She added, "We didn't really get a chance to *talk* at the luncheon on Tuesday."

To my way of thinking, we'd said plenty to each other—probably too much. "So," I asked, "what can I do for you?"

"Meg," she said, "I seem to recall—though I *may* have had a few drinks by then—I think that we found ourselves on different sides of the fence regarding, you know, the election."

I told her, "I've long thought of you as a dear old friend, but no two people can agree on *everything*." I laughed it off.

"And it's *charming* that you're able to dismiss our little set-to so easily. But I just *can't*, Meg. It really bothered me."

"Then I *do* apologize. I'm sorry, Bebe—it won't happen again. Okay?"

"Not exactly. You see, this morning I received the most *peculiar* piece of paper, delivered by special messenger."

In the background, I heard a voice say, "*Mother.*" It was Gene, and his tone carried a ring of warning. "Don't do this..."

"Will you *shush*, Junior?" Returning her attention to me, Bebe said, "It's a copy of a notarized codicil, apparently from Eugene's estate plan. Very concise. It mentions crimes and secrets—and it apparently grants me permission to contest your inheritance."

Trying to mask the panic in my voice, I told her, "You're right, Bebe—that is a *very* peculiar document. It makes no sense at all to *me*. Eugene was apparently 'not well' when he wrote that."

"Maybe," she said. "But you know what? I'd be a *fool* not to take this up with my lawyer."

CHAPTER
FIFTEEN

First thing I did was excuse myself from the bedroom, leaving Ashley looking bewildered as I went downstairs, returned to the library, and shut the door. By the time I sat down, I had already sent a text to my "nephew" and attorney, Adam Hudson: URGENT. PLEASE CALL.

He was one of only two people with whom I'd shared my complete backstory, the other being my therapist, Faye Rubin.

When the phone buzzed in my hand, it was Adam calling back. I connected. "Thank God I reached you, Adam."

"What's *wrong*, Aunt Meg? Are you all right?"

"Physically, never better. But emotionally, bad news."

He said, "I'm in the car, on my way to a meeting. But if you need me there, I could cancel."

"No," I told him, "that's not necessary. I just need a minute or two to tell you what happened—didn't want to put it in writing, in a text."

"Understood. And my meeting doesn't start till three, so we have twenty minutes. Take your time—and try to relax."

I took a few deep breaths, which didn't relax me much. In fact, it made me light-headed. So I just blurted my news: "Bebe's got the codicil."

"Um ... let me pull over." I heard the *ticktock* of his direction signal as he parked somewhere. Then: "Aunt Meg, did I hear you correctly? Bebe has the codicil to Eugene's estate plan? How do you know this? Where did she get it?"

I explained, "She phoned me—just before I texted you—and she told me that a copy of the codicil had arrived by messenger. She didn't say who sent it. I assume she doesn't know."

"Did she read it to you?"

"No, but she described it, and it rang true. She was mystified by it, so I played along, telling her that I'd already seen the codicil but could make no sense of it. I suggested that Eugene wasn't in his right mind when he wrote it—which may not be far from the truth. His own lawyer, Ronda Trask, wasn't sure what to make of it."

"And what did *Bebe* make of it?"

"Whataya *think*? She sees it as an opening for a cash grab. She plans to talk to her lawyer."

"Christ..." After a pause, Adam said, "I'll have to review the copy you gave me, but I'm thinking that Bebe has no grounds to invoke a challenge—assuming you haven't publicly revealed any 'secrets' regarding the insurance scheme. You haven't, correct?"

"Of course not." That very afternoon, however, I'd teased an eager reporter with the prospect of a blockbuster exposé, which would lack credibility without details of the long-ago fatal scam.

As if thinking aloud, Adam said, "We understand Bebe's interest in the codicil—simple greed. But what about the person who sent it to her? What was the motive for doing that?"

"No idea."

"Who even *knew* about the codicil?"

I said, "Unless I'm mistaken, the only person with knowledge of it, other than us, has been Ronda Trask. But my instincts tell me that she did *not* tip Bebe off."

"Why not?"

"This may sound odd, and I know that Ronda *herself* is plenty odd, but I doubt that she would deliberately make trouble for me. At *some* level…I think she likes me."

Adam laughed. "If *I* were a lesbian, I'd have you in *my* sights, Aunt Meg. What a *catch*."

He couldn't see it, but I might have blushed. I asked, "So it *is* true, then? Ronda is in fact a lesbian? I've always assumed that, but I lack the 'inside' perspective."

"Mm-hmm. As a long-standing, card-carrying member of Fairview's gay community, I can confirm that Ronda belongs to the tribe. She's pretty much a loner, though. If she has a partner, I've never seen—or even heard of—anyone."

Pondering this, I said, "So if Ronda didn't alert Bebe to the codicil, who did? Who would even *know* about it? And what would be that person's *motive* for passing it along?"

Adam suggested, "Maybe this goes back to your break-in. You told me that nothing was stolen—except for Eugene's computer. You said they seemed to be looking for something—something like information. Could they have been looking for Eugene's estate plan—and the terms of his will?"

"The timing would fit," I agreed, "but who would even *care* enough about the estate plan to go to all that trouble—staging a daring break-in on the top floor of a high-rise?"

Adam reminded me, "You said there was a possibility that the sheriff's department might've been involved. And that's scary."

"It is indeed. But their involvement is merely theoretical. Even if it could be proven, why would they bother to search out a copy of Eugene's will on his home computer—and then send the demented ramblings of the codicil to his first wife? That does *not* add up."

"You're right, Aunt Meg. The plot, as they say, thickens."

Though there was little humor in the situation, I had to laugh. "Thank you, Adam."

"For what?"

"For pulling me back from the verge of a panic attack."

"Hey," he said, sounding serious, "anytime you feel that things are spinning out of control, just call—and I mean *anytime*. Meanwhile, I'll write up notes summarizing this conversation and add them to your file, just to 'memorialize' these developments. I've also assigned a private investigator to do some digging into Wentworth's campaign, but so far, he hasn't found much."

"I'm not surprised. I get the feeling that anything Wentworth wants to hide, it's all protected by the so-called deep state."

"*Huh?*"

"Sorry, just kidding." At least I *hoped* I was kidding.

When I got off the phone with Adam, around three o'clock, I noticed that I'd received a text from Everett Burke, downstairs at the Towne Club. He'd written: CALL ME?

After I tapped his number, he answered on the first ring. "*Hello*, Meghan—I mean, good afternoon, Mrs. Auric. Thank you for getting back to me."

"What can I do for you, Everett?"

"Nothing at all, Mrs. Auric. I just wanted to thank you again for such a splendid afternoon yesterday."

I'd lost count of his thank-yous, but there had been several too many already.

He continued, "I've gained an entirely new appreciation of Flemish portraiture. I can still *smell* it—the varnish, the warmth, the love."

Oy. "It was my pleasure, Everett."

"But the reason I asked you to phone: Chef has added a special entrée for dinner tonight and tomorrow, which I know you've enjoyed in the past, *boeuf bourguignon*. Very autumnal, don't you think? He thought it would be especially appropriate for the last night of September and the first night of October. Would you perhaps care to join us?"

"Well, I already have plans for this evening"—and in spite of the day's darker developments, I found myself getting cheerier by the hour, anticipating dinner *chez* Dustin St. James—"but I'm free tomorrow night, Everett. Could you reserve for me an order of the *bourguignon* and a table for one?"

"Certainly—that's why I reached out. Would you enjoy your usual booth in the barroom? Seven o'clock?"

"Yes, please. And thank you."

Ashley left at three thirty that afternoon, and I thought I might lie down for a short nap before putting myself together to visit Dustin and little Nova at his studio. But the nap was nixed when Detective Nick Gamarra phoned, asking if he could pay me a visit—he had "developments" to report. Twenty minutes later, I was waiting for him as the elevator door slid open in my entry hall.

He said, "Thanks for making time for me, Meghan, and sorry for the short notice."

I assured him, "I'm grateful for *your* time, Nick. Please, come in." Leading him through the living room and up the stairway, I suggested, "It's such a pleasant afternoon—let's sit on the terrace."

We stepped outside through a pair of heavy glass-and-steel French doors, which I closed behind us. Part of the roof garden on the top floor was set back from sections of the terrace on the floor below, but upstairs, the most expansive outdoor entertaining area occupied the full width of the building, with a thirty-floor drop beyond the balustrade. I seated Nick in a comfortable chair with a prime view, extending all the way to Consensus. Through the dry, pristine air, the capital's faraway buildings looked like miniature models—tiny toys, close enough to touch.

Nick set his briefcase on the chair next to him. I sat on a cushioned bench, across from him. Oddly, there was no breeze, and in the stillness, it seemed the world had gone silent.

"I have some disturbing findings regarding the break-in," he said quietly—but the words rang in my ears. "Everything points to the involvement of the department."

I gulped. "I assume you're referring to the *sheriff's* department."

"Unfortunately, yes. It's infuriating. And the way forward is uncertain. As you can imagine, this creates a delicate situation. I believe the complicity extends all the way to the top."

"Sheriff Hewitt?" I asked. "You think he *himself* is involved?"

Nick nodded. "And that's why I've been so reluctant to issue a report from the investigation—none of it looks good for the department, the deputies, or the boss. If the report went public, it would create an absolute firestorm. And you can bet there'd be furious pushback—against *me*. At the very least, character assassination."

I noted, "And you wouldn't be the *only* one in trouble."

"Exactly. If this blows up in my face, can you *imagine* what the Wentworth campaign would do with it? I'm the husband of their opponent, who'd be stuck with 'guilt by association.' Celia would get absolutely *smeared* by Wentworth, the department, and the press. With the election not five weeks away, it would be impossible to turn things around in time."

I cocked my head, curious. "But if you *did* file your report, why would you assume that Hewitt's pushback would be successful? The report could easily result in *his* undoing."

"Yes, it could, and it *should*. I've always thought that Stan Hewitt is a bit of a showman and a crank, but now I'm also convinced that he's a *dirty cop*. He has no business wearing a badge, let alone running the department. He deserves to go down. But in the words of Emerson, 'When you strike at a king, you must kill him.'"

I flinched.

Nick clarified, "I have no desire to harm Stan *physically*. To sink him, though, I'd need more than the threads of circumstantial evidence that I have now. I would need to nail him with absolute, incontrovertible *proof* of his malfeasance. It might be out there, but so far, I haven't been able to find it."

"I asked, "What's your current understanding of the break-in?"

"We've managed to trace an electronic trail of communication relating to passcodes for the freight elevator"—Nick pointed at it, on a side extension of the terrace—"and as we suspected, these passcodes were intercepted by guards in the security office of Auric headquarters, downstairs in this building. Significantly, all of these intercepts occurred during the night or on weekends, when off-duty sheriff's deputies were there. In effect, these passcodes gave the sheriff's department the key to your penthouse. It was that simple. Or rather, the 'how' was simple. We still don't know exactly *who* did it, or *why*."

I asked, "And you think Sheriff Hewitt was aware of all this?"

"He *had* to be. The scheme involved so many violations of department protocols, no one would have *dared* participate in the scheme without Stan's go-ahead."

"I've *never* liked that guy." Then I recalled, "Tuesday, at Celia's luncheon, I had the strangest encounter with him. Remember how he was sort of making the rounds, table-hopping, chatting up his constituents?"

Nick nodded. "The man in uniform ... working the room."

"Right. He came to our table and circled around it, all smiles and bullshit with everyone—until he finally came to *me*. Get this: he didn't say a word, but he just gave me a weird grin and shook a finger at me, as if I'd been 'naughty.' I got the impression that this had resulted from my assumed involvement with the *Times* story—as the 'credible source' who disputed Wentworth's Oxford credentials. I took Hewitt's finger-wag as a warning."

With a pinched expression, Nick wondered, "What the *hell* is he up to? That almost sounds like ... *taunting* ... like when the intruder left that mess of ice cream in your kitchen."

"One other thing: When Hewitt shook his finger at me, I noticed a ring he was wearing. It looked like one of Eugene's—a clunky thing, the type that guys in a club might wear. I found it while I was going through his clothes."

"Stan always wears that," said Nick. "He seems to be proud of it—some good-old-boy clan of some sort." Nick paused before adding, "No offense to your late husband."

I rolled my eyes. "Trust me—I've said worse about him."

Nick grinned. "But the *point* of all this is simply to caution you, Meghan. I know you don't go out often, but even here at home, be on guard—and *stay* on guard until we figure out what's really going on."

With a sigh, I noted, "At least the elevator codes have all been changed by now."

"So? I'm sure those codes are monitored by Auric security—then sent merrily along to sheriff's headquarters."

A lull drifted over our conversation, but it wasn't passcodes that were vexing me. "Nick," I said, "something strange happened earlier today. Some sensitive information from Eugene's will was delivered to his first wife, which could cause me some trouble. I don't know if there was anything illegal about conveying this information, except that it might have been obtained from Eugene's home computer—the only item known to be stolen during the break-in."

"*Well*, now," said Nick, suddenly on high alert, "that's an angle worth exploring. Did anyone have access to the computer after Eugene passed away but before it was stolen?"

"I had access, of course, and so did Ashley, my helper, but neither of us ever *touched* anything on Eugene's desk. He was very particular about that." Then I paused, recalling, "His lawyer, Ronda Trask, was up here the morning after he died, explaining his will, getting signatures, and such. While she was here, she did some digging in his computer for a while, which was fine with me. And I'm sure she wasn't snooping for his estate plan—because she *wrote* it."

Nick made note of all this. He told me, "I'm sorry I wasn't able to deliver better news today, but we *will* get to the bottom of this, Meghan."

"Thank you, Nick. I believe you." But ... I wasn't so sure.

He reminded me, "And anytime you're interested in sharing that recording you told me about—the phone call with the threats—I'll be *most* eager to hear it."

"I haven't forgotten. Shouldn't be much longer." But ... I wasn't so sure about that, either.

A very bad day, I told myself, was about to get much better as I waited for Dustin St. James to pick me up at the residents' entrance. It was nearly six o'clock as I stood with the doorman just outside the building, with a cooler at my feet containing gelato—more than enough for three.

In the distance, a massive safari-style cruiser appeared, its crimson finish aglow in the light of September's final sunset. As it approached from the next block, I felt the worries of that day ... evaporate.

When Dustin pulled up to the curb, the doorman helped me climb into the vehicle, then passed the cooler to me and closed the door. Both Dustin and I leaned over the wide console to greet each other with a kiss—not on the cheek, but a quick, deliberate kiss on the lips. Six days had passed since the night we'd spent together, and this evening's kiss seemed to acknowledge—to affirm—that what had happened last week was no fluke that would be brushed aside and dismissed as the embarrassing aftermath of too much booze.

He asked, "Would you believe that I've missed you?"

"Mm-hmm. You've crossed my mind as well—once or twice."

We didn't say much else during the five-minute drive to his studio. There was *so* much to say, but small talk would have felt foolish.

After we parked, Dustin led me to the entrance to the converted warehouse. He opened the door and stepped aside as I entered his home. Something smelled *wonderful.*

"Meghan!" said Nova, skipping over from the kitchen for a hug. "Welcome back. Is that gelato?"

I handed her the cooler. "You bet. Hope you like spumoni."

Warily, she asked, "Is there candied fruit in it?"

"Nope—no evil surprises inside."

She smiled. "Great." And off she went with it.

Dustin took my coat, a light wool jacket, tweedy brown. He offered, "Can I get you a drink?"

"Sure," I said. "Wine, please. Whatever's open."

Amid Dustin and Nova's to-and-fro, amid our chitchat, I stood momentarily adrift—expected to do nothing, but not yet invited to sit—so, naturally, my attention drifted to the studio area of Dustin's quarters.

The core *purpose* of my visit that evening was to see Dustin's latest sketches for Eugene's portrait. Standing near his kitchen now, stealing sidelong glances into his work area, I didn't know what, realistically, I expected to find. His studio space was huge, and I had no knowledge of where he might tuck away a few sketches, presumably no bigger than an artist's newsprint pad.

There was, however, one aspect of his studio that I could not recall from my two prior visits. The clutter of easels bearing various works in progress had been cleared in front of the rear wall, which was now draped with a paint-spattered canvas tarp. Had he been experimenting with a new Pollock-inspired phase of his *oeuvre*? Or had he simply tacked up the tarp to cover something? I wondered...

"Here," said Dustin. "Taste."

I turned to find him standing behind me with two glasses of wine.

"We're having chicken Marsala," he said, "but Marsala's too sweet for drinking—at least for me—so I opened a nice pinot noir to go with it." He handed me one of the glasses.

I swirled and sniffed—nice, indeed. "Cheers," I said as we clinked, then tasted.

He raised an inquisitive brow. "Should I dump it?"

I laughed. "Fat chance." Then I took a *serious* swallow.

Watching me, but calling to his daughter, he asked, "Can you finish setting the table, sweetie?"

"Already on it, Dad."

Still watching me, he said quietly, "May I show you something?"

"Please do."

With his glass in one hand, he wrapped his free arm over my shoulders and strolled me into the studio. "Stand ... *here*," he said, positioning me about twelve feet from the back wall. He stepped away to switch on some extra lighting, then moved to the wall and carefully tugged the tarp free of two nails that served as hooks.

As the tarp fell to the floor, I gasped.

He turned to me, grinning. "I got excited about the sketch, so I scaled it up—full size."

I said nothing.

He added, "But if you don't like it, I'll start over."

"Holy *Christ*." I clapped a hand over my mouth. Wine sloshed in my glass.

Nova giggled, watching from the kitchen. She told Dustin, "Back to the drawing board, Dad."

"*No*," I said, twirling to address both of them. Setting my glass on one of Dustin's taborets, I told him, "I think it's *astounding*."

Carefully, Dustin suggested, "But maybe a tad too irreverent?"

What I saw was clearly a sketch, nothing like a finished painting on canvas, but Dustin had drawn his sketch—in paint, eight feet square—on the freshly whitewashed wall. Showing through the image were the faint lines of a pencil grid he had used in scaling up the original sketch, which was on newsprint and hanging nearby, attached to the wall with masking tape at its upper corners. The composition reflected the ideas he had previously discussed with me: Eugene (who was *recognizably* Eugene) in Napoleon garb, standing next to a horse with his arm draped over the beast's rump, which directly faced the viewer. In the background, idyllic golden wheat fields parted like the Red Sea, revealing a path to the faraway ruins of a skyline dominated by a fanciful tower.

"Irreverent?" I asked. "I don't think so—but give me a few days to consider that."

"Take as long as you like. I want you to be totally comfortable with the results. I want you to love it."

"I already love it. But I probably *should* consider the 'legacy' angle—both his and *mine*." Mumbling, I elaborated, "Wouldn't want to be remembered as a bitter old bitch."

Nova giggled again.

Dustin said, "Whatever you decide, I'm at your service."

Dinner was faultless—in its preparation, its presentation, and in the easy, cozy chemistry that the three of us enjoyed at the table. Dustin was his forever-charming self, and Nova displayed, once again, surprising maturity for a ten-year-old, while never tempting us to forget that she was, at heart, just a kid.

She was excited about her after-school dance class. "There's a big recital next *spring*, so we've been working on some stuff from *Appalachian Spring*—ever heard of it?"

Dustin sputtered a laugh.

"It rings a bell," I said.

"I'd like to play the bride—but I'll probably get stuck with the ugly old pioneer woman."

I told her, "I'm sure you'll be *lovely* in either role." And I thought of the importance of dance—of *all* the arts—in Nova's young life.

Which of course brought to mind Petro Yorba's vision of The School at Fairview Institute of Arts, where creativity and personal expression would be *built into* the entire academic program, rather than being relegated as after-school "activities." Perhaps Nova could attend high school there. If things went well, it could be up and running by then—unless my future plans were upended by malevolent forces like Bebe Auric, Julian Wentworth, Sheriff Hewitt, and God-only-knows who else.

But I tried not to dwell on such disheartening possibilities, focusing instead on the here and now. My companions were cheery. The Marsala was superb. And the spumoni was a hit.

When Nova got up to clear the table, I said, "Let me help."

"Of *course* not," she said. "You two, enjoy yourselves."

A few minutes later, Nova came back to the table—with a practiced yawn. "I've got a test in the morning, so I think I'll go to my room and study awhile, in bed. Good night, you two." She gave me a hug, kissed her father, and headed up to her room, where she disappeared behind a closed door.

Dustin checked his watch. "It's *only* eight o'clock."

I laughed. "What a minx."

Neither of *us* was inclined to call it a night, so we lingered over another glass of wine, quizzing each other about the minutiae of our lives, resuming the process of getting better acquainted. Eventually, the discussion led to past relationships.

Dustin said, "I hesitate to darken such a pleasant evening with an unpleasant topic, but I'm guessing you might have questions about the circumstances of my wife's death, then my husband's."

I shrugged. "You said you were 'unlucky in love.' I'd say, '*tragically* unlucky.' I'm sorry for your loss—or rather, losses."

"It's just that, well, there's been some 'talk' about what happened. So you might as well hear about it from me. I've already told you that both my wife, Crystal, and my husband, Brad, died within a couple years of marrying me. But I didn't mention that I had substantial life-insurance policies on both of them, so the insurance companies got suspicious and opened an investigation."

"How horrible for you," I said. But this, of course, was not news to me.

"On the surface, what happened *did* look bad. But here's the part that wasn't so obvious: My *father* bought both of those policies for me as wedding presents. He gave Crystal and Brad policies on *my* life as well. Dad is just 'that kind of guy'—an obsessively cautious provider. Crystal died very suddenly of an aneurysm, which clearly had *nothing* to do with me, and the insurance paid up. Then, when Brad came along, Dad was all the more convinced that insurance policies were in order. Brad and I actually joked about it, how 'lightning never strikes twice.' Turns out, his parents never told him about a congenital condition— a heart anomaly—because they thought it would only 'upset' him. Instead, it killed him. And once again, I was the beneficiary of a generous payout. It was beyond tragic: it was also embarrassing and suspicious. Hence, the investigation."

I shook my head. "What an ordeal."

"In the end, the investigation fizzled. But things like that seem to have a way of not *going* away. Some people still wonder about it." Then Dustin reached for my hand on the table. "I hope you haven't found this distressing."

"No," I said slowly, somberly, "of course not."

Suppressing a grin, I found that these added details had given me *quite* a boost. Dustin's explanation of his double windfall was soundly plausible, and I was happily willing to believe every word of his story that night.

But that didn't mean I wouldn't hire someone to verify it.

CHAPTER
SIXTEEN

On the first of October, dawn arrived later and darker than usual, with daybreak delayed by cloud-clogged skies, threatening rain. That Friday morning brought an abrupt change from the long streak of glorious autumn weather that had marked the end of September, but I was not inclined to read much into this—omens, portents, entrails, and tea leaves had never been high on my list of rational concerns.

And it would take more than a bit of gloomy weather to dampen my spirits after a deep, restorative night's sleep—made possible by the camaraderie of the prior evening. My time with Dustin and Nova had been the perfect antidote to toxic developments of a difficult day. Then, around ten, when Dustin delivered me to the residents' entrance at Auric Tower, our good-night kiss was lengthy enough to cue the doorman to back away from the vehicle.

Because I slept so soundly that night—and because there were no shafts of early sunlight to rouse me on that gray morning—I was still in bed when Ashley entered the room shortly before nine, intending to start her workday but discovering, mortified, that she had woken me.

"No need to apologize," I croaked groggily. "I should have been up *hours* ago."

Coyly, she asked, "So? How'd it go last night? He must've *really* worn you out." *Wink-wink.*

"He did nothing of the kind."

"I'm sorry to hear that."

I threw a pillow at her. "Could you *possibly* get a pot of coffee going?"

Within half an hour, I'd showered and thrown myself together for a morning at home—not quite presentable for guests, but I wasn't expecting any, and at least I felt human again. The coffee, handed to me while I was still in the bathroom, helped.

Walking out from my dressing room, I saw that Ashley had already made the bed and was now busily occupied, again, sorting and folding more of Eugene's clothes, which were stacked near a carton for my review.

I set down my coffee mug and went at it—going through all the pockets, finding nothing, setting most of the items inside the carton, and tossing others aside as trash. Bored and frustrated, I thought aloud, "Will this *never* end?"

"Eventually...," said Ashley, but her tone lacked conviction.

I picked up my coffee again and downed a few slugs. "Oh," I said, "did you finish with that box that came from the hospital yesterday?" After going through the envelope of Eugene's personal effects, I had abandoned the rest of the box when Bebe phoned me about the codicil.

Ashley rose from the floor, where she'd been sitting while folding clothes on the carpet. Standing, she clapped imagined grime from her hands. "I put Mr. A's watch and stuff on the tray in his dressing room, but I left the clothes in the box—thought you'd want to go through those yourself." She popped into the dressing room for a moment, then reappeared in the bedroom, carrying the open Bankers Box, which she set on the bed for me.

The day Eugene had gone to the hospital—for the last time—he'd left from his downstairs office at Auric headquarters, driven, I believe, by Ronda Trask. His various ailments had been worsening for about a week, and that day, at the end of an afternoon meeting, he told Ronda, weakly, "Seems I'm in need of another tune-up." When they left, he didn't even have his briefcase, just the clothes he was wearing.

And here they were. I set everything out on the bed, then immediately trashed the underwear and socks. I handed the shoes to Ashley, who put them with dozens and dozens of other pairs, all custom-made in London. The white dress shirt, also from London, needed to be laundered but was worth handing down, so it was placed in the appropriate pile.

Which left the three-piece suit he'd worn that day. I removed the flashy silk handkerchief—peacock blue—from the breast pocket of the jacket; Ashley put it with others that needed pressing. By now, I'd had plenty of experience finding all the hidden pockets, so I quickly retrieved some change, a wad of Kleenex, and a couple of spare collar stays for his shirt (he had an inexplicable preoccupation with those).

The vest, I'd learned, was a dandy place to tuck things away and forget about them, so I felt the watch pocket. (Does *anyone* still carry a pocket watch?) There was something inside, but from the feel of it, I couldn't imagine what it was—certainly not a watch of any description.

I pulled it out, holding it between two fingers, and examined it. Recognizing it as some sort of computer thing, I asked Ashley, "What *is* this?"

She took it. "It's a flash drive, sometimes called a thumb drive."

It was, in fact, about the size and shape of a thumb—plastic, with a metal plug at one end.

Ashley said, "It's a handy little gadget for moving files around, from computer to computer. Just stick it into a USB port."

"I knew *that*." But I didn't. "Can we find out what's *in* this?"

"Sure. I've always got my laptop with me. Come on. I'll set you up with it in the kitchen."

Sitting on stools at the center island, Ashley opened her laptop for me, booted it up, and plugged in the flash drive. On her home screen, a folder icon represented the inserted drive. She clicked on it. "It contains just one file," she told me. "It's a video recording, and it seems to be a Zoom meeting—you know, like everyone was doing during the pandemic."

"Not *everyone*," I assured her.

"This file was created about five months ago."

Thinking back, I said, "That would put it between a couple of Eugene's hospital stays—before things got terrible for him."

Ashley asked, "Do you want me to leave? This might be … personal."

I had no idea whether it was personal or not, but I thought I should probably be alone when I found out. I said, "Thank you, Ashley. How do I *do* this?"

"Just click and play."

I waited till I heard her footfalls retreat across the party room, toward the main bedroom suite. Then I heard that door close.

When I clicked the file, the screen filled with the images of three participants in a video conference that was just beginning. Across the bottom was a larger image of Eugene, who had called the meeting. He was sitting at the desk in his den in the penthouse—there was no mistaking the brightly colored corner of a LeRoy Neiman painting on the wall behind him. In the upper-right of the screen was a smaller image of Ronda Trask, seated in her office downstairs at Auric headquarters. Upper-left in the screen—I winced—there sat Julian Wentworth, but I couldn't tell where he was located.

Eugene cleared his throat, saying, "...now, in case you didn't notice, the red dot just lit up, which means I've started recording this—locally, not in the cloud. You can do the same, if you want, and I hope you will. We'll be talking about things that no one else can *ever* know. The existence of the recording ensures that this discussion will remain strictly among the three of us—because, if it doesn't, we will *all* find ourselves in one fucking-serious shitload of legal jeopardy."

"Eugene," said Ronda, "I have some problems with this. I love ya to bits, but I'm technically an officer of the court. I know, I know—you scoff at that concept—"

"*Bah*," he interrupted, sounding angry.

"See what I mean?" said Ronda, tossing her hands.

"Just shut up and *listen*, dammit. I have a *problem*, and it needs to be *solved*. Pronto."

Wentworth asked, "What's the problem, Eugene?"

"Senator Grady Vaughn is the problem."

Ronda reminded Eugene, "But you *love* that guy. You put him in office."

"Exactly. So wouldn't you expect that son of a bitch to under-stand that he owes me some fucking *loyalty*? Everything he's got, he owes to me. And I want that pipeline to *happen*."

"He does, too," said Wentworth. "So what's the issue?"

"He's backing the wrong *map*. Of the many pipeline routes that have been proposed, only two remain, both running through this state: Map Twelve and Map Nineteen."

Looking enlightened, Ronda said, "And *you* have an interest in Map Twelve."

"Damn right I do. Nearly a hundred miles of pipeline would pass through *my* land, and the rights to dig it up would be worth *billions*. This is payback that Grady *owes* me, and I've told him so—more than once. He seems, however, to be under the mistaken impression that the choice is ultimately *his*. And guess what: he's throwing his support to Map Nineteen. Why? Because 'promises have been made.'"

"Oops," said Ronda.

"*Oops?*" said Eugene, pounding both fists on his desk like a spoiled baby. "That motherfucker *really* fries my ass!"

"Okay...," said Wentworth, "I guess we understand the 'problem' now, but how do you think we can 'solve' it?"

Without hesitation, Eugene told both Wentworth and Ronda, "Grady Vaughn needs to be removed from office."

Ronda laughed. "How the fuck is *that* gonna happen? It would take a year to mount a recall campaign—and voters seem to like the guy, so it would probably fail."

Eugene leaned close to the screen and calmly clarified his meaning: "Grady Vaughn needs to *die* in office. Quickly. And then—"

"Time-out," Ronda interrupted, gesturing with her hands. "I *cannot* hear more of this. Whatever you're driving at, Eugene, I advise you against it. And for your own protection, I'm signing off." When her section of the screen went black, a caption appeared: R. TRASK HAS LEFT MEETING.

Then the black square disappeared, and the images of Eugene and Wentworth rearranged themselves, filling the screen.

"Well," said Eugene, "it's just us, Mr. *Wentworth*." He made air quotes with his fingers, signifying his knowledge that the other man's name was previously something else.

Wentworth asked, "Isn't 'dying in office' a bit...extreme?"

Eugene laughed. "Don't try to tell me you've suddenly grown some scruples."

Wentworth also laughed. "I wouldn't go *that* far. So let's get specific. What do you want done? And what's in it for me?"

"I've already said what I want done: Senator Vaughn needs to die in office, quickly. Let's say, within a month. You've been trained. If you need any assistance or technical backup, just talk to that numbnuts lard-ass."

"I *assume*," said Wentworth, "you're referring to our dedicated public servant, Sheriff Hewitt."

"Who *else*? He'll do what he's told, but I'm trusting *you* to figure out the details—there can be no evidence of foul play." With his orders now understood, Eugene calmed himself. Adopting a more enticing tone, he said, "Regarding what's in this for *you*, how would you like the sound of 'Senator Wentworth'?"

"I think I'd like that *very* much."

"Of *course* you would," said Eugene. "I can do plenty to help make that happen. And then, after 'considerable study and reflection,' you'll decide that the pipeline will be good for the people, and you'll also decide that the best plan for advancing the project is Map Twelve. Got it?"

Grinning, Wentworth leaned forward with a thumbs-up.

The video abruptly ended.

And with a shaky hand, I closed the laptop.

PART THREE

Scream Like a Girl

Knowledge, as they say, is power.

But consider *this* bit of newfound knowledge: my late husband, long revered as a builder and visionary, had conspired with a man who had once betrayed me, and together they were responsible for the murder of a sitting member of the United States Senate. The thumb drive I now had in my possession did indeed give me the *power* to end Julian Wentworth's quest to join "the world's most exclusive club," but watching the video had left me feeling anything *but* empowered—because revealing what I had learned would expose me to multiple dangers.

Just for starters, I now knew with certainty that I had been dealing with people who did *not* kid around. I had already received a death threat, and the video made it clear that I should take the threat seriously. *Very* seriously. If my husband and Wentworth, assisted by a crooked sheriff, could blithely decide to snuff out an elected, high-ranking federal official—over a tiff about a pipeline—what chance did *I* have of surviving an attempt to expose them?

At a deeper level, while I now understood that Eugene's sterling reputation as a businessman deserved to be tarnished by the truth that he was a narcissistic thug, I had to consider that I'd stood at his side for twenty-five years, serving as his trophy wife and hostess. Could I have been that blind? Yes. But news of the extent of Eugene's depravity would lead some to conclude that I had served his purpose with—at the very least—"emotional complicity." This sort of guilt by association was *not* how I wished to be remembered.

But perhaps, I now feared, this was exactly how I *deserved* to be remembered. And it all traced back to my youthful stupidity in an insurance scheme. I had played a role in the loss of life. Turns out, Eugene had done the same.

What a match we made…

So. The video on the thumb drive did empower me to settle a long-festering score with Julian Wentworth, a.k.a. John White, but the recording was far from a surefire checkmate, a conclusive *coup de grâce*, because I would face such a heavy price for making it public.

With all of this in mind, what was I to do?

First, I watched the video again, making mental notes of who'd said what. Then I removed the thumb drive from the laptop, picked up the computer, and took it back to Ashley in the bedroom.

As I entered, she looked up from a stack of folded shirts she was sorting by color. With an uncertain expression, she asked me, "Well…?"

I moved to the bed, sat, and patted a spot next to me, suggesting quietly, "Sit down, Ashley."

As she did so, I handed her the laptop, which she set aside. I pivoted to face her; she mirrored my position. Showing her the thumb drive in my palm, I said, "This was… mind-blowing."

Cautiously, she asked, "Anything you'd care to share?"

Leaning an inch or two closer, I said, "I want to share it *all*, Ashley. But right now, I just can't. I *do* trust you—I hope you know that—but there's a real possibility of danger to anyone who sees this. Do you trust *me*?"

"Of *course*, Meghan. Completely. How can I help?"

"The person who made this video—and it is, as you thought, a Zoom meeting—he says at the start that he's recording it 'locally, not in the cloud.' What does that mean?"

Ashley said, "'Locally' refers to his own computer, the one he used during the meeting. Instead, he could've had Zoom save the recording for him on their servers, but it seems he was trying to prevent anyone else from getting hold of it."

"That makes sense—he did *not* want this to get around." I set the thumb drive between us on the bed. "If he put the video recording on this gadget, did that remove it from his computer?"

"That was entirely up to him. He could have simply *copied* it to the thumb drive, or he could have *moved* it, which would delete it from his computer."

I thought aloud, "Then *that's* what they were looking for."

"Hmm?"

I clarified, "During the break-in, when they tore up Eugene's office, they took his computer."

Ashley raised a brow. "Then ... the 'he' you've been talking about, on the video, 'he' was Mr. A?"

I nodded. "Just let it go at that, okay? And don't repeat it."

She gave me a three-finger Scout salute, which I interpreted as a pledge of secrecy. Then she repeated her earlier offer: "How can I help?"

"Can you make a copy of the video from the thumb drive—on another thumb drive? No 'cloud' stuff."

"Easy. First I'll need to copy it, temporarily, to my laptop, but then I'll move it to a new thumb drive and delete the copy on the laptop."

"Perfect."

Then Ashley asked, "You do know, don't you, that nothing's ever truly *gone* from a computer, unless it's been completely wiped. With the right tools and savvy, you can resurrect almost anything."

I shrugged. "Then we'll just have to take that chance. And the copied thumb drive, by the way, is for *you*. Don't open it, don't look at it—*please*. But at some point, I *might* ask you to post it on the internet. Could you do that?"

"Well, *yeah*. If it's truly 'mind-blowing'—your phrase—I'd *love* to add it to my vlog. Sounds like it might be primo clickbait."

"Yes," I agreed with an air of understatement, "it might draw a bit of attention."

We settled on a plan. She had a spare flash drive in her backpack, so she could copy mine and return it right away. Her copy was to be hidden away but always accessible on a moment's notice. I would notify her if and when I wanted it made public. Meanwhile, she would set up an online post as a vague, generic teaser, something along the lines of: WATCH THIS SPACE, BE THE FIRST TO KNOW. She would supply me with a direct link to it. Then, later, if I gave her the go-ahead, she would replace the teaser with the Zoom video, and I in turn could send that link— along with a link to the recorded phone call with Wentworth's death threat—to Detective Nick Gamarra, reporter Chase Unger, and my lawyer, Adam Hudson.

While Ashley got busy making the copy of the thumb drive, I tried snagging an extra appointment with Faye Rubin. After the revelations of that morning, I really needed to meet with her before our regular session next week.

It was after ten o'clock that morning when I phoned down to Faye's office and, as expected, the call was answered by her receptionist, Marlene. She was never at her best when confronted with last-minute requests. As if treading water, wondering how to make me go away, she asked, "Is this an emergency?"

"It's not a *suicide*-level emergency, but yes, it qualifies as a crisis in the making—I was confronted with an extraordinary development this morning and I *need* some professional advice."

"We'll ... it's *Friday*," she explained (as if I didn't know what day it was), "and Dr. Faye was hoping to slip out early this afternoon. Her last session ends at twelve thirty today."

"You mean, the rest of her afternoon is *open*?"

"Appointment-wise, yes. But she may have other plans of her own."

"Don't be *silly*," I said with an airy laugh. (No wonder I always sensed that Marlene didn't quite care for me.) "Please tell Dr. Rubin that I'll bribe her with double fees, lunch, and gelato if she can join me in the penthouse any time after twelve thirty. Could you let me know?"

"I'll ask her at the conclusion of her current session, Mrs. Auric. Thank you for calling." Her tone, while studiously polite, had all the warmth of a put-upon bureaucrat.

Waiting to hear back from Marlene, which I assumed would be after eleven, I considered phoning Nick and Adam with an update. The detective and the lawyer would surely want to know what I'd discovered on the thumb drive—but I hesitated. At present, they weren't even aware that the thumb drive existed, let alone that it contained explosive information regarding the death of Senator Vaughn. Both Nick and Adam represented the law, though from different perspectives, and they would each feel compelled to take immediate action after being presented with new, decisive evidence. I simply wasn't ready for that. If I were to update them now, I could not supply the most pertinent details—certainly not the actual recording of the Zoom meeting—so I would only be tantalizing them, once again, with hints of what they *might* learn from me later. I understood how frustrating they would find this (and how ditzy I would appear), so I decided that they could wait awhile to learn of my discovery.

When Marlene phoned back, around eleven thirty, she informed me that Faye would be happy to come up to see me at a quarter to one.

I had already told Ashley to take the afternoon off, so I was alone in the penthouse when I went to greet Faye at the elevator.

"*Meghan*," she said as the door slid closed behind her, "I've been so concerned—what's troubling you?"

Before launching into it, I suggested, "Would you *maybe* like a glass of wine?"

She considered this briefly, then grinned. "You're my last appointment of the day, so my weekend has nearly begun. Why not?"

I led her up to the top floor and into the kitchen, where I opened a chilled bottle of French rosé, a perfect anytime wine, and poured it generously into oversize balloon glasses. When we lifted them, I touched mine to hers. "*Thank* you for being here. It's been a rough day."

"Let's see if we can't make it better."

Taking a first sip, I smiled. "Wine always helps."

There had been no rain yet, but the sky was still completely clouded over, so lunch on the terrace seemed like a bad idea. Since the dining room was much too stuffy for a casual lunch for two, the only remaining option was the kitchen, which had a comfortable breakfast alcove with a table for four—plenty of room for Faye to spread out her notes while we ate the quiche I'd whipped up. Then we settled back for some serious conversation.

Faye said, "Our last session was on Monday, and then I saw you again at the Towne Club event on Tuesday. Would you like to give me a chronological update, or would you prefer to start with whatever happened today?"

"You deserve to know why I wanted to meet so suddenly, so let's start with this morning."

"Good." Faye set aside my folder and opened her notepad to a fresh page.

"I was going through some of Eugene's clothes that were sent back from the hospital yesterday. In the watch pocket of a vest, I found a hidden computer thing, a thumb drive—are you familiar with those?"

She nodded. "Sure. A little flash drive."

"Right. And my helper, Ashley, set me up with her laptop so I could find out what, if anything, was contained on the drive." I paused.

She said, "I assume you found something disturbing."

"Very. And I have to be honest with you, Faye. The mere knowledge of what's on that drive could prove dangerous—to anyone who's in the loop. Do you want me to continue?"

She set down her pen and spoke through a soft smile. "You wouldn't have asked to see me if you didn't want to share this. And I'd be a lousy therapist if I didn't want to hear what you have to say. So: tell me."

"The thumb drive contained the recording of a video conference Eugene had several months ago with his lawyer and Julian Wentworth."

Faye's brows arched. "And Julian Wentworth is the man you once knew as John White. Is that past incident what they talked about?"

"No. That never came up. And I only wish it were that simple. What they *did* talk about was far more serious—they were plotting the murder of Senator Grady Vaughn."

Faye flumped back in her seat. "Good heavens."

"The lawyer dropped out of the conversation as soon as she realized where it was headed, but Eugene and Wentworth wrapped it up together. Senator Vaughn had refused to do Eugene's bidding regarding that ridiculous pipeline project, and there was some *serious* money on the line. So Eugene decided that Vaughn needed to 'die in office.' He ordered Wentworth to figure it out, 'within a month,' which is consistent with the timing of Vaughn's death. Plus, get this: Eugene said that Wentworth could depend on Sheriff Hewitt for assistance and backup because, quote, 'He'll do what he's told.'"

Stunned, Faye asked, "And Wentworth just went *along* with all this?"

I explained, "Eugene promised to help get him elected to the open Senate seat."

Faye grasped the edge of the table with both hands, steadying herself. "The level of corruption here—to say nothing of the murder scheme—is simply beyond belief."

"Believe it," I said flatly.

"I'm confused, though. They had this clandestine meeting to hatch this clandestine plan—so how does it happen that a video recording even *exists*?"

"The reason is *so* perverse, and it is *so* Eugene. He himself recorded the meeting and encouraged the others to do the same. Because they were all culpable, he concluded that they were each equally motivated to enforce the others' silence—sort of a peremptory groupthink."

Faye noted, "This is sounding so ... Machiavellian."

"That's my Eugene: just when you think you've heard the worst, there's always more."

Faye paused to clear her head—and to down some more wine. "Okay. This happened. You made this awful discovery. But what's next?"

"That's the question I meant to ask *you*."

"If you're asking for advice, I can only tell you what *I* would do if faced with the same circumstances: I'd take this evidence to the police. Right away."

I reminded Faye, "In Fairview, 'the police' is the sheriff's department, and the sheriff himself seems to be neck-deep in the murder scheme I've discovered."

"Oh." Faye had another slug of wine. "That *is* an extenuating circumstance."

"It's also a pisser." I poured her another slosh of wine, laughing softly.

She said, "I'm glad you're able to find humor in this situation, but frankly, I don't get it."

"Not exactly humor," I said, setting down the bottle. "It's more like irony. Think about it: When we met two sessions ago, I had just discovered that the man who'd betrayed me, John White, had somehow resurfaced and transformed himself into Senate candidate Wentworth. My 'issue' at that point was simple. I wanted to get back at him. I wanted payback."

"You wanted revenge."

"Such an ugly word," I mused aloud, "but yes, that pretty well sums it up. Trouble was, I had also recently learned of the codicil to Eugene's will, so making trouble for Wentworth could also make trouble for me. Meaning, I would just have to stew about it—and not rock the boat."

Faye skimmed back through her notes. "But then, the next time we met, the situation had evolved in unexpected ways."

"*Very* unexpected," I agreed. "At our last session, I reported that I had recently been threatened by both Wentworth and his campaign manager. By then Wentworth knew that I had figured out who he was and that I could expose harmful secrets from his past. Therefore, I was a problem. I had also seen through his shallow, two-faced campaign to win at any cost. So my 'issue' at that point had become more complicated—and less selfish. The desire for revenge was still there, but now my main concern was for the common good, hoping to thwart his campaign for higher office."

Faye noted, "Yes, your motives to thwart him had evolved in their complexity. But at the same time, your reasons for *not* getting involved had also mushroomed."

"Right," I said. "Previously, the codicil—the threat to my inheritance—was the only thing holding me back. But when Wentworth started making *threats*, it became much more serious than a game of gotcha. At that point, I was facing a true life-or-death dilemma."

"And now, today," said Faye, "the complexity of your situation has grown exponentially. It seems that your 'Wentworth problem' has also been—all along—a 'Eugene problem.'"

Placing an elbow on the table, I held my forehead in my hand as I recalled, "Hearing him this morning—watching a video of my husband ordering the murder of a friend over nothing more serious than wounded vanity and a perceived lack of 'loyalty'—I had to wonder how this could possibly be coming from the man I thought I knew, warts and all, for twenty-five years. I mean, if I missed *this*, what *else* don't I know?"

Faye reached across the table. I lifted my head and took her hand. She said, "I think you must've hit bottom today—no more surprises regarding Eugene. As dreadful as these revelations have been, at least you've learned the worst of it. And now, you can start finding your way forward."

Sitting taller in my chair, I flicked something from the corner of my eye and realized that it was a tear. Managing a smile, I said, "See? I really *did* need to talk to you."

"I'm glad I had an open afternoon."

I suggested, "Gelato?"

"Sure—that was part of the deal. What flavor?"

"More like *three* flavors. I made spumoni to take to dinner at Dustin's studio last night—but I didn't take it all."

"Delightful," she said. When I got up to serve the gelato, she asked, "And what was the 'nature' of that dinner?"

Turning to her from the refrigerator, I said, "It was *not* what you're thinking, Faye. Dustin had worked up a new idea for Eugene's portrait and wanted me to come over to see it. It was a school night for Nova, so she was there, and our dinner was just a comfortable family-style supper. Dustin had me home by ten— and we parted with a lovely good-night kiss."

With an approving nod, Faye was taking notes. "So you managed another excursion from the building this week—excellent."

"Actually," I said, bringing the bowls of spumoni to the table, "that was my *second* outing this week. Earlier, on Wednesday, I went to the museum. Ashley drove me." I sat again.

Picking up her spoon, Faye asked, "Board work? Committee meeting?"

"No. Have I ever told you about Everett Burke? He's general manager at the Towne Club—handsome man, mid-fifties, widower."

Coyly, Faye said, "I do recall that you've *mentioned* him in the past—a few assignations, I believe. And I got a good look at him at Tuesday's luncheon. Handsome, indeed." She winked.

I sighed. "He's a really sweet guy. Refined. Courteous, to a *fault*. And since Eugene's death, Everett has made it known to me that he'd be open to 'taking things further.' I'd been putting him off, so I suggested an innocent afternoon 'date' at the museum."

"How'd it go?"

"I sorta ditched him."

Faye licked her spoon. "The spumoni is *marvelous*, by the way. But why did you ditch Everett?"

"Petro Yorba, the museum director, got word from the staff that I was on the premises, so he tracked me down and mentioned that he'd been wanting to talk to me about a development plan he's been cooking up. I feigned an urgent interest in this, so Everett took the hint and bowed out."

With a laugh, Faye told me, "I must admit, Meghan—I'm impressed. When it comes to men, you certainly have options. If it were up to me, *I* wouldn't send Everett packing so quickly." She laughed again. More precisely, she twittered.

Hmm.

"Anyway," I said, "after Everett left, Petro filled me in on his big idea: The School at Fairview Institute of Arts."

Faye asked, "What sort of school would it be?"

I gave her all the details, speaking so quickly that I realized I was gushing. I slowed down, explaining, "Petro's vision for the school resonated with me—strongly. I haven't felt so energized about a project in many years."

"How wonderful," said Faye with a smile. Then her tone turned more serious as she asked, "But do you think your reaction might have been compensating—maybe *over*-compensating—for the recent stress factors in your life? You've experienced the death of a spouse, the reappearance of a past nemesis, and various threats. Could the school project simply be a 'shiny new object' that distracts you from all the crap you've been dealing with?"

"Maybe," I admitted. "But the scope of the project is very long-range, at least five years, so I'll have plenty of time for second thoughts if my sense of commitment fades. Honestly, though, I don't think that will happen. I would *love* to see this through—and truly make a difference in the lives of young people. That's worth doing on its own merits. But at a deeper level, there's more: by engaging in selfless 'good works' that have a lasting impact, I might be able to begin working my way through the guilt I've been carrying. There's no way I can ever fully atone for the lives that were lost in that insurance scam, but a little altruism can go a long way toward ethical redemption—or at least, partial redemption."

Faye bobbed her head, assessing my words. "I think ... you *are* seeing this clearly. And perhaps the school *would* give you a rewarding sense of purpose. It sounds as if you'd be making a lifetime commitment."

"According to Petro," I said, "this could be my 'legacy project.' As you can imagine, something of this scope would involve a substantial portion of my assets—so I can't proceed with it *at all* until I know with certainty that my future finances are secure. Eugene is no longer in the picture, but the codicil is still hanging there, and Bebe could conceivably wipe me out."

While Faye wrote her notes, I added, grimly, "Money isn't the only issue. If and when this Wentworth business blows up, my own past could come back to haunt me with legal jeopardy that could literally lock me up. Worse yet, I've had threats of retribution from bad people with powerful interests who play for keeps—with deadly results."

As if on cue, the first rumblings of thunder pulsed from the gray sky and rattled the doors to the terrace outside the kitchen.

With a laugh of disbelief, I said, "Now, *that* did not sound good."

"Don't be silly. It's only weather—doesn't mean a thing."

Faye was right. I knew that. But still ...

"So," she said, "as your crisis has developed, Meghan, your dilemma has deepened. You've encountered many wrongs that you, as a clear-thinking person of good will, want to thwart—simply because it's the right thing to do. At the same time, however, that clear-thinking brain of yours is warning you not to act—simply because doing so could produce consequences that are decidedly *not* in your best interest. The 'issue' that drives you was once quite basic: revenge. But the circumstances have evolved, and your 'issue' has become far more complex. Unfortunately, you can't just peel away parts of the problem and deal with them piece by piece. That's not an option. Which means that now, Meghan, your 'issue' is to weigh *all* the risks and try to sort out the actual price of exposing ... *everything*."

Pondering this wisdom, I tossed my arms. "No doubt about it. I am totally, irreversibly *fucked!*"

Thunder exploded beyond the windows as lightning scorched the sky.

Faye grinned. "Mind your language, Meghan."

By the time Faye left, the leading edge of the storm had passed, and the steady rain had started, driven in sheets against the glass. At two in the afternoon, the sky was the color of mud.

The events of that day had left me exhausted. I faced a dilemma that offered no clear path to resolution, and I was tired of thinking about it, talking about it, worrying about it. The mental fatigue, coupled with the dark sky, nudged me toward the bedroom.

I couldn't remember the last time I had succeeded in taking a nap. I had long thought of a midday snooze as a self-indulgent luxury, something to be relished, a stolen hour of repose. But today I absolutely *needed* to lie down. To sleep ... perchance to dream.

Ashley had tidied the bedroom before leaving, but there were still cartons of Eugene's clothes lined up against the baseboard of an interior wall. Fewer than before, they signaled that the arduous process of decluttering was at last nearing its end.

I drew all the curtains closed against the outer wall of glass, cutting off what was left of the anemic daylight, but I could still hear the incessant pelting of the rain, a sound I now found oddly comforting and restful.

Taking off my clothes—everything—I opted not to put on pajamas or one of my silken karate gis. I pulled back the bedding and slipped in, between the sheets, naked and fetal, curling into a warm blob in the darkness. I closed my eyes.

Given my state of consternation, I wondered if I would be able to fall asleep—but these doubts proved groundless. In my next moment of awareness, in a second or a minute or an hour, I knew that I was sleeping because the dream had begun:

I'm in my bed, not naked, but wearing a gi, not one of the pretty ones I often use as night wear, but the sturdy canvas one that I wear when training with Gus. I'm not curled into a ball, but lying flat on my back, eyes to the ceiling, but closed. There are unknown sounds, and when they find their way into my consciousness, my eyes open. I listen in the darkness. I am alone in the penthouse, but I hear the sounds of intrusion—a rattle, a jiggle, a scrape—sounds that are muffled and not meant to be heard, not meant to rouse me. I sit up in bed, then swing my feet to the floor. I stand. Then, placing one foot in front of the other, I slowly make my way to the bedroom door. I reach to open it ...

And with a blink of my eyes, I awoke from my nap in the here and now, naked and fetal, sweating under a sheet. I gasped, taking stock of the reality surrounding me on that Friday afternoon.

Except, when I threw back the covers and switched on the bedside lamp, I saw that it was no longer afternoon. It was six o'clock, and I had slept for several hours. I swung my feet to the floor and sat up, running my fingers through my hair. I had a dinner reservation, solo, at the club at seven—*boeuf bourguignon*, if I recalled correctly. I didn't need a mirror to confirm that I looked like hell, but I was feeling refreshed, and I had a full hour to put myself together.

After the nap and a shower, I was in a better frame of mind and was able to set aside, at least temporarily, that morning's revelation that my late husband had been not only a builder, developer, and all-around local tycoon, but also, apparently, a crime boss.

And what did that make *me*—his moll? I had asked myself that question facetiously, but it may have lingered in the back of my mind as I decided to wear a red cocktail dress that night— not generally my color, but I thought it would look good in the ruddy confines of the club's barroom.

On a Friday evening at seven, the main concourse on the ground floor of Auric Tower was quiet, as there wasn't much activity in that part of the building after business hours. However, when I arrived at the top of the staircase leading to the second-floor entrance to the Towne Club, I saw at once that the venerable old joint was hopping. The doorman greeted me by name, adding, "Mr. Burke asked me to let him know when you've arrived. He saved a booth for you in the bar."

So I stepped inside the club's crowded lobby, waiting for Everett to appear. I drew a few glances—probably the red dress. I doubted if anyone would have sufficient nerve to ask me about it, but I almost hoped it would happen, as I had a line ready: *Yes, my period of mourning was brief.*

In truth, though, I was far from the center of attention. That distinction went to Governor Swaine, encircled by a gaggle of well-wishers as he bantered amiably, sipping a brown cocktail with a cherry in it. Now and then, he would nod and wave to anyone who spotted him. Not a member of the club (no man was), he seemed to be with the Keatings, a couple I did not know well.

"*Meghan,*" said Everett, approaching me with a broad smile. "Delighted you could join the festivities tonight. I've been shooing invaders away from your booth—so let's get you situated." While escorting me to the barroom, he leaned to tell me, "You look just *smashing* in red." I gave his arm a squeeze, a silent thank-you.

Though the bar was busy, it wasn't mobbed, so the dimly lit setting was conducive to mingling and conversation. Everett had ordered me a champagne cocktail, which sat at my place setting. "People tend to ignore the RESERVED sign," he said, "but a drink on the table usually scares them off. If you'd like something else, I'll get it for you."

"This will do nicely, Everett. Thank you."

He seated me, bobbed his head, and stepped away.

As I sipped the cocktail and set aside the menu (I already knew what I was having), the Keatings entered the barroom with the governor in tow. Everett had reserved a table for them in the middle of the room, but they told him they'd rather have a drink at the bar first. Once again, Everett bobbed his head and stepped away.

While the Keatings were getting situated at the bar, Governor Swaine turned and spotted me, flashing a smile. He mumbled something to his hosts, who looked over and acknowledged me—he with a nod, she with a wave. Swaine then walked over to my booth.

I started to rise. "Good evening, Governor."

Gesturing with his hands for me to stay seated, he said, "Hello, Meghan. And please—it's 'Howard.' May I join you for a moment?"

"Of course, Howard. Please do."

He squeaked on the curved leather banquette as he slid in across from me at the tiny round table. When one of his knees brushed mine, he said, "Excuse me," and jerked it away. "You're looking *lovely* this evening, as always."

"That's very sweet of you, Howard. Thank you." A man in his sixties, trim and avuncular, with a slicked-back crop of silver hair, he had the look of a dashing actor who would top the casting call for the role of any governor. I asked him, "Where's Olympia tonight? As if I couldn't guess ..."

He laughed. "She's in DC, naturally. When she agreed to serve as interim senator for a few months, we both assumed the job would be largely ... what, ceremonial? Not at all, though. I don't think we've spent a week together since."

"When you talk to her, be sure to extend my greetings."

"Certainly, Meghan. She'll appreciate that." Then his expression turned serious. "Since the loss of your dear Eugene, it's been ... what, two weeks?"

"Fifteen days—but who's counting?" It wasn't intentional, but I was sure my tone came across as far too glib.

"Uh, yes," he said, clearing his throat, "and I just wanted to tell you how devastating his loss was to both Olympia and me. Needless to say, we offer our heartfelt sympathies."

"That's such a comfort. Thank you, Howard."

"We sent a card, of course, through Auric headquarters—not sure if you received it."

"There were so *many*. I haven't been very good about thanking people. And that was such a warm tribute you gave—your quote in the *Times* obituary."

He assured me, "No thanks are necessary—just wanted you to know that you've been in our thoughts. Also, I noted that there won't be a memorial service until next spring. When you decide on a date, could you let me know? If you'd like for me to be there and say a few words, I'd be honored."

"Really?" I tried to mask my astonishment at such a fulsome offer. "The honor would be entirely ours—or rather, Eugene's. I'll be sure to keep you informed." I presumed that, by next spring, he would forget all this. God knows, I would.

Wistfully, he told me, "Eugene was *more* than our state's leading business figure—to me, he was always sort of a *father* figure. When he had a problem, or when I had a problem, we'd just pick up the phone and talk it out, more like *brothers* than father and son, despite the age difference. Olivia and I have often commented that both you and Eugene felt like family to us."

This struck me as an odd remark, which I didn't quite believe. He and Olivia had been guests in the penthouse several times; in turn, Eugene and I had attended a handful of events at the executive mansion in Consensus. Yes, I had always counted them as friends. But "family"? Not even close.

"Family," repeated the governor. With a chuckle, he added, "Or, as some might say—*famiglia*."

Now, *that* was sounding just a tad too godfatherish.

Everett appeared at our table, setting a refreshed brown cocktail—with a cherry—in front of Howard. "From the Keatings, Governor." I half expected Everett to do a full-blown bow and scrape, but he simply backed away.

Howard raised his glass to me; I tapped it with my champagne cocktail. He said, "To Eugene's memory," then drank.

Eyeing him over the rim of my flute, I pondered his *famiglia* comment. That morning, I'd learned that my husband had exhibited defining traits of a mafia don, ordering a hit. Was the governor also ... "in on it?"

He reminisced, "Eugene was such a natural *leader*. I know, I know, his heart belonged to his business—and to you, dear Meghan—but I always wondered why he'd never tried his hand at politics. He could've given *me* a good run for the money."

I reminded Howard, "At eighty-five, Eugene was getting a bit old for a new gig."

Howard laughed, nodding. "I *meant*, when he was *younger*, he could've chosen a very different path—and he could've gone far with it."

I shrugged. "We each contribute in our own way, I guess."

He nodded, thinking, elbows on the table, holding his cocktail with both hands. I noticed the governor's ring, a simple wedding band—no massive diamond, no cryptic engravings. Perhaps he wasn't *famiglia* after all.

"Speaking of politics," he said, "I understand you've turned into a big backer of Celia Gamarra—she's a good woman, a great candidate, period."

"That's *right*," I said, recalling, "she was appointed labor commissioner by *you*. Turns out, it was just the leg up she needed to get into this race."

"And now that she's in it, she's going to need all the help she can get. Are you familiar with her opponent?"

"Familiar?" I said. "That's one way of putting it."

Howard leaned closer over the table. "He's a *slick* bastard, don't you think? For him, the race is *about* him—he doesn't *believe* in anything else. And sad to say, some internal polling shows that he's running slightly ahead."

"Eek." I cringed. "That *is* troubling."

"Celia's campaign has asked me to write an endorsement, to run in this Sunday's *Times*. I mean, my support is pretty obvious, but maybe it'll help swing a few votes."

"God, I hope so, Howard. Um ... are you aware that Eugene was sort of a mentor to Wentworth?"

"Oh, sure. He cashed in a *heap* of favors to get Wentworth that spot on the county board. God knows why, though." He paused before adding, "Don't get me wrong, Meghan. I flat-out loved Eugene. But just like the rest of us, he had a few—shall we say—effing *strange* ideas."

I chortled. "He certainly did ..."

"Well," he said with a laugh, "I'd better get back to the Keat-ings—or I *might* end up buying my own dinner."

I reminded him, "Your money's no good here, Governor. But if you're left in the lurch, *I'll* sign your chit."

He winked. "Thanks, Meghan." He patted my hand, then got up from the booth and returned to the bar, where he was quickly surrounded by a clutch of hobnobbers, eager to bend the ears of power.

A few minutes later, after placing my dinner order, I saw Bebe

Auric enter the bar with her son, Eugene Junior. As they passed, Gene acknowledged me with a grin and a nod, but Bebe looked away as she slid into the booth next to mine, sitting back-to-back with me. We were so close, I could practically hear her breathing, but she spoke not a word, not even to her son.

It would be a chilly night in the Towne Club.

But the *boeuf bourguignon* was warm and delicious.

CHAPTER
EIGHTEEN

By Saturday morning, the clouds had cleared, and with the brighter sky came a suddenly cooler breeze. Autumn had arrived in earnest.

So I shrugged into a heavy velour robe—it was chocolate brown and gave me the unflattering, tubby look of a teddy bear. Then I took my coffee and newspaper out to the terrace, where I found a comfortable area to sit, protected from the wind but exposed to full sunshine. Steam rose from my cup, brilliant and sinuous in the morning light.

That day, October second, was a month before the day of the special election in November. I assumed that this timing would be noted in that morning's edition of the *Consensus Times*, and as I removed the paper from its delivery sleeve and unrolled it, my hunch proved correct.

Page one contained two photo layouts depicting highlights of Julian Wentworth's and Celia Gamarra's recent campaign activities. Wentworth was shown greeting people and speaking at churches, garden parties, and the chamber of commerce. Gamarra was similarly engaged at libraries, a union hall, and a campus rally at Lindencrest University. A boxed sidebar story carried the headline: ONE MONTH TO GO. The text beneath it, which carried no byline, told readers:

The statewide special election to fill the remainder of the late Grady Vaughn's term in the United States Senate is now just one month away, on November 2, with early voting scheduled to begin two weeks from Tuesday.

Tomorrow's Sunday edition of the *Times* will feature endorsements from Governor Howard Swaine as well as the *Times* editorial board, on our OPINIONS page. Sunday's paper will also feature letters submitted by readers in support of both candidates, Julian Wentworth and Celia Flores Gamarra. Letters will be accepted for future publication until a week prior to the election.

Senator Grady Vaughn had represented the people of our state in Washington for nearly seven years at the time of his sudden death this summer, while on recess at his home in Consensus. The circumstances of his death, originally attributed to heart failure, were recently revisited, and the death has subsequently been ruled a homicide. State and federal investigations are now underway.

The shocking development has greatly heightened public interest in the special election to fill Vaughn's seat, now held on an interim basis by Olympia Swaine, wife of Governor Swaine. Polling of the current contest between Wentworth and Gamarra suggests that election results will be extremely close.

Turn to the *Times* for ongoing coverage.

I was particularly interested to note the story's reference to Senator Vaughn's death as a homicide. I had learned of this a week earlier, in confidence, during one of Detective Nick Gamarra's visits to the penthouse. Now, though, the story was out there, with predictable results: the election to replace Vaughn was no longer a mere curiosity or a dry civics lesson, but very hot news.

That said, the revelation of Vaughn's murder was not news to *everyone*.

Julian Wentworth knew about it—because he himself had arranged it and was probably the person who performed the deadly deed.

The late Eugene Auric had known about it—bless his blackened soul—because he himself had given the orders that led to Vaughn's demise.

And a third person knew about it, Ronda Trask—because she had participated in the early part of a video conference called by Eugene to plan the hit. She'd bowed out before Eugene and Wentworth got down to specifics, but she'd heard enough to understand exactly what outcome to expect.

Then, a month after the video conference, it happened—Senator Vaughn "died in office."

And now, I had a recording of that video, retrieved from my dead husband's clothing, on a thumb drive. Since finding it yesterday morning, I'd been debating whether or not to discuss the recording with Ronda, who surely presumed that I knew nothing of its existence. If I confronted her, how would she react? We were chummy enough, but she had advised me not to "rock the boat," and if I did so, I thought she might be capable of... anything.

However, I'd also had an unrelated matter on my mind, a financial question I'd been wanting to discuss with her, which now gave me a pretext for a meeting—during which I could assess her mood before dropping any bombs.

I glanced at my watch—a few minutes past nine. On a Saturday morning, I had no idea where to reach her, so I sent her a text: HEY, RONDA. ANY CHANCE WE COULD DISCUSS SOMETHING? SOON, I HOPE. SORRY TO BUG YOU OVER THE WEEKEND.

Setting my phone aside, I reached for my cup to finish what was left of the coffee, but it was cold. After hesitating, I drank it anyway.

Then my phone buzzed with Ronda's reply: HAPPENS I'M IN THE OFFICE TODAY. SLAMMED THIS MORNING. MAYBE MEET AT NOON? PENTHOUSE? OR DOWN HERE?

I replied: GREAT. HQ AT 12.

Ronda: TEXT ME FROM LOBBY ON 17. NO ONE AT DESK.

I sent her a thumbs-up.

So I wasn't rushed. I had plenty of time to go inside for a *hot* cup of coffee and read the rest of the paper before an extended workout in the gym. Then I did some more sorting of Eugene's clothes. When I finished what was stacked in the bedroom, I went into his dressing room and switched on the lights, ready to haul out another armload of his stuff, bracing myself for whatever I might dig out of his pockets *this* time. But ... could it be? It seemed, at long last, this task was done. Stunned, I drank in the sight of his empty closet, closed my eyes, and breathed a bit easier.

By a quarter to twelve, I was cleaned up and put together for the day. Before leaving the penthouse, I considered taking a purse—but what did I actually need to have with me? Just a key card and my phone. So I placed them in a simple leather clutch, went down to my entry hall, and summoned the elevator.

Arriving in the residents' concourse on the eighteenth floor, I switched elevators and went down another floor, to the seventeenth, occupied entirely by Auric headquarters.

The elevator door closed behind me as I stepped into the small public vestibule, separated by a glass wall from the company's dimly lit lobby and reception desk. As Ronda had mentioned, there was no one at the desk.

Before digging out my phone, I tried the double doors in the glass wall, but as expected, they were locked. I made a mental note to ask Ronda if I could get a key card—after all, I *owned* the place, right? Pulling out my phone, I texted her: I'M HERE. She immediately sent a thumbs-up.

Within a minute, she chugged her way out from the back offices and rushed up to meet me at the glass doors, one of which she swung open. "Come on in, Meghan." Seemingly preoccupied, she began leading me back through the lobby and around the desk.

"Uh," I said, barely keeping up, "do you suppose I could, maybe, get a *key* sometime?"

"Sure, sure ... Ralph can take care of that."

I had no idea who Ralph was.

As we took several turns through hallways, we encountered a security guard who was making his rounds. He greeted Ronda by name—with a playful little salute. I thought he looked familiar, but if he recognized me, he didn't let on. Unless I was mistaken, he was one of the sheriff's deputies who had accompanied Detective Gamarra to the penthouse after the break-in—and now, here he was, off duty, playing weekend rent-a-guard at Auric headquarters.

Nearing Ronda's office, I noticed the assistant's desk outside her door. It was now piled—literally *piled*—with files and boxes and stacks of paper. I recalled the fey young man with indigo hair who was sitting there the last time I'd visited Ronda, and I pitied whatever was in store for him on Monday morning. (Was *he*

Ralph? To my mind, he didn't look like a "Ralph." Rolf maybe, or even Rufus, but not Ralph.)

Ronda led me inside her office and closed the door. She went straight to her desk and sat down, as if collapsing there. The room seemed even more disarrayed than before, but I thought little of it, attributing the state of Ronda's surroundings to her bullheaded, gangbuster sort of personality and drive. I needed to remove a box from a chair and pull it over to her desk, where I set down my phone and handbag. After I was seated, facing her, she checked her watch and asked, "What's up, Meghan?"

With a half laugh, I asked, "Am I *keeping* you from something?"

She echoed my laugh. "Of course not. Please—what can I do for you?"

"As you know," I said, "I've been on the board of directors at Fairview Institute of Arts for quite a few years now. It's a superb organization. I'm truly honored to be a part of it, and—"

"Yeah? Yeah?" She leaned forward on her elbows, as if prodding me to pick up the pace.

"Well," I said with a shrug, "long story short—they want to build a school, and I want to make it happen for them."

"What sort of school?"

I gave her the details.

"How much?"

I gave her the amount, adding, "But it wouldn't *all* be paid up front. The project would be built in phases over five to ten years."

She didn't even flinch. "So what's your question?"

"Am I—financially—in a position to do this?"

She laughed. "You're fuckin' *loaded*. Of course you can do it. Plus, it's all deductible, every penny. Very shrewd, Meghan."

While this was precisely the answer I'd hoped for, it failed to address an underlying concern. I explained, "I'm worried about the codicil. It leaves open the possibility that Bebe could wipe me out. And if that were to happen, I'd hate to leave the Institute in the lurch after committing to build the school and getting it started. It could bring down the entire organization."

Ronda signaled time-out (as I had seen her do during the video conference). "The probability of that happening is *very* slight—I'd say, negligible."

"Not anymore," I assured her. "On Thursday, Bebe phoned me. She's aware of the codicil, and she intends to talk to her lawyer—for all I know, that's already happened."

For once, Ronda was dumbstruck. She managed to ask, "How? When?"

"Bebe said that she'd received a photocopy of the codicil by special messenger that morning. It was sent anonymously." Summoning a bit of pluck, I told Ronda, "I assume *you* didn't do it."

"Swear to God, Meghan—no, I had nothing to do with this."

Without elaborating, I said, "My hunch: it had to be either someone in the sheriff's department or someone in Wentworth's campaign."

She blew a noisy sigh, nodding. "I won't ask you how you reached that conclusion, but I do agree with you. More specifically, I think it must've been Wentworth."

I reminded her, "The morning after Eugene died, you came up to the penthouse, and we took care of some business in Eugene's den. Then you spent some time digging around in his computer. Were you looking for his estate plan? The codicil?"

She shook her head. "No. That was stored on the computer, naturally, but I didn't touch it. I was looking for something else."

Just as I'd thought.

She added, "What I *was* looking for—not important."

I looked her in the eye. "I think you were searching for Eugene's recording of a video conference that included you and Wentworth. I found it on a thumb drive that Eugene had squirreled away. And I've watched it—over and over."

Never had I witnessed anyone's face turn so pale, so fast. It was as if the blood had drained from Ronda's head—with a *whoosh*. She stammered, "Oh, boy... sweet Jesus... fuck me."

I asked her, "Is *that* what you were looking for on Eugene's computer—evidence of the plot to assassinate Senator Vaughn?"

She pronged her fingers on her forehead. "Yes. And I found it, and I deleted it. Because I knew that Wentworth was also aware of the recording. And when your place was broken into, I assumed that was *his* doing, probably with help from the sheriff's guys. They wanted that video, but couldn't find it, so they took the computer. Later, they must've found the codicil instead—and now Wentworth is trying to screw you with it because he knows that *you've* figured out his past."

I nodded. "Now that we're on the same wavelength, Ronda, I hope we're through playing games and keeping secrets. So, then: What do we *do* about this?"

"First," she said, "I want you to know something, Meghan. I've always liked you. A lot. And it kinda broke my heart, all those years ago, when Eugene forced you into that marriage. I thought it would never last, but you surprised me. And frankly, I think you surprised *him* when—somehow—you made it work. Believe it or not, you made him a better person."

"He ordered a *hit* on a *senator*."

She raised her hands in surrender. "I know, I know. But I never went along with that—or with lots of other stuff he did. The problem was, I was in *so* deep, there was no way I could stop him without getting *myself* locked up for life, so I didn't make waves. Because I couldn't. This'll sound lame, but for whatever it's worth: I'm sorry."

"*Sorry?*"

"I don't expect you to forgive me. But at least I tried to give you a heads-up. The day after the break-in, I suspected who was responsible, so I told you that Wentworth was your old pal John White. The rest of it? You've managed to piece it together on your own."

I cleared my throat. "Returning to my original question: What do we *do* about this?"

"Sorry to say"—she gave me a feeble laugh, a forced smile— "I have no fucking idea what *you* should do about this. But I know what *I* need to do."

Through an accusing squint, I asked, "What?"

"Well, it's not an official job description, but Eugene used to call me his 'fixer.' Have you ever *heard* such a thing?" She laughed.

"Yes, I'm familiar with the term."

"So here's the deal: I've spent a lot of years making things happen, making problems go away. For instance, back at United Insurance, when Eugene offered to fix things for you and John White, *part* of how that worked was to make John 'disappear.'" Proudly, she added, "*I* did that."

Dryly, I replied, "I figured."

"And it was really pretty *cool*, pulling that off—the documentation, the strings that were pulled, the plastic surgery, the specialized training that *he* got. I mean, he came out a totally new person, ready to start over."

"Congratulations. Mission accomplished. But you created a monster."

She nodded. "And that's why I was so pissed off when he ended up running for the Senate. As far as I was concerned, that was never part of the plan."

"But," I said, "it seems it was part of *Eugene's* plan all along, propping up 'Wentworth' to do his bidding."

Ronda agreed, "It was full-blown evil. And I'm glad I'm not answering to Eugene anymore. But I *am* grateful for the experience of fixing people's problems when they're in a serious pinch. Because now, *I've* got a problem. I'm too old for this, and I need to retire—to disappear." She eyed me meaningfully.

I eyed her askance. "What ... are you up to?"

"The way I see it, there is no way this situation has a happy ending—for *me*. Therefore, let's just say that 'arrangements have been made.' After this weekend, Ronda Trask will cease to exist. She will have simply disappeared."

"You're not thinking of ...?"

She shook her head. "When Auric headquarters opens for business on Monday morning, its key executives will find on their desks a letter from me repenting for past wrongs and informing them that I have taken my own life. They'll learn that I employed a shady ex-military pilot to fly me several hundred miles out over the Pacific. Then I'll explain that with the help of heavy tranquilizers—and a gentle nudge from the pilot—I ended my guilt by tumbling from the plane at low altitude, to be swallowed by the briny deep. Cool, huh?"

Horrified, I asked, "Not really ...?"

"Hell *no*, doo-doo-brain. Yes, there *is* a pilot and a flight on standby, but I'm not saying where it's headed or what happens next, except that it involves new documentation, strings that have been pulled, and a rather astonishing physical makeover. I'll be a new person, with a new identity, ready to begin again. I wish I was able to share all the details and then show you the results—but that would sorta defeat the purpose, wouldn't it?"

I tossed my hands. "Were you planning *not* to tell me this?"

"Actually, I was trying to figure out how to break the news, and then you called today's meeting, so I got a lucky break."

"Yeah … lucky *you*."

"The reason I came in today was to sorta clean things up."

I glanced around. "I'd hate to get a look at your *house*."

"*Excuse* the mess—things have been a little hectic. I haven't been cleaning up the *office*, but cleaning up the details. I told you about the 'suicide' letters, but there's also a shitload of memos to get out—mostly recommendations for the succession of jobs. When I walk out of here today, I'll never be seen again."

I rolled my eyes. "And to think—I put *you* in charge. I *ought* to fire you."

She flipped her hands. "Too late."

"So. The succession. Who do you think should take over?"

"Ralph."

"And *who* in God's name is that—your secretary?"

"No way. Ralph Naiman started here about a year ago, degrees in law and business, smart guy. Eugene never cared for him, but I do, and I managed to get him promoted twice. He is *not* part of the old guard—no shenanigans—so he's exactly the right person to move things forward in a fresh direction. I'm proposing that Ralph take over as acting president and CEO. But *you're* the corporate chairman, Meghan—or *chair*, if you prefer—so the final appointments are up to you. Give Ralph a chance. You'll like him."

"And why do you say that?"

"He's gay, late thirties, unattached—I've *seen* your artist friend."

Interesting, I thought. I asked Ronda, "Will someone keep me in the loop and alert me to the next meeting of the executive board? I've never attended one."

"I'm instructing Ralph to do that, and he's smart enough to understand that it's in his best interest. Trust me, you'll hear from him." While speaking to me, Ronda had opened one of her desk drawers and was now tossing miscellaneous crap into either of two piles—stuff to take (on the top of her desk) and stuff to trash (on the floor).

I asked, "When does your escape plan actually *launch*?"

She stopped what she was doing and paused in thought. "Now, *that's* a good question. I'll leave the building no later than three today, and I *had* planned to leave Fairview early tomorrow morning, meeting a driver at the edge of town. That's just the first step in a complicated process that makes me 'disappear.' I'll be constantly on the move for about two weeks, sorta covering my tracks, till I go into seclusion—far, far away—where every aspect of my past begins to be rebuilt. It'll be about a year before I'm able to circulate in society again, somewhere else, as *someone* else."

My shoulders slumped. "That sounds ... daunting."

"Yeah, *tell* me. But here's the hitch: What do you plan to do with the video on that thumb drive?"

"Honestly? I don't know yet. If I go public with it, there'll be serious consequences for a lot of people, including myself. Wentworth has already threatened my life—he can't afford to have his past identity exposed, let alone his role in Senator Vaughn's death. And Bebe has threatened my fortune—she's itching to invoke the codicil, and if Wentworth's past is revealed, that'll lead directly to my role in the fraud scheme at United Insurance."

"And yet," said Ronda, hunching forward over her desk as she looked into my eyes, "something tells me you'd just *love* to nail Wentworth."

I nodded. "That's putting it mildly. He betrayed me with that insurance scheme and abandoned me to face the aftermath alone. He's committed murder, and he's threatened me with the same. But the worst of it? As things stand right now, he's got a better than even chance of winning a seat in the United States Senate. So, yeah—you *bet* I'd like to stop him."

Ronda said, "I totally get it, Meghan. And the surest way to stop him is to go public with that video. If you do, when do you think it might happen?"

I felt sick and frightened saying it: "*If* it happens, it'll probably be soon."

"Okay," said Ronda. "That gives me some concern, regarding my disappearing act. Plan A, as I told you, is to ditch Fairview tomorrow morning, but there's always been a plan B—to get out of town this evening." She raised a finger, as if asking me to wait a moment. Then she pulled out her phone and punched in a number. When someone answered, she said, "It's me. Looks like we should do this tonight." She paused, listening, then said, "Great. We're on." Tucking her phone away, she told me, "Six this evening, I'm gone. Can you hold off that long to make your decision?"

"Yes." I was suddenly exhausted. "I'll need at least that long to think this through properly. But what's the reason for *your* hurry?"

"Wentworth knows the recording was made, but he doesn't know for sure if it still exists. If and when you lower the boom, however, he will instantly become one *very* desperate man. Are you aware that he's a *trained* killer?"

I swallowed. "The Zoom video alluded to something like that."

"Uh-huh. And once that video is 'out there,' I'll rise to the top of his kill list."

"But you bowed *out* of the video before he and Eugene got down to business."

She shook her head. "Doesn't matter. Eugene is dead, so I'm the only other living soul involved with that meeting, and prosecutors will want me as their prime witness. I didn't hear everything that was said *that* day, but oh, brother—I've got enough dirt on Wentworth to stick him with *ten* life sentences. And he *knows* that."

My tears had been welling up and now flowed freely. "And I'm stuck alone ... *again*. I don't know how to deal with this. It's too much. And the worst part is the *guilt*."

With a tone of maternal concern not natural to her, Ronda said, "Oh, *honey*. What are you talking about—what 'guilt'?"

"The scheme. The insurance fraud. People died. This has been hanging over me for more than twenty-five *years*."

With my head bowed, I felt Ronda's eyes on me, watching me, but she said nothing while long seconds passed. When I looked up, she was chewing one of her fingernails.

"Meghan," she said, removing her hand from her mouth, "when you first watched the Zoom video, how did you feel?"

"Horrified, of course. I saw the man who had married me plotting a political assassination with the man who had once betrayed me. Even though I was shocked that Wentworth would go along with this, I wasn't much surprised—it only confirmed the evil in him that I'd recognized long ago. But my reaction to Eugene's role in this was another matter completely. I was *stunned* to realize that I had never really known Eugene at all. I was appalled to discover the extent of his depravity."

Ronda nodded slowly.

I continued, "I found and watched the recording yesterday morning, then I spent what seemed like most of the afternoon talking about it with my shrink. And together, we determined that this terrible revelation about Eugene contains one tiny, *tiny* bright spot: Now, at least, I know the worst about him. He's incapable of hurting me more deeply."

Ronda had a *very* odd look in her eye. "Meghan sweets," she said, "if only that were true."

"Huh?"

"For a *long* time, I've wondered if I should tell you about something. Mostly, I figured, 'No, don't tell her. It'll upset her all the more.' But now? Hearing how agonized you are by this guilt, I think you need to hear just one ... remaining... *minor* detail."

Warily, I gripped the arms of my chair, bracing myself.

Ronda collected her thoughts. "Think back. When Eugene rode in like Sir Galahad, offering to rescue you from the fallout of John White's fraud scheme—how did you react?"

"I was skeptical that Eugene could actually make my problem go away, but somehow, he did—and I guess I owe *you* a measure of gratitude for that."

She squirmed. "Well, yes, I did play a role in that situation. But there's this little ... *wrinkle* that you're not aware of."

I sat back in my chair. "Try me. I'm all ears."

She cleared her throat. "In a nutshell: the insurance scheme wasn't John White's idea. Eugene himself dreamed it up."

I cocked my head. "*What?*"

"Eugene recruited your then boyfriend, recognizing in him a taste for dirty dealing. He lured John with promises of big things to come—a new life spent in the service of the great Eugene Auric himself. Simple enough. But there was a 'part two' to this bargain—Eugene also wanted *you*, Meghan, as his submissive wife, which of course wouldn't interest you in the least. So the scheme was to entrap you, with John's assistance, in a made-up fraud, convincing you to take part in it as a means to more comfortably feather your future with John."

"Um," I said, "I don't get it. I know that Eugene was a big client at United and also a partner in the firm, but why would he go to so much trouble, just to deny the payout of a few insurance claims? To Eugene, that was spare change."

Ronda shook her head. "You're not *listening*. The scheme *itself* was a fraud, a ruse, an elaborate game. The documents you altered—they were all fakes to begin with. So were the policyholders—they didn't exist. No one *died*. You weren't in trouble. You were tricked into *thinking* you needed Eugene to 'rescue' you, when in reality, it was an invented crisis of his own making that had supposedly placed you in legal jeopardy."

"My God," I mumbled, struggling to comprehend this, "you mean, all these years, everything I've been dealing with, the shame of my hidden past—none of that actually *happened*?"

Ronda shrugged. "None of it. You were skunked."

"And *that*," I asked, "that's supposed to make me feel *better*?"

She explained, "It's supposed to assuage your guilt."

"Well," I admitted, "that *is* a refreshing angle. But Jesus *Christ*. Eugene! Could that fucker possibly *be* any more vile?"

"Nope," said Ronda. "Now you've heard it all."

I heaved a disgusted sigh. "I'd better go."

"Wait," said Ronda as I started to rise from my chair. When I sat down again, she warned me, "Be on guard, Meghan. Take Wentworth's threats seriously. Even if he doesn't know you have the thumb drive, he's feeling *highly* motivated to make sure you keep quiet. And that security detail hired by his campaign? They're sheriff's guys. While you're deciding what to do—keep *all* of that in mind."

Phew. I stood, removing my phone and handbag from Ronda's desk.

She stood. "Uh, do I get a hug?"

I grinned. "Sure." And we met beside the desk.

Holding me close, she said, "So long, Meghan. Have a good life." She sniffled.

"You too, Ronda. Good luck."

And a moment later, I was out in the hall, pulling her office door closed. I made my way to the lobby and out through the glass doors. Then I punched the button to summon the elevator.

When I stepped inside it and the door slid safely closed behind me, I checked my phone, smiled, and stopped the voice recorder.

CHAPTER
NINETEEN

After returning to the penthouse, I went upstairs to the kitchen, a corner of which was set up with a small desk that I often used for keeping track of household accounts, shopping lists, and occasional correspondence on paper.

Sitting at the desk, I took out a sheet of stationery, an envelope, and—how quaint—a stamp. I also took out my checkbook and set it aside as I wrote a short missive:

> *Dear Dustin,*
>
> *Thank you for the delightful evening at your studio on Thursday. Dinner was wonderful. Nova was a delight. And your full-size "sketch" of Eugene's portrait was, and is, sensational.*
>
> *You suggested that I should take some time before giving you approval to begin the actual painting, fearing that I might later regret this somewhat "irreverent" approach to depicting Eugene.*
>
> *Please accept this written document as my full, final, irrevocable approval to proceed. Have fun, Dustin, and don't hold back— let him have it!*
>
> *Yours truly,*
Meghan Daley Auric

I then wrote out a check to Dustin, covering the full amount of the finished project. I attached a sticky-note to the check, instructing him: *Please cash this at your earliest convenience—do not wait until completion of the portrait, which should not be rushed.*

My purpose was twofold: With regard to the painting, I hoped Eugene would turn in his grave. With regard to the payment, I wanted Dustin to secure the funds before Bebe stood a chance to freeze my assets in an attempt to bankrupt me.

When the ink had dried, I placed the check and the folded note inside the envelope, then sealed it, addressed it, and stamped it. A quick elevator ride took me down to the residents' concourse, where I slipped the envelope into the OUTGOING MAIL chute.

Next, back in the penthouse, I revised, but did not send, the earlier text I had initially prepared for Detective Nick Gamarra, containing a link to the recording of Julian Wentworth on the phone, threatening my life.

I expanded the list of recipients, which now included Nick Gamarra, attorney Adam Hudson, reporter Chase Unger, and Ashley Factor, my house manager. My brief message to them: PLEASE REVIEW THE CONTENTS OF THESE THREE LINKS. YOU WILL KNOW WHAT TO DO. The message was followed by hyperlinks to: the recording of Wentworth's phone threat, the recording of my conversation in Ronda Trask's office that afternoon, and the video of the Zoom meeting regarding the assassination plot, to be posted on Ashley's vlog.

Shortly after four o'clock that afternoon, I phoned Ashley to give her a heads-up.

She answered on the second ring. "Hey, Meghan. All's well?"

"Not really," I replied, choosing candor over sugarcoating. "I think the whole 'situation' might be coming to a head—maybe as soon as tonight."

"How can I help?"

"Be ready for me to alert you to post the video from the thumb drive. I wish I were able to tell you when that's likely to happen, but the timing isn't entirely under my control—it could be late in the night."

"No problem," she assured me. "I'm behind on a lot of video editing. It's very time-consuming, so I like doing it late, when I won't be disturbed—except by *you*. Feel free to call or text anytime. When I finally *do* go to bed, I'll set my phone loud enough to wake me."

"You are a *treasure*, Ashley."

"Awww"—she laughed—"I try."

"Here's what to expect." Then I explained that she was one of four people who would receive the text, which I read to her, including a description of its three links. "So," I said, "if and when I send the group text, the first thing you should do is upload the thumb drive to your vlog. Then, immediately, you should phone Detective Gamarra to confirm that he's received everything— but do *not* phone me. Okay?"

"Got it."

"*Thank* you, Ashley." I gave her Nick's direct number, adding, "I'll let him know that he might be hearing from you."

"Sounds like a plan, Meghan. Meanwhile, can I bring you anything—or just come over to keep you company?"

"That's really sweet of you, but I should be alone tonight. I've got a *lot* of thinking to do—about important decisions. So just sit tight. If anything happens, it won't be till after six o'clock, possibly much later."

After we hung up, I checked my watch: four fifteen. I could relax a bit. Nothing would be decided about a course of action until at least two hours from now.

Six, of course, was the hour at which Ronda planned to launch her disappearance—a point of no return for her. After that, it would be highly unlikely that she would ever pay a price for any wrongdoings committed in the service of Eugene's fiendish plots and whims. But she would not escape unscathed, having lost her self-identity along with her past. What, I wondered, would it feel like, being forced into the body and spirit of someone else— someone new, invented, and unreal?

Naturally, that long-ago philosophy degree reared up in my mind, nettling me about the ethics of allowing Ronda a head start on her race against justice. But now that I understood the scope of Eugene's heinousness, I was willing to cut Ronda some slack—much like me, she had been a victim of his manipulation. Plus, her intent was not only to escape the long arm of the law. Her more immediate concern was to escape the lethal cunning of Julian Wentworth and whatever dark forces were aligned behind him.

Around five o'clock, I phoned Detective Gamarra. He picked up at once. There was noise in the background—the noise of many people talking and jostling—as he asked, "What's up, Meghan?"

I said, "You sound busy, Nick. Do you have time for an update?"

"I'm at an event for Celia at the Little League ballpark—good crowd, but it'll break up soon so folks can take care of dinner."

"Are you there as a supportive spouse? Or in a police capacity?"

"Both. I have a deputy with me—a friend, one of the good guys—helping to keep an eye on things. The campaign has no budget for security, so we're doing it gratis."

"Uh, the reason I called ..."

"Yes?" he asked.

"My situation with Wentworth—it's heating up, and I might want to send you something later. If I do, I'm sure you'll want to take action."

"Are you talking about the recording of the phone call, the threat?"

"That, yes, and now there's plenty more—including a short video that's nothing less than explosive. It's all self-explanatory. If everything moves forward, you'll get a text with the links from me, followed by a phone call from Ashley, my assistant, to make sure you received everything. It could happen anytime after six, or well into the night. Or not at all."

"Okay..." He sounded as if he was thinking aloud, making mental notes. "Is there a chance I'll need backup for this? If so, I'll talk to my buddy here. He and I both brought cruisers to the ballpark; we'll keep them overnight."

"Yes," I said, "you might want to do that."

"Anything else I should know?"

"Nick," I said, lowering my voice as if there were spies in my kitchen, "not a word to your boss. Sheriff Hewitt cannot be trusted."

He digested this for a moment. "Understood." Then he asked, "Do you need—or want—protection?"

"Thanks, Nick. But I'll be fine." At least I hoped so.

It proved to be a long evening—with a conflicting brew of anxiety and boredom. Six o'clock came and went. Ronda was now out of the picture, as was the artificial deadline I had set for resolving my dilemma. Would I summon the courage to send my text with its evidence-laden links, blowing the whistle on Wentworth and bringing him down? Or would I cower in my tower, poor little rich girl, afraid that telling all would threaten not only my fortune, but also my ability to spend it on worthy deeds that would absolutely fry my late husband's fat ass?

I'd eaten almost nothing that day, so I fussed in the kitchen, putting together a decent sandwich with ingredients scrounged from the fridge: fried bacon, a breaded chicken breast, Havarti, pesto, and a couple of thick slices of dark whole-grain bread. I considered slamming a drink or two—but thought I'd better not. Some Saturday night.

I killed more time by cleaning up the kitchen, including the oven, which didn't need it, but going through the motions allowed me to avoid tussling with the issue that would, eventually, need to be decided.

Around ten thirty, growing ever more frustrated—and exhausted—I began turning out lights and headed toward the bedroom. Nothing, after all, *demanded* that I resolve everything that very night. Why stress myself out over a meaningless, self-imposed ultimatum? Better to deal with this in the morning—with fresh eyes and a clear head.

After tending to my ablutions in the bathroom, I went to my dressing room and decided to wear a gi to bed that night. As the weather had gotten chilly, I didn't choose silk or flimsy cotton, but the sturdy canvas gi I sometimes wore for workouts. I'd always found the nubby texture of the fabric strangely comforting against my skin—and I could use plenty of comforting that night—so on it went.

Moving to the bedroom, I padded over to the control panel and activated the security system. It beeped to the pulsing of a tiny yellow light while the readout counted down from ten. It then went silent as the yellow light turned red. The readout informed me: SYSTEM ARMED.

Then I got into bed, made sure my phone was charging on the nightstand, and switched off the lamp. In the darkness, I closed my eyes, thinking that the jitters of that day would forestall sleep. But I was wrong.

Beeping. Gentle but insistent, the beeping woke me.

Disoriented, I wondered if I was dreaming, as had happened during my afternoon nap a day earlier. A glance at the bedside clock informed me that I had slept for three hours—it was now nearly two on Sunday morning. This wasn't a dream, and the beeping wasn't coming from the clock, but from the security panel.

I got out of bed, retrieved my phone from the nightstand, and slipped it into the jacket pocket inside my gi. Snugging the belt, I moved over to the control panel.

Flashing red on the readout were the words UPPER TERRACE. I had the option of pressing a winking button marked ALARM, but I did not. The system was constantly in "passive" mode, and if someone was out there, the cameras were watching—and recording—what was going on, even after I pressed the DISARM button. If the intruder was the man I suspected, I didn't want to scare him off. I wanted to hear him admit something.

Turning no lights on, I left the bedroom and moved through the main space of the party room, making my way toward the French doors to the terrace, near the kitchen.

I saw the silhouette of a figure in a hooded sweatsuit trying one of the doors—but since the prior break-in, these were now always locked at night. He circled his hands to his face and pressed them to the window, trying to see inside, but I knew from experience that the tinting of the glass would make this impossible when the room was dark and the terrace was lit, as they were now.

I moved closer as he set a plumber's bag on a nearby chair and took out a few tools. Trying to figure out what to do, he swept back his hood and scratched his head in thought. I saw his face clearly, and as expected, it was none other than Senate candidate Julian Wentworth—up to no good while taking a late-night break from his politicking.

Within a foot of the door now, I pulled the phone from my jacket and opened the group text I had prepared. I knew that the time had arrived—now or never. I could do the right thing and reveal all that had happened. Or I could wimp out, posing no risk to my inheritance, and hope that someone *else* might bring him to justice.

I pressed SEND.

Then I switched on the phone's voice recorder and returned it to my inside pocket.

Out on the terrace, Wentworth set down the tools he'd been handling. He must have decided to see if perhaps some other door had been left unlocked, offering a less flagrant means of entry, because he now stepped out of view—carrying a gun as he disappeared around the corner of the terrace near the freight elevator.

Quietly, I unlocked the door, slipped outside, and closed it behind me.

Browsing through Wentworth's tools, I grabbed a wrench and moved silently—I was barefoot—to a dark nook near the elevator.

Wentworth *wasn't* barefoot. His combat boots clomped on the terrace pavers as he returned from his fruitless search for an open door. Crouching in the shadows, I waited for him to appear, and when one of his legs was within striking distance, I smacked the wrench—*hard*—below his knee.

He yowled as he fell face down and lost hold of his weapon, which skittered away and vanished beneath a bulky, cushioned chair.

Stepping forward, I taunted, "Awww, did the big *man* lose his big *gun*?"

"I don't *need* a gun," he assured me as he got back on his feet—albeit with difficulty. He winced.

I grinned. "How will you explain that limp to your bimbo, Ivy Quick?"

"*Shut* up." And he grabbed the wrench from my hand. Fortunately, he tossed it aside. Unfortunately, he still had ample strength to grab *me* and then drag me over to the ornate stone balustrade at the edge of the roof garden.

With my butt pinned against the top surface of the railing, I glanced over my shoulder—and felt faint at the sight of the street, thirty floors below. "Uh," I said, "we need to talk."

He laughed. "It's your nickel, Meghan. Let's hear it—your famous last words."

"Well, for starters, did you ever really love me, back when you were John White?"

He started talking smack about what an idiot I was, what an idiot I'd *always* been, but I didn't care about any of that. I just wanted to get him talking and keep him talking while I struggled to inch us a few feet along the railing, where he would be more closely framed by one of the video cameras. Word had apparently not gotten back to the wrong people at the sheriff's department that the penthouse had been fitted with a security upgrade—it was privately monitored by the firm that had installed it, not by the sheriff's goons. Wentworth seemed totally unaware that he was being watched as I got him closer to lining up with a camera.

The video would have no sound, but that was being recorded by my phone.

When he finished trashing me for being an idiot, I asked, "Just *where* have you been all these years? Ronda Trask says *she* was the one who pulled all the strings and arranged for your new life."

With an indignant snort, he said, "*That* cunt—don't get me started." And he launched into a rant about *her*.

While he foamed and blathered, I continued sidestepping along the balustrade, with only a foot or so to go. Even with his bum leg, he was still a powerfully fit man as he held both of my arms. I didn't have the strength to escape him outright, but by squirming, I managed to keep moving him sideways. Eyeing his hands, I noticed the ring he was wearing—exactly like Eugene's, exactly like the sheriff's.

When I had him where I wanted, I said, "But enough about Ronda."

"Exactly. She's outlived her usefulness. Now she simply knows too much—just like you do. Her days are numbered."

I countered, "You'll have to find her first."

Derisively, he asked, "Think I *can't?*"

Answering with an innocent shrug, I changed the topic: "And what about Senator Vaughn? Ronda says—"

"Hold *on*," he interrupted. "Don't tell me she's trying to take credit for *that*, too. She didn't have *shit* to do with Vaughn's death." Leaning within an inch of my face—close enough to kiss—he bragged, "*I* killed that worthless old scumbag."

And I had the audio I wanted.

Closing my eyes, I slipped into that Zen moment that Gus had told me about, calling up something that felt second-nature and unpracticed. It was as easy and inborn as taking my next breath.

Wentworth was midsentence in a new diatribe when I grabbed *his* arms and stopped him cold with the Magnuström Method—knee to the balls, foot to the ankle.

It was perfectly executed, a flawless doozy that brought him down, rolling on his back, gasping in pain, sputtering misogynist invectives—including a few I'd never heard.

As he struggled to stand, I easily spun him into *my* previous position, with his butt pinned against the balustrade, and when he was finally, vertically on his feet, I let him have it again—knee only, straight to the groin.

He looked at me with disbelief, pleading with his eyes as I reached behind his calves and tossed his legs in the air. He teetered for a moment on top of the railing—then he screamed like a girl as he flipped over the edge.

I yelled, "*So long, asshole!*"

And after the thud, he moaned. I looked over the railing.

I had positioned him for a fall that landed him not on the street, but on the lower-level terrace of the penthouse, where Julian Wentworth now sprawled in my patch of autumn lettuce, with one of his legs bent at a gruesome angle. He was moving, but not much. I felt a satisfied smile spread across my face.

I would never be capable of condemning someone to a thirty-floor plunge. But fifteen feet and a few broken bones?

Yeah, I could do that.

Satisfied that he wasn't going anywhere, I sauntered over to the stuffed chair, tugged it aside, and retrieved his gun. Returning to the balustrade, I wagged it at him as a warning not to move. Then I placed it on the ledge, within easy reach—just in case.

I took a deep breath before pulling the phone out of my jacket. After confirming that the voice recorder had been running, I switched it off. And I noticed that a number of alerts had arrived during the last few minutes.

First, I opened a text from Detective Gamarra: ON OUR WAY.

I replied: NO RUSH. WENTWORTH UNDER CONTROL AND READY FOR PICKUP. PLUS … NEW VIDEO, NEW AUDIO, COMING SOON.

There was a text from Ashley, including a thumbs-up: BUSSIN' ZOOM FOOTAGE, MEGHAN!

And from Chase Unger: THANKS FOR THE EXCLUSIVE!

From the lower terrace, Wentworth feebly asked, "Help?"

I ignored him as my phone buzzed with an incoming call from ADAM HUDSON, ATTORNEY. When I connected, he asked, "*Aunt Meg*? Are you all right?"

"Yes, sweetie. Didn't mean to alarm you. Nick Gamarra is coming over—but I'm fine."

"What a *relief*. And hey—I've got some great news. I just listened to your talk with Ronda Trask from this afternoon. She told you that the old insurance scam was *itself* a scam, with Eugene behind it. I realize how jarring you must have found that. But consider: the words of the codicil stipulate that your inheritance can be contested if you reveal details of 'crimes' that *you* committed at United. Aunt Meg, *you* committed no crimes whatever; you yourself were victimized. And as I've already mentioned, I found *nothing* in the record that pertains to the alleged scam. Bottom line: any challenge to your estate would be laughed out of court."

Elated as I was to hear this, it was now very late, so I thanked Adam and asked if we could talk again in the morning. Then we each wished each other a fond good-night.

As I was tucking away my phone, Wentworth shouted from below, "Help me!"

I leaned over the balustrade, barking, "*Quiet*, down there—or I'll give you something to *really* cry about." And I aimed the gun between his splayed legs.

He whimpered.

"Just *kidding*," I told him.

Lifting my head, I laughed into the star-specked October sky, where the sound of my voice melded with the wail of approaching sirens.

CHAPTER
TWENTY

Sunday morning's *Consensus Times* was already being printed when Wentworth was removed from my lettuce patch and taken into custody. Therefore, when the paper was delivered that day, it contained no news of what had happened, and the two editorials offering senatorial endorsements appeared on the OPINIONS page as planned: Governor Swaine extended his ringing support for Celia Gamarra, while the paper's editorial board, which tended to speak not so much for the people, but for the one-percenters, mouthed its predictable (though tepid) endorsement of Wentworth.

However, before dawn on that same day, cub reporter Chase Unger had gathered his facts and the evidence I supplied— which by then included video of Wentworth's rooftop antics as well as audio of his bragging that he had assassinated the revered Senator Vaughn. Chase was ready with a draft of his blockbuster exposé when he phoned his managing editor at home, roused him from a deep slumber, and sounded the alarm.

Within an hour, an emergency Sunday meeting of the editorial board was called (including the managing editor, editor in chief, and publisher) at the *Times* newsroom in Consensus. After reviewing Chase's source materials and draft, they cleared the following day's front page, as well as two inside pages, for the story. In addition, they immediately penned a new editorial, rescinding their endorsement of Wentworth "with feelings of shock, disgust, and betrayal," while throwing their full support to Gamarra, described as "a faithful public servant who has both the integrity and the intelligence to lead us out of this quagmire and represent us in Washington."

A story this big could not possibly keep until Monday morning, so everything was posted on the *Times* website well before noon on Sunday. By midday, it had been picked up by every wire service and major news outlet in the nation, and each time it appeared or was referenced, it carried a credit: *As first reported by Chase Unger, Consensus Times.*

Later that day, Chase, who had worried about getting a week off in January for a trip to Mexico, approached his editor with the request, which was not only granted on the spot, but sweetened with a bonus and first-class flight upgrades for both Chase and his companion. (Ashley, of course, would be charmed and dazzled by his cleverness.)

By the following afternoon, Monday, as details of the story continued to emerge, Sheriff Hewitt found himself suspended and the subject of county, state, *and* federal investigations—all of them cooperating in the pursuit of speedy justice. Recall petitions were already in circulation.

Needless to say, from that point forward, results of the special senatorial election were never in doubt. Ballots had been printed, and early voting would begin in two weeks. Wentworth had not been allowed bail, but even from his detention cell, he refused to step down from the race. With election day less than a month away, our friend Celia Gamarra could simply continue her dignified campaign while sticking to her stump speech and letting the clock run out. Not much else needed to be done—other than planning the victory parties.

Because more than three-quarters of the state's voters resided in Consensus County, celebrations could be limited to the capital, by far the state's largest city, and Fairview, which was not only the second-largest city, but also Celia's home.

The main event would begin in Consensus that evening at the stroke of seven, when the polls closed, since the contest would probably be called in Celia's favor at once.

She would remain there with her husband, Nick, until nine or so, then drive back to Fairview, arriving by ten o'clock. Her local headquarters was at the university, where a large, youthful crowd was expected in the main field house, which happened to be only a few minutes' drive from downtown.

So I had offered to host a late reception at the Towne Club, a more subdued setting where Celia and Nick could actually relax and unwind—while hobnobbing with some of her most generous supporters. The Gamarras were scheduled to arrive anytime between eleven thirty and midnight. With a week to go, our plans were set.

And now, at last, it was election night, November second. Celia was quickly declared the winner, and as the evening wore on, with actual vote tallies rolling in, it became evident that she had not only won the race, but crushed it—with over two-thirds of the vote.

Dinner service at the Towne Club had ended around nine that evening. Then the facility closed for a couple of hours, doing a reset for the late festivities. When the doors opened to invited guests at eleven, I had already been there for some thirty minutes, reviewing the arrangements with Everett Burke.

The main gathering space was the ballroom, where the stage was set up for a brief victory speech. A twelve-piece band was tuning up, with most of the floor space left open for dancing and mingling, while the perimeter of the room was ringed with tables—open seating, except for the table that was reserved for me, where I could coordinate with Everett and the campaign.

Balloons were used as centerpieces on the tables and as garlands crisscrossing the room overhead. Food stations offered hors d'oeuvres, which would also be passed, along with champagne. For those needing a "real drink," there were full bar setups at both ends of the room, and the barroom itself was open. The lighting was dim and dreamy. The music was stylish. It was all very... civilized. Such was the Fairview Towne Club.

I had invited about twenty guests of my own, but the party was open to any of the club members and their guests as well. Given the late hour, on a Tuesday, there wouldn't be a mob—a hundred or so at most.

When the guests started filing in, the band struck up a cheerful medley of old tunes, and the Armani-clad serving staff dispersed through the crowd with their trays. The room rang with laughter and greetings as I circulated and welcomed people— the dutiful hostess.

Ashley trailed me, at beckoning distance, in case I needed help with names or introductions. Chase Unger was not far behind, as he and Ashley were now frequent companions. I tried not to pry, but it seemed they were now an "item," if not quite yet a "couple." Perhaps their torrid Baja escapade would seal the deal in January.

The Hudsons arrived—my old college friends, Theo and Lila, with their son, Adam, the attorney. With hugs and kisses all around, they told me that they'd just left the party at the Linden-crest field house; the senator-elect would soon be on her way.

By the time we all had drinks in our hands, I noticed a man enter the room, looking adrift, and I asked Adam, "May I introduce you to someone?"

Noting the direction of my glance, he replied, "*Sure.*"

"C'mon, then." While walking Adam across the room, I explained, "Ralph Naiman is now the acting president of Auric Development & Holdings. He's also gay."

"I, uh, don't suppose he's single?"

"Yes," I said blithely, "I believe he is."

"Mrs. Auric!" said Ralph. "Thanks for inviting me tonight. I've never been in here—and I've always been curious."

"Consider yourself 'at home' now, Ralph. And please—we're *family* at Auric Development—so do call me Meghan."

"I'd be delighted." He smiled. And it was a very handsome smile—not lost on Adam. They couldn't keep their eyes off each other. Although Ralph was nearly ten years older than Adam, and in spite of their racial difference, it was easy to imagine them as a well-matched couple. This was promising, to say the least. So, after getting them properly introduced and sharing some obligatory commiserating over Ronda Trask's recent "suicide," I left the boys to get acquainted.

Petro Yorba had been to the club many times before—and frequently in recent weeks as we met for lunch to discuss plans for The School at Fairview Institute of Arts, plans that were becoming more detailed with dizzying speed. And I was all in.

"*Meghan,*" said Petro, spotting me and rushing over. "It's so fabulous you're doing this tonight—and congratulations on your candidate's victory."

"It's a victory for *all* of us," I assured him as we each pecked both cheeks, Euro-style. After a brief hesitation, I said, "I have this *little* idea that I'd like to discuss with you ..."

"Of *course*. What is it?" And when I finished explaining it to him, he told me with a wink, "I'm sure that can be arranged."

I saw Eugene Junior at one of the bar tables, so I excused myself from Petro and went over to greet Gene. After a quick hug, I asked, "So Bebe stayed home?"

He nodded. "Mom's never been the 'good sport' sort of loser. Even after everything that's happened, she's still lamenting the downfall of Julian Wentworth. According to her, 'He's one of *us*. He's part of *our crowd*.'" Leaning close, Gene said into my ear, "And she blames *you* for his loss."

"I'm so pleased to hear that." And I meant it. We both laughed.

As Gene moved on, I felt a tug on my sleeve and turned to find Nova St. James standing behind me with her father, Dustin.

"*Hello*, sweetie," I said, crouching for a hug with her. "Aren't you up a bit late for a school night?"

"Yeah!" she said, loving the night life.

Dustin said to me, "I thought it was important for her to witness this—and to remember this night. Told her she can skip school tomorrow, but she insists she'll be there. Talk about *energy*."

He and I shared a kiss, which I enjoyed with no qualms (because, by now, his explanation of his late spouses' insurance policies had been discreetly looked into and verified). I told him, "Glad you're here. Both of you."

Nova had drifted off to the dance floor. Feeling the music, she began moving to it, improvising a graceful solo that was soon noticed by older couples who abandoned their box steps to stand and watch.

Dustin chortled. "Virginia Smokehouse—what a ham."

"Guess what," I said. "I just had a little chat with Petro, from the museum. Since I couldn't be more *thrilled* with the progress you're making on Eugene's portrait, I'm now thinking it would be a shame to keep it hidden away from the public—upstairs in the lobby at Auric headquarters. So let's give Eugene the attention he's always craved, especially now that the world appreciates what an evil turd he truly was."

With a grin, Dustin said, "I'm almost afraid to ask, but *what* are you up to?"

I returned his grin. "My offer to Petro: I'd like for the portrait to be unveiled, with press and fanfare, in the lobby of the museum, where it will remain on indefinite loan from me. The scale will be perfect in that space. And given the notoriety now being 'enjoyed' by Eugene during his afterlife years, I'm sure the painting will draw not only interest, but crowds. Petro *loves* the idea."

"Frankly," said Dustin, "so do I. *Thank* you, Meghan." And again, we kissed. He asked, "Care to dance?"

"I would—but I *just* spotted someone I need to talk to."

"Then we'll save a dance for later. Meanwhile, maybe Nova would be willing to share the limelight with her dad." And with a wave of his fingers, he moved toward the dance floor.

I turned to Dr. Faye Rubin, who was walking up to me. "You *made* it," I said. "Welcome."

"Sorry I'm late—a patient in crisis—averted, thank God."

"Well, then, let's get you a drink."

No sooner had I summoned a waiter when there was some hoopla near the door—and in walked our newly elected senator,

Celia Gamarra, in the company of her husband, Detective Nick Gamarra, and Celia's campaign manager, Xolani Vahdat. Faye had already met them at the September luncheon, so she joined me as I walked over to greet them. The band struck up a corny arrangement of "Happy Days Are Here Again." People cheered. Balloons popped.

Celia and I exchanged a gush of jolly sentiments, and then she made her way to the stage as everyone gathered toward the front, applauding.

But Nick held back, looking whipped. He told Faye and me, "It's basically the stump speech again—and I've heard it so often, I could recite it in my sleep."

So the three of us slipped out to the lobby, then into the barroom. Nick ordered Scotch, Faye had her first glass of champagne, and it was time for me to switch to water. We carried our drinks from the bar to an open table, and I was glad to sit after standing for so long.

We made a few toasts to the occasion, then we drank and set down our glasses. "Well," I said to Nick, "you've *done* it. Now what?"

He laughed. "We need to get Celia sworn in and settled in DC, and then—I guess—we'll *both* be taking lots of plane rides to see each other when we can. I'm sort of mid-career at the department, and with the sheriff on leave, this is *not* the time for me to jump ship—even if I wanted to, which I don't. So Celia has a mission now, and so do I, and we'll need to give each other some space for a while."

Dr. Rubin went into work mode: "And how do you feel about that? Both of you?"

"Surprisingly, not bad. I mean, it's a little scary, sure, but it's also, what ... invigorating?"

Faye nodded. "Looking forward. New challenges. *Good* challenges."

"Yes. Exactly." Nick turned to me. "And how about you, Meghan? You've been through a *lot* lately. But some people are calling you a hero. And I agree with them."

"That's ... *nuts*," I said. "I was convinced that Wentworth was propped up by a sprawling cabal of faceless, evil money lords, but now we know that it was just Eugene and his inane pipeline project. The conspiracy went no further than the three custom-designed 'club' rings that were made—for himself, Wentworth, and our hee-haw sheriff. That was *so* Eugene, always into the 'trappings.' But now Eugene and the pipeline are dead, and Wentworth and the sheriff are screwed."

Nick nodded. "Like I said—you're a hero, Meghan."

"I don't *feel* like a hero."

As Faye's brow wrinkled with concern, a huge burst of applause came from the ballroom. The band started playing.

Nick sighed. "That's my cue. Sorry, gotta run." He slammed the remainder of his drink, gave us a salute, and traipsed off.

I said to Faye, "I guess we should get back, too."

She nodded. We picked up our glasses and returned to the ballroom.

But unlike Nick, who was now onstage with Celia, holding hands aloft, Faye and I hung near the back of the room, removed from the din. Soon, the stage lights dimmed as Celia and Nick stepped down to the dance floor, where the crowd parted, allowing them a slow and tender spotlight dance.

Faye turned to face me. "Why *don't* you feel like a hero, Meghan? You deserve to."

I shook my head. "No. I don't. I'm still *stuck*. My damned 'inner ethicist' won't let me off the hook. Yes, things have ended nicely, I guess. But *I* still know two things: Way back then, I made the wrong decision and agreed to participate in the insurance scheme, whether it was real or not. And now, more recently, the threat of the codicil—it feels as if I sidestepped financial ruin on a mere technicality. There was nothing *heroic* about that."

Faye set down her drink and placed her hands on her hips. "Pardon me while I roll my eyes." She rolled her eyes. "We've already talked through the timing of these events, *ad nauseum*, and *this* is the essential truth: In the moment when you decided to send your text with all the links that would bring down Wentworth, you *thought* you were risking everything. It was a brave and noble act. Turns out, thank God, you *did* get off on a technicality—the lame wording of the codicil itself. You should simply *accept* that. And be grateful for it."

"But that's like *cheating*."

Faye growled. Then she calmed herself. "You were raised Catholic, right?"

I nodded, but reminded her, "It didn't stick."

"Even so, they're big on guilt—they've got it nailed. But they're also good with forgiveness. You know—confession or contrition or whatever?"

"Yes ...?"

"So here's the thing." She patted her fingers on her chest. "Just think of me as kindly old Father Rubin, okay?" She smirked. Then she lifted her hands in front of me, saying, "By all that's holy, I forgive you, Meghan. I *absolve* you of the ill-considered sins of your youth. You have fully atoned for them. You have learned from them. And now—you are freed from your guilt." She lowered her hands. She paused. Lifting two fingers, she mimicked blessing me with the sign of the cross.

I sputtered a laugh. "You got the vertical part right, but the horizontal part—backwards. Sister Mary Grace would *not* approve."

With a shrug—and a Yiddish lilt—she said, "So sue me."

I hugged her. "Thank you, Faye."

Everett ambled by, tending to something, but stopped to ask, "Has everything been satisfactory this evening, Mrs. Auric?"

"Yes," I said with complete honesty, "it's been more than satisfactory. It couldn't have turned out better."

"Ah! That's *very* kind of you."

Then I noticed Faye eyeing him, and I recalled that during a recent session, she had twittered like a schoolgirl when I mentioned him. "Uh, Everett," I said, "have you met Dr. Faye Rubin?"

He offered his hand to her. "My pleasure, Dr. Rubin. I'm Everett Burke, club manager. I recall noticing you at one of our luncheons, and I may have seen you in the building, as well."

"*Yes*. My offices are upstairs, on eleven."

Sensing some electricity, I backstepped and disappeared into the crowd.

By one o'clock, the party had petered out. The Gamarras were long gone—I couldn't begin to fathom *their* exhaustion. Nearly everyone I knew had also called it a night, and come to think of it, I had seen neither Faye nor Everett in quite a while. (Had they perhaps skulked up to the eleventh floor?) In the ballroom, a cleanup crew was stomping on balloons.

A few die-hard drinkers had moved to the barroom, and as I walked through the club lobby, I thanked the remaining staffers I encountered.

Before leaving, I stepped over to the checkroom and asked the attendant, "By any chance, did I leave a topcoat here a few weeks ago?" Because I lived in the building, I never wore outerwear to the club, but occasionally I was coming from, or going to, other appointments. I added, "Camel hair, I think?"

"Let me check," she said, stepping away. A few seconds later: "Here you go, Mrs. Auric. Sleep well tonight."

"I'm sure I will, thank you." Tipping was not expected or allowed in the club—but I slipped her a twenty.

With the coat draped over one arm, I walked out through the club entrance, placing me at the top of the curved staircase in the building's main atrium, which was dead quiet—even the splash of the fountain in a reflecting pool had stopped. The snap of my heels echoed in the vast space as I descended the stairs to the ground-level concourse.

Reaching the floor, I would normally have turned and walked over to the elevators in the residents' lobby, but that night, I paused. I felt the corners of my mouth stretch into a soft smile. Then I walked straight ahead, through the grand entrance that faced Auric Boulevard.

"Good *evening*, Mrs. Auric," said the doorman with a look of surprise as I stepped out of the building and into the night air. Standing together under the canopy, he told me, "I hope your party went well tonight."

"It did, Clarence, thank you."

"Is ... someone picking you up?"

"No, just thought I'd get some air." Since I was carrying my handbag, I asked, "Could you help me with my coat?"

"Of *course*, ma'am." He snapped into action, as though apologizing for neglecting his duties. He even held my purse while I buttoned up, including the collar—the night had turned cold.

Grinning, I wondered how he would react when I told him, "I think I'll take a little walk."

His eyes bugged. "Would you like me to accompany you? I could call someone from the break room if—"

"No, Clarence, of course not, but that's very kind." An important moment had arrived. I paused to consider it before saying, "Good-bye. See you in a bit."

He bobbed his head, smiled. "Good-bye, ma'am. Enjoy your stroll."

I found the old adage to be true: the first step was the hardest. Moving out from under the canopy, off the carpet, and onto the glittery concrete of the sidewalk, I inhaled deeply. The frigid air filled my lungs—oddly refreshing, even exciting, in the stillness of that dark hour.

I hesitated, looking back over my shoulder, and found Clarence leaning out from the building, watching me. I smiled and waved. He did the same, then ducked back into his alcove.

Moving on, I picked up my pace, increasing my distance from the doors, but still walking alongside the building. When I reached the corner, I faced a decision, then crossed the street, leaving the building behind. The sidewalk no longer sparkled. But each step proved to be slightly less challenging.

I should note that in Fairview, during the wee hours following a Tuesday night, there was no one to be seen, anywhere. Traffic lights flashed through their cycles, but without purpose, as nothing moved on the streets.

In truth, then, my little foray wasn't much of a test.

But it was a start.

Michael Craft is the author of twenty-one novels. The first installment of his Dante & Jazz mystery series, *Desert Getaway*, was a 2023 MWA Edgars nominee for the Lilian Jackson Braun Award. The second installment, *Desert Deadline*, was a Gold Winner of the IBPA Benjamin Franklin Award, as was his 2019 mystery, *ChoirMaster*. Four of his novels have been honored as finalists for Lambda Literary Awards. In addition, his prizewinning short fiction has appeared in British as well as American literary journals.

Craft grew up in Illinois and spent his middle years in Wisconsin, the setting for many of his earlier books. He now lives in Rancho Mirage, California, near Palm Springs, which provided the setting for his more recent Dante & Jazz mysteries.

In 2017, Michael Craft's professional papers were acquired by the Special Collections Department of the Rivera Library at the University of California, Riverside.

Visit his website at www.michaelcraft.com.

ACKNOWLEDGMENTS

While writing *Not Our Crowd, Darling*, I relied on a number of friends for their generous assistance with various plot details: David Grey (who knows a lot about the law), Lynne Messner (who knows her medicine), Gary Mihalik (who knows more than *anyone* about gelato), Michael Quimby (who knows more than most men do about ritzy women's clubs), and Jim Stout (who unknowingly inspired the title).

M.G. Lord, Barbara McReal, and Larry Warnock served as early readers of the manuscript, lending countless suggestions for improvement, while Jim Thomsen's astute editing was invaluable in polishing the text.

As always, Mitchell Waters, my longtime literary agent, has been tireless in guiding me through the obscure byways of the publishing world. And finally, my husband, Leon Pascucci, has remained a steady font of patience, support, and good cheer.

Heartfelt thanks to all.

— *Michael Craft, 2025*

AUTHOR'S NOTE

This novel is something of a departure for me. Most of my earlier books have been murder mysteries, and most of those have featured gay male protagonists. But *Not Our Crowd, Darling* is not a whodunit, and its main character is a straight woman, newly widowed, who serves as the story's first-person narrator. So this one is different.

Although the plot involves a murder—with the possibility of more to come—these crimes are not, ultimately, what the story is "about." Rather, the arc of the narrative is far more "interior," dealing with struggles of the central character, Meghan Auric, as she tries to overcome the emotional consequences of a very bad decision made many years earlier.

Readers often ask me where I get the ideas for my books. The sources of inspiration vary: items in the news, or snatches of overheard conversation, or motives that intrigue me, or technological advances that seem fertile for abuse, or an idea for a character's name, or anything else that might pop up and surprise me with an "aha" moment.

In the case of this book, inspiration struck at a New Year's Day brunch when someone asked our host about someone else, who wasn't there. With a knowing scowl, he replied under his breath, "Not our class, dear," a phrase that had apparently been bantered about in more than one BBC streaming series. Everyone laughed.

The phrase caught my ear and stuck with me—its condescension, its ennui, its clubbiness. *How delicious*, I thought. When I altered it a bit to make it sound less British and more American, I knew that I'd found the title of my next novel, *Not Our Crowd, Darling*. Then? All I had to do was write a story that fit the title.

The text of this book was set in Garamond Premier Pro, a 2005 interpretation and expansion of Adobe Garamond, which was designed in 1989 by Robert Slimbach as a digital revival of Claude Garamond's original array of metal typefaces dating from the mid-1500s in France. Garamond is a serif typeface classified as "old style," meaning that its strokes and serifs have a slightly more organic, handwritten feeling than transitional or modern serifs.

Known as the most conspicuous example of French Renaissance typography and one of the key font families worldwide, Garamond can be easily recognized for its elegant forms and excellent readability. Its smooth curves and simple serifs convey a classic and easygoing beauty, well suited for long blocks of text. Among print designers, Garamond is often favored as a timeless choice for text that is authoritative, highly legible, and slightly dressy.